I AM ISTANBUL

I AM ISTANBUL

BUKET UZUNER

TRANSLATED BY KENNETH J. DAKAN

DALKEY ARCHIVE PRESS
CHAMPAIGN / LONDON / DUBLIN

Originally published in Turkish as *İstanbullular*
by Everest Yayınları, Cağaloğlu, 2007

Copyright © 2007 by Buket Uzuner
Translation copyright © 2013 by Kenneth J. Dakan
First Edition, 2013
All rights reserved

Library of Congress Cataloging-in-Publication Data is available.
ISBN: 978-1-56478-891-7

This book has been supported by the Ministry of Culture and Tourism
of Turkey in the framework of the TEDA project

In cooperation with Barbaros Altug and Everest Yayınları

Partially funded by a grant from the Illinois Arts Council, a state agency

www.dalkeyarchive.com

Cover: design and composition by Mikhail Iliatov

Printed on permanent/durable acid-free paper

1
I AM ISTANBUL

I am Istanbul, city of cities, mistress of metropolises, community of poets, seat of emperors, favorite of sultans, pearl of the world! My name is Istanbul and my subjects call themselves "Istanbullu." And of all the world's cities, I am without doubt the most magnificent, mysterious and terrible, a city upon whose shores Pagans, Christians, Jews and unbelievers, friend and foe alike, have found safe harbor through the ages, a place where love and betrayal, pleasure and pain, live side by side.

I, daughter of Poseidon, miracle of the Argonauts, Empress of Medieval Cities, the harbinger of a New Age, whose star shines anew in the twenty-first century, am the city of prosperity and ruin, of defeat and glad tidings. Istanbul is my name. It is I! Place of extremes, the full gamut of human emotions experienced at one and the same time, from the sublime to the basest, the loftiest to the lowest. I! My name is Istanbul, eternal archangel and goddess of cities. They come and go, leaving their mark on my soul; I have seen them rise and fall, be born and decline; I harbor their jumbled relics in my underground cisterns and vaults.

Blue as hope, green as poison, rosy as dawn, I am Istanbul; I am in the Judas tree, in acacia, in lavender; I am turquoise! I am the unfathomable; the muse of possibility, vitality, creativity.

My name is Istanbul. That's what they call me, what they have been calling me for a century past; but I have been Constantinople, city of Constantine; I began as Byzantium, and have had many names since: The Gate of Heavenly Felicity, Dersaadet, Dar'üssadet, New Rome, Asitane, Daraliye, He Polis, Tsargrad, Stamboul, Konstantiniyye . . . Mortals are like that, forever changing names, laws and borders! I laugh at these mortals taking themselves so seriously in their fleeting mortal world of false illusion, fears and shadows. Had anyone thought to consult me, I would have chosen "Queen of All I Survey," which is what I am anyway. I am Queen of Queens, City of Cities; I have walked with emperors and sultans, shared the confidences of travelers and poets. Aspiring authors still line up to write about me. In fact, here comes one now!

But even the soul of a great and noble city can feel the strain. Of late, I've been feeling restless. Lest I harm myself and the fifteen million people who reside with me, I seek distraction. That is why I've chosen this day to turn my attention to Yeşilköy, my old "Green Village," now my modern face, home to what they call "Atatürk International Airport."

The original name was Ayastephanos. That was back in 395 or 495, I can't quite remember now. On the night of that terrifying tempest, my Byzantine guests were still living here, and the small boat that was to transport St. Stephanos's remains to Rome was forced to find refuge in this port. I remember it as though it were yesterday. They had caused me great distress, which had, of course, caused the storm. It was indeed a terrible night, a blinding squall. The remains of the saint languished in the port waiting for fair weather, but his body never left, and the church in which he was finally interred was called Hagia Stephanos, hence the neighborhood: Ayastephanos.

Many years later, in 1926 or 1927, long after the arrival of my Turkish guests, the author Halit Ziya Uşaklıgil, who was fond of the place, renamed it Yeşilköy. And that's how it stayed.

The reason I've turned my gaze on the airport today is to revel in the return of an Istanbullu, who many years ago packed her bags and imagined she'd left me for good. I'm in the mood for a little fun. She's been angry with me for exactly thirteen years, had fled far from me, and here she comes running back. She'll be touching my tarmac shortly. Her name is Belgin. It gives me particular pleasure to welcome back those mortals who, like this one, have stormed off, vowing never to return. They inevitably find some pretext for doing so. In this case, Belgin of Bebek claims to have fallen in love with the sculptor Ayhan of Adana, now also of Istanbul.

I've seen it time and time again; what they're really addicted to is my *love. But it is no mortal love, this love of Istanbul. They carry me always in their hearts, and to me they must return: homesick, pining, missing me to death, their hearts ablaze with an unquenchable love, solace for which can be found nowhere else. Once an Istanbullu, always an Istanbullu. I am the last song on the lips of dying exiles; I am pain and poetry; even to those who imagine they have left me of their own accord, I remain forever their lost home; for I am the smell of earth, the tang of sea, the stuff of dreams. I am Istanbul. City of magic, city of enchantment, object of the world's desire.*

And for millennia, no one has ever really left me. I will not be abandoned! Will never be deserted! My name is Istanbul.

2
FINAL RETURN

The pain of returning to a city that so resembles oneself can only be compared to the pain of coming to terms with one's own mistakes. It's like the excitement, the suffering yet supreme passion of returning to a never-forgotten lover.

Only one of the passengers on the plane now descending into Istanbul was making a "final return." No one else on the Turkish Airlines airbus that had been cruising from New York at 8575 km per hour for ten and a half hours knew that this particular passenger was making a final return. And if anyone had known, they wouldn't have cared. Far below, Istanbul was languishing through an ordinary summer day, reclining across two continents and heedless of the planes buzzing about in her airspace.

The passenger making her final return to Istanbul appeared to be a calm sort of person, the kind who doesn't easily lose control. Her tiny upturned nose was like a comma, scrawled in the middle of her face as a bit of a prank, as though to provide a contrast with her cool composure. With black shoulder-length hair spilling onto her forehead, arched ebony eyebrows curving to her temples and tapered side locks seemingly plastered to her cheekbones, she looked just like Belgin Doruk in her Gina Lollabrigida phase. It was a retro hairstyle in the summer of 2005. And yes, some would have identified it with Gina Lollabrigida, Doruk, Sophia Loren; while others wouldn't have been reminded of anything at all. This passenger was an attractive woman. Clear-complexioned, about five and a half feet tall, a size twelve, she looked somewhere on the younger side of forty. Her classic navy-blue boat-collar dress was sleeveless and ended just above the knee. It must have been chemically treated, for its razor-sharp lines were not in the least bit wrinkled from the long journey. A second look would also have revealed that she was tense as a bow, her hazel eyes hauntingly beautiful. Her name was indeed Belgin. And in order to convince herself that she was really coming back

13

to Istanbul for good, and for the better, she repeatedly whispered the words "final return." The handsome elderly woman sitting beside her concluded that Belgin must be praying, because afraid of flying, while long experience led the cabin crew, accustomed as they were to dealing with all sorts of people, to ignore this passenger apparently talking to herself.

"Final return!" Belgin whispered. "This is it. Now it's for real. I'm returning to Istanbul, and for good!"

As the pilot prepared for descent, a female voice announced in Turkish that seatbelts were to be fastened, seats brought to an upright position and tray tables folded. The same instructions followed in carefully enunciated American English. Flight attendants began roaming the aisles to ensure that all had complied.

"I'm making my final return!" Belgin whispered to herself once again. "My *kesin dönüş.*"

The Turkish for "final return" seems so much less linear than the English, she mused. The English word, though of course meaning, literally, to "turn again," never really refers to anything more than the act of going back to A from B and back, whereas the word "*dönüş*" really does refer—again, literally speaking—to a "gyration" or "rotation." A final "rotation," like turning around, coming full circle, and arriving at the end—the end of what? Yes, it was this business of "ending," the finality of that "final," which was the more difficult burden to bear—perhaps implying defeat. Did her return indicate a failure of some kind? She suddenly felt weighed down, embarrassed at the thought of someone noticing.

"Have I really done it? Is this really it?" Just the thought made her stomach churn. "Am I ready for Istanbul? Ready for its terrible, splendid chaos?"

As the plane banked and wheeled, the monitors that had been showing news programs, travel documentaries and two Hollywood films had long since automatically retracted. The "fasten your seat belts" and "no smoking" signs just below the overhead baggage compartments were the only sources of illumination. Even seasoned travelers wore noticeably tense expressions, worn out as they were by the ten-and-a-half-hour flight, biological rhythms disrupted by jet lag, and a diet of airplane food that even at its best never manages to be as appetizing as what one gets on land. But, above all else, what really weighed on the planeload of travelers was the humiliation of the series of intrusive security checks they'd been subjected to, which after 9/11 has completely taken the joy out of travel.

"Am I really starting a new life in Istanbul, returning to the city to become an Istanbullu once more?" Belgin wondered. "Of course I am. And I'm returning by choice!" she told herself. "This isn't a case of a woman who's disrupting her whole life, sacrificing everything for a man. No, that's not it at all!" Her tone was now combative. "I just want to live in the same city as the man I love, and I was in love with the city long before I fell in love with the man." Despite this inner dialogue, her face remained impassive, continuing to signal to the world that all was well within. This ability of hers was a blessing and a curse, and had shaped the course of her life; but those who accused her of being unemotional, and even punished her for it, never stopped to think that she herself disliked this trait. How could they know that she was taking after her mother?

The elderly female passenger in the next seat suddenly began to speak with great enthusiasm: "There's no place like home. Even though it sometimes drives us mad, even though we criticize it, even though we settle in other countries for whatever reason, this wonderful Istanbul of ours makes us tremble with excitement every time we return . . ." She sounded as excited as a child.

Belgin almost thought she must have imagined this timely interjection, but no, the woman in the next seat, who had been silent up to now, and whose ageless beauty Belgin had admired from the start, turned her head and continued in a dreamy tone:

"Even when we're forced to live with twin passports, away in other cities, our compasses always point to Istanbul . . ."

Since she came from a "good family," and so had been saddled with that distinguished burden known as "good manners," Belgin automatically flashed a gracious smile at the woman. The smile still lingered on her lips as she found herself subjected to the inevitable question. Unsure of what she'd respond, it was a question she'd hesitated to ask herself.

"Are you an Istanbullu too?" the woman inquired.

There was a moment's silence.

"Am I an Istanbullu?" Belgin echoed uneasily. "Who can really claim to be 'of Istanbul'? What does it take? If it just means being born in Istanbul and living there, can I still count myself an Istanbullu after an absence of twelve years? But if it really means *belonging* to the city, I may well still define myself, culturally, by way of Istanbul . . . Or do I now belong somewhere else?"

The faraway voice from the next seat was now tinged with a note of pride. "Well in my case, I was born and raised in Istanbul . . ."

"I'm going back!" Belgin sighed. "I'm going back, returning to Istanbul! Would you believe I'm really making a 'final return'? Going back to the city to which I vowed never to return, except for holidays and other short visits, I mean . . . going back to the city of betrayal, of hypocrisy, of loneliness."

She flinched. Why was she telling all this to a stranger?

"My dear girl, still so young, and with so much still ahead of you! The longer we live, the more we experience. Oh, the vows we break; the things we spit out only to lap up later!" said her fellow passenger, smiling more joyfully than ruefully. "My dear," she added, "even someone like me, who prides herself on her principles and her patriotism, often end up spending half the year in America just to be with her daughter and grandchild." But Belgin's attention was wandering, her thoughts focused on her return to Istanbul . . .

"*Dönüş* . . . to turn, one needs an axis; to orbit, a trajectory." Belgin's thoughts were in free fall, spinning out of control. "It's a simple act. Motion in space. So why is it causing me such pain?"

"Ah, but is it really as simple as that? A final return isn't just a question of movement, a one-way voyage. You don't think it's as straightforward as that, do you?" the elderly voice asked.

"Isn't it?" asked Belgin.

16

"But of course not, my dear!" replied the woman, raising an eyebrow. "For example, let's examine the metaphorical meaning of the word *dönme*, or 'turning,' as used by the Sufi; that is to say, let's look at the two concepts involved: axis of rotation and cycle of existence. First of all, let me remind you that the ritual spinning practiced by the Mevlevi and Sufi orders is called the *sema*—no doubt known to you by more colorful names, like 'the dance of the dervishes.'"

"Yes, of course . . ." said Belgin, feeling slightly ashamed that only now did she understand what the old woman was getting at. She may have been living in America for twelve years, but she felt certain she hadn't become quite so ignorant of her own culture. She'd never been one of those Turks who slip into the unfortunate affectation of speaking Turkish with an American twang by their second year abroad, as well as "forgetting" words they've used all their lives.

"Sufism is extremely popular in America these days, and we Turks often learn more about it over there! This, unfortunately, is yet another dramatic example of the ways our culture has been hijacked . . ." the woman added.

As Belgin was wondering whether this complaint was directed at herself, the beautiful old woman in the next seat returned to her lecture.

"Now, don't get me wrong, it isn't as though I have any personal experience of any religious cults and so forth. I'm a Kemalist: a secular, Republican patriot. My grandfather on my mother's side may have been a Mevlevi sheikh, but all of his granddaughters received modern educations, went on to have careers, and became thoroughly secular and civilized Atatürkist members of society, praise be to Allah! Look at me, a retired history teacher!"

Bewildered by the twists and turns of their conversation, Belgin nodded vacantly in a bid to stall the old woman. It was perhaps the perfect moment to respond with, "Pleased to meet you; I'm Assistant Professor Belgin—I'm a geneticist." But Belgin didn't bother. In any case, the title of assistant professor doesn't exist in the Turkish academic system, its closest approximation being "deputy university lecturer." And then, Belgin was still quite tense at the prospect of her "final return."

"Being a civilized nation doesn't require the rejection of one's own culture and traditions! An Eastern-Western synthesis is best for us, I think—or rather, absolutely essential! We must unite our local values with universal ones. Does it not follow, my dear, that we shouldn't abandon our great philosopher and poet, Mevlana, to the Americans?" the retired history teacher asked.

"Rumi!" said Belgin absentmindedly. "The West calls him Rumi . . ."

"Yes, of course they do. And if we don't claim him as our own, that's just how the foreigners will steal all our values!"

They fell silent as the plane glided over the Sea of Marmara.

"You spoke of a 'turning back' to Istanbul," resumed the former history teacher. "The *sema* ceremony of the dervishes involves turning, but is in fact a metaphor for the circular movement of history. Not only do they whirl on their own axes, they also simultaneously revolve around the sheikhs. 'Turn,' 'return,' 'whirl,' 'spin,' 'revolve'—they're all the same word in our language, as you know."

Looking out of the window at the billowing clouds, Belgin imagined dervishes in white robes and conical red hats whirling with the clouds, spinning, eyes closed, heads tilted to the right, one hand extended palm upward toward the sky, the other downward toward the earth. She envied their serenity, felt a yearning for absolute calm, the spiritual purity that comes from balancing the earthly and the divine. And, for a fleeting moment, she felt bathed in cool whiteness, afforded a glimpse, however brief, into a mystical experience of wholeness and safety. Reassured, the color flowed back into her face, and she even smiled.

"One must reach ecstasy!" exclaimed her neighbor, startling Belgin, who had already forgotten all about her. "You can't turn without it!"

"Really," murmured Belgin. "So I have to reach ecstasy to return?"

"What I mean is that you must rejoice. You do see, young

lady, that a soul that is not rejoicing in purity can't whirl. To 'turn' you must rejoice."

"So," thought Belgin, "that must be what's missing from my final return to Istanbul—joy! I'm failing to rejoice. Do I have enough energy and joy for Istanbul? Do I have enough desire and courage for the wonderful man who is waiting for me down there in the airport? Do I have the joy I'll need to start a new life with this man I love? Without it, how will I survive Istanbul? Or love? Or does defeat and disappointment await me in Istanbul, yet again?"

"Of course, for those who can't rejoice, *tecavud* will do just as well," threw in her neighbor.

Belgin nodded automatically. It was as if this beautiful old woman were reading her thoughts. Then she realized she wasn't certain what the word *tecavud* meant, and frowned.

"Which is to say, it's permissible for those who can't truly rejoice to appear to be feeling joy," the old woman explained.

Belgin laughed, incredulous. "What do you mean? How can I fake joy?"

"Surely you don't mean to say you've never done that, at least on occasion?"

"Am I to understand that you're asking me if I've ever faked it?" stammered Belgin, somewhat taken aback. The incredulity she felt was as great as that of her Western friends when they learned that she had been born and raised in a country in which some women were still subjected to virginity tests.

"I think you understand exactly what I mean. After all, you're not a child."

Belgin shook her head dispiritedly. She was just past forty, and very sensitive to any references to age.

"I mean, you must be at least thirty-five," the history teacher hastily amended.

"You're too kind—I'm forty-one, you've shaved off quite a few years!"

"Some people are just born lucky," smiled her companion, before continuing where she'd left off: "We were discussing the concept of turning. Angels whirl around the throne of God, faithful Muslims circle the Kaaba, planets orbit the sun. The ritual whirling of the dervishes reflects the divine nature of circularity. Do I make myself clear? But then again, according to some legends the dervishes whirl and whirl until they are lost in the sky . . . Keep that in mind when arriving at a decision about your own situation and all the turning involved . . ."

They both smiled, one of them reflecting on the dervishes whirling up into the clouds, the other imagining herself whirling into oblivion in Istanbul. For a moment, the two of them were lost in their separate thoughts . . .

"If Istanbul is the axis around which I turn, is love some kind of centrifugal force? How can it be that after telling myself I'd never fall in love again, couldn't possibly share a future with anyone, I find myself head over heels—and at my age, no less? And why, all settled in the organized convenience of New York, do I find myself returning to the chaotic magnificence of Istanbul? Why go back to those twin nightmares: Istanbul and love, love and Istanbul! Am I out of my mind? Where did I find the courage to open my arms to love, let alone love in Istanbul? And if I really am ready to face both city and man, why this sinking feeling? And then, after having had my life repeatedly turned upside down by defeat and failure, why do I persist in asking such childish questions?" As someone who had confided in a mere handful of others her entire life, Belgin couldn't believe she was posing these questions to a total stranger. She swallowed hard and bowed her head, fearing that her confidences had been unseemly. Inside, storms raged; but her face remained impassive: not a leaf stirred.

"Ulviye," exclaimed the passenger in the next seat by way of introduction. "Ulviye Yeniçağ! Ulviye New-Era! My dear late father, may he rest in radiance, chose this family name for us because it was both modern and purely Turkish."

"Nice to meet you," Belgin said, back in control. "I, of course, am named after the famous movie star, Belgin Doruk. My mother and father adored her. And my surname comes from my great-grandfather, a silversmith. So my full name is Belgin Gümüş.

Belgin Silver. I suppose my names are quite ordinary."

"Don't say that, Belgin *Hanım*! First of all, silver is a precious and noble metal. Pay no mind to the provincials, those *nouveau riche* and their obsession with gold. They're just copying the Arabs. We Turks are a people who have been known for centuries for the creativity and skill of our silverwork. Silver ornaments play a very important part in our culture."

She indicated her own silver ring and the brooch decorating her collar, and after a lengthy disquisition on each, returned to the subject of Belgin's name:

"Your mother and father made a very appropriate choice!" she said. "Indeed, I'm certain that there's not a single person of our generation who didn't grow up enthralled by that shining star of the silver screen, Belgin Doruk! Who could remain unmoved by her elegance, her sophistication? And who could forget Ayhan Işık, our own Clark Gable, her debonair leading man in those black-and-white romantic comedies of the '60s? Ah, Belgin and Ayhan! Ayhan and Belgin! Yes, she was the personification of everything a young lady should strive for and so few have attained, then or now. At the same time, the word *belgin* means 'clear, open and pure'—all three highly desirable qualities. Your forename and surname are both superb. Even more importantly, a name has the power to bring its owner good fortune, you know."

"Good fortune, eh? Luck and love . . . happiness and prosperity . . . So is happiness just a matter of luck?" wondered Belgin. "Is it destiny that brings me back to Istanbul? Perhaps that's what the turning turns upon: destiny."

"Returning," said Ulviye Yeniçağ, resuming their earlier discussion, "is like remembering; it involves going back to one's history, community and personal experience. A remembrance of things past is an essential part of returning. And furthermore, only those who understand the past can comprehend the present, Belgin *Hanım*!"

Belgin had been burdened by the prospect of this final return for weeks, and the musings of her traveling companion had lightened her spirits by confirming that returning is never easy. She gave her neighbor a closer look. Yes, Ulviye Yeniçağ had something—a feminine beauty that belied her years; her brightly twinkling blue eyes gave her a coquettish air that burned to cinders any and all ageist preconceptions.

Perhaps it was an abundance of nervous energy, or it may have been the result of having been cooped up in a confined space for so long, but Belgin felt bold, even chatty enough to venture a personal remark:

"Speaking of turning, who knows how many men have been smitten by those eyes of yours, how many heads you've sent spinning?"

"Ah-ha!" chortled Ulviye Yeniçağ. "You should have seen me in my youth, my dear . . . I inherited these eyes from my mother. My grandfather's side of the family hails from Thessalonica. They migrated to Turkey following the Population Exchange Convention of 1923. But on my father's side, we've been born and bred Istanbullu for generations!"

"Here we go again with being an Istanbullu!" Belgin said to herself. But the face she turned to Ulviye Yeniçağ was affable, the tone she employed eminently reasonable: "My family has been settled in Bebek for many generations, Ulviye *Hanım*, but I don't think birth certificates are the measure of who belongs to the city . . . nor of who is a true Istanbullu. Let's take a certain fellow I met two years ago. He's incredibly clever, creative and passionate; as an artist, he's represented Turkey abroad. He also happens to have been born in a village in Adana, the seventh child of a mother who couldn't read or write even in her mother tongue, which was Kurdish, and a father who had only an elementary school education and worked all his life on manual labor. Against all odds, while still a child, this man came to Istanbul to study, all alone. He has always tried, through his work and his example, to appreciate and even to contribute to the culture, history, and art of Istanbul. Doesn't this man, who has adopted Istanbul as his home and Turkish as his language, have at least as valid a claim to being an Istanbullu as you and I?"

"And just who is this artist?" snapped Ulviye Yeniçağ.

Annoyed that Ulviye Yeniçağ had reduced the entire story to a name, Belgin nearly shouted, "The sculptor Ayhan Pozaner! And if you're saying that . . ."

"My dear Belgin *Hanım*," interrupted Ulviye Yeniçağ, "does the fact that you've formed some sort of attachment to this man, and are therefore unable to see certain things clearly, suddenly eliminate the importance of background and bloodline? Really, my dear, surely you haven't forgotten who stabbed us in the back during the War of Liberation?"

Although a bit mystified by the turn the conversation had taken, and unable to see its connection with Ayhan and Istanbul, Belgin, ever the victim of "breeding," instinctively sought common ground:

"But Ulviye *Hanım*, surely you'll agree that it is the mixing of peoples and races over such a wide and bountiful geography that has made us such a unique and distinct nation? Furthermore, as a scientist, I can tell you that a diverse gene pool is healthy and desirable." But Ulviye Yeniçağ was having none of it, and had turned her head away in a fit of pique as Belgin persisted.

"Look at any map and you'll see that we have blood-ties to nearly all of our former colonies, near and far. You have genes from Thessalonica and the Balkans; mine are from Georgia and the Caucasus; Ayhan's are Kurdish and Persian . . . Apart from the Ottomans, none of the other great European empires can boast as much open and honest diversity. You're a historian, and perhaps know better than me . . . But did the people of those other empires ever properly intermingle? Think of how recently they've finally learned to celebrate diversity. How many of the Dutch have a secret Indonesian aunt; how many Englishmen have a conveniently forgotten Indian great-grandmother?"

"Now you've gone too far! I won't have it," said Ulviye Yeniçağ. A dark shadow swept over her lovely face, darkening those playful blue eyes and threatening to coarsen her seeming refinement. She had turned into someone else. "I would never have thought it of you! First of all, the Ottomans had no colonies. They were our *principalities*, and organized according to a system completely different from the colonial model. Secondly, you ought to bear in mind the case of the Irish and the Scots, who are citizens of Great Britain and speak English, not their mother tongues, even at home. Their literature too is in English! Most importantly of all, it's unbecoming for a well-educated, intellectual young Turkish woman like yourself to be mouthing the platitudes of the 'Second Republic'—that's thirdly! Everyone in Turkey is Turkish, end of story; no good can come to any of us from ethnic separatism!"

Belgin recoiled as though she'd accidentally stepped on a stranger's foot. She was speechless. And more than a little upset . . . Slumping slightly, she drew back into her seat. Then she tried to understand what she had said to give so much offense.

"We're perfectly aware that well-intentioned young people such as yourself, who have lost their sense of history due to living overseas for too long, often end up as pawns of the West! But we're not letting go of so much as a handful of soil from this land of ours, every square inch of which has been watered with the blood of our ancestors, Belgin *Hanım*! While we've got breath in our bodies, our breasts shall be as shields against those traitors!"

"Good grief!" sighed Belgin, clasping her head in her hands. What does she mean by "we?" And just who does she consider a "traitor"? At that very moment, she felt a migraine coming on. Yes, a migraine, that most treacherous of traitors, repeatedly announcing its intentions as it creeps toward the head of its victim, hooks at the ready. Ulviye Yeniçağ misinterpreted Belgin's grimace and grew even more affronted. In fact, Belgin was simply preoccupied with the migraine now stalking her, and the thought of meeting Ayhan, who was probably at the airport even now, waiting to greet her. How would she manage the reunion she had fantasized about for weeks, the rapidly approaching moment when he would clasp her in his arms? She glanced down at her stomach and found herself inexplicably astonished with herself. As though whatever she'd seen there had astounded her, and she wasn't at all sure what to do about it. Then her two hands were on her stomach, holding it tight, as though to keep safe whatever was inside.

"Look, I may have spoken a bit harshly," the old woman

prattled on, "but ours is the generation that was brought up on tales of how, during the First World War, our grandmothers and grandfathers heroically defended our beloved homeland against those invading, latter-day crusaders. It may be a joke to you, but it was our ancestors, yours and mine, who inspired the slogan *Çanakkale geçilmez:* 'The Straits of Gallipoli,' as your Westerners would have it, 'are impassable.' But if you divide our people into Kurd, Laz, Circassian, Balkan, Arab, and Persian, the National Pact of 1920 will have come to naught. If the great Atatürk had favored such a model, surely he'd have introduced it—he wasn't stupid, you know. God forbid! He must have known best, may he rest in peace in the company of angels!"

Belgin was dumfounded by the continuing verbal assault; her hands, which a moment earlier she'd been surprised to observe cradling her stomach, were now massaging her temples as she braced herself to withstand the hooks about to plunge into the base of her skull. At the same time, she was trying to understand the process by which she had been branded a "pawn," "ignorant of history," and an "enemy of Atatürk." Like most Turks, she and her family were fervent admirers of Atatürk, and had grown to love him even more as the details of his personal life had begun to emerge. But Belgin was tired of all this. In a few moments she would be reunited with a most extraordinary man, the love of her life; all she wanted was to savor the moment. Not only that, but she would soon be back in Istanbul, the city she had abandoned so long ago. And all this with an impending migraine and the reproaches of Ulviye Yeniçağ, a retired historian she'd known for a full fifteen minutes, ringing in her ears. Belgin was very cross indeed with her fellow scientists for having failed to find a cure for migraines.

"Western imperialists and missionaries are plotting to take what slipped through their fingers in the Treaty of Sèvres! Ah, if you had any idea what sorts of plot they're hatching behind our backs!" said Ulviye Yeniçağ in a rasping whisper. "You're an intelligent woman, please don't let yourself be a pawn in their game. Do you think being an Istanbullu is easy? You think just anyone can move to the city and claim to be an Istanbullu?"

Belgin had had enough. One hand at her temple, the other clutching her side, she said, "Don't be ridiculous, Ulviye *Hanım*! Don't try to make me complicit in your paranoia. There's more to belonging to a city than a family tree. I was a New Yorker for years; Ayhan has been an Istanbullu since childhood: everyone has the right to choose their own city!" But when she turned toward her neighbor, she saw that Ulviye Yeniçağ was fast asleep.

Belgin was astonished. How had she fallen asleep so quickly? Looking up, she found herself eye to eye with a flight attendant:

"I've been waiting for fifteen minutes to collect her headphones, but she was sleeping so peacefully I didn't want to disturb her," the attendant smiled. "We've nearly reached Istanbul. She'll have to wake up soon."

"She's been sleeping for fifteen minutes? That's impossible. We've been chatting for half an hour."

The plane dipped steeply landward, the attendant back at her station, leaving Belgin to stare at Ulviye Yeniçağ's face, beautiful even in sleep. If she's been asleep, who have I been talking to all this time? she wondered. Or am I the one asleep and dreaming? That's when she spotted the elegant black case stowed under her neighbor's seat. It was clearly labeled with the words: "Ms. Ulviye Yeniçağ; Büyükada-Istanbul-Turkey."

The THY airbus gently caressed the tarmac. They had landed in Istanbul. Much to the surprise of the foreign passengers, the Turks wildly applauded the captain and crew. They'd arrived in Istanbul. Belgin had returned to Istanbul. The final return.

3
ALONE AT THE BAR

"I've got a real bone to pick with whoever designed the legs of these barstools! What the hell! It's bad enough having to line up side-by-side like at a public urinal just to get a drink. But it's even worse at an airport bar, which is a place specifically designed for sitting and waiting! In this false world of ours, as we wait it out in this world of illusion, what could be worse than even more unnecessary waiting? I've never liked bars; not when I first came to Istanbul and not after university either. I never got used to them. Anyone who appreciates a proper table for drinking could never get used to a bar. And to make matters worse, they stick stork's legs onto an ordinary stool and call it a 'barstool.' That's what really gets me. Are we Turks such a long-legged race that we're expected to perch comfortably on one of these lousy things just to have a drink? May heaven strike me down if I'm not telling it like it is!"

Beer mug in hand, a dark man with short, blue-black hair and '70s-style sideburns fidgeted on the edge of a barstool in the arrivals hall of the international terminal of Atatürk Airport. The muscles rippled in his arm as he impatiently turned his dark eyes to his watch: Belgin's plane wouldn't have landed yet.

"We're a stocky people, *hodja*. All those migrations on horseback have given us wide asses and short legs. They say the new generation has turned into a race of long-legged lions . . . What a bunch of nonsense! How's their diet any different from ours? Is there less poverty? Is there more milk and meat to go with their bread? I wouldn't mind being taller, but I don't mind being as I am . . . 178 centimeters tall, not even 180 . . . and then only if I draw myself up to my full height. Why should I want to be any taller? When I was a kid we weren't exactly living off the fat of the land. Take Japan. They say children are getting taller all the time over there. What idiocy! Doesn't anyone think to ask, 'Just how many people are there in this new tall generation of ours, and what about all the stunted boys and squat girls we see every day outside of our 'exclusive' European neighborhoods, I mean in the real streets of this country?

"It's true that we were plenty poor, nine of us fed on lots of bread to make the cucumbers and tomatoes last longer. But did we have terms like 'starvation level' and 'poverty line'? It may have been patched, but at least we had underwear on our backsides; maybe the soles were hobnailed, but we had shoes on our feet; and even if it was only made with plain water and a few vegetables, Mother could always give us soup. One thing's for certain: we were never barefoot and selling paper handkerchiefs out on the street! Of course, tissues weren't even around back then, damn it! This diabolical 'use it once, throw it away' mentality was embraced by our country precisely with the introduction of the disposable handkerchief. That's what really bugs me! Is a friend annoying you? Has your lover become old hat? Is your spouse past his or her sell-by date? Don't worry—just toss them aside! As long as you've got some money, there's always a new hankie waiting just over there, on the corner . . . in the hand of a child abandoned by its own mother. What's more, there's always a new variety . . . improved, colorfully packaged, cheaper, thinner, multilayered: tissues, lovers, friends . . . That's right, pal, this world's a cheap fabrication!

"They said we were one of the seven self-sufficient countries, food-wise, a land of plenty, with the reddest tomatoes, the roundest grapes and melons, the sweetest wheat and fish, the snowiest cotton and the whitest rice in the world. And that was only, what, fifteen years ago; okay, let's make it twenty. But please, let's drop this 'disposable society' mentality . . . That's not us—we're not like that! No, we're the kind of people who name a neighborhood *Vefa*, fidelity; who write the poetry of *hüzün*, melancholia and loss, as well as epics in praise of merit and worth! This fiendish 'use it and toss it' mentality has made us lose our sense of 'us,' we're not what we used to be, damn it! . . . Not since the founding of the Republic have we shared one dream in common! And then we get all this talk of getting taller, our growing civilization, and our supposed entry one day into the European Union, and on and on! Fuck them all!"

Glancing at his watch again, he saw that only two minutes had passed. He lit another cigarette. To the outside observer, he looked more like a soap star than a professor of fine arts, a sculptor with numerous national and international exhibitions to his credit. Ayhan Pozaner was wearing blue jeans, white sports shoes and a blue polo shirt with no insignia. He wasn't conventionally handsome, though his strong dark features were still what you might call "sexy." The permanently upturned corners of his mouth, which remained curled even when he was fast asleep, lent him a puckish air and smoothed the rough edges of his features. The contrast between his bold black eyes, which promised he was "up for anything, anytime," and his face, which seemed always on the verge of softening into a smile, only added to his charm.

"And to think that it was here, in Turkey, that the divan, the most comfortable seating apparatus in the world, was invented—and now, in the name of modernization, our bar culture is simply reproducing an endless line of those stork-like American stools they sip their whiskey on! What's more, those outsiders, those Starbucks and the rest, come along and hijack our divans and sofas to fill their own cafes with them! I've got half a mind to take one of these stools, saw off the legs and do a good deed for my country.

"When it comes to a drink, a real drink, this beer smelling of piss and whiskey smelling of a distant sea just don't cut it: the shah of drinks is 'lion's milk.' End of conversation! The name of the drink is rakı, and it's milky white . . . and the name of the best football team is Beşiktaş, and their colors are black and white! Whoa there, get a grip on yourself, Ayhan my boy. Cool it. She's on her way, your one and only. Just cool it!"

He looked at his watch again and saw that another two minutes had passed. He muttered the juiciest curse he knew, but this time it did nothing to ease his agitation. He had no idea how to pass the time. Actually, at that moment, it wasn't anticipation he felt; it was fear. He was afraid; he, Ayhan Pozaner, a man who'd picked himself up by his bootstraps and braved Istanbul, was terrified. That's why he'd left home so early in the morning, arriving at the airport a full two hours before Belgin's flight was scheduled to land. A barman who'd been observing Ayhan closely ever since he took a seat came over with a smile to replace an ashtray. But Ayhan didn't even notice. The barman's light brown hair was gathered into a ponytail. He wore a single earring, and this young, green-eyed, fair-skinned barman had a tic, an involuntary twitching, in his right shoulder.

"Would you like another one, *beyefendi*?" he asked Ayhan, eyeing the nearly drained beer mug.

"No thanks, *hodja*, I'd better take it nice and slow—I'll be here for a couple more hours . . ."

"Waiting for someone?" asked the barman in a bid to start a conversation.

"Someone?" asked Ayhan, offended. "No, not just 'someone'! A beauty is descending from the clouds—young man, my own little lady is on her way! She's coming!"

He lit another cigarette, carefully jetting a stream of smoke out of the corner of his mouth to ensure that it didn't blow into the barman's face, then frowned and sighed deeply.

"Yes, she's most definitely on her way . . . It's just . . . Well, I'm not sure how happy I am about it. It's kind of like the sense of inadequacy . . . or uneasiness . . . you'd get if you hit the jackpot with someone else's lottery ticket . . . Know what I mean?"

The barman searched Ayhan's face to see if he was joking, and suspected him, ingenuously enough, of being drunk. Ayhan instantly forgot all about the barman, who stood silently by; instead of answering what he assumed to be a rhetorical question, he made a show of straightening the bar counter, and waited.

"Daughter of a hotshot diplomat, and what's more, she's a professor and she's dropping everything in America, getting herself transferred back to Istanbul just for me . . . It had me dizzy with joy . . . but . . . look . . . it terrifies me, too . . . Joy and terror, mixed. Damn it, I'm scared!"

The barman may have been young, but he was experienced

enough to know that a sympathetic ear for the troubles of strangers was part of his job description. Even so, such a serious confession, and on a single beer, and well before noon, fell outside his experience. What's more, the man across from him looked like a typical 'Anatolian,' not at all the type to go in for public declarations of love. Besides, in the year 2005, 'real men,' even in the great metropolis of Istanbul, still considered displays of emotion to be frivolous and inappropriate and—let's be frank—womanish. And it was, last he checked, still the year 2005.

At that moment Ayhan noticed the earring in the barman's left ear, read the name on his tag, and gave him a closer look and a friendly smile.

"Baturcan İ. Uzunçay, huh?" he asked.

"That's right, sir," replied the barman, composing himself.

Ayhan looked as if he was racking his brain, trying to remember whether or not they'd met before. Perhaps the barman resembled one of his students. Acting with the forthright ease of a university professor, he launched his next question.

"Tell me young man, where does 'Baturcan' come from?"

"Excuse me, sir?" stammered the barman.

"What I mean is, were you named Baturcan after your grandfather, or maybe your uncle?"

The barman stared blankly for a moment, with the discomfort of someone who's suddenly been caught out and needs to buy himself time. He took in the nonjudgmental smile still lingering on Ayhan's lips, cleared his throat and swallowed. He shifted his lower jaw first to the left, then to the right. The tic in his right shoulder became more pronounced.

Perceiving that his question, or the way it had been asked, had somehow discomfited the barman, Ayhan realized he'd opened an old wound, and himself felt troubled. He wanted to right whatever he'd done wrong. Marshalling his forces, he flashed his aforementioned amazing smile and reached out his hand.

"Nice to meet you then. I'm Ayhan!"

Having decided that Ayhan's easy manner was not of the variety actually intended to intimidate, the barman politely shook the extended hand, but did not say a word. Instead, he began wiping down the bar with a cloth to look as busy as possible. After a moment, having surreptitiously glanced to the left and the right to make certain that the few customers at the bar weren't listening in, he finally spoke, albeit in a very low voice.

"That's not it at all!"

"What's not it?" asked Ayhan, now the discomfitted one.

"My name's got nothing to do with my relatives . . . Actually . . . you see, Ayhan *Bey* . . ." The barman cleared his throat at length, coughed and whispered: "My real name isn't Baturcan at all."

Ayhan took a deep drag on his cigarette and cursed himself for having gotten into this business of the name. Was this really the time to get caught up in the story of a bartender? Belgin was coming, was returning to Istanbul: Belgin . . . soon!

Leaning closer to Ayhan, the barman checked again that no one else was listening. He wanted so badly to unburden himself. He looked the very picture of a penitent, a confession on his lips:

"My real name is İlyas, but they gave me that name without asking. So I go by the name Baturcan, which somehow seems more fitting."

"Because they gave you your name without asking, huh?" Ayhan repeated, with a puzzled smile.

"It's a bit complicated. You see . . ."

"Of course I see, young man! Excellent! Good for you, Baturcan! Defying those who named you without your consent!" said Ayhan, with a loud chuckle.

Encouraged, the barman opened up.

"Over there . . . in Trabzon, in our village of Tatavlacık, the sea shines and the vegetation is so bright it's almost flashy, but the people are really conservative. Actually, we came to Istanbul many years ago—we're considered Istanbullu now—but these things take time . . . What I mean is, sometimes it's not easy to be yourself, to do what you want, even in a place like Istanbul . . . Do you know what I mean?"

Ayhan, upset, as though each cigarette he stubbed out extinguished a human life, kept his eyes, which were narrowed against the smoke, on his latest "dead cigarette" as he thought to himself:

"Ah, poor thing, do I ever . . . We've all become accustomed to doing things in secret, to keeping our broken arms concealed in our sleeves and hiding behind the tough-guy bluster . . . How many 'he-men' there must be out there, eager to taunt you over your earring, your job at a bar, your long hair and certain other aspects of your private life . . ."

But he saved those thoughts for later, having decided to offer some words of encouragement first.

"Don't let it get you down, Baturcan. It's all about people! It's a treacherous world out there, and there's no saying 'oh, it can't happen to me.' Don't condemn or judge anyone unless they trample on someone else. You know, it's like that old story about the hunter and the hunted. Starting out life as the hunter means nothing; anyone can become the hunted at any moment, and there's always the possibility that a lamb will turn into a wolf. I'm babbling on here, *hodja*, but what I mean to say is: Be what you are! You can't live in fear, hiding. Surely that's not what you'd call 'living'?"

Ayhan swigged the last of the beer from the bottom of his mug. Then he looked at the barman, who was watching him expectantly, as though he'd left out a key sentence.

"So that's why I say—good for you! You've done the right thing and dared to live as you are!" added Ayhan with a radiant smile.

The barman had clearly relaxed, but the smile he returned was guarded. A customer asked the barman for his check, and Ayhan was left alone with his thoughts. He stared long and hard at a cigarette stain, as though he wanted to wipe it away. His eyes remained fixed on it.

"Look, Baturcan, our Taurus Mountains, in Çukurova, are a fertile paradise, just like your corner of the Black Sea, but we still left our homes to come to Istanbul. Why did we come to this cruel city, a city that welcomes none of us with open arms, that, in fact, pushes and shoves away all newcomers; what is it that draws us? Have you ever considered that? Huh?"

When the barman returned, Ayhan pursued this train of thought aloud.

"We don't migrate to this shrew of a city, Istanbul, just to earn our daily bread. No, *hodja*, we race toward the light, the bounty, the streets paved with gold! We come here because sometimes this magnificent, magical Istanbul really does enable those with courage and a bit of luck to pursue a dream, the dream of making their own choices and living their own lives! What we come here for is the 'Istanbul Dream.' That's the real attraction: 'The Istanbul Dream'! Here you're no longer İlyas from Trabzon, and I'm no longer Ayhan from Adana: we became citizens of Istanbul and found the opportunity to be ourselves. That is to say, those who somehow manage to carve out a place here get that chance, don't they? Just look at me! Without answering to anyone, I have the freedom to cherish stone, to caress and sculpt it. Here, in Istanbul . . . Anyway, give me another cold beer, Baturcan. I'll stay here and think things over a little longer while I wait for Belgin . . ."

Biting his lower lip, the barman listened. He looked absorbed but uncertain. "Does Istanbul make your dreams come true, or does it awaken you from your dreams, Ayhan *Bey*? I haven't decided which one it is . . ." he murmured. Then, silent as a sleep-walker, he was gone, serving a new customer before returning to place a full mug of cold beer in front of Ayhan, who was once more lost in thoughts of Belgin.

"Five years after we migrated to Istanbul," the barman said, "when I was in middle school, they cut my father's throat and tossed his body into an empty field . . . Right in the belly of Istanbul, a father of four, no danger to anyone . . . He drove someone else's taxi at night—they slit Dad's throat for fifty lira, Ayhan *Bey*! Istanbul doesn't have a conscience—or whatever it did have is long gone!"

When talking about his father, Baturcan seemed strangely

distant, as though he was describing a scene in a film, albeit a profoundly shocking film of an event that had marked him permanently. Ayhan pictured Baturcan, distraught and stock-still, standing near the body of his father, its head nearly detatched, and he recoiled. A statue flashed before his eyes, body of bronze, decapitated head of Afyon marble, eyes staring . . . He willed the image away.

"It was Dad who wanted us to move to Istanbul. He thought life would be better here than in the village. But are we better off now? I couldn't really say . . ."

Breathing deeply, Baturcan frowned and bit his lip. For the first time, Ayhan became aware of the music playing in the bar. Jazz. He'd first been exposed to jazz back when he was a student at Darüşşafaka High School, and had mocked as "affected" those who claimed to appreciate what to his ears was nothing more than a discordant racket; later, when he found out that the blues was originally the music of African Americans, the musical expression of a downtrodden people, he'd made an effort to understand and appreciate the strange rhythms and melodies, and had grown to love jazz more than ever now that it was one of the interests he shared with Belgin . . . He loved jazz as much as *türkü*, Turkish folk music. He often used the example of jazz in his lectures, pointing out that you can grow to love something as you get to know it better, and that love clears the path to true understanding.

"Listen, it's 'Mack the Knife.' The Louis Armstrong version's best," he said, but this time it was the barman who'd become lost in thought.

"I suppose I'm better off here . . . If we'd stayed in Trabzon, they'd have married me off long ago, and that would have been a pity, for both me and the girl . . ." Baturcan said with a distant look in his eyes.

That last sentence had slipped out; he winced and fell silent. He hadn't intended the mention of his father's tragic end to lead to revelations concerning his own personal drama, but the human mind inevitably finds a way to divulge unresolved issues, astonishing even the speaker himself, who is powerless to stop it. And that's exactly what had happened.

"This is serious stuff . . ." Ayhan mumbled awkwardly. "If I read you right, you're talking about some important things here, Baturcan, my friend!"

Although nothing and no one save Belgin was important on this day of all days, Ayhan's sense of compassion meant he still found himself obliged to commiserate with anyone in need of sympathy, no matter the circumstances. "You're hopeless, Ayhan!" he thought, but he was in too deep now to change the subject.

"Actually," Ayhan continued, "there are many cases like that, but of course it's always kept under wraps, hushed up . . . For example, I suspect that a lot of those girls who mysteriously commit suicide out there do so because they've been married off to men who aren't interested in women . . ."

He stopped talking and weighed the effect of his words. He didn't want to go too far. Actually, he too had been born into, and was still part of, a culture of machismo. He'd unquestioningly ridiculed homosexuals as "faggots," demoting them to the status of women, who were in every way considered inferior, while believing his own status as a man to be thus elevated. It was easier that way, and even advantageous. And this went on up to his days as a student at the academy, when a talented and earnest classmate had become so oppressed by his terrible secret that he'd chosen to end his life. Yes, it went on, but only up to that day . . . Ayhan had been shocked by the death of his young friend, and realized for the first time that social pressures can be deadly. For the first time, he imagined what it would be like to be one of those homosexuals he had ridiculed. After that, he never again told a faggot joke or allowed one to be told in his presence.

And then, one day, during a workshop class, when he'd maintained that "men can be feminists, Christians can fight anti-Semitism, whites can stand up for the rights of blacks, Muslims can oppose the destruction of a church and veterans can join hands with conscientious objectors . . ." a student not unlike himself, back when he was an ambitious but penniless country boy, had taken exception, ribbing him with, "But Professor, is it possible for the wolf to lie down with the lamb? Can a man and a woman be 'just friends'? How long can fire and gunpowder rest side by side without there being an explosion? I'm surprised how quickly a villager like you has forgotten the laws of nature!" And the kid had smiled. And Ayhan had smiled too because he'd been flippant and carefree once himself, and had relied entirely on this determinist line of reasoning. "You're right," he replied, looking directly at this student who was at least fifteen years his junior. "That is, you're right as long as you think like a wolf. But you're here in this class as a person, to study sculpture. People are born people, but one's humanity is learned. Did you know that? The education you receive here is to teach you humanity. After all, creativity can't be taught—it's assumed that you got into this workshop because you've got some natural talent already. All we can do is guide you, and try to give you the skills you'll need in addition to that talent. Without a sense of humanity, you may become a successful sculptor, but you'll never become a true artist . . . or a good man," he'd said. The kid had been quite dismayed by this speech, delivered as it was in front of the female students, and his smile became a scowl.

Ayhan had wanted to think about Belgin, to lose himself in excitement and fear while he waited at Atatürk Airport, and he was angry at himself for reminiscing with Baturcan. But Ayhan was Ayhan, and although even he sometimes disliked his own tenacious refusal to leave anything half-finished, he knew it was part of the package.

"There are some things in life you just can't force, Baturcan. And how," he asked, taking a drag on his cigarette, "do you explain that to homophobes and the women who encourage them? We haven't come to terms with our own history—we're still too embarrassed to talk about those young men that were reserved for the pleasure of our sultans! No, all we talk about are the women of the harem, and the number of women we've bedded ourselves! We're still that insecure! Why?"

The barman listened, barely breathing. It's true that many of the men who stopped by the bar had been eager—especially after a couple of drinks—to air their half-baked ideas, but no one had ever been as blunt and outspoken as Ayhan. Even so, Baturcan thought it best to proceed with caution.

"When my dad died, I had to drop out of school. I began bussing tables at a *meyhane* where someone from back home worked, and my sister got married, my big brothers found new jobs, my mother took in ironing at home . . ." he said softly. "What I really wanted was to study, become a draftsman or something, so I could work for an architect in one of those fancy offices . . . But being a bartender is fine too—you get the chance to meet people . . ."

Frowning and sucking on his cigarette as he listened, Ayhan was observing that the tic in Baturcan-İlyas's shoulder, which caused him to twitch as though he was doing the *horon*, a traditional Black Sea dance, became even more violent when he was excited. The mind of a sculptor is accustomed to observing muscles and sinews.

"That virago we call Istanbul always chooses her victims from the ranks of the newcomers, from us all, the bitch!" he said, taking his eyes off the barman's shoulder and bowing his head. Suddenly desolate, eyes burning, he missed Berfin.

Neither man spoke as they pondered the victims that had already been sacrificed and those that surely would be.

"But you know what really gets me? The ones selling tissues out on the streets, the little ones who've died and the others who are going to die from sniffing glue. They're being sacrificed by their mothers and fathers . . . If I ever track one of them down, I swear they'll have to pry them out of my hands!"

"But they're just victims of fate too, Ayhan *Bey*," said the barman in a voice too low for Ayhan to catch. "We've all known victims, the victims claimed by Istanbul. She demands a sacrifice to cross her borders, like a savage goddess!" he sighed, essentially to himself.

Baturcan-İlyas was summoned by his supervisor. Not for the first time, he was given a severe warning not to spend too much time with one customer at the expense of others.

"I've offered up a sacrifice of my own, this city took some-one from me too, Baturcan—someone who was my heart and soul, my flesh and blood: Berfin!" said Ayhan, once Baturcan was gone, knowing he wouldn't hear, perhaps even preferring that he didn't. Ayhan quickly shook off those memories and began instead to think about the woman who would soon be stepping off a plane and into his arms. He found himself trapped in a kind of Araf, a Muslim limbo, a borderland between paradise and hell reserved for those whose sins and virtues are evenly balanced. He was caught between his longing to see Belgin and the desire to flee before they met.

Some time later, as he served Ayhan a third mug of beer, Baturcan asked:

"You mentioned stones . . . are you an engineer, Ayhan *Bey?*"

"No way! There's no way I could bring myself to cut and shape stone for buildings and bridges. God forbid! For me, stones are living things, Baturcan! I stroke them, cherish them, lay bare their beauty, even hear them . . . Each piece of stone conceals a jewel, each has its own story and history . . . Each is unique, like people. Stones are our mothers and our fathers, like fire, water, air, and earth . . . They're also our legacy. And stone, would you believe it, surrenders itself only to those able to understand their language! I'm a sculptor, a shaper of stone."

As he talked, Ayhan's face lit up . . . hands lifted to caress an imaginary block of stone, he was off in another world. Uncertain whether or not the man who claimed to love stone was putting on an act, Baturcan was more than a little confused and wary, but listened appreciatively nonetheless. At times like this, the tic in his shoulder was stilled.

"Look," Ayhan continued, "there aren't many people who hear the language of stones! Not just because they don't take the time . . . It's simply that most people are deaf to it. Take Rodin, for example: he knew them through and through. One of my child-hood idols! His statues give you the feeling of being so close to reality that it pains the soul. You know, in the early days, his work disgusted the bourgeoisie—there was *too much* reality, in fact. I loved that kind of thing when I was young, provoking the bourgeoisie, being a rebel. I was poor, a peasant really, and determined to become the next popular hero, like Yaşar Kemal's Memed from *Memed, My Hawk*, or the 'Ugly King' himself, Yılmaz Güney. No one bothered to tell us that the important thing was the hard work, patience, and strong sense of right and wrong that went into creating a character like Memed or a persona like Güney—that we should look further than the gallantry, the defiance and the drama. Anyway, these days I'm more interested in the nature of art itself than in grand gestures, both in my work and in my daily life."

The ability to listen attentively to customers is said to be intrinsic to the art of bartending. Baturcan was a master of this art.

"I was obsessed with Rodin's *Gates of Hell*. Seeing the original, touching it, seemed to me a magical thing; photographs, magazines and books just wouldn't do! Those who don't strive to reach the works of their master can never become artists! An enthusiastic student in my final year, I borrowed and scraped for busfare to Paris, where I spent three hungry days at the Musée d'Orsay, spellbound in front of that gate, before returning to Istanbul without having had so much as a glimpse of the Eiffel Tower! It's true my older brothers were workers in Europe, and helped me out a bit, but what's important is total determination, the ability to completely dedicate yourself to something, to art! The following summer, even though I was barely getting by on an assistant's salary, I made prints and did any other odd jobs I could find to save up for a trip to Florence to see Michelangelo's *David*. Amazing! I had a professor at the academy, Baturcan: Vasıf Esmer, a great sculptor! (May he rest in peace!) He changed my life. 'Look, Ayhan,' he'd say, 'if you're going to be an artist, first read Dante's *Divine Comedy*; only then will you understand *The Gates of Hell*. Do whatever it takes, but find it and read it, then come back to me!' Would I find it? If you look hard enough, you can find anything in Istanbul. Well, I did find it, read Dante until my head split and my eyes glazed over, but then I found myself more confused than ever. 'Confusion opens the door to development,' Vasıf Hodja told me. Later, after reading the poetry of Baudelaire and the works of Freud, I felt I was finally getting somewhere. But you know what, Baturcan? Sometimes I think *The Gates of Hell* will always remain a bit of a mystery—at least to anyone who hasn't been shaped by Christian culture.

"It's true that without some understanding of Western art, we can't create universal art, but if we expect everyone, even the uneducated, to develop an appreciation for art, we need statues, paintings and music rooted in our own culture. We can't create our own art without first being in touch with our own folklore, regional stories and religion; otherwise, this is all we'll ever amount to! We still don't have the freedom to use our Prophet or stories from the Koran in our art . . . It's still taboo, still sinful! But that's why we're still in thrall to the West!"

Although much of what Ayhan said had gone over his head, Barman Baturcan listened attentively, affected as much by Ayhan's charisma as by his words. Taking leave to serve a new customer, he returned, excited:

"I'm proud to have met someone like you, Ayhan *Bey*. Especially considering your background and how you managed to make it as a sculptor in a place like Istanbul."

Ayhan laughed and lit another cigarette. "Don't make so much of me! For all our complaints, remember, we live in a country where a shepherd can become president and the child of a farm hand can become a professor."

"That may be true, but those are pretty rare occurances, Ayhan *Bey* . . ."

"So, you're saying the Istanbul Dream is still elusive, are you?" Ayhan asked, smiling.

Neither of them spoke, and during these moments of silence, neither man had any idea what the other was thinking.

"My father was gone before he ever had a chance to feel proud of me," Ayhan announced, sporting a new smile. He scrunched up his face, as though he had an unpleasant taste in his mouth, and bowed his head as though he wanted to plunge it into his mug of beer.

Wanting to comfort him, the barman asked, "Where'd he go?"

"He moved along to the other side . . . you know, disappeared for good."

"Allah's mercy on him, Ayhan *Bey*!" Baturcan said softly.

"What do you mean 'Allah'? I don't believe in any of that stuff!" said Ayhan.

The barman was horrified. "Bite your tongue! Vow never to say anything like that again, Ayhan *Bey*! What kind of way is that to talk?" Baturcan drew back a few steps. "We'll be struck down here and now . . ."

"Dad was already forty-eight by the time I was born; it's considered a ripe old age in Anatolia for someone who's toiled out in the fields all his life just to fill his stomach. Living that long is quite an achievement . . . If you call it 'living' . . . He never did have enough money for food, just frittered away his life producing children! He just kept making more kids; seven of us survived; who knows how many others miscarried or were made to miscarry or died soon after they were born. That was my father, just thinking of himself, never thinking of poor mother, even though birth control was being handed out to the poor! He smoked a lot, and whenever he got hold of ethyl alcohol, he'd even drink that . . . I suppose it's no surprise he passed away so young." Ayhan's ever-present smile turned bitter as he stubbed out his cigarette. Meanwhile, Baturcan was silently reciting the first verse of the Koran, in order to avoid divine retribution.

"As for me, I was crazy about rocks and stones as a kid, and only Mom understood. At first, on account of my age, no one in the village gave me any shit about it. But when they saw I was still carving stones at age ten, everyone—including Dad—made fun of me: 'Like a woman doing her knitting,' they'd say. But I was so obsessed with the different textures and grains, the way the rocks felt in my hand, the energy hidden inside, their forms . . . You know, I'm still in love with the energy in stones," Ayhan's smile returned to its previous luminosity.

"So a person can fall in love with a rock, then?" asked the barman, showing a genuine and growing interest in Ayhan's story.

"Of course they can, Baturcan—of course, *hodja*! It's like the passion writers feel for words, or poets feel for sound and rhythm, or painters feel for shapes and colors. A writer friend of mine once told me that as she watched the letters form on the page, she felt a sensation akin to walking on air, to floating. The whisper of pen touching paper, the joyous hush as ink flows from pen, shaping a letter, produced a spiritual explosion in her, an orgasmic thrill. The profound pleasure I feel as I work with stone, as I caress and carve it, is something like that. It's an intensely pure love that nothing else can compare with . . . For example, it's far more overpowering than the hopeless love that binds a man to a woman."

Baturcan's face clouded over during this last sentence, and when his shoulder started twitching Ayhan paused, slapped his knee with his hand, scratched the back of his neck, raised his eyebrows, and pursed his lips. He looked as sorry as he felt.

"Or to put it more correctly, it's stronger than the hopeless love one human being can feel for another. That's better, isn't it? Love is love, young man!"

The barman avoided Ayhan's eyes as he echoed his smile. He clearly appreciated the revision.

"But except for my mother, not a single woman has ever understood, forgiven or failed to make me pay for my passion for stone. Not my ex-wife, not my girlfriend, herself an art historian . . . Or any of the others . . . Every single woman felt threatened by this love and proceeded to completely screw up our lives because of it! One of them even said, and I swear on bread and the Koran that these were her exact words: 'It's the rocks or me!'"

The barman was pleased that Ayhan wouldn't be going to hell after all, for despite having declared himself an unbeliever, his frequent references to Allah and the Koran suggested to his listener that he wasn't entirely serious, at least, about his lack of faith.

"But isn't jealousy only human?" the barman suggested. "Of course lovers get jealous, even of stones. There's no difference between the living and the nonliving when it comes to jealousy!"

Ayhan was too wrapped in thought to hear him.

"And then there came Belgin . . . An angel, soaring high above the clouds even as we speak. That was two years ago, at a mixed exhibition in New York. The most melancholy eyes in the world . . . A woman as intelligent as she was beautiful . . . Listen carefully, intelligent *and* beautiful, I said! Just for your information, there aren't many of those around!"

He paused, studying the barman to make sure the young man appreciated just how difficult it is to find intelligence and beauty in the same woman.

"Don't say that, Ayhan *Bey*. Some beautiful women just choose to appear stupid—it's a supply and demand thing, you know . . ."

Ayhan was surprised. He hadn't expected Baturcan to produce such a comment. But the barman acted as though he'd merely stated the obvious, and was at that moment busily scratching his ear with his pinkie. Noting the disbelief in Ayhan's eyes, he elaborated.

"Women open up when they talk to gay men . . . That's how I know . . ." He lowered his eyes and waited for his words to take effect. "Actually, Ayhan *Bey*, if you heard some of the things women said about men, you wouldn't believe your ears! The apparently mindless chatter, the forced laughter at crude jokes, the pretense that certain things just go right over their pretty little heads . . . If you knew what women really know about men, your views on the fairer sex would shift fifty degrees, I can guarantee you that!"

This time it was the realization that the young barman had a certain perspective on women he himself would never enjoy that caused Ayhan to study Baturcan anew. He'd never imagined he would envy a gay man. It appeared that in certain ways Baturcan had achieved a far more intimate contact with women than Ayhan ever could, the same Ayhan who had always prided himself so on his success with women and his ability to read their deepest thoughts. But why had Baturcan spoken of a fifty-degree shift in perspective, not 180?

"Well, you're never too old to learn," Ayhan said, mostly to himself, but his words brought him no comfort. He cracked his knuckles grimly, one by one, and lit another cigarette.

Gleefully counting a large tip left by a customer who'd gone out following the announcement that the plane he was meeting had landed, the barman once again took up his post across from Ayhan.

"So, Ayhan *Bey*, you were in the middle of telling me about that exhibition. I'm dying to know what happened . . ."

Ayhan noted that the barman had already forgotten about his own comment on women, which confirmed that Baturcan had seen it as a self-evident truth.

"Now, where were we, Baturcan? Ah, you were ruining my story!"

"No, I wasn't. We were at the best bit. You know, the meeting at the exhibition . . . Well?"

Unsure exactly how many beers he'd drunk before coming to the bar, Ayhan was hit by another wave of panicked anticipation of his approaching reunion. A new smile, this time heralding a sense of helplessness, crept across his face as he settled down to tell his story to a barman he'd only just met. He told himself he had plenty of time and would never see the barman again anyway . . . And, really, in the final analysis, did he actually give a damn about any of it?

"Belgin was at the exhibition, but we hadn't met yet. It was an opening at Türk Evi for an exhibition of works by Turkish artists, and it was only my second time in New York. I was considered to be a bit of a 'hick,' ha! Just imagine, I was the youngest sculptor there. The others were all urban types, the children of 'good families,' college kids—and there I was, a poor villager, son of a day-laborer. If Dad had heard that Ayhan, son of a cotton picker, a boy crazy about stones, was representing Turkey abroad, he'd have burst with pride. But it was too late, of course: he'd never know . . .

"So there I was, completely smitten with the New World,

bowled over by New York, knocked out by the time difference; in short, a total mess! I'm not one for show and ceremony, those cocktail parties suffocate me, frighten me. So, I'm holding a silly wineglass, moving through the crowd like I haven't got a care in the world. All dressed up, but a bit stiff—as you can imagine—the village boy from Çukurova working his way through a bunch of ladies and gents reputed to be experts in the world of plastic arts. Oh! What's that? I look over and I see a woman, a woman with the most melancholy eyes in the world, hazel eyes so plaintive that anyone who looks into them is tied up in knots, captivated. A woman—a stunning woman, mind you!—is studying my statue, is talking to it: 'You,' she says, 'you hear it!' I swear on bread and the Koran, that's exactly what she said! She's standing there talking to the stone, just like me! She's looking at the statue I sculpted out of stone, touching it, caressing it, and—would you believe— seeing all my secrets, deciphering all my codes. And those eyes . . . I was riveted to the spot, clutching that silly glass. For the first time, I swear it, a woman other than my mother understood my love for stone! I didn't know where she'd come from, but there she was! A woman, quite tall . . . age, status, and stature all greater than mine. The daughter of a diplomat, a pampered only child educated in private colleges, waited on by servants, wrapped in cotton wool and doted upon . . . Marble-white skin and an old-fashioned hairdo with jet-black bangs . . . But it was her nose that got me. I've never seen anything like it: shaped like a comma, a slightly upturned, elegant little nose placed right in the middle of her face, like it'd been hand-carved. A great sculptor had worked on it, that much was clear! And that woman with the tiny nose and the world's most melancholy eyes understood my secret . . . And what's more important, instead of being jealous of my stones, she admired them, and me; she understood me, Baturcan!"

"Wow, what a love story, Ayhan *Bey*, like something straight out of a movie . . ."

"You can say that again, Baturcan. It is, isn't it? Then I snatched her away, smuggled those melancholy eyes into a place just round the corner, one of those New York cafés, the pretext being coffee and a chance to discuss art and sculpture. The following evening began with a group of artists from the exhibition and ended up just the two of us at a bar, food and drink and those melancholy eyes . . . On the third day, the melancholy eyes permitted me to touch that comma of a nose, and on the last day, her arms wrapped round my neck, her scent pervading my very being, those melancholy eyes were stored away forever, just here, in the palm of my hand. Look!" Ayhan's smile became joyful, momentarily, as he saw the barman examining the palm of his extended hand, as though whatever was hidden there would actually be visible.

"Wow, Ayhan *Bey*, what a story!"

"So you said, so you said! But maybe that's what's worrying me, that it's too good to be true . . ."

"Don't put yourself down, Ayhan *Bey*, you're a fine-looking man, a real dish!" said Baturcan, briefly running appreciative eyes down from Ayhan's thick black eyelashes to his broad chest.

"I might be, *hodja*, but this woman of mine's not accustomed to contenting herself with a single dish; she's been dining at a banquet her whole life. I suppose what I'm getting at may sound a bit old-fashioned, but it's what we call 'class difference'! And leaving that to one side, I still find even the mention of the words 'serious relationship' terrifying. Everything's been perfect for the last couple of years: Visiting her over there to spend a few weeks together in New York, a series of short holidays in London, Athens, Rome, supposedly to attend exhibitions and conferences, but each of them more like a honeymoon really. Living together will be different . . . And what's more, me—a guy constantly accused of being relationship-weary, relationship-wary, a relationship-casualty—I was the one who put the idea in her head, did all I could to convince her! Can you imagine that, me, who's always avoided long-term relationships . . ."

Like a runner out of breath, he stopped. He gulped his beer, held it in his mouth for a moment, and swallowed. Then he scrunched up his face again, as though his throat burned. Meanwhile, Baturcan went off to serve some other customers, then returned and replaced the ashtray.

"Do you think the love I feel for Belgin could ever equal the passion I feel for stone, Baturcan? If you stumble across a woman you love as much as stone, as much as Istanbul, as much as your own mother . . . If you found a woman like that . . . what would you do? Well that's just what I did, damn it! Instead of regretting it for the rest of my life, I stepped forward like a man and blurted out, 'Let's be together, come be my woman!' Me, can you believe it? I all but begged this terrifying woman . . . 'Wait,' she said. 'Let's wait a bit—we've only known each other a year.' The more she hesitated, the crazier I got. We'd reversed roles! I'd met my match, a woman even more of a man than I! Then, finally, she gave in, gave up her job, transferred to a university here in Istanbul, and now she's on her way . . ."

"You see, she's in love with you, too," the barman enthused.

"What a joy for you, Ayhan *Bey*: a girlfriend brave enough to take risks, and such a huge risk, just for you. My lover turned out to be a total coward. He's married, and too much of a weakling to tell his wife he's fallen for another man. In fact, his wife came over and threatened me, saying she'd send my picture to the newspapers. Can you imagine anything so primitive?"

Ayhan's eternal smile regained its former bitterness . . . He lit another cigarette, stubbing out the first one without finishing it.

"Unless courage is used at the right time, it can blow up and take you with it," he said.

They were silent, both of them pondering darkly on how to elaborate on that grim sentiment. While they were still thinking, new customers arrived in the bar and gave Baturcan their orders, which he delivered with his own smile. When he returned, Ayhan was still deep in thought.

"Ready to start on your fourth one?"

"What do you mean fourth?" asked Ayhan, a bit alarmed.

"I just meant your fourth beer . . ."

"Ah . . . No, I'd better cool it. There's no sense in spoiling things, is there, Baturcan? Besides, if a man's determined to get drunk, even water can do the trick, can't it?"

"Perhaps I'm out of line here, Ayhan *Bey*, but I still think you're a lucky guy . . ."

"Lucky? I'm not just lucky, I've hit the jackpot, Baturcan! Like I said before, I've won the lottery, I've won, but I wonder if I'm ready to be rich?"

They laughed.

"Baturcan, you know what the devil's whispering to me, what's really tempting: just get up and go, split while you have the chance . . . Belgin can go back to the US on the first plane, to her work, to her life, to her friends, to her own world . . . We could cut our losses now, while there's still time, before either of us ends up getting hurt . . ."

"How can you say that, Ayhan *Bey*, and about the first woman you've met who isn't jealous of your rocks . . . ?"

He laughed. Looking into Baturcan's eyes with a new tenderness, Ayhan joined in. Seizing the moment, the barman was forward enough to ask: "So, is Ayhan your real name?"

"Well, it's not my stage name! Why do you ask, anyway? I'm Ayhan, Ayhan Pozaner."

"Well you did say you were from a village and all, and the name Ayhan does seem a bit, well, flashy. Please don't take it the wrong way."

"No, of course not. My name's real enough, but what a reality it reflects! I wasn't one of those kids named 'Ayhan' just so it rhymes with the names of his brothers. You're right, my big brothers and sisters have good honest names like Ali, Hasan, Mehmet, Hatice and Ayşe. I suppose mine is kind of classy compared to theirs. Before I was born, my mom would go to work in the cotton fields with my father, and it was there, in an outdoor summer cinema showing Turkish films, that that illiterate mother of mine, who'd never even had a chance to learn Turkish, who got by with five or ten broken sentences, went and fell head over heels for the king of heartthrobs himself, Ayhan Işık! She didn't have enough money for tickets, of course, so the poor thing would watch from outside, watch the film backward from behind the screen. Adana already had its homegrown 'Ugly King,' Yılmaz

Güney, so why shouldn't it have a handsome one as well! Right, right, who were we, and who was Ayhan Işık, even with all his charisma . . . But anyway, my mom takes one look at Ayhan Işık and goes 'Now that's what I call a man!' Of course, if she'd said that in front of Dad, the dearly departed would have broken her nose for her. You know, over in Adana, we don't go in for things like platonic love!"

"It's like that everywhere . . . up in the Black Sea, a woman's forbidden to imagine she might even think she's attracted to another man, but husbands are allowed to do whatever they want, Ayhan *Bey*!"

"But once a woman's made up her mind, there's no stopping her, Baturcan. My mother plotted and schemed and finally ended up naming her next baby boy Ayhan. She talked my dad into it by saying, 'We'll name your son Ayhan, so he grows up to be a great man!' These women, Baturcan, they're indomitable, believe me."

"And you did grow up to be a great man, Ayhan *Bey*: exhibitions in America and everything . . ."

Ayhan chuckled.

"Who am I to claim greatness, Baturcan? Greatness is too much for me, look at me, a scared little man, still afraid of Istanbul and even afraid of Belgin!"

Baturcan was called by his boss and reprimanded once more for spending too much time with a single customer. He listened in silence, acknowledging he'd been wrong, but after serving another new patron he was right back in front of Ayhan, who was busy with a newspaper crossword.

"Quick! A neighborhood in Istanbul . . . Seven letters? Where do you live, anyway, Baturcan? In what part of the city did you become an Istanbullu?"

"In Cihangir, of course," replied Baturcan-İlyas, with considerable pride.

"Of course?"

"The best people live there, you know . . . Artists and such . . ."

"Cihangir's nice enough, but isn't it a bit expensive?"

"It is, but I wanted to live there so much. I mean, I really loved Cihangir . . . So when I was working as a waiter in Kumkapı, I met a real gentleman, the wonderful man who got me this job. He's your typical Istanbul '*beyefendi*,' lives in Maçka. He helped me out, made it possible for me to take a correspondence course. I've got a roommate, a friend who works as a bartender. So anyway, now I'm *Cihangirli* . . ."

"So not only have you become Istanbullu, you're Cihangirli too, are you?" Ayhan asked, his smile having turned affectionate. "Where do you live?"

"I'm both *Ortaköylü* and *Acıbademli*. My home and my atelier are in Ortaköy, so I'm *Avrupalı*, a European; but I teach in Acıbadem, so that makes me *Asyalı*, an Asian. I have it pretty good, so don't ask me what I'd really like. If you did, I'd tell you I wanted to move to Kabataş, just to be near the Istanbul Modern. Just imagine the luxury of living right across the street from a world-class art museum! Just imagine, getting up in the morning and saying to yourself, 'Okay, Ayhan, hurry up and get shaved and then off you go to the Istanbul Modern for a cup of coffee in that wonderful café looking out on the historical peninsula, before taking in a few of the new exhibits. How could a day like that go wrong?'"

"I know all about it. Erol *Bey*, that gentleman friend I told you about, just loves art and insisted I go with him when I had a day off. After wandering through the museum with him I couldn't understand why museums had always bored me!"

"Bless you, Baturcan, you really are something else, you know that? Hey, wait a sec, Belgin's never been to the Istanbul Modern. How could she, when it's only just opened and the poor girl's been away for thirteen years?"

"God willing, you'll be happy with Belgin *Hanım*, Ayhan *Bey*! I don't go in for referring to friends' wives as 'sister-in-law,' that's why I didn't call her *yenge*."

"Belgin *Yenge*, ha!" laughed Ayhan, roaring so loud that some of the other customers looked over. "Turkish! What a language we've got, this chatty, chummy, poetic language of ours! You know,

Baturcan, when I was little, we spoke a lot of Kurdish and just a little Arabic and Turkish at home—at school we spoke Turkish, and at the mosque we were taught Arabic. The only language my mother knew was Kurdish. She'd picked up a bit of Turkish, like I said, but only enough to get by, thirty or forty words, tops. Dear Mom wanted to read, always wanted so much to be able to read a Turkish newspaper. When I first started talking to stones, it was in my mother tongue. But I've forgotten it all now, damn it!"

They burst out laughing. Then they laughed some more. They laughed long and they laughed hard, not even understanding exactly what it was they found so hilarious. They laughed and laughed until the supervisor of the airport bar looked over at them, alarmed.

Two men in a bar in the waiting area of the international terminal at Atatürk Airport had talked like old friends, with a rare openness, about even the most personal subjects, and then they'd roared with laugher. But then, most men don't like exchanging confidences, do they; any talk about their feelings is excruciating.

"Believe it or not, Ayhan *Bey*, because they didn't use to send girls to school, back when my mother and her sisters were growing up, my mother only knew Laz! It wasn't until we came to Istanbul that she learned Turkish. What I mean is, back before I started school my Turkish was as bad as yours!"

"You're kidding!" Ayhan smiled. "Who'd ever believe it?"

Oblivious to the stares of onlookers, they continued their laugh, and the longer the two men laughed—these two men who'd begun learning Turkish only in school, but had each gone on to become Istanbullu; these two men born at least a decade apart in villages so obscure as to be barely noticeable on maps of the Black Sea and Çukurova—the more they laughed the more they bonded, reaching out to each other with the sound of their laughter, their true colors shining in their eyes, and finally, there in the airport bar, they became compatriots.

"Hey Baturcan, bless you, you've straightened me right out! But there's something puzzling me—what you said about my view of women changing fifty degrees. What did you mean by that? Why not 180 degrees? Why fifty?"

Barman Baturcan looked confused for a moment, then, with what Ayhan would have had to describe as a mischievous gleam in his eye, responded:

"*Haçen*, you mean you haven't heard that Laz joke, Ayhan *Bey*? You know, the one where Dursun goes, 'Have you ever been on a plane, Fadime?' and she says . . ."

Only one hour was left before Belgin's plane would land in Istanbul.

4
CLEANLINESS THROUGH GODLINESS

"This is Istanbul to me, the place where I spend eight hours a day, cleaning the porcelain thrones city folk rest on to do their business. These days they're made of porcelain back in the village too, but look, you're still meant to squat over a hole in the ground like God intended. The public ones used to have '100' on the door, but now you're more likely to see 'WC.' You know, like when the television shows university students holding up two fingers like a fork, to make a *V*, and the cops come over to club them. Well, if you stick two of those *V*s together, you get a double *V*, but for some reason the foreigners call it a double *U*. Anyway, stick a *C* just after the double *V* and you get what this place is. There it is on the door: 'WC.' Some people call it a washroom or a toilet or a restroom, but Turks pronounce WC 've-je' and foreigners say 'dah-bull-yu-see.' The tourists understand only if you say it like they do. I suppose that makes it easier for everyone.

"I don't call the toilet a *hela* anymore, even at home. It's not that I'm trying to be like one of those refined ladies; I do it for my girls. I want them to grow up city girls, nice and polite. We all want so much! Ever since we came to Istanbul, I've been using the word 'toilet.' My husband makes fun of me for changing my language. 'Hasret girl,' he says, 'it doesn't matter if you're rich or poor, you end up going to the same two places: one of them is the *hela*, the other is the funeral slab, and may Allah ease your way in both!' My man's like that, doesn't mince his words and doesn't know how to put things proper. So be it, but I still want to speak nice. Some things should change when you come to Istanbul, know what I mean?"

Hasret Sefertaş was a cleaner at one of the women's lavatories at the international terminal of Atatürk Airport. Having just replaced some rolls of toilet paper and emptied wastepaper baskets that were mostly full of soiled maxipads, she leaned against the wall near the door to rest her legs, for though only thirty-six, she suffered from varicose veins. According to the new regulations, it was forbidden for bathroom attendants to sit around while on the job. Every hour of their eight-hour shift they were required to vouch for the cleanliness of their demesnes by signing off on a check-list hung on the back of the door. The old custom of sitting on a low stool and accepting tips had been banned. Workers were none too pleased with the new regulations, which meant they were able to sit down only at mealtime; but, then, finding a steady job in Istanbul was something of a miracle, and it didn't do to turn your nose up at a miracle.

"Praise be to Allah," Hasret sighed matter-of-factly, natural as breathing, as she smoothed the blue tunic and trousers that comprised her work uniform, and tugged at the ponytail into which her thick black hair had been gathered. Like all the other girls in the village where she'd been born, she hadn't appeared in public without a head scarf since the age of ten, but this plump-cheeked, black-browed, black-eyed, softly rounded young woman was now an airport janitor, and went bareheaded to conform to those same regulations.

"For as long as I can remember, that's the way things were done back home," she thought to herself. "Boys were circumcised as they trod the path to manhood and young girls took to wearing a head scarf. That was our way, all we knew, just as it had been for my mother's family and my grandmother's family. But there was none of this worrying over whether a single strand of hair was showing, this wrapping your head up tightly in a kind of skull cap under a scarf, hair gathered in a bun like you were being taken in for an X-ray. That's new. In my day, we just followed tradition. Of course, girls change when they move to the big city. Just look at my kids. They've changed too, but there's no wearing head scarves. They've been city girls for a while now and wear jeans and all that. I just don't get it. How can they say that without a head scarf you're not a real Muslim—God forbid! Who would think such a thing? The very idea. Look, all I can say is: *Elhamdüllillah*—Glory Be to God; I'm a True Believer. Even if they threaten to chop off my head, I'll say there's only one Prophet, and Mohammed is His name! So what's all this fuss about head scarves?

"One day I heard that some women who'd moved to Istanbul from my village had found work at Atatürk Airport, with health and retirement benefits no less. I wasn't about to miss out on a chance like that. Cleaning house just won't cut it; there's no worker's comp, health benefits, or pension. And as for our husbands, well, none of them bother to hold down a job. What a bunch of worthless lumps they turned out to be, hanging out at the teahouse all day, smoking pack after pack of foreign cigarettes. And as for rakı, 'lion's milk' is what they call the damned stuff! Can you believe that? So, anyway, we wives sat our men down and told them straight, we need a good job and this is why. My guy's as lazy as they come, but he's no dummy. 'Okay then,' he said, and gave me permission just like that. And now I've been working here as a cleaner for two years. Praise God, I couldn't be more pleased. At first, it wasn't easy working without anything on my head. I just wasn't used to it. I'd been wearing a scarf for years, like a second skin. But we've all got to earn our daily bread, and there's nothing wrong with an honest day's work as long as you get your husband's permission first. Anyway, we all tie on a scarf before we leave home in the morning, wear it on the service bus, and take it off only in the employee changing room when we put on these blue uniforms. And when we finish work in the evening, the scarves go back on our heads until we get home. Working here at the airport is kind of like being at home anyway, and I have to admit that I look pretty good in my work clothes. My curves show a bit, but that's to be expected: women have breasts and round bottoms, there's no getting around it!"

Sighing deeply once again, "Praise God!" exclaimed Hasret, her hand automatically traveling to her hair to adjust the absent head scarf.

"I'm so used to it. My hand just goes up there. At first I felt naked, but I've begun to adjust. Even so, when I'm here at work bareheaded like this, I feel all funny; even when a woman looks at me, I get embarrassed and a little resentful. Like they're going to tell my superiors on me: 'Look, Hasret's taken off her scarf; for shame!'"

At that moment, a toilet flushed and a large, elderly tourist emerged from a stall. Hasret took in the foreigner, at least thirty years her senior, eyeing her from head to foot: the Bermuda shorts riding up between generous thighs, the backpack and the rubber-soled shoes.

"If she were back in our village this old lady wouldn't be running around, she'd be laid up in bed lording it over her daughters-in-law. Get a load of her, though, walking around straight as a broomstick, just amazing! These foreigners are nothing like us. The women think of themselves first, just like the women of Istanbul, and the men can't get away with being a pack of good-for-nothing lumps all the time. Well, all I can say is, good for them! Ah, ah, in this false world of ours nothing beats being born a city woman. That's fortune for you . . ."

As the foreign lady washed her hands, wearing the studiously benign but curiously vacant smile of the well-intentioned stranger in a strange land, she peered at the mirror image of Hasret, the first Istanbullu woman she'd ever laid eyes on. The woman's gray hair fell loosely to her shoulders; she was dressed in a comfortable oversize T-shirt and orthopedic sports shoes that clearly cost a mint. Her eyes remained on Hasret as she dried her hands.

"That's it, smile. Smile away! You've got plenty to smile about! I bet you've got our countrywomen cleaning your WCs back home, too. Who's going to smile if not you, mother? My sister-in-law tells me everyone from our village who migrated to Germany is cleaning either toilets or streets. And even our men, who are normally so lazy—they'd stay in their mothers' bellies forever if they could swing it—work like donkeys once they get to Germany. That's what really burns me up. We get saddled with all their troubles, but when they land a foreign woman they manage to get along just fine, all sweet as can be. Ah, ah, how could you know what our men are like, living off their wives' earnings, sitting all day on asses like a bunch of leaky tires, at home, in the teahouse, and in the fields, while our brainless women slave away and are still expected to pull a nightshift in bed! It's been ten years since we moved to Istanbul. My husband's still unemployed. My oldest daughter and I work to make ends meet so we can survive here in the cruel city. That's right, smile, smile for all you're worth, smile with those bow-tie lips. You've got plenty of money and your salt's dry, so smile away . . ."

As she walked out, the foreign lady bestowed upon Hasret a new, frozen smile and an American dollar. Hasret took it without hesitation, nodding her thanks but omitting to smile in return.

"I really shouldn't have taken it, but, well, I need it! I've got to pay for my youngest girl's school. I'll do whatever it takes so she can study and doesn't turn out like her mother. If just one of my girls can get an education, so she doesn't have to depend on her husband! My dad didn't send me to school, married me off when I was young. And look how that turned out!"

The thought of it always got to Hasret, who, barely able to contain herself, would have to get up and pace, muttering to herself to calm down. That's what she did now, marching around the empty restroom, flushing toilets one by one and tugging at her blue work apron.

"When I first came to cruel Istanbul, I got a job at an apartment building where my sister-in-law worked as all-round building super and janitor. Seven days a week, I cleaned, did laundry, ironed, and wiped floors. There was a teacher lady in that building. She didn't have much money, but she'd still have me over to clean every fifteen days. May everything she touches turn to gold for saying to me one day: 'Look, Hasret, you're a smart woman. Not knowing how to read and write in this city is like being a fish that can't swim. You should take adult literacy classes in the evening. I've got friends in the civil service; they'll get you enrolled in a six-month course.' She kept at me, and would you believe it, I ended up going to reading and writing lessons for five months because of her! At first I lied to my husband, told him I was spending evenings with the teacher lady knitting things to sell for extra money. I figured he'd be against it, since he himself only ever finished elementary school and wouldn't want me getting ahead, but then I worried he'd find out anyway and divorce me or something. One thing I will say for my husband, he never beats me, but I was worried he'd want a divorce. It's really shameful back home to be without a husband, and being divorced is worse than being dead! That's not how we do things. We live in Istanbul, true, but we still follow the village ways. Anyway, it's not as if we can ever be like Istanbullu! That's too much to expect; it's not as simple as changing cities or moving house. You know, my girls always say, 'Divorce him, leave that drunk. He takes all your money for cigarettes and booze, has never been a real father to us, blames you for not giving him a son . . .' But I can't do it . . . Look, maybe I'm not afraid to get rid of my head scarf, but I'm terrified at the thought of being all alone without a husband, especially here in Istanbul! They'd all gossip—'divorced,' they'd whisper, and I'd be too ashamed even to leave the house to go to work. He thinks he's so high and mighty, too good to shine shoes or hold down a job, the lazy bum. But at least he never hits me. Ah, I know what the other women go through; just about all of the wives from the village get beaten. But mine doesn't lift a hand and doesn't care about my head scarf. In the end, what more can you expect from a husband?

"Praise be to Allah!" Hasret sighed, smoothing her imaginary head scarf yet again. Then, she checked again that all of the supplies were in stock.

At that moment, the door opened and a young woman clicked in on designer high heels, bottom swaying in an ultra-mini that accentuated her long legs and narrow hips. Fresh from the hairdresser's, her thick black coif lay in sticky clumps and the heavy makeup she was wearing on this hot summer day failed to mask the traces of acne on her cheeks. She wore tiny diamond earrings and carried an expensive briefcase and a dossier. She wasn't what one would call pretty, but she was young, full-lipped, and radiated an animal sexuality. She was perfectly conscious of the effect her youthful long legs had on men, but so high were her heels and so short her skirt that they didn't seem to have anything to do with each other—or even her.

"Just look at that hussy, all her airs and graces!" Hasret muttered. "May Allah keep my girls from going down that path, God forbid, and perish the thought!"

Giving her a condescending look, the woman handed the dossier to Hasret:

"Hey there, keep an eye on this for me, would you?"

"Sure. No problem . . ."

"Thanks. You can't imagine what it's like lugging around the boss's stuff in this heat!"

"My oh my, doesn't she work hard for her money, the rude thing!" Hasret thought, trying to work out what was written on the dossier as the woman disappeared into a stall. Without realizing it, she sounded out the syllables, as she'd been taught at the literacy course.

"EN-TEK Trade, Inc. Mi-nutes of Mos-cow Meet-ing of Turk-ish and Rus-sian Bu-si-ness-men. 15 July. Tİ-JEN DE-RYA . . . *Tijen*? What kind of name is that?"

The woman sprang out of the stall and furiously grabbed at the dossier. "It's confidential," she scolded.

Noting that the woman hadn't flushed or even bothered to wash her hands, Hasret knit her black brow and stared in disgust.

"Confidential!" the woman repeated. "You can't go reading it aloud in public!"

"Yes, yes, you've been entrusted with top secret documents, eh, you little bitch?" Hasret thought, staring in silence at this airport patron. "And aren't you something, anyway, haven't even learned to flush, running around with shit on your hands!"

Oblivious to the daggers boring into her back, the woman— who was indeed named Tijen Derya, by the way—plucked a lipstick out of her Gucci handbag, resting on the marble countertop, and applied a fresh coat to herself, warbling out snatches of a song in English as she did so:

"Everyway that I can . . ."

"Oh my, just listen to her. Sings in a foreign language and all! I know her type: fresh out of the egg, but turning up her nose at her own shell! Well, what do you expect from someone who leaves a fresh dump in the toilet bowl. She probably brings her shit home with her. Look at her, painting those lips with that dirty hand, then kissing some lucky guy with the same lips. The Travels of a Turd, ha-ha!"

Sensing the bathroom attendant's less-than-charitable thoughts, Tijen Derya made no effort to conceal her disdain. Calvin Klein perfume, Yves Saint Laurent blusher, and a hairbrush lined up in front of her, she painstakingly refreshed her makeup.

"That's it, Tijen *Hanım*, just keep painting! Who knows how much that paint costs; who knows where you get the money for it at your age; who knows why you go round half naked? I may be ignorant, but I'm not stupid, and I've seen your type on television, oh yes I have, sniffing at some rich man till both of them are doomed. O Lord, watch over my daughters, *Yarabbi*!"

"Praise the Lord!" she cried aloud, smoothing her hair and feeling, at that particular moment, truly blessed. Tijen Derya was startled by this sudden pronouncement, but grew even more agitated a moment later when it was announced that the THY flight from Moscow had just landed.

"Ahhh, he's here! Better get there to meet him!" thought the object of Harset's scorn, quickly gathering up her things and racing out of the restroom. In her panic, it transpired, she had forgotten her cell phone in the stall, resting on the toilet-paper dispenser.

"That's it—run, baby, run. Your boss can always get you a new phone. A big boss like him must have a long life behind him and pockets full of cash . . ." Hasret thought, shaking her head as she examined the phone, testing various buttons as she tried to turn it off. Once the screen went dark, she put it in her pocket. Then she turned her attention to the mirror, mimicking Tijen: lips puckered into an exaggerated moue, she applied imaginary lipstick with her finger. She expected Tijen Derya to come back for her phone, and, a moment later, that's just what happened:

"Excuse me, did I leave my phone here?" Tijen asked in a wheedling tone. She seemed deflated, somehow reduced, shorter, even her eyes smaller below their thick coat of dark blue shadow. Under layer after layer of foundation and blusher, her pocked cheeks were distinctly pale.

"I really couldn't say . . ." said Hasret, looking around. "So many come in and out of here, this being the toilet and all. Have a good look round; if it's here, you'll find it . . ."

Tijen began searching frantically.

"This is like the third time I've done this! How can I tell him I lost another one, damn it!"

Ignoring Tijen, Hasret began singing a folk song as she checked the wastepaper baskets:

"Deer felled by a hunter, way back yonder, beyond the mountains . . ."

Expecting Hasret to help, Tijen Derya politely prodded her:

"Excuse me, you do remember me, don't you? I was here just a minute ago. You looked after my dossier for me. Remember?"

"Are you talking to me?" asked Hasret, feigning surprise.

"Yes. Remember me, Tijen? You were reading my dossier . . ."

"Pardon me, Miss, but we get so many people in here. It's enough to make me forget my own face, let alone the ones I only see once . . ."

"It was a very expensive phone, damn it! And I had the sound switched off, so I wouldn't even hear it ring . . ."

"This is Istanbul, lady. If you give them your hand, they'll steal your whole arm. You can't trust anyone! You've got to keep your eyes open. You might have left it here, but with so many people coming in and out, there's no way to be sure . . ."

"God Almighty, the plane's landed. Mehmet Emin *Bey* will have a fit if I'm not there to meet him," Tijen groaned. Shoulders slumped, pouting, she looked much younger, almost vulnerable. Her hand automatically reached into her bag for a cigarette, as it always did in moments of stress or joy, but was withdrawn when she remembered that smoking wasn't permitted in airport restrooms.

"Fuck! And it was so expensive. WAP, camera, Bluetooth, MP3 player, USB port, multimedia . . . the works."

"I feel really bad for you now. Why don't you go to the lost and found? You never know. Some good-hearted soul may drop it off there. Your dad's sure gonna be angry with you though . . ."

"Not my dad; Mehmet Emin *Bey*, my boss. I'm his personal assistant."

"You don't say? A young girl like you. Why, I thought you were a student. And here you are, an assistant and all . . ."

"A personal assistant! And I'm twenty-four years old! I finished university a year ago," Tijen snapped.

"Sure thing, sure thing. What do I know? I'm just an ignorant old woman. Aren't you a lucky girl to find work in a city like Istanbul. You know, my sister-in-law has this friend in Armutlu. They scraped together barely enough money and even went hungry to send their son to university. He did them proud, graduated with honors. But guess what, he still couldn't find a job. When you live in the outer slums a diploma isn't always enough, I guess. Anyway, he got mixed up in one of those protests and the police took him away, beat him up real good. I can't remember exactly what it was all about. Might even have put him in one of those new isolation cells, 'F-type' I think they call them. So he joined one of those hunger strikes in prison. Wasted away day by day, nothing anyone could do, until, I tell you, that boy died of starvation. Right in front of everyone. How his mother must have suffered! Her heart gave out and she hasn't been right since. Now if only that boy'd had some of your luck, enough to become a personal assistant or whatever it is you say you do. Well, I guess it wasn't meant to be. Just put him down as another victim of cruel Istanbul!"

"I don't live in a place like Armutlu!" Tijen hissed. "My father used to work at Antalya Marina, before he retired. And anyway, I'm an Istanbullu now!"

"Well good for you, miss. With your dark hair and black eyes, I thought you might be from Anatolia, like us. We moved to Istanbul from a village in Kayseri. It's so pretty out there. Nothing like it, even in Europe. But we came to Istanbul to find work. What can you do?"

"My family's blond, it's just that I take after my father's mother. We're from Antalya! Anyway, what am I doing wasting my time with you! I've got to go meet Mehmet Emin *Bey*. If you find my phone, drop it off at lost and found, would you?"

"Don't you worry your head about that. I'll be sure to run right over the minute it turns up. Don't you worry."

"What do you expect from a peasant?" Tijen thought to herself as she fussed with her hair. "She's old and jealous. And, oh-so-interested in my father and my boss. It's none of her business. Typical village cunning, acting dumb and stringing me along. Does she think it's easy to become a personal assistant at my age? Comparing me to the lefty slum-dwellers of Armutlu! Fuck! If it weren't for my English and my diploma, I wouldn't be where I am today. Doesn't she know how many girls are out to snag a boss like mine? And even when you do beat out the competition, you have to spend twenty-four hours a day beating the other girls off. But how's she supposed to know any of this, locked up in the can all day. Fuck!"

"Why don't you leave your number? I'll call if your phone turns up."

"Don't bother. I'll send someone from the company over to lost and found," said Tijen, suddenly deciding to touch up her makeup again.

"What if this peasant woman stole my phone? I wouldn't put it past her. She doesn't like me and could have done it out of spite. The sneak! I'll have her sacked and back in her village in two seconds flat! I'm sick and tired of her sort, always playing morality police. 'He's old enough to be your father,' they say. Well so what! What am I supposed to do, slave away all my life, unable to move to America or Europe until I'm forty or even older? We've all seen what happened to the older generation of women who thought everyone should 'stand on their own two feet.' And how did that fairy tale end up: they all lost their husbands to girls young enough to be their daughters. So much for hard work. Struggle, toil, wear yourself out. For what? The city's crawling with professional women as attractive as they are lonely, sad sacks with sterling characters and great clothes. Well, that's not going to be me twenty years down the line. Besides, Mehmet Emin is young at heart, likes me well enough, and does everything I ask. Whose business is it anyway? Look at Woody Allen. He married his own stepdaughter, thirty-five years his junior, and the ground didn't open up and swallow him. Besides, do they think handling an older man is easy? First of all, men over fifty are all total megalomaniacs. That's what mine is: pure ego through and through. Thinks he's done everything and always knows best. And then there's the smell of an older man . . . No matter how often they shower, how much aftershave they wear, there's no getting rid of that smell, the stale stink of an old man! Well, you can't expect to get something for nothing. It's that simple. And if the buyer and seller are both happy, what's it to anyone else? When Mom got sick, he had her brought over from Antalya, from a neighborhood like Bahçearası, straight to a five-star hotel, then chauffeur-driven to a private hospital for her operation! He found a job for my cousin. He's always given me everything I've desired and things I'd only dreamed about, too: restaurants, dining at private clubs, the chance to meet famous people. He moved me from my rented flat in Beşiktaş—700 lira a month I paid for that dump—to one of his apartments in Nişantaşı. And when we get married, I'll be moving into a triplex with a sea view. What more could I want? He's experienced and cultured; I suppose it's only natural that he's a bit arrogant. My grandmother used to say that all men are 'suckers for praise.' Too right! All you have to do is lay it on a bit thick. You know, the usual lines: 'You're really something in bed. My ex-boyfriend was so inexperienced. You make me feel like a real woman. I've learned so much from you.' That's it, nothing to it. You'd think he'd have doubts, but no, he laps it up just like a man, any man! So if that's what men want, that's what they'll get, a good dose of it, administered at the right time, in the optimum amount, and all with a straight face. And of course, you have to put on a bit of a show in front of his married friends, play 'horny but freshly fucked,' complete with bashful giggles and dirty words whispered into your man's ear. The other guys go green with envy while 'daddy' plumps up his feathers and struts. Oh, you should see him, the idiot. But the next day, daddy's good little girl is sure to get her reward. What a laugh!

"Yes, he might snore, secretly use Viagra, chew with his mouth open, doze off in front of the TV, and have a squishy middle, despite the dietician and trips to the health club. But his tailored shirts hide his flab; anyway, I always close my eyes when we're naked. He's clueless about foreplay and oral sex. 'Good sources' tell me he habitually cheated on his ex-wives and only hires female employees he wants to get into bed. So, sooner or later, he's going to cheat on me too. Well, so what? Our mothers all expected honesty and dependability. And look where that got them! All I have to say is, fuck them all!"

The end of Hasret's shift was signaled by the arrival of a new attendant in a blue smock. Greeting her coworker, Hasret ticked off each of the items on that list behind the door: floor, mirrors, washbasins, toilets, hand soap, wastepaper baskets, paper towels. Then she scrawled *Hasret Sefertaş* in large shaky letters and scratched in her signature with all the attention of a calligrapher, a joyous act of defiance against the old days of ink-stained fingertips.

As usual, the empty restroom was suddenly filled with a wave of visitors arriving to meet the next plane. It resounded to the sounds of clicking heels, splashing water, laughter and conversation.

"Have a good one!" said Hasret to her colleague, also calling out a "May God grant you abundance!" to Tijen, who was putting her paints and perfumes back into her handbag.

Instead of going straight to the changing room on the floor below, Hasret headed for lost and found, her hand wrapped around the cell phone in her pocket. She'd drop it off before she changed clothes, put on her head scarf, and go home. She hurried along at a brisk pace, such was her fear of being tarred with the sin of stealing when all she'd intended was to teach Tijen a lesson. But, afraid or not, she couldn't help smiling wickedly at the thought of the prerecorded message Mehmet Emin Entek must have heard at least half a dozen times by now: "The number you have dialed is not available at this time. Please try again later." It was a message Hasret had heard all too often when she called her husband on his own, second-hand phone.

5
ISTANBUL, MOTHER OF FREE TRADE

"See here, gentlemen, what's with all this démodé yammering about 'the people and the nation'? What's with the panicking—why all this agitation? It defies reason! Here we are, trying to integrate with a globalizing world, and there you are, up in arms over a so-called 'fire sale of our national resources.' Just stop it, for God's sake. Our leading economists have all talked themselves silly on the talkshow circuit, trying to bring the masses up to speed. But they refuse to get it! What a nation we are, in a class of our own, nothing like us on the face of the earth! There's no point in getting overwrought, gentlemen. I'll put this as simply as possible: We have no choice but to embrace a liberal economy; you can't have democracy without privatization; free countries have free markets.

"And then they label us *liboş*—imagining they've coined a withering insult with that adorable distortion of the word 'liberal'! Enough with your peasant innocence, gentlemen! If you ever bothered to study a little history, you'd realize that globalization is nothing more than trade without borders, which, incidentally, makes Istanbul the mother of globalization. But no, it's much more fun to play the nationalist card than to pick up a book from time to time. So tell me, while the state's resources were being flushed down the toilet, what did you accomplish with your populist cries of 'the people and the state'? Those days are behind us now. Sorry to break the news, but it just didn't work out. The era of unwieldy state banks, of Sümerbank and Etibank, is over; there will be no more 'Buy Turkish' weeks, with catchy slogans like 'Local Goods are the Nation's Goods—All Turks Should Use Them.' It's over, I tell you! Gentlemen, the time has come to build a bright new future!"

A business-class passenger aboard the THY flight just arriving from Moscow, Mehmet Emin Entek averaged twenty such business trips a year. It was his habit to rehearse an indignant analysis of his homeland's economy every time his plane spiraled down to Istanbul, addressing an imaginary audience at a chamber of commerce or a business dinner. For him, economics was the end-all and be-all of life; everything else fell into three broad categories: waste of time, unexploited potential, or general weakness of character.

"Did you really think you could run one of the most closed economies in the world for five decades, failing to boost per-capita GNP even as much as $2,500, at the same time as secretly pining for EU membership, of course, and all the while pumping up the people with slogans lifted from the heady days of the Turkish National Movement? For God's sake! It's just not possible. You can't opt for a capitalist economy and then play at being socialists. Look, even the Russians get it. This isn't the time or place for nostalgic yearning for socialism. The age of the nation-state is over, gentlemen!"

Even as a child, Mehmet Emin Entek had never traveled economy class, and even as an adult, he never traveled unaccompanied. While he'd occasionally forego the company of a young executive assured of a bright future at Entek, Inc., or of an experienced middle-aged executive, he would never have considered, even for a moment, dispensing with the services of a presentable secretary, better known, these days, of course, as a "personal assistant." It was essential that he be accompanied by at least one attractive young woman, for he was of the opinion that a man's attributes are most effectively thrown into relief by the presence of a pretty lady. He was also accustomed to hearing his chauffeur and retired human-resources manager outdo each other in an enthusiastic chorus of "Welcome back, sir!" the moment he stepped into the arrivals hall. This time, though, he was traveling alone.

Whether they arrive on long- or short-haul flights, are disgorged from first, business, or economy classes, all passengers descending upon Istanbul from the four corners of the globe are, for a moment, however brief, treated equally: Everyone is expected to queue up together for passport control. Everyone, that is, except for a select group of individuals determined by law to be Very Important Persons, and so get accorded access to the VIP lounge. Whether an individual is deemed important enough to be exempted from the other great Istanbul equalizers—water cuts, power outages, traffic jams, and the occasional earthquake—is, of course, another matter altogether.

Yes, the great mass of people straggle through passport control, trudge off to claim their baggage, and then opt either to rent a handcart or to engage the services of a *hamal*. It should be duly noted that airport personnel prefer, in this day and age, to be addressed simply and literally as *taşıyıcılar*, "carriers," rather than *hamallar*, "coolies," a vaguely Oriental word that evokes the image of a rough laborer bent double under an iron stove. The main complaint of these modern-day bearers of burdens, however, is the simple fact that so many passengers now choose to wheel off their own baggage, unassisted. As recently as five or ten years ago, that would have been unthinkable, but we can agree that the relegation of the *hamal* to the pages of history is an inevitability that might also be interpreted as a general triumph for humanity.

Businessman Mehmet Emin Entek was alone on this particular trip for the simple reason that he was involved with two women, each of them unaware of the existence of the other. The price of being greeted at the airport by the Turkish one was the absence in the seat next to him of the other. Mehmet Emin Entek craved praise and affection, and ensured that any displays of such were so genuine that he himself quite forgot that they had essentially been purchased, would even get quite choked up as he protested, "Ladies, gentlemen, you're embarrassing me." Big business, big deals, big demonstrations of love were the oxygen upon which he thrived. He had never in his life troubled himself with the details of "petty deals," which he mocked, leaving them to the weak. There was no place in his life for details or weakness, and never had been. Even his hobbies were chosen for their usefulness rather than pleasure.

His great-grandfather had been an astute and ambitious ironmonger who migrated from Ankara to Istanbul, opened a small hardware store in Karaköy, and then, acting on the principle that "all's fair in business," proceeded to expand by crushing everyone who got in his way and by snapping up assets left behind by non-Muslims fleeing Istanbul in the wake of the riots of September, 1955. In no time at all, he had opened several building-supply shops in Perşembe Pazarı, eventually bequeathing to his three university-educated sons the core of what would become the leading construction firm Entek, Inc. Two generations later, in Nişantaşı, Mehmet Emin Entek arrived in the world as the eldest son of a prosperous mercantile family, his future assured and the distant exploits of his grandfather whispered proudly into his ear as he grew up. As the most ambitious, fearless, and ruthless of the siblings and cousins that comprised the Entek clan, he had for a considerable time held the position of chairman of the board of Entek, Inc. Except for a few early minor business setbacks and a love affair gone wrong in his youth, he liked to boast that he had never been "stung," even as he proudly recalled that he himself had done a considerable amount of "stinging." But every time he bragged that he had never permitted—and would never permit—anyone or anything to weigh him down, he was struck by a sudden bolt of lightning represented by the memory of Belgin.

The key to Mehmet Emin Entek's character lay in the two things he'd admired since childhood: success and numbers. He'd been seduced by the concept of success right from the start. As the years went by, the act of succeeding developed into a growing addiction to success itself, just as the act of falling in love seemed to occur quite independently of the partner involved, where he was concerned. He'd been raised by a family driven by the pursuit of success, and had become insatiable for this very quality, reluctant to set aside precious time even to enjoy such success, once achieved. With loud guffaws, he'd proclaim himself a "hyperactive, adrenaline-driven" kind of guy as he raced toward the next target, the next "well done, sir!" "I haven't got time for this," he'd announce, never realizing how insulting he was being to the people left behind as he rushed to his office, where he found a kind of peace, sitting at his desk, even if he was only idly surfing the Internet. He lacked the self-knowledge to realize that he was essentially a greyhound forever focused on the elusive rabbit, instead fancying himself to be another Alexander the Great, forever pushing outward, forever expanding the boundaries of his personal empire. He was his own biggest fan and he demanded the same unreserved admiration from his friends, his wives, his lovers, and his children, twenty-four hours a day. Anything less, and such personal relationships were severed. Business relationships, on the other hand, were entirely different. He'd taken to heart his father's oft-repeated maxim: "There's no such thing as hurt pride, in business." There's no taking offense when you're dealing with someone you might have to work with, someday.

No, he only took real offense with people at home. For all the bluster, the swagger, the posturing, Mehmet Emin Entek was as sensitive as a little boy when faced with criticism of any kind, totally unnerved by and resistant to the slightest hint of faultfinding. The simple truth was that he had never grown up; nobody had helped him along the path to maturity. For narcissistic reasons of her own, his mother viewed this eternal boy wonder as her crowning achievement, beyond reproach or even guidance; and his father had simply never had time for the children. So Mehmet grew and, of course, learned, but his emotional intelligence remained a child's. And it was only at home that he could punish perceived transgressions with injured silences—first directed at his mother, when still a child; then at his wives and lovers, much later, as a man.

The Entek family viewed even personal relationships through the prism of success. For example, even though his mother knew her husband to be systematically unfaithful, she had never considered divorcing him. Six years ago, when his father had suffered a fatal Viagra-induced heart attack in the arms of a girl, his mother had keened and lamented with all the intensity of a miner's widow. Even the most successful of her three sons was quite impressed. Divorce would have been an admission of failure and, in any case, the only thing more difficult than gaining admission to the Entek family was receiving permission to leave it. Only one

73

person had flouted this unwritten rule, a person who had never fit in right from the start. Even while married to Mehmet Emin, Belgin had never managed to be an Entek, and after their divorce she'd had little to do with any of them. Thus, she represented the singular great failure for both Mehmet Emin Entek and his family: she, Belgin Gümüş!

Throughout his fifty-five years, Mehmet Emin Entek had never really learned to love anyone, even his mother. He wasn't a bad person, necessarily; he simply lacked the capacity to love anyone but himself, to love anything but success and numbers. He was also realistic enough to believe in, and even to approve of, the idea that everyone who loved him, including his mother, expected something in return. All but one person, that is. In his entire life, Mehmet Emin had met only one person who seemed to love him for himself, no strings attached. One person. Belgin. Belgin Gümüş. His ex-wife . . .

Numbers. Now they were something else! He worshipped them. Numbers, figures, statistics . . . He'd never been interested in letters or other shapes. In fact, he instinctively distrusted anything that was open to interpretation, which was why writing and painting struck him as suspect, emotional, feminine, three qualities he regarded as inherently unstable, unbalancing, threats to potency and power. Mehmet Emin Entek felt that numbers were entirely different. Numbers were their own language; they do not require translation or interpretation, cannot be incorrect, deficient, or excessive; they don't exaggerate or raise false expectations. Numbers never disappoint.

Most importantly, scale can only be measured in numbers. Amounts of money, quantities of moveable and immoveable goods, goals scored, countries visited, and units of sexual prowess, well, more or less, all came down to numbers and more numbers . . . Even when choosing gifts, his primary considerations were cost, size, or quantity. His Istanbul career in industrial engineering was driven by numbers, as was the MA in Economics awarded him in London. Power and success could only be quantified and defined through numbers, rendering meaningless anything that could not. For that reason, everyone and everything as divided into the countable and the uncountable; the measurable and the immeasurable. To date, he had rarely been let down by what he considered the magic key to any door: the simple question "how much?" And as an accomplished locksmith, he boasted an international array of keys: "How much?" "*Kaça?*" "*Combien?*" "*Cuanto?*" "*Hvor mye?*" "*Çend?*" "*Skolka?*"

Everyone called Mehmet Emin (*Bey*) by his first and middle names, everyone, that is, but his mother and his ex-wife, who called him "Entek." Belgin. The one woman he'd failed to conquer. Melancholic, lovely Belgin. A woman who always held back, who looked into her husband's eyes as they made love, yes, but never quite surrendered. Proud, aloof Belgin, the one person to shake off the Entek family name unscathed and without incurring major debts. Belgin Gümüş. The one person to give Entek the slip.

This was the same Mehmet Emin who frequently held forth on the subject of Man and Woman at crowded tables, the same Mehmet Emin with the loud, self-assured guffaws, the one never without an attractive young female employee at his side lending weight to his words, giving him a sort of raffish gravity: "Women are like money. Intimate knowledge and skill with the one gives you a head start in handling the other; the real victory for poor saps like us who claim to run the world will be the day we finally get a handle on the fairer sex! Ah, but who among us will ever be so skilled in the dark arts!"

Still, each time he trotted out this dinner-party chestnut, he would remember the look in Belgin's eyes. That memory left a sour taste in his mouth, removed the spring from his step, took the wind out of his sails. He wanted to shake free and instinctively sought to protect himself from the ghostly presence of the real woman who'd loved him without question or calculation. So he idealized her memory until her reality was lost. Thus he protected himself, secretly and determinedly. He knew that in order to get away from him, Belgin had fled Istanbul, and he realized that he had given her as much pain as had the assassination of her father. He knew, but the admission would have caused irreparable damage to the picture he nurtured of his own perfection. That is why he had screamed at Belgin as at no one else: she was the first person who had made him feel that he was just like anyone else. He had, of course, kept tabs on her, knew that his ex-wife was now a professor at Columbia University and had never remarried. One of the first steps he'd taken in the long process of mending his wounded ego was remarriage, the faster the better, to hurt Belgin, and with a shallow young woman of limited imagination to boot. This, his second wife, was a personal assistant who'd been recruited on the old principle that she was "eminently beddable." The young woman was as surprised as anyone by her meteoric rise from the ranks of executive secretary to the next Mrs. Mehmet Emin Entek, and many tears of gratitude were shed by her parents, who had not previously subscribed to a belief in miracles. At the first opportunity, Mehmet Emin took his bride to New York to meet the woman who had been his wife just weeks earlier. But Belgin had merely replied, "True to form," and walked off. Her melancholic eyes had said, "This is just what you deserve—I was always too good for you, Entek!" But there were no histrionics, no rage, no grievances . . . Just Belgin: proud, icy Belgin!

Some ten years into Mehmet Emin's second marriage, which had produced two sons, Başar Emin and Yener Emin, his wife suddenly decided she'd had enough of his frequent affairs. Ten years had been ample time for her to learn the ways of the world, and to realize that the same process which had so surprisingly rocketed her to matrimonial success would inevitably dredge up her replacement.

She hoped it wasn't too late to take steps. Her mother-in-law advised finding consolation in the Entek surname; advice that was spurned. Futile efforts to reclaim her wayward husband had progressed through numerous tearful scenes, visits to the shrines of holy men, and consultations with a modern-day shamans, culminating at last in the loss of her last bargaining chip, their two sons, custody having been granted to Mehmet Emin Entek during a hushed-up and hasty divorce that netted her a car, some jewels, an apartment, and, to some degree, her good name. Mehmet Emin believed himself quite upset as he cut out, for his personal archives, a tabloid account headlined "IRRECON-CILABLE DIFFERENCES END IN SPLITSVILLE FOR PHILANDERING CONSTRUCTION MAGNATE MEHMET EMIN ENTEK," complete with a photo in which he appeared to be gravely contrite, or at least a little sad. Some months later, having dared to take up with a young man approximately her own age, the mother of his children was warned that she would forever be an Entek, and was expected to behave accordingly. Shortly afterward, for reasons of her own, she moved to İzmir with her mother. She was gone, but *she* had not left *him*. No woman ever had; no woman ever could. Who could walk away from that "scion of Nişantaşı society," the "brilliant economist" and "trail-blazing businessman" whose "youthful good looks" belied his age? Well, there had of course been one—that one woman. She of the beauty he never tired of describing as "melancholy": Belgin. The beautifully melancholic Belgin Gümüş!

A senior partner in one of Turkey's foremost family-owned construction companies, Mehmet Emin Entek had begun traveling with increasing regularity to Moscow, as well as to Libya and the republics of Central Asia. On this particular trip, his "official girlfriend" and "personal assistant" of two years, Tijen Derya, had been left in Istanbul and in the dark over his affair with a Russian engineer. He'd employed the tried-and-true tactic of ensuring that the cheated party was tied down with a mission of his own devising; she'd truly believed that he trusted her and her alone to represent him at a company meeting while he was abroad.

In fact, Tijen had no real complaints. She was one of the thousands who crowd into Istanbul from small cities to attend university. To her credit, the girl was diligent and disciplined, but that's not what had first captivated Mehmet Emin Entek. No, he had been tickled and titillated by the odorless, colorless, and invisible—but nevertheless palpable—lust for power streaming from the corners of her mouth, her nostrils, her underarms, and even her inky pupils and dead eyes. While still in her final year at a business-administration school, Tijen Derya had been awarded a student internship at Entek, Inc. She may not have been as pretty as some of her predecessors, but she was young and long-legged and bold enough to go out on a limb, no pun intended, to attract the attention of the "big boss" at a company dinner. The audacious don't always succeed, but they certainly manage to get themselves noticed. It was there, at that dinner, that the big boss not only noticed this young intern for the first time, but recognized something of himself in her naked ambition.

Mehmet Emin Entek's libido as much as his gambler's instincts were stirred by a woman's lust for power. And if the woman happens to come from the aspirational classes, so much the better: the relative size of the prize makes her that much more compliant, that much more willing to raise the stakes and go for broke. He felt it wrong to compare such women to prostitutes: whores never go home empty-handed. But women who view men as so many stepping stones forego not only love, but—if they play their cards wrong—remuneration of any kind.

Belgin had been the exception. Her ambition baffled a man like Mehmet Emin: she seemed to be competing with herself. When she was a young assistant professor at Bosphorus University, she didn't envy her peers; she offered them heartfelt congratulations on their successes. She wasn't consumed by ambition but kept it in check, a controlled flame that enabled her to work for days without sleep. The advisor who helped her with her dissertation, Professor Yannis Seferis, would praise her as follows: "This girl's got a burning love for science . . . but she seems so dispassionate about everyday life!"

What was so praiseworthy about that? She was an odd girl, that Belgin . . . She, her friends and her family . . . Impossible to pin down, a bit aggravating, annoying . . . Perhaps annoying precisely because she was impossible to pigeonhole? Yes, Belgin had always been different. Mehmet Emin Entek may have held Belgin above and apart from all other women because he saw in her certain qualities that he secretly wished to see in himself. Perhaps what made her sacrosanct was that she had become his other and better self.

When Mehmet Emin Entek first took an interest in Tijen, he knew she had been dating a young man who was shoved aside the moment she sensed his interest. He also knew that she had had the presence of mind to keep the young man in her orbit, at arm's length, but always firmly in her grasp, should things go wrong. "Yet another young thing bent on rising above her station," Mehmet Emin had chuckled. As he got to know Tijen better, he came to realize that she had the makings of an ideal wife. For one thing, she knew she was no great beauty, and, like any woman, would have to compensate for that great shortcoming for the rest of her life. Everyone knows that beauty always beats brains. Secondly, she adapted quickly, embracing the company as her own; in no time at all, she took to referring to it as "our company," or "our project," and her loyalty would only grow the more she was praised and petted. After months of appraisal, Mehmet Emin Entek began to take Tijen Derya with him to invitational events, deliberately introducing her simply as "my right hand at the firm" or "a promising young assistant." It was his way of assessing her self-control and reserves of patience. How long would it take before she became possessive and began pestering him with cries of "come on, boss"? It was a little game he played, prolonging for as long as possible the pleasure he took from observing her "stealthy" quest to be promoted from "boss's assistant" to "boss's wife." He freely admitted that the pleasure he took was perverse—"It's something like peeping at a woman while she's masturbating or shaving her pubic hair!" he'd laugh to himself from under his moustache. But Tijen had unwittingly bared not her body, but her soul, as her boss patiently waited for greed to force her hand, to push her into the fatal error of pushing him prematurely.

But Tijen did nothing of the kind. By never questioning him about their relationship, she had revealed the magnitude of her ambition and her capacity for taking risks. It was also this show of backbone that had caused Mehmet Emin Entek to start asking himself whether she might even be "the one." After all, she did seem to appreciate his intelligence, youthful looks, and boundless energy. Unlike Belgin, she didn't get seasick when they went yachting, nor did she object when he got behind the controls of his private plane. She deferred to him in every way, and as she stealthily clawed her way into his world, she appeared to lay no claims to a world of her own. She was always on call, at his side whenever he needed her, as dependable as a shadow. How unlike Belgin in every way!

And Tijen had the youthful energy and drive required to adapt to him and to the Entek family. It's true she had her faults, was gauche and reckless; but those same traits could be used against her if necessary. She also had more serious faults: there was no denying her ignorant and frankly vulgar pretension, but Entek was confident he could mold the girl to his liking. In fact, her training had already begun. First she'd been transferred from a cheap flat in Beşiktaş to a fully furnished company flat in Nişantaşı. Then came a series of modest gifts: a laptop, a three-day holiday in Italy, courses in English and diction, a state-of-the-art iPod, cell phones to replace the ones she kept on losing, shopping privileges at cosmetics and clothing shops with the simple caveat that she furnish the invoices for all purchases, medical treatment for her mother in a private hospital . . . Yes, Tijen Derya had every reason to continue circling, biding her time. Her "prey," Mehmet Emin Entek, simply waited and watched, biding his own time, testing her mettle, reeling her in.

"I'll pop the question in a few months, maybe on her birthday. She's a Scorpio, isn't she? That's right, how many times have I heard her tell me: 'Don't forget, I'm a Scorpio!' A simple wedding at the end of the year, and that's that!" he was thinking as he made his way to the baggage carousel. He'd called Tijen repeatedly since landing, but always got the same recorded message.

"The idiot's lost her phone again!" he said aloud as he checked the monitor to find out where his bags were waiting. Waving to one of the carriers in dark blue uniforms, as though hailing a cab, he held up two fingers to indicate the number of his carousel. The carrier nodded and dutifully fell into line behind him.

A tall, trim man striding along in a black Italian suit and English shoes, Mehmet Emin Entek's brisk manner announced that he was a force to be reckoned with, and his leather laptop case, Gucci sunglasses, and Rolex watch all underscored that message. While his clothing testified to his financial power, his body attested to his willpower—and all this was achieved at quite a price. A private trainer supervised his thrice-weekly home workouts, a dietician his calorie intake. His gray hair had been tinted a distinguished silver, his nails buffed to a high sheen. Full medical check-ups were scheduled every six months, and his private physician not only regularly monitored his blood sugar (diabetes ran in the family), but also partnered him twice weekly in squash. Creams and rejuvenators were applied to his face and hands at night, sunscreen to any exposed skin on sunny days. When Mehmet Emin Entek looked into the mirror, he saw well-deserved success. God knows he'd worked for it.

"Come on, answer!" he shouted.

"You talking to me, sir?" asked the surprised carrier. Entek shook his head as he redialed, still grumbling. "What an idiot! If you've lost your phone, call from a pay phone. Is that so difficult? And she's probably panicking. That girl still needs some training, some serious training!"

Just as he was approaching the baggage carousel, a woman with short gray hair, struggling with an enormous suitcase, a box, and two bags, came up to him. A traditional hand-embroidered head scarf was draped over her shoulders like a shawl, she wore a mercerized white cotton sweater over a black skirt so long it nearly concealed her orthopedic sandals.

"Excuse me, brother, is this for the bags from Berlin?" she asked. Certain the question had not been addressed to him, Mehmet Emin Entek ignored her.

"Brother, did you just get off the Berlin plane too?" she asked, sidling still closer with an earnest smile.

"Yet another idiot!" he thought. "She's probably been a worker up there for years, and most certainly knows how to read. But her mind's still Eastern! There's a huge display panel right over there;

just go and check it. It's this mentality that shames us all in the eyes of the West!"

"This is the first time I've been all alone in Istanbul . . . I'm afraid of losing all my things . . . This *is* for Berlin baggage, isn't it, brother?"

Mehmet Emin Entek replied in the negative, Turkish-style, with a sharp click of the tongue, eyebrows raised, head thrown slightly back. The woman continued smiling expectantly. A cell phone rang.

"Ah, finally . . ." thought Mehmet Emin Entek, his relief turning to dismay when he realized that the ringing phone not only belonged to the woman, but that she was using the same Nokia ringtone as him!

"Ha, yes, Hasan Hüseyin, it's me, Sabriye. Fine, thanks. I've landed safely in Istanbul. I'm waiting for my baggage right now. Fine, fine, everyone in Berlin is fine. Seyit Ali is well; Ali Ekber kisses your hand. I'll tell you all about it when you come. Don't you worry, I've got a nice fellow here helping me. See you later, Hasan Hüseyin. All right then. Bye."

"It's me, Sabriye," she said, as though the caller didn't know whom he just called. Women! "Every one of them an idiot!" fumed Mehmet Emin Entek, shaking his head resignedly as he called Tijen yet again. Then he froze: Could it be that he was the helpful "brother" she'd referred to? There she was, still smiling at him, still waiting. "This can't be happening!" he groaned inwardly. Then he spun on his heel and marched to the other side of the carousel, pressing the redial button as he did so. But Sabriye plodded along behind him. Finally, he snapped.

"This is for the flight from Moscow! Now leave me alone and go find the carousel for Berlin!" he shouted, startled at the rage in his own voice. Under the disapproving stares of strangers, he immediately regretted his lack of control. The outburst had been unforgivable, and beneath him to boot. It was all Tijen's fault. She was the reason he was so wound up. He tried again, adopting a neutral, paternal tone.

"Look, Sabriye *Hanım*, see that panel over there, that screen like a TV, all lit up? Well, it'll tell you where your baggage is. Just find the carousel number next to Berlin." He allowed himself a deep sigh of relief, certain he was free at last. But Sabriye was still there, rooted to the spot, her eyes suddenly wide with fear.

"How did you know my name?" she asked. "Are you with the police, brother?"

At the end of his rope, he turned his back and began looking for his carrier, who had wandered over to the next carousel along. Phone still pressed to his ear, Mehmet Emin Entek was ranting to himself.

"We're supposed to get into the EU with people like that? Not in a million years! That woman's been in Germany for years; the baggage carrier is employed at an international airport; and Tijen, the idiot, is an employee of Entek, Inc., for God's sake! And each of them is worse than the other! No sense of responsibility, no brains . . ."

Walking toward a suitcase that had been left against the wall, guarded by an airport official, was a man in a bowtie, a digni-fied man, well-dressed and commanding. And he looked familiar. Someone he'd done business with, or seen on TV? He looked so familiar. Now who was he?

"Ah, Erol Argunsoy! Belgin's uncle!" His heart started beating faster. "Yes, that's him. That great friend of the environment, the architect Erol Argunsoy! Well, what do you know? Spends what little money he makes lecturing on the environment, and claims to be in love with Istanbul! The guy who socked me in the jaw when I got caught cheating on Belgin! Well, I won't acknowl-edge him. Not that he's going to want to talk to me, either . . ." Mehmet Emin quickly turned his back on Erol Argunsoy. Then another thought struck him:

"Could he be here to meet Belgin? No, don't be silly. She'd never come back to Bebek, to Istanbul . . . Settled in a place like New York, why would she? Besides, didn't she say she'd never live in the same city as me . . . ?"

"Brother, if you're from the force," the woman went on, "I want you to know that Hasan Hüseyin didn't have anything to do with those riots in Gazi. And Zeynel Abidin was just a boy at the time. Leave us alone, brother. We're respectable citizens, both in Europe and here in Turkey. And we're true believers, just like you!"

Mehmet Emin Entek had long forgotten Sabriye, and was more than a little disconcerted to find her still stalking him. The conveyor belt began rolling; the crowd jockeyed for position. But Sabriye stood her ground, nervously eyeing Mehmet Emin Entek. He turned his attention back to his phone, and when he couldn't get through, glanced over at the baggage carousel only to see Sabriye hoisting three enormous suitcases off the belt, completely unassisted. Puzzled, he checked the electronic display overhead. Berlin! Weighed down by her baggage, panting, Sabriye trudged over to him:

"Can I go now, brother? Look, I'm clean. Okay?"

Mehmet Emin Entek simply nodded, anxious to get rid of her and unable to bear the thought that a woman who did menial work in Germany had been right when he'd been wrong. Actually, it didn't even matter that she was a woman, or what she did for a living. He'd been wrong! Wrong! That was enough. And it was all Tijen's fault. If she'd been waiting for him, none of this would have happened. He'd show her! He watched out of the corner of his eye as Sabriye slowly advanced to the customs area, tired and tense, a forced smile on her face, SABRİYE BEKTAŞ-BERLIN-ISTANBUL written in bold capital letters on tags attached to each of her suitcases.

6
HOME IS WHERE THE HEART IS

"These days, Kurtuluş is one of the most nondescript neighborhoods in Istanbul. Gone are the market gardens, friendly neighbors, and the distinctive bay windows of the Greek houses. Notions of respect and consideration have gone too, and along with them the very soul of the neighborhood. These days, Kurtuluş is nothing but the dreary district behind Harbiye, of no consequence to those who can't remember the old days, when it was 'Tatavla.' Istanbul is a lesser city without Tatavla, but it would do just fine without Kurtuluş. This is the new Istanbul, and these are its residents: the slipshod, unaesthetic, joyless New Istanbullu!"

Turkish passport in hand, Professor Yannis Seferis sat in the departure lounge of Atatürk Airport waiting for the next flight to Athens. His beige cotton suit was coordinated with an Italian tie, blue-and-white striped, and a white shirt that had retained its crispness even on this hot summer day. A dapper man with a graying moustache, he looked more like a 1960s Parisian than a twenty-first century academician of Eastern Mediterranean extraction.

"And why exactly was Tatavla renamed Kurtuluş, meaning 'liberation, deliverance, salvation'? Had it been 'liberated' from its former residents, 'delivered' from its old culture? Or was the name changed simply to obliterate all traces and memories of the past? Well, a city without a memory is a city suffering from senility, barely able to stand on its own two feet and certain to get lost! I suppose all cultures have their own 'liberation' metaphors and myths; man has always managed to find himself in need of salvation! Anyway, even if it hadn't been renamed Kurtuluş, it wouldn't be the same Tatavla. People still wouldn't greet each other with cries of '*Merhaba*,' '*Kalimera*,' '*Shalom*,' and '*Parev*'; for that matter, people don't greet each other on the street at all nowadays, in any language. The old ways and the old residents are all gone, off to other lands or the next world—some moved, others fled.

85

I suppose the new ones get along just fine, manage as best they can. What else do they know? Most if not all of them migrated to Kurtuluş from uniformly conservative little towns . . . How can they be expected to understand and appreciate the meaning of *metropolis*, the richness in diversity, the essence of what made Istanbul Istanbul? Look, it's not easy for them, either: most have little or no education. What are they supposed to do, the poor things? And even when they do migrate to the big city, the education they get in Istanbul is superficial at best. They're not encouraged to use their minds, let alone their imaginations. I see the result in my own students at Bosphorus University—bright kids stifled by a 'good education,' in many ways less broad-minded than their fathers. They're so busy wrestling with the individual pieces and components that they fail to grasp the idea or theory; today's youth have lost sight of the big picture . . ."

Punctual to a fault, Professor Yannis Seferis sat on a wooden bench between the currency exchange bureau and a wireless computer available for public use, waiting for the announcement that would direct him to his gate. A careful observer would have noticed the perfect manicure on the hand with which he held a copy of *Gates*, the airport magazine that he was too preoccupied to read.

"How can people be happy if they don't love the place where they live? The newly arrived haven't formed neighborly relations, among themselves or with the old-timers: there's no sense of community. It's the same everywhere: in Athens and Istanbul, in Thessalonica and Smyrna. If you haven't grown up in a neighborhood where the auntie next door offers you a glass of water when she hears you cough, where neighbors distribute pita for Ramadan, red-dyed eggs for Easter, and matzah for Passover, where you get a scolding from the uncle at the corner grocery the first time you get caught smoking, and where a gang of brothers share a swig of rakı to celebrate your first kiss, how can you be a Kurtuluşlu? Indeed, how can you ever be a true Istanbullu?"

Lined with shops and dotted with wooden benches, the waiting area beyond passport control is designed to resemble a wide pedestrian walkway. In a nod to "old Istanbul," wrought-iron streetlamps stand at regular intervals outside duty-free shops. Wooden "street signs" also list shop names and provide a brief description of their wares. But in English only, perhaps on the assumption that any Turk who's made it this far surely has sufficient mastery of that language to shop. Duty-Free, Food Court, Gourmet Corner, Food Hall, Golden Touch, Bazaar, Children's Wonderland, as well as the international brands, some of them Turkish, that have girdled the globe, and play a pivotal role in making it go round: Rolex, Burberry, Bvlgari, Hugo Boss, Fossil, Lacoste, Silk & Cashmere, Versace, Hermes, Bally, Empire, Desa, Mavi Jeans, Vakko, and others. Ironically, in this Disneyesque Istanbul, signed and posted in English, the shopping bags carried by foreigners and Turks alike attest to the popularity of shops selling Turkish coffee sets, Turkish *çini* tiles, handcrafted silver and gold jewelry, "Nightingale's Eye" traditional color-twist glasswork, Turkish leather coats and handbags, and, of course, the national drink, rakı.

A middle-aged man of medium height with a receding hairline, a Roman nose, golden-brown eyes, wheat-colored skin, a Greek name, and a Turkish passport, the Professor was typically Mediterranean. The worn but chic leather briefcase resting next to him on the bench was full of articles and papers on "gene technology," in Turkish, English, and Greek. Professor Seferis was now staring absentmindedly at the pictures of Athens in his magazine.

"Excuse me, where did you get that?"

Startled, Professor Yannis Seferis gawked at the tall, middle-aged blonde pointing to the magazine in his hand. Yes, she was talking to him. Buttoning his jacket, he straightened slightly and pointed to a nearby newsstand as he responded, in English: "You'll find one over there, Madame—just over there."

The woman looked to be in her forties, and her accent immediately identified her as an American. Depositing an apparently heavy piece of hand luggage at his feet, she asked him to "keep an eye on it," and was off to get a complimentary copy of *Gates*.

"What a woman!" Professor Seferis smiled, shaking his head. "Only an American in Istanbul would surrender a piece of luggage to a complete stranger."

"Thanks. My Turkish is far from perfect, but I'll still give it a try," she said, likewise smiling as she sat down next to Professor Seferis, chatting and rapidly flipping through the pages of her magazine. Yes, she was an American, easy and confident.

"Hi, I'm Susan. Everyone calls me 'Istanbullu Sue.' What's your name?"

Professor Seferis stiffened imperceptibly under this reckless introduction, then instinctively responded in the manner expected by his own culture. Rising to his feet, he fastened another button on his cotton jacket and extended his hand:

"And I, Madame, am Professor Seferis, Yannis Seferis. Pleased to meet you."

Clearly delighted by the performance, Istanbullu Sue giggled and extended a hand of her own, which Professor Seferis gently clasped in his own and kissed. The confident smile on his lips was positively rakish. Professor Seferis may have cultivated a courtly charm, but he was worldly enough to have studied its effect: a brush of lips on skin, if applied with finesse and respect, invites a woman to be a woman. Or so he believed.

And the Professor wasn't entirely inexperienced on the subject of women: he'd been engaged once; he'd had lovers since. But his sex life had been halting and unfulfilling, haunted as it was by the exhortations of Aunt Eleni, who had drummed into his boyish mind the conviction that expectations of premarital sex were deeply insulting to any woman worthy of the name. He was also overly meticulous, fastidious, and something of a hypochondriac, traits that didn't necessarily endear him to women. He had, as stated, succeeded in losing his virginity. But that encounter, one of several with the Widow Marika, back in Tatavla, while he was still at university, was a source of sinful shame rather than a treasured memory of fulfilled lust. For many years now, Professor Serferis had been alone, a confirmed bachelor in the eyes of his university colleagues and relatives in Athens. But while everyone else had given up on him, he hadn't given up on himself. He still hoped to meet the woman of his dreams: She would have soft curves, a smile as inviting as ripe fruit, a gleam in her eye that for all her independence demonstrated that she was nevertheless indulgent of male failings; she would be generous and unrestrained; ardent in bed, skilled in the kitchen, hearty in her embrace of life—well, that was how he put it all to himself.

This picture of the perfect woman bore an uncanny resemblance to the Widow Marika, actually; she had simply been updated over the years to become more "modern" and "cultured." It was when the Professor was away from Istanbul that he would most frequently indulge in his fantasies of the perfect woman, always half-expecting her to appear in person soon after his return. But, always, she eluded him; but, always, she remained forever stationed at the corner of his ungleaming eye, on the tip of his tongue.

"Oh my, haven't you turned into the real Istanbul gentleman!" cried Susan, her former giggle replaced by a proper laugh, now, with an unmistakably feminine ring. The kiss had worked its magic. "I used to be a San Franciscan, but I've been an Istanbullu for ten years now!"

"One becomes an Istanbullu only when one truly understands the soul of Istanbul, Madame. And once you do that, you'll never belong anywhere else!"

"You don't need to call me 'Madame.' The name's Susan, Istanbullu Sue."

Susan's American accent lent a slightly childish quality to the Turkish she'd learned at Tömer—textbook Turkish now punctuated with expressions she'd picked up on the street. Professor Yannis Seferis was quite bowled over; this Susan was the most exotic thing he'd ever seen.

"You're right. Every city has a soul, and you can't figure out the city without understanding its soul. The only thing is, once you understand Istanbul's soul, you find you can't leave! Actually, that's what you just said, isn't it?"

"Exactly, *hanımefendi*. It's that old paradox: 'can't live with her, can't live without her.' Even if you're not happy in Istanbul, you won't be happy anywhere else. Only a few cities can cast such a spell: Paris, London, Rome . . . They say the same of New York, but I'd imagine it's too young for that. Anyway, I haven't been to the New World yet . . ."

"Well, San Francisco's pretty young too, but it's a cosmopolitan place and it's definitely got a feel all its own, a real northern California vibe. Compared to Istanbul and most cities in Europe, everything in America's new. I mean, it's just amazing, think of all those civilizations, over thousands of years. Why, look at you. You're *Rum*, Yannis, aren't you? A Greek-Turk?"

Confirmed bachelor Yannis Seferis was known in the neighborhood as *Bay* Yannis; his colleagues and students called him Seferis *Hodja*; social and academic circles referred to him as Professor Seferis. It had been years since anyone but Aunt Eleni, who raised him when he lost both parents in a car accident, had addressed him by his first name. The easy familiarity of the breezy American woman struck him as overly forward, but he was nonetheless intrigued. In fact, he was getting quite worked up as he hid behind the dry, measured tones of his response.

"I am first and foremost an Istanbullu. Yes, to the world, I am Greek; to the Turks I am *Rum*. You just indicated you find 'all those civilizations' to be 'amazing.' Can I then safely assume that you're familiar with the origins of the word *Rum*?"

"Well, I know that Greeks in Turkey are called *Rum* and Greeks in Greece are called *Yunanlı*. It's never made much sense to me. Oh, and someone told me the Turkish word *Rum* actually comes from the Arabic word for 'Roman.'"

Professor Seferis cleared his throat and launched into a brief lecture:

"*Rum* does indeed mean 'Roman.' But I'm Greek, as you observed, so why would Turks refer to me as a Roman?" He paused for effect. "Well, back when the Byzantine Greeks controlled all the lands that are now modern Turkey, they considered themselves to be the continuation of the Roman Empire, and called themselves *Rhomaioi*, Romans. The modern Turkish *Rum* is a derivative of *Rhomaioi*, going back to the time when the Byzantine Empire was known to the Arabs and others as 'the land of Rûm.' When the Seljuk Turks swept into Asia Minor, they even retained the term, renaming their new territory the Sultanate of Rûm."

"I get it now!" Sue responded, every bit like a prize pupil: "When Turks refer to you as *Rum*, they're acknowledging your Roman descent, not in the sense that you're Italian, but that your ancestors ruled the Eastern Roman Empire!"

"Precisely. Interestingly, Turks call Greeks born in Greece *Yunanlı* because ancient Greece was known to the Arabs as Yunan—which is to say, Ionia. So, in conclusion, to the Turks, Greeks born in Asia Minor and Cyprus are *Rum*; Greeks born in modern-day Greece are *Yunanlı*. Any questions?"

"Fascinating!" cried Susan. Encouraged by her enthusiasm, the Professor continued on a more personal note.

"As I was saying, I'm an Istanbullu first, a *Rum* second. In Athens they say I'm 'from the land of the Turks.' Here in Turkey, my homeland, I'm a 'non-Muslim,' a member of an 'ethnic minority.' I've got two mother tongues, but I'm a stepchild in each of my mother countries. Let's just say I'm a true Istanbullu, and leave it at that!"

Then he paused again, before whispering in a confidential tone:

"And please, call me Yanni, not Yannis. In Greek you omit the final *S*."

"Oh, I see. Well, Yanni, you've taught me a lot, not only about being a *Rum*, but what it means to be an Istanbullu. I try to explain when I'm in America, but they just don't get it. They've got this image of women shut up indoors, forced to take the veil, stoned to death if they don't obey a bunch of black-bearded men! Granted, some women don't have it all that easy, especially in the east, out in Eastern Anatolia. I travel all over Turkey for work. But the east is no more representative of Turkey than this is," she said, indicating with a wave of her hand the well-heeled shoppers strolling by.

Professor Seferis was pleased she'd defended Turkey, and by extension Istanbul. With a shy smile he straightened his tie, adjusted his collar, and smoothed the fabric of his trouser legs. Having satisfied himself that all was in order, he allowed himself to relax slightly. Taking no notice of him, Susan popped a piece of chewing gum into her mouth:

"The Romans, the Byzantines, the Seljuks, and the Ottomans all came here, one after another. That's what makes Istanbul so magnificent."

"Of course it is . . . But that's not how my Aunt Eleni sees it!" Professor Seferis let slip.

"What's that?"

"My Aunt . . . My Aunt Eleni," he explained, a bit angry at himself. "She migrated to Athens many years ago. Even among all her new friends and relatives she's still lonely, still misses Istanbul. She was born here, spent her girlhood here, grew up with the songs and legends of this city . . ."

"That's Istanbul for you. She never lets you go, makes you miss her like a lover."

"Bravo Susan *Hanım*! Beautifully put. But look, Aunt Eleni is getting on in years. She calls me twice a week, and it's always the same. 'Yanni,' she says, 'stop being so emotional—Istanbul's not our home anymore. Come over here to Athens, my little darling.' She says she's got one foot in the grave and no family left but me, the son of her 'black-eyed Yerasimos,' may he rest in peace. 'Come to Athens,' she says, 'come to your home, your country, your family. It's time to leave Istanbul.'"

Susan pulled a bottle of water out of her bag and took a sip. She was all ears.

"I listen. What else can I do? I listen and I sigh. She's very old, my Aunt Eleni. That's why I fly to Athens like this so often, why I spend so many days a year waiting in airports. Istanbul-Athens, Athens-Istanbul. Circling up out of Istanbul, circling down into Istanbul. A vicious circle! And I always take Olympic Airlines. God forbid I should take Turkish Airlines! My aunt can barely see, but she still inspects my ticket to make sure. I used to try and tell her Olympic was fully booked, that I couldn't get a seat. But she just wouldn't hear of it. You know, if she wasn't my aunt, the only relative from Istanbul I have left, I'd never put up with it. Anyway, we were brought up to respect our elders—a traditional Mediterranean upbringing!"

"Well, my childhood was spent in California, and I'm sure it was a lot different from yours. But my relatives are a mixed bag too: French, Welsh, Jewish Romanian . . . Take my surname: Constance—I'm Susan Constance. Do you know where that comes from? The Romanian port of Constanta, biggest on the Black Sea; known to the Turks as Köstence and to the Greeks as Constantia. My father's mother would have been a citizen of the Ottoman Empire, may even have considered herself Ottoman. I'd like to think so, anyway . . ."

"Aunt Eleni has always been a difficult woman, and the older she gets the worse she gets . . ." Professor Seferis continued, as though he hadn't heard a word Susan said. "On and on she goes every time we talk on the telephone: 'I suppose you've forgotten those black days. After all the Turks did to us. Have you just erased it from your memory? You were about ten back then, weren't you? Surely you remember the events of the 6–7 of September?' But what she'd like to say is, 'Remember the rioting that happened in Istanbul after those rumors that the Greeks had bombed Atatürk's birthplace in Thessalonica? They attacked our houses, our churches, our shops, our tavernas, smashing and burning and plundering!' But she's still afraid to let go, afraid to let her anger boil over. She's grown used to downplaying such things, so all she says is, 'They say seventy-eight churches were destroyed, including the Armenian ones. I think it was more than that, though—perhaps as many as 200. And for what? Why? Because someone said something had happened to the house in Thessalonica where Atatürk was born. And we, the *Rum* community of Istanbul, were made to suffer the consequences. Officially, three thousand houses were wrecked. What nonsense! It was at least ten . . . But that's nothing compared to what they did to our hearts and minds. Overnight we became outsiders, unwelcome, living in fear. How can you still call a place like that your motherland? It's not home anymore! Come to Athens, come home to me, Yanni, my darling Yanni!'"

At that precise moment, Professor Seferis had a violent coughing fit. He expected it to end quickly, but when it didn't, was more worried about the spectacle he was making of himself in front of an attractive woman than about suffocation. He squirmed and his face turned red; he flinched as Sue thumped him on the back, Turkish-style, waving away her offer of water. Several minutes passed before he consented to drink from Susan's open bottle. Aunt Eleni would not have approved their sharing the same vessel. His fit had lasted long enough to attract the glances of strangers, but now the Professor was more concerned about the possible transfer of germs from the American's mouth to his own than with the stares of strangers, or even with how to thank Susan, who was now bending over to retrieve his fallen ticket from the ground.

"Isn't this a Turkish Airlines ticket, Yanni?" she giggled or laughed.

"Don't ask," was his hoarse reply, as he fussed and fidgeted with his tie and jacket. "I love my dear Aunt, and who am I to argue with an eighty-four year old? I keep an Olympic Airlines ticket stub in my pocket just in case. I'll hide the Turkish Airlines one in my wallet the moment I land in Athens. What can I do? She's getting on in years," he added, perhaps secretly pleased that he had an aged relative around to make him feel relatively young.

"You're okay now, aren't you? Your color's come back," said Susan, studying the Professor's face.

"I'm quite all right, thank you very much. Quite well, *maşallah!*" he claimed with a scowl, still regretting the coughing fit. The two passengers, both of them non-Muslim, but both of them sufficiently steeped in Istanbul culture to use expressions like *maşallah* and *inşallah*, sat for a time in silence.

"My mother thinks your country is a wild and dangerous place. She's not all that old, but I know she's worried and maybe even a bit angry that I've chosen to live here . . ." Susan signed.

"My Istanbul is completely different from hers. I remember coming here for the first time, as a tourist. I know, it's such a cliché, but it really was the light and the colors that got me first, all those colors dancing like the tail of a kite: red and white, gold and green . . . Gray and earth, and blue, so many shades of blue . . . For me, Istanbul was an incredible mixture of colors. The pale face of the Virgin Mary in Byzantine icons; the gorgeous reds and blues of İznik tile work. Magnificent Ottoman architecture, so much of it destroyed or in disrepair, but so much still here. Mosaics and tiles, crosses on churches, crescents on mosques, stars on synagogues. And the streets, those chaotic streets: a 4X4 jeep roaring past a street corner beggar, children selling tissues to ladies carrying Louis Vuitton bags. The call to prayer, vendors hawking sesame rolls and stuffed mussels, the scrap dealer pushing along his cart: the chorus of Istanbul! Crowds everywhere, mostly young, bursting with life, edgy and energetic. And things you'd never see back home. Girls with covered heads and slingbacks, boys with master's degrees from America, come back to find a good virgin wife . . ."

Professor Yannis Seferis was impressed by Susan's Turkish, which grew more fluent the more she described Istanbul. He'd also had a stunning realization: the Istanbul she described was precisely the Istanbul he wanted to believe in, the Istanbul he needed to hear spoken of again and again. But he didn't pursue that thought, focusing instead on Susan, as he concluded that skinny and small-breasted as she was, her blue eyes were undeniably lovely.

"You're probably thinking, 'How can an American possibly understand a city like Istanbul'? Well, I'll have you know that the British writer Mark Girouard once wrote that the 'wonder and amazement' European migrants felt at their first glimpse of New York was exactly the same sensation experienced by Europeans as they sailed into Constantinople. See what I mean, Yanni?"

Professor Seferis suspected he would never forgive Mark Girouard for comparing Manhattan to Istanbul, although he was inclined to be tolerant of Susan's having cited him.

"A cousin of mine, from Athens, said something along those lines the first time he came to Istanbul . . ." he mumbled, or perhaps muttered. "That was back before the earthquake of 1999, back when relations between Greeks and Turks were a lot worse; believe me, they're much improved now! My visiting cousin embarrassed me in front of my colleagues. The Greeks have never forgotten the Ottoman invasion, and the textbooks in both countries keep alive every injustice, perceived and real. Well, my cousin immediately hit a raw nerve by constantly referring to Istanbul as Constantinople. As you know, the Turks have a real phobia about Greece's supposed designs on Istanbul. What a scene it was! Shouting and insults . . . Fortunately, my cousin stormed out of the room before worse could happen. But for all the bad blood, bear in mind that the Greeks were the first to extend a helping hand after the earthquake. I believe both sides have grown tired of the enmity, certainly the people have . . . Besides, Greece is the strongest supporter of Turkish membership in the EU."

Professor Seferis's tone was grave, but Susan was smiling mischievously. "Well what do you think, Yanni? Do the Greeks really believe they're going to take Istanbul back one day?" she laughed. "It's only been, what, 550 years? That'd be like the Native Americans making the rest of us return to Europe. Just imagine that!"

"I believe nothing of the kind, Madame. Yes, there are extremists and nationalists on both sides, but what's done is done," he replied. Americans were really too much sometimes, blunt to the point of tactlessness . . .

"Well, we've got more than our fair share of fanatics and nationalists, too. Just look at the Bush administration. 9/11 just gave them room to become even worse zealots than they already were. I wouldn't be surprised if they criminalized abortion. It's funny, abortion isn't even an issue in Turkey."

"So you're a Democrat?"

"Me? No, I'm an Independent. I try to keep an open mind. I've never been one to blindly accept the status quo. I suppose you could say I'm a bit of a rebel, Yanni! It's not like what most Turks think—not all Americans are fans of Bush. There are so many different views back home, and most people tolerate that. You certainly don't have that kind of tolerance here! I used to be married to a Turk. He was downright liberal when we met, but the older he got the more conservative he became. Finally, I couldn't take it anymore, and divorced him. You all believe in fate here . . . well, that must have been my particular fate!"

Professor Seferis laughed. Here was an attractive woman, and one who spoke openly and freely. Not only that, he'd just learned she was a divorcée. It was at that moment that he forgave her for having made him drink from her water bottle. His ability to forgive and forget so easily, at least when it came to Susan, also surprised him, uncharacteristic as it was. But it was a pleasant surprise. The kind that happens only rarely, and indicates we're ready at last to let go of long-held prejudices and hang-ups—you know the type. The Professor felt strangely refreshed, light and carefree. But the moment didn't last long: Imagining what Aunt Eleni would make of Susan, he suddenly felt guilty of nothing less than frivolity.

"When Mom found out I'd gotten a divorce, she assumed I had no reason to stay here, that as a single woman I'd go right back to the US."

Professor Yannis was thrilled that Susan regarded herself as "single." In Turkish, the word for widow and divorcée is the same; and on the part of women, at least, "singleness" still implies virginity. Yes, he was quite ready to overlook her small breasts and thin arms.

"But . . . but I don't live here because of a man . . . or a woman or a child. I just love Istanbul. You know what I mean? There's just something about this city. Something about its chaos, its refusal to compromise or fall in line, its willful rejection of its glorious past and headlong rush into its uncertain future, its instinctive revolt against established rule. Yes, its nihilism and, above all else, its cocky self-assurance and ability to carry on, regardless of oppression and neglect! I love Istanbul just because it believes in itself. Istanbul loves itself! You could write a novel about it! I love the squawking seagulls and the drone of the ferryboats, the hushed silence inside the inner courtyards of the mosques, the profoundly mystical colors of Sufism . . . and I love the openness of the people. I love it! What more can I say? What does 'homeland' mean, anyway? I'm an Istanbullu!"

"Homeland?" wondered Professor Seferis.

"Yes. What is it? What does it mean, anyway?"

As they spoke, hundreds of people were listening to announcements telling them which planes would take off at what times to which cities in what countries. Hundreds of passengers were rushing to gates that would take them home, or take them far from their homeland.

"Ah, that's a question I'd like to ask my Aunt Eleni. But it would hurt her, and I couldn't do that. And even if I could squeeze all my childhood memories into a suitcase and haul them to Athens—the kites I flew with neighborhood kids, the footballs I kicked, the marbles I won, the balloons I let go, the Tatavla funfairs, those pre-fast feast days of Damascus sweets, flavored gums, walnut pastries, and *salep*—even if I could squeeze all those memories into Athens, where would I put the Istanbul I'll carry forever in my heart? If Istanbul *isn't* my homeland, how could Athens ever be? But if Istanbul *is* my homeland, what of my childhood friends? With Tasos in Athens, Nikos in Thessalonica, Silva in America, and Varojan in Paris; with the cobblestones of Akarca covered in asphalt and Yeni Atlas cinema long closed; what's left for me here? Is your homeland your earliest, fondest memories, or is it where your friends and family are? Tell me, which is it?"

Professor Yannis resorted to another sigh and lapsed into silence. Thinking, eyes focused straight ahead, oblivious to the hum of the crowd and the announcements being made in two languages, he felt himself positively smothered by this new silence and suddenly very alone.

"Sometimes I'm about ready to despair. But I tell myself it's just part of growing old. 'You're getting on, Yanni,' I say to myself. 'That's all it is. Everything will be all right, don't worry, don't give up!' Anyway, forgive me for burdening you like this with my personal troubles . . ."

Just like a Turk, Susan smiled as she tilted back her head and clicked her tongue in gentle protestation. The Professor understood, and was grateful.

"I think many Americans understand how you feel, Yanni. Remember, we Americans are all immigrants—we've all left homelands behind. Perhaps that's why I feel so at home in Istanbul? You know, I've got a travel agency here . . . I've set up my own business and I've met an awful lot of people. It's funny, so many seem to feel the same way you do. They all say they love Istanbul. But it's such a mournful love, a love so tinged with nostalgia . . . it's like they're . . . yearning somehow!"

"So, you're in tourism. I'm a geneticist: I teach genetic biology. I don't know if it would interest you, but if you'd like to visit a school with the most wonderful view in the world, you'd be most welcome to visit me at Bosphorus University. I mean, of course, once we're both back in Istanbul. We could meet and talk. That is, if you'd like to?"

Painfully aware that for the first time in years he was attempting to arrange a rendezvous with a woman, the Professor felt himself flush; beads of sweat actually formed on his forehead. Suddenly anxious to change the subject, he clutched at the first thing that came to mind.

"An old student of mine is planning a final return to Istanbul some time around now. She got a doctorate in genetics in America, became a professor there. Dear Belgin, I knew her back when she was an undergraduate. Even after all those years in America and her vows never to return, she's coming back. She must have missed Istanbul. She's just like us, an Istanbullu caught between two countries. I'd like you to meet her. Why don't the three of us have coffee one day?"

Susan watched the Professor with a playful smile, his romantic intentions now apparent; she thought his bashfulness sweet, if a bit old-fashioned. She also thought it best to take the first opportunity to mention her young Turkish business partner, who was also her lover.

"That'd be nice, Yanni. Let's meet up, the three of us, and

celebrate the fact that somehow we've all ended up in Istanbul together!"

Having grown a little overexcited by what he took to be the acceptance of a date, Professor Seferis returned to the topic of Belgin, which was safer ground.

"You'll love Belgin. Such a clever girl, and from such a good Istanbul family. Her diplomat father was assassinated, which was terribly difficult for her, of course. She graduated from my university, worked as my assistant while she completed her master's degree. She also had an unfortunate marriage . . . well, anyway, I got an e-mail from her some time ago, telling me she planned a 'final return' to Istanbul and asking about a position. I was overjoyed. With an academic background like hers, she'd be welcome at any university. We'll be thrilled to have her. And it's so nice to become the friend and colleague of a former student . . ."

Susan had grown a bit bored with the long description of Belgin, but had homed in on one particular detail of her biography.

"When Turks speak of an 'unfortunate marriage,' what they really mean is that the husband cheated on his wife. Is that what you meant, Yanni?"

Professor Seferis had never warmed to American bluntness, and found the question deeply inappropriate. He had no choice, however, but to reply.

"Unfortunately, in our society, like in any other, some men distress their spouses. And not everyone is faithful," he allowed in an injured tone.

"Ah-ha! Gotcha! You sound just like a typical Turkish man," said Susan, with a smile that softened this reproach. "What is it with this war between the sexes in Turkey, anyway? I'm going to be frank with you. In the same way there's still a race problem in America, one nobody talks about and few acknowledge, there's a not-so-secret problem in Turkey too. But it isn't friction between Kurds and Turks, or Sunni and Allawi. And it's not about the head scarf either, Yanni. The real problem in this country is the relationship between men and women. Wherever I go, even if I'm with members of the so-called elite, educated types who believe in democracy, the men and women always end up in separate groups, just like in the palace in the days of their grandparents . . ."

Professor Seferis was taken aback at finding himself expected to defend Turkish men. After all, the separation of men and women had never been part of his cultural tradition. And he didn't consider himself the least bit sexist. No, women were like flowers, to be handled with great care and affection . . .

"Like I told you, I've traveled all across Turkey, to Van, Mardin, Kayseri, Trabzon . . . you name it. I mean, I like Turkish men—many of them are incredibly good-looking. But most of them are such misogynists! Sometimes I go to parties in Istanbul, parties with a lot of smart, young career men. And what do you know, after a few drinks the men are all gathered in a separate group, joking about sex, making fun of women, and gay men too! And these are the modern, well-educated ones!"

"But surely every country has people like that!" protested Professor Seferis, smiling, but feeling awkward and overly defensive.

"Typical macho men! Well I've had it! In America and Europe, anyway, the younger generation of men aren't like that, Yannis. I just don't get Turkish men. Why are they so terrified of women?"

Professor Seferis hadn't objected when Susan pressed her water bottle to his lips, and he had been perfectly prepared to overlook the easy familiarity with which she'd barreled down on him in search of that magazine, but this attack on his Istanbul brothers was really going too far. He sensed that his reservoirs of tolerance were nearly depleted, even as he noticed for the first time that Susan had crow's feet around her eyes. Istanbullu Susan wasn't as young as she looked.

"Surely women must accept some of the responsibility," was his clipped reply, his voice tinged with disappointment.

"I have to admit you got a point there, Yanni. Turkish women are like geisha girls. They're subservient right from the get-go!"

Professor Seferis had had enough. "Well then, I suggest you go back to your beloved homeland and marry one of your cowboys!" he nearly shouted. At that moment, passengers on the Turkish

Airlines flight to Athens were advised to go to Gate 215. Taking a deep breath he rose and turned to Susan to say a saddened good-bye. But the seat next to him was empty. Looking around him, he saw that directly opposite sat a tall, attractive American woman, her legs stretched out on the next seat. Confused, he timidly drew closer to the woman. Eyes closed, lids twitching lightly, she must have been dreaming. And the dream must have been a good one, for she smiled. Professor Seferis's eyes were drawn to the label on her hand luggage. It read: Susan Constance / Istanbul–San Francisco.

7
THE HOMECOMING

"Yeşilköy. That's what we called it; no one ever said 'Atatürk Airport.' It happened there, in Yeşilköy, in the '70s. Mother turned to me, reproachfully, as though it were all my fault: 'Hold your head high and don't cry. You're a Turkish girl, Belgin! Make your father proud!' But cry I did—I sobbed, completely without shame, though shaming my mother and my father in his coffin . . .

"'Yeşilköy.' That one word was enough: one went to Yeşilköy to board a plane. Back then, the important thing wasn't the distant places you would visit—the adventure was the plane itself. Our set considered it 'vulgar' to acknowledge or display what we all felt. Adults can forget how easily children decipher body language and tone, and we knew perfectly well that our parents were just as thrilled as we were. Yes, as difficult as it was to go abroad back then, the act of flying was the point, a reason in itself, not the arrival in a new place. Flying was much more than a means to an end in those days . . . Those hazy, insular days in a patriarchal state, when the ends always justified the means. The 1970s . . .

"When mother announced 'your father is at Yeşilköy,' as she so often did, I'd proudly picture my giant father emerging from the inside of an enormous metal bird. He was indeed a big man, tall and heavyset. 'Maşallah, strong as a lion,' his mother—my grandmother—would say. 'Big, strong body, but a heart soft as cotton,' she'd always add. Kete, my beloved nanny, would then chime in with that bashful smile and gentle voice: 'A wonderful father, heart like cotton!'

"My earliest memories of my father all center on Yeşilköy, the arrivals into and departures out of. 'Official duty,' they'd explain. The other children all had fathers who worked in Istanbul; mine had a 'duty' thousands of kilometers away. That was always how they explained his absence, and why I grew up missing him so much. I blamed everything on that mysterious duty (and on mother). I learned much later how much mother had relinquished when she took on the 'duty' of marriage. One day, the piano to which she had dedicated so many hours of her childhood and maidenhood was carried, along with the rest of her dowry, to their new home. Mother had forsaken the dream of becoming an internationally acclaimed musician; becoming a wife was more important. Did she hesitate to abandon her desires and dreams? Was it really so easy? When, as a child, I felt overwhelmed by life, at fault, lonely, or inadequate, when I needed to get angry with someone, it was always my mother. I never had trouble finding a reason, but the one I cited to myself most frequently was her failure to choose a father without a duty, or at least to persuade my father to work in the city. I was also angry with Mother for having given up the opportunity to lead her own life and have her own career, was angry with her for being so much at loose ends once father was gone, furious that she'd surrendered herself to depression and housework, squandering the education she'd received at the finest conservatory in the country. I fumed and I railed, and I failed to appreciate that, unlike the mothers of so many of my friends, she hadn't been the crushing center of my existence, hadn't competed with me in any way, had in fact steadfastly but silently supported me so I could grow up to make my own decisions. But like any daughter who fears growing up to become her mother, I secretly seethed—but not at my father, never at my father!"

Belgin's plane had touched down, but was still taxiing. Astounding the foreign passengers with their total disregard for instructions, some of the Turkish passengers were already switching on cell phones and taking their baggage out of the overhead compartments.

"When I was seven, it was also my father's 'duty' that caused us to leave behind my grandmother, my aunt, my Uncle Erol, and our neighborhood. The penalty for a reunion with Father was separation from everyone else I loved. It was a heavy price, but it only increased my awe of him. He was nothing like the other fathers I knew. A hulk of a man, he visited only a couple of times a month, bringing toys none of the other children had. Whenever

I overheard grownups talking about his mysterious duties, they'd knit their brows, purse their lips, and nod profoundly. 'It must be difficult to do your duty, much more difficult than it seems, especially during these tough times for Turkey . . . ' they'd cluck. It was only much later that I came to the conclusion that Turkey has always, and will always, be going through 'tough times.' But I'm forty-one now. I know a lot more. And as I sit in this plane on the runway in Yeşilköy, looking back on those times, remembering the mysterious nature of my father's absences, the secrecy in which everything seemed to be shrouded, I see how much it shaped my character. I've always been determined to get to the bottom of things, to research and to deduce and to leave no mystery unsolved. That's probably how I ended up a genetic engineer . . .

"One day, mother, Nanny Kete, and me got onto a plane and flew to one of those distant cities to which my father's duty had taken him. We were served refreshments on the plane, and everyone was smiling. I looked around us at all the happy people and it dawned on me that perhaps, far away from us, father was fine—and that people who are fine don't miss those they leave behind. One of my first great disappointments was the happiness I too felt there on the plane. But I did what happy people do: I postponed that sense of disappointment to a later time, to a time when I would feel bad anyway and wanted to make myself feel even worse. At that moment, as we flew toward a new life, a new roof under which we'd live with my father, I completely forgot those we left behind. Even all these years later, Yeşilköy is still a place I associate with my father, with reunion and separation . . .

"My first foreign address was gloomy Copenhagen; 'Kopenhag' in Turkish, stubbornly called 'Köpenhagen' by mother in a typically futile effort to assert herself, to show that she was more than just a wife and mother. Later, as a widow and mother, her attempts at self-definition became increasingly random and riddled with inconsistencies. My mother never forgave herself for her perceived errors and deficiencies. Nor did I help her to do so. I was never able to conceal my anger, and I was distant to the end. A spectator, I allowed her to take full responsibility for the tragedies and dramas of our lives, unable to forgive her when she most needed it . . .

"So many memories of my mother, too, center on airports. My mother and airports: mother getting dressed to go to the airport, boarding a plane, on a plane, waiting for a plane to land, seeing mother off at the airport . . . Elegant mother at the airport . . . I can see her now, getting off the plane in Copenhagen. There was that deep blue hat with the white crown, chiffon bow, and wide rim with large white polka dots. She was an attractive woman with false eyelashes and beautifully shaped, bold eyebrows. She wore a navy-blue skirt and jacket inspired by Dior and modeled on Jacqueline Kennedy, ten years her senior, whose husband had been assassinated just months after I was born. Mother identified even more closely with Jacqueline Kennedy after she later lost her own husband to an assassin's bullet. Had she left it at physical appearances, her obsession would have been quite amusing, but mother went way beyond identification and empathy: she began to see herself as the Turkish version of the former First Lady, would read up on said former First Lady's every move, searching for clues to the course her own life might take. It was disturbing—really quite spooky. We'd jokingly called her 'Jackie,' but over time the moniker grew a hyphen: she was known for the rest of her days as Jackie-Halide *Hanım*. Her fixation had begun many years earlier, actually, when she met father for the first time at a family gathering and pointed out that their names—Halit and Halide—were not unlike the Turkish version of Jack and Jackie. That joking comparison was later interpreted by mother as an omen, and she managed to convince me, when I was still a child, of the existence of such signs and auguries (with the consequence of forcing me to reject all such mystical beliefs in later life, however reluctantly).

"She was an attractive woman, my mother; absolutely radiant when father was around, her luster fading the longer he was away. And when, finally, he was gone, never to return, she grew more intractable, more stubborn, duller, until she disappeared

106

completely. Right up to that traffic accident I've always suspected was suicide . . . Right up until then . . .

"We were welcomed at Copenhagen Airport by my father and several men in black, taken in a big car, also black, to a two-story house, white. Father, enormous father, was as jolly as ever, more child than grown-up. The more childish his behavior, the older mother seemed.

"'It's nothing like Yeşilköy, is it?' asked father, giving my mother a meaningful look. No, it wasn't. Not at all. He must have been talking about the airport, but I thought he meant the neighborhood. Even today, I think of Copenhagen as a dark, distant city. It makes me tremble inside—or my insides tremble. The first thing to strike me was the flatness: it was completely flat as far as the eye could see! There wasn't a hill, or a mountain, or even a slope in all of Copenhagen. It was a narrow-hipped city, no breasts, no crown—a city level and straight, stripped naked, no mysteries to hide now or ever. Clean, organized, calm, and rich—it terrified me, me who'd just arrived from a city of shimmering heat and the smell of figs, from late summer in Istanbul to early autumn in Copenhagen. Smells, colors, and sounds had disappeared: citrus sunsets, hawkers pushing wooden carts piled high with bunches of grapes and pomegranates, stray cats lazily licking paws and haunches, lavender cologne, the pit-a-pat of Grandma's slippers, that strange song rising from the mosque on the seaside (I later learned that it was called the *azan*, the Arabic call to prayer), high windows framing ferryboats gliding along what I saw as an endless blue river, the Bosphorus, dust and laughter under the sycamore trees on those rare occasions Mother let me skip rope with the local kids . . . That I believed all of Istanbul lived as we did in Bebek, that all Istanbullu were wealthy, educated, and European, was not simply the product of a childish mind. Everyone cultivated this illusion, my entire family, my relatives, and my neighbors. But the dream was gone; it evaporated in Copenhagen, where they began treating us like Africans, Arabs, or Asians just as soon as they learned we were Turkish. They were astonished to find that my mother played Mozart, that my father had read Andre Gide in high school, that in Istanbul we swam in the sea and walked on the beach in our swimsuits. And we were astonished in our turn, my mother, Nanny Kete, and me . . . Who were we, after all? Why were we being treated like this?

"I started primary school in Copenhagen, at an American school. For four years I spoke English at school, Danish on the street, Turkish at home, and Kurdish with Nanny Kete, but the latter only when my mother, who worried that I would spoil my Turkish, wasn't around. I was happy that my father was now a regular part of our family, but the city remained as foreign as ever. That was when I learned how painful it is to be a stranger to a city, to not love a city and to feel rejected by it—and the two usually occur simultaneously and reinforce each other. I was still little, and knew nothing of assimilation, adaptation, or the implications of one's relationship with his or her environment, but I knew the fear of a city for the first time. It was only much later, after I came to associate Istanbul, too, with rejection and betrayal, and to fear it as well, that I became immune to the threat of any city, anywhere.

"After four years, we packed our bags for South America, never to return to Copenhagen, even for a visit. I now knew that my father was a diplomat, and expected that, as his daughter, I would spend my life in foreign countries, forever leaving behind classmates, friends, and loved ones. 'In return,' Mother would point out, 'you've already learned English and Spanish, you've learned all about different cultures, and while still a young girl you've seen the original works of great artists and listened to the best performers in the world. Belgin, you've experienced things your friends can only dream about!' She was trying to raise my spirits, but unable to raise her own. Nothing is more important for a child than love and the sense of security that comes from a fixed routine. My mother never accepted that my early upbringing might have contributed to my lifelong insecurities. In her eyes, my childhood as the daughter of a diplomat had been idyllic. How was she to know any different?

"As it turned out, I didn't spend the rest of my childhood moving from country to country. After just three years in South America, we returned to Istanbul. This time, father wasn't sitting on the plane with us, holding my hand in his, pointing out clouds shaped like animals, telling me stories from Nordic mythology. He was returning to Istanbul with us on that plane, but in a casket, wrapped in the Turkish flag. I was thirteen, and returning to Yeşilköy with my father, but without my father. Father had been killed in the line of duty. And here I am now, about to disembark from a different plane in Yeşilköy, at Atatürk Airport.

"Mother was dressed all in black, with a veil like Jackie's, head unbowed, not a single tear, gripping my hand so tightly I would have cried if I hadn't already been sobbing. 'The terrorists killed your father, Belgin. He's a martyr now.' Then mother turned to me, reproachfully, as though it were all my fault: 'Hold your head high and don't cry; you're a Turkish girl, Belgin! Make your father proud!'

"It's been the same ever since. The same sense of loss and loneliness and guilt every time I arrive at this airport. If it were possible, I'd always take a train, or a steamboat—or just stop traveling altogether."

The plane had ground to a halt, engines cut out as stairs were wheeled up to the main exit. Baggage strap hanging over her right shoulder, Belgin flexed her stiff neck and arm joints as she shuffled down the aisle, smiling and nodding at the flight attendants. As she stepped off the last rung of the stairs onto Istanbul soil, she felt a rush of exhilaration and foreboding, but her face was impassive as she looked up at the sky, glanced at the brand new terminal, and boarded the shuttle bus.

Smoothing her curls into place, navy-blue dress unwrinkled, face impassive as she stepped onto a moving sidewalk, Belgin was however feeling a little worse for wear; the strain of intercontinental travel had taken its toll. Even so, a smile crept across her face as she remembered the way her father would pinch her cheek and praise the curls she'd had even back then, at age thirteen. Her hand reached once again to smooth one of them down.

Somebody on the moving sidewalk mistook the smile for a greeting, and smiled back: Ulviye Yeniçağ, who had somehow found the opportunity to refresh her makeup.

"You slept like a baby!" she sang out.

"Slept? Me?" wondered Belgin.

Belgin decided that Ulviye Yeniçağ was at least sixty-five, and although still a beautiful woman might be a bit senile and prone to imagining things. She also decided it would be rude to point out that it was Ulviye who had slept, not her.

"Allow me to wish you and Ayhan *Bey* the best of luck. I do hope you'll be happy together."

"If she was asleep, how does she know about Ayhan?" Belgin thought. She took a closer look at Ulviye Yeniçağ, who was nodding vigorously, lips curled into a knowing smile. Then it hit her. Ayhan! Lost in memories of her childhood, she'd relaxed, forgetting the impending migraine on the plane and even pushing to the back of her mind her reunion with Ayhan, now only moments away! He must be there waiting for her now, just a hundred meters or so behind passport control. She was back in Istanbul, back for a new life with Ayhan in this city that terrified her so. She, who had declared repeatedly that she would never again trust a man, never again fall in love. Ayhan had been as enticing as Istanbul, as full of promise. This time, her hand traveled to her stomach. But she immediately drew it away, as if neither the hand nor the stomach was her own. But this was reality. She was in Istanbul, she was in love, and she was pregnant.

"Are you all right, Belgin *Hanım*? You look a little pale. Could it be your blood-sugar level?" asked Ulviye Yeniçağ.

"I'm fine, just fine!" Belgin snapped.

"I think you'd better sit down. I'll give you a sweet. It must be all the excitement. That's love for you!" declared Ulviye, rummaging through her handbag.

Belgin was annoyed at being mothered, and eyed the caramel suspiciously, in its colorful wrapper.

"Just pop it under your tongue, dear . . . I may not be all that young anymore, but I haven't forgotten the excitement of

110

love . . . As a matter of fact," Ulviye confided, lowering her voice, "I'm quite excited myself. I'm having dinner with an old flame this evening, a gentleman who lives on Büyükada Island, same as me. A retired journalist, most distinguished. We haven't seen each other for years! My, my, you don't look at all well, my dear! Here, take this."

"But it's just a migraine!" grumbled Belgin, accepting the caramel automatically.

"No, no, it's love!" proclaimed Ulviye, arching her eyebrows and nodding sagely.

They were just reaching the end of the first moving sidewalk. In a desperate bid to rid herself of Ulviye Yeniçağ, Belgin excused herself with the words: "I think I'll sit down and rest for a moment. Good luck Ulviye *Hanım*!"

Stepping onto the next moving sidewalk, Ulviye Yeniçağ turned and waved. "Good luck to you too, dear. And don't forget to enjoy life. Don't forget, all the fuss and worry is never worth it. Never!"

Even as Belgin heaved a sigh of relief, she realized that part of her was sorry to see the back of Ulviye Yeniçağ. What a strange lady . . . not at all a bad person, interesting in her way, and with much to say. But so typical of women of her station and generation, relishing the self-appointed role as a guiding force for enlightenment and modernity, forever instructing and chastising.

Belgin turned her attention to her migraine, banishing all other thoughts from her mind. She sat down on a metal bench, pulled a pillbox out of her handbag, and swallowed a tablet without water. Closing her eyes, she massaged her temples for a few moments. The tablet had left a bitter taste in her mouth, so she followed Ulviye Yeniçağ's instructions after all, and placed the caramel under her tongue. It wasn't long before she felt better, well enough even to think about Ayhan . . .

It'd been two years since they'd met, two months since she'd last seen him. Now Ayhan was here, waiting for her, the sweetest, warmest person she'd ever known. A real human being, a real man. And waiting for her now!

"It's crazy—love's crazy," Ayhan had said. "And it's as rare as it is crazy, as miraculous as it is rare. Think about it, Belgin. What's the likelihood of ever meeting someone you can really fall for? You've got to love the feel of their skin, the touch of their hand, the way they smell, and the sound of their voice, not to mention their hair, teeth, feet, and fingernails. You've got to learn to love the smell of their sweat, their pimples, and moles. There's the way they dress, the jokes they tell, how they laugh, look, and walk. And even though you may not agree on everything, you need to respect their view of the world and their place in it, their understanding of art and politics. It can't bother you too much if they throw their leg over you in their sleep, if they snore, have dandruff, or are going bald. Just think how much you take on board, Belgin, if you want to fall in love. And you have to throw caution to the wind: there's no holding back, no defense against possible disappointment. And then let's say there is someone like that, one in a million. What are the odds you'll ever meet? Most people never meet 'the one,' that special someone they can get up to mischief with, completely relax with, develop a common language with, make love with. The truth is that simple, Belgin, and that brutal. And here we are, you and me, Belgin and Ayhan, and we've met. We've met, but we're afraid. Afraid! We have separate lives on different continents, we've burned our mouths on love, burned our mouths so badly we blow on our yoghurt before we eat it . . . We've had it with 'long-term relationships,' had our fill of tales of 'true love' and 'perfect couples,' and even if we ached sometimes, deep inside, we didn't believe in real love anymore. You were busy with your genes, me with my rocks, making do, getting by, managing . . . And just when we think we're 'managing' just fine, what happens? We meet! But look, Belgin, we've got to give it a try. We may never get another chance like this!"

That had been his appeal, both reasoned and emotional: perfect . . . And add to that Ayhan's incredible powers of persuasion . . . But it was the power of love itself that had worked its magic, that had hypnotized Belgin into turning her world upside down . . .

She'd thought it through, weighed it up again and again, but now that Belgin found herself in Yeşilköy, at Atatürk Airport, she felt unprepared for the intensity of Ayhan's love. Belgin was scared, of Ayhan as much as Istanbul. She stopped massaging her temples and tried breathing exercises.

It had all been under control. Ayhan's visits to New York, their long talks on the telephone, the e-mails they'd exchanged, full of sweet nothings, jokes, and sex. It had all been so comfortable, so easy, so fearless. And even when they had disagreed, there had been no enmity, no sting, no battle of wills, or pitting of views. They'd stood their ground, even as they were finding common ground over which to advance, together, toward this moment. They had succeeded in so much, more than either had ever been able to do before. But was it going to be enough?

Both had suffered failed relationships, failed marriages. But that only made their relationship more precious. Yes, this time it would work. It had to! Belgin had finally met a man she could trust, one who didn't loathe women and wasn't even afraid of them. Because Ayhan had a conscience, he was courageous and uncomplicated enough to admit when he was wrong, and to apologize. Ayhan was different . . . He was . . . wasn't he?

"I could hide in the restroom, wait for a few hours, wait until Ayhan thinks I haven't come, gives up on me and returns to his old life . . . And I'll take the first plane back, back to my old life . . . before anyone is hurt . . ." thought Belgin, choking at the thought, swallowing hard several times.

Her fellow passengers had passed through passport control and were now officially in Istanbul. Some had even claimed their baggage and were mired in Istanbul traffic. As Belgin continued to sit on that uncomfortable metal bench, nursing a migraine, paralyzed with fear, a new wave of tired travelers started streaming through the arrivals hall. She raised her head and watched them rushing off toward passport control. A dark-haired woman of medium height stopped right next to her:

"Belgin? I don't believe it! It is you, Belgin, isn't it?" she very nearly screamed. "Don't you recognize me? Have I really changed that much?"

"Ayda?" asked Belgin. "Is that you? It is you! What a coincidence, Ayda!"

Some of the travelers being conveyed down the long corridor on the moving sidewalk looked on with smiles as the two middle-aged women embraced each other with cries of joy.

"Of course it's me. *Je suis* Ayda Seferyan, Dame de Sion, number 215!"

"Oh, Ayda! I've missed you so much! And here you come, as always, to the rescue."

"I still can't believe it. Tell me I'm not dreaming. You said in your last e-mail that you were planning to return, but you didn't say when. I thought you'd changed your mind again. All those years away, you must be a real New Yorker by now. Let me get a good look at you: Are you really here!"

They laughed. Running into Ayda was good for Belgin; Ayda had always been good for her.

"I suppose you've just come back from Paris?" asked Belgin.

"That's right . . . but this time it wasn't so much to visit my brother as to settle Sibel in. Would you believe she's as tall as me and beginning university over there? My daughter's off to university! We're getting old, Belgin. *C'est la vie.* Sibel's all settled in with my brother, and I'm back in good old Istanbul. And what's up with you? I see you've still got the same curls, still beautifully dressed Belgin with her curls!"

"I don't think so! Just look at me. I'm a mess, I've got a headache, and if I could slip into bed I'd sleep for at least twelve hours."

"Ahhh, those famous migraines of yours. I'll never forget Madame Rosignol, accusing you of making excuses just to miss class. Remember?"

"How could I forget? The worst teacher at Dame de Sion, and did she ever have it in for me!"

"Well, you've got to admit you were a bit of a handful, especially to people who didn't really know you. Such a cool customer, but what a lot going on inside. I've got students like that now—they

114

remind me of you sometimes. Anyway, I've really missed you, Belgin. I'm so glad you're back. Especially now, when I've just sent my daughter off to Paris. Let's get together, just like old times, pajama parties and all! We'll have tea in Bebek, pudding in Pangaltı. We've got so much catching up to do."

"Well, we'll have plenty of time. I think I'm returning to Istanbul for good."

"You're kidding! Are you serious, Belgin? *C'est vrai?*"

Ayda studied Belgin's face carefully, then let out another of her unlikely screams and hugged her.

"This is such great news, Belgin! I was worried you'd turned into an American, that we'd lost you, too, to the brain drain. I mean, look at my big brother and cousins, all living in France now. So many people in the West for careers and all that . . . Well, Aret'll be thrilled you're back. He's coming to pick me up. I still can't believe it. There's nothing like old friends, and here's my best friend, back in Istanbul!"

"You're right about that . . ." Belgin said with a sigh. "Only old friends stand the test of time. Do you remember, when we were little, how Aret would cup his hand and tell us how he was holding 'time' inside it?" She smiled at the memory of Ayda's brother.

"*A la recherché du temps perdu.* Well, our friendship has certainly stood the test of time . . . and Aret's the same old Aret, not bothered at all by things like the passage of time, or the search for lost time, or the remembrance of things past, or what have you. Or maybe he just pretends. Anyway, don't let all this talk of time get you down, Belgin. I'm forty and I've never been happier. Really, there's no better age for a woman: you know yourself, you don't care so much about what others think, your kids are grown up. And look at you! Gorgeous as ever! I've put on weight but you're as slim as ever. You must take after Auntie Jackie-Halide!"

Belgin's return to Istanbul after the death of her father had been difficult, and Ayda had been a ray of sunshine in those mournful years. The two girls had been inseparable, with a friendship that started at Dame de Sion and continued over the years in Bebek and Pangaltı.

Ayda's father, Armenian watch repairman Artin Seferyan, had been able to send his girl to the prestigious high school only because of a full scholarship. The sense of guilt he felt toward the 'martyr's daughter,' orphaned by the Armenian terrorist group ASALA, made him doubly protective of Belgin and her relationship with his daughter. On weekends, he'd travel by bus all the way to Bebek so the girls could see each other, and even managed to persuade Jackie-Halide *Hanım* to permit Belgin to spend the occasional night in Pangaltı, at the Seferyan's. Belgin was always present at family dinner celebrations for Christmas and Easter, and would receive the same modest gift as his daughter. On Muslim holy days he would be certain to take the long bus-ride to Bebek to present Belgin's mother and Nanny Kete with a box of traditional Kandil sesame rings. Prior to her husband's assassination, Jackie-Halide *Hanım* had never given much thought to the ethnicity of friends and neighbors, but the "tragic event" had sensitized her to such differences. Still, the sincerity and warmth of the Seferyans was incontestable, and she acknowledged in her heart of hearts that the crowded, bustling home in Pangaltı was far preferable to the oppressive atmosphere of her own household. Belgin always returned from Pangaltı in high spirits, and would chatter away to Kete about how much fun she'd had.

Artin Seferyan always made the final, short leg of his trips to Bebek by taxi, so Halide *Hanım* would never be aware that he was too poor to take a cab all the way. Belgin was in on the little deception, and it was through her travels on the bus with Artin that she saw a side of Istanbul she would otherwise never have seen.

"I'll never forget those days," Belgin found herself saying aloud. "It's just like Ayhan says, the goodness we see in others remains a part of us for the rest of our lives . . ."

Realizing she'd inadvertently mentioned Ayhan, Belgin cleared her throat and continued in a matter-of-fact tone:

"Oh, by the way, Ayhan's a sculptor friend of mine. He has some interesting ideas."

116

Ayda knew Belgin far too well to be taken in by her flat delivery. "Must be an interesting character, this Ayhan of yours. Sounds like he has a real way with words!" she interjected, grinning meaningfully.

"But isn't it true what he says, Ayda? We remember every wrong and slight, because they hurt us. But goodness we forget, because it actually becomes a part of who we are."

"Stop trying to change the subject, Belgin Gümüş, number 555. You're hiding something from me! Number one, if this Ayhan isn't a candidate to be my brother-in-law, my name's not Ayda! And number two, we may forget good deeds, but they're never lost, never disappear. So where do they go? Anyway, *qui est,* Ayhan? Who is this philosopher sculptor! Come on, let's get through passport control and into Istanbul. Then you and I are going to have a nice, long talk!"

"I . . . Ayda, would you mind terribly if I just sat here for a while? I'm battling a migraine . . ."

"Don't be ridiculous, Belgin. What are you going to do, sit on this hard bench all afternoon? There'll be plenty of time for that in Istanbul. Come on! They've opened separate counters for 'Turkish Citizens' and 'Foreigners,' just like in Paris, where we have to queue in the 'Non-EU Member' lines." We'll be through in no time at all!"

"That's right, someone told me about that in New York."

"And the passport people are nothing like the old days. They actually smile, and they don't bat an eye when they see I'm an Armenian," Ayda blurted.

At that last reference, however oblique, to the "taboo of the century," something intangible rose up between the two women, an imperceptible ripple of discomfort, something tinged with shame and ancient suffering. But whatever it was, this thing, they knew how to banish it.

A moment passed in silence. Then Ayda extended her hand and Belgin took it. Anyone watching them at that moment would have seen nothing more than two female friends, holding hands, faces sad, mourning together.

At that moment, a cell phone broke into the "A la Turca" march.

"Hi," Ayda cried out, as gaily as ever. "How are you, Sibel? How's it going? . . . Yes, everything's fine, we landed just fine. Sibel, you'll never believe who's standing next to me right now. Your Aunt Belgin! Really! And she says she's back in Istanbul for good . . . When you come home for a visit, we'll have a balcony party in Bebek, just like the old days . . . What do you mean you don't remember? Well, you were just a baby, I suppose. No, I guess you wouldn't remember. What's that? You met someone? *Le bon homme*, you say? But you met another boy just yesterday. What's the rush?"

"I'm back for good," Belgin whispered to herself. "News of my final return has now traveled as far as little Sibel, as far as Paris." She sank back onto the bench. She felt broken. If she could only stretch out here and sleep, sleep for hours and days.

Ayda had finished talking to her daughter, but was still grumbling to herself. "What if this girl of mine falls in love with some French boy and doesn't study? What would I do if she dropped out and had a baby? You'd think she was picking out apples from the market! I'm telling you, Belgin, having kids is trouble! Believe me, sometimes I envy you for not having any . . ."

Belgin was abruptly reminded of the baby in her womb, the baby she'd been trying to forget . . . the baby conceived with Ayhan. At the same time, she remembered Ayda's decision twenty years earlier to marry an Istanbullu Muslim, who she'd since divorced. And she remembered the number of people who'd unexpectedly opposed the marriage, supposedly for the sake of the children as yet unborn. It was strange; back in school, Ayda had never seemed particularly strong-minded or resolute, but when it came down to it, she'd shown her true colors. And when she was pregnant with Sibel, she'd cried out to Belgin: "No one's stronger than a woman carrying the child of the man she loves!"

Perhaps she should tell Ayda everything, here and now, all her fears . . . or should she simply run for it. It wasn't too late. Should she cut her losses and flee? Then the migraine kicked in again. Belgin suddenly found the company of her oldest friend intolerable.

"Hey, why are you sitting down again? I told you, you're coming with me, Belgin! I'm not leaving you here. Get up, get up. Surely you didn't come all the way back to Istanbul to live in the airport! . . . You know, you really *don't* look well. You've gone all pale. Come on, Belgin, let's get you out of here!"

"Can I call you tomorrow? You've got Kete's number, anyway. I've got to get to a restroom. I'm going to be sick," Belgin gasped, struggling to her feet. Ayda helped her to the nearest bathroom and very reluctantly agreed to leave Belgin there. But Ayda's mind remained with her friend as she hurried off to passport control, assuring her brother, who was having parking problems, that she would soon be meeting him in the arrivals hall. Alone in the bathroom, Belgin locked herself into a stall, hung her handbag on a hook, and sat on the closed toilet seat with a deep sigh. She huddled there, palms pressed against her eyes.

"What am I going to do?"

8
A BUMPY LANDING

"Taurus Mountains and wild thyme, that fresh smell forgotten after I moved to Istanbul! For Istanbul is the scent of lavender. It doesn't matter who you are, or where you're from: first the lavender goes to your head, softly and sweetly, then, suddenly, you're reeling. Yes, Istanbul seduces with her perfumed charms, gently enfolding, softly bewitching . . . then moving in for the kill. That's the first thing I remember about her: a whiff of lavender. The sweet smell of lavender! I grew up with the scent of thyme, pine, violet, and citrus, but she smells of lavender, of Judas, of acacia and tulip. That's Istanbul: scent of lavender and Judas, a hint of acacia and tulip. That's Istanbul, smelling just like the woman I love . . ."

Ayhan was just knocking back his fourth beer with Barman Baturcan when the announcement came: the THY plane from New York had landed. He hastily paid the check and, with a quick good-bye to Baturcan, raced to the display panel. On the wall next to the panel was the well-known picture of a smiling Atatürk framed in the window of a train. Ayhan was in too much of a panic to notice.

"Hundreds of smells greeted me when I first arrived in Istanbul, but that one really struck me: lavender. It was lavender that permeated me. Lavender was splashed into the palms of my hands, lavender scented my dreams and mingled with the smell of my sweat. I gave up so much for lavender, the elusive scent of lavender that infused my hopes and my imagination, making them Istanbullu. From the street corners of Beyoğlu, Şişli, and Bahariye, women not unlike the dark beauties of Adana spread the scent of lavender on the streets, into the doorways, inside trouser pockets and brassieres—we exchanged lavender-scented glances; our dreams and desires were drenched in it, and whatever was left was sold tied up in tiny sachets. That was the scent of Istanbul, the very essence of Istanbul for me then. To become an Istanbullu, you must submit to the lavender spell. But I wasn't yet an Istanbullu! I was just getting acquainted with elegant lavender, with that wonderfully coddled, flirtatious perfume so far away from the smells I grew up with.

"'This is Istanbul, Ayhan. Keep your eyes open and take a good look round! This is Istanbul. It's no joking matter. Don't let me down!' My teacher, Emin, from my primary school, had led me by the ear to Darüşşafaka Lycée. I was a tiny boy, far from his mother, his school, Adana, the Taurus Mountains, and the little girl next door. I would have sobbed for my mother had I allowed myself to, had I not been taught from babyhood that 'men don't cry.' Well, they do! Even donkeys cry, so why not men? Damn it! It's the ones who can't cry that should worry, not me! I'd cry myself to sleep there in the dorm when I thought all the other fatherless boys had fallen asleep. I missed my mother and the mountains, but more than anything, I missed the days when I was free to carve bits of stone. Then I'd picture my teacher, standing there in front of me. He'd always say, 'Look, son, if you really want to carve stones and make things people want to buy, if you want to make a living doing what you love, first you have to study! Your natural talent won't make you a sculptor, Ayhan! You need to learn about the world first; you have to understand poetry, literature, music, and art.' I remember reading somewhere that one of life's greatest miracles is having the perfect teacher while still a child. I couldn't agree more! That was the miracle that made me a sculptor, an Istanbullu and, most importantly of all, made a man of me! May Teacher Emin rest in paradise, if there is such a place. If he hadn't brought me to Istanbul and arranged that scholarship, who knows where I'd be today. Probably a bum or a mafioso or just another lost soul . . . And there are so many clever village kids who haven't been as lucky as me, whose lives have gone down the drain thanks to our educational system!

"Lucky me! But some luck! I may have been knee-high to a grasshopper, but I knew life was going to be tough and was already on my guard. Little kids who are poor and pushed around wise up to life pretty quick. There's no messing around, no time for mistakes or tantrums. I had one option and one option only: study and make a man of yourself! I'm still not comfortable with luxury. My food sticks in my throat when I haven't fed a stray dog or helped some kid go to school. I still feel a bit guilty when I'm out having fun. Maybe that's why money just slips through my fingers.

"Poverty is hell! It's hell when you can't look after your family, when you have no insurance and no union to rely on! It's hell anywhere in the world. It takes the shine out of your eyes and leaves you with nothing but despair. What's worse than despair? Shame on anyone who forces others into poverty!

"The biggest decisions are often made early in life, but executed many years later. First I had to leave my mother, my home, and everything I loved. Separation, homesickness, and loneliness! It's a certain kind of loneliness. Like you're invisible, even among millions of others, all of them happy and successful and surrounded by friends . . . The long nights, aching to touch and be touched. But no one to touch but yourself as you ache for the real thing . . . Feeling even lonelier afterward.

"Desperate for warm flesh you find yourself in a brothel, crying out to a body bought with borrowed money! Then, finally, when a girl does seem to like you, worrying that she'll realize you're the kind of man who pays for it, and finding yourself driven to the brothel yet again out of respect for her virginity, but all the while desiring only her . . . not making love, not even 'sleeping together,' just spilling yourself into a stranger's body. Coming like an animal and feeling even worse when you're done! Paid barely enough for food, you skip meals to take your hungry young body to the brothel yet again. However hard you try to hide it, your gestures, your clothes, even the corners of your mouth give away your village background. Homesick migrants call the city 'cruel Istanbul.' They battle on, try to bring the city to her knees, but it only makes things worse . . . And then, finally, comes the realization that you can become an Istanbullu only if you play by Istanbul's rules . . . The painful realization that you will live with loneliness and homesickness until you let go of your old home, until you sacrifice everything you knew, your whole way of life . . . Only then will be you be embraced by Istanbul.

"As for me, I was young, ugly, scared, and lonely. That's why I couldn't go near a girl until I was eighteen. I was a scrawny kid, terrified no one would like me. And when someone did, I never quite believed it. I still don't. My mother was the only one who ever liked me as I was. If my arms and body are in shape now, it's only because I work out, but my mother loved me as I was back then. I was her lamb. It was only when I had the courage to start working with stone, when I laid myself bare and confronted my fears and dreams, that girls seemed to like me. As I sculpted and shaped, as I chiseled away, revealing things about myself, to myself and the world, women started coming after me. I understood the beauty and appeal of honesty. That's how I lost my fear of Istanbul and of women. And yes, it's true that women love creative men. Could it be because all women are creators, and find something of themselves in artistic men? Or could it be that they expect passion from creative men? Are women really that romantic? Yes, unfortunately for them, many are . . .

"Darüşşafaka was a wonderful opportunity. I entered the school, looked around, and saw that it was the real thing. And it still is. I'm talking about a school that was established way back in 1863. Considering the 'greats' it's turned out, being a DAÇKA alumnus is no mean feat. By the time I started, it had become coeducational. The girls, the female students, had adapted to Darüşşafaka so quickly and so thoroughly that it was with some astonishment that I learned, some months later, that they had been barred from its gates for a full 108 years. I'd have hated going to an all-boys' school. I've never understood—and am even alarmed by—places off limits to women. A gathering without women is just that much more competitive and cutthroat. And places brimming with men smell like unwashed socks—not unlike their manly conversations!

"Darüşşafaka welcomed me with open arms, became a home and a family. I can never repay them! And I've got a few choice words for anyone who sneers at it as 'a school for orphans.' I still may not be any good at saving money, but over the years, whenever I did have a bit extra, it would go first to my daughter, Berfin, then to Darüşşafaka. My only hope is that somewhere in Anatolia another kid who loves stones, or words, or colors, or science, or music will be rescued like I was . . .

"I met Belgin far from Anatolia, in a foreign city of towering buildings. The language and culture were also foreign to me. A grand total of two of my sculptures were being shown in a well-known Manhattan neighborhood at a mixed exhibition of 'Turkish Plastic Artists' held at the Turkish House. Even thousands of miles from Istanbul, there in that vertical city, she smelled of lavender! I swear I could smell lavender; even there, in New York, Belgin smelled like Istanbul! I couldn't believe it. The moment we met there were two things that just knocked me right out! First, she said, 'You understand it, you speak the language of stone'; secondly, she smelled like Istanbul! I felt like I'd taken a punch to the gut, but, determined to be a he-man, I didn't let on. Belgin and I became lovers about a month later. Lying in my arms, all woman, all Istanbul, she suddenly came out with: 'Ayhan, remember when we met? There's something I noticed then that I haven't been able to figure out. I don't remember when it happened exactly, but you went all pale, even seemed to sway, as though your blood pressure had suddenly dropped or something. What was it? Did one of those snobs at the opening upset you?'

"That's Belgin for you, she never misses a trick! That's my girl! I could never put one over on her. That's Belgin! If you truly want an equal relationship, she's the one. But you'd better have the balls . . .

"'Oh that,' I laughed. 'It was because you smelled just like Istanbul!' That smell, so out of place in that distant, vertical city. She was thrilled when she learned I loved it and gave me a bottle of Rebul lavender cologne, like the one she'd taken with her all the way to New York. I haven't used lemon cologne since then. I've even been handing out bottles of the stuff to friends, and am sure to tuck one into my bag whenever I travel. 'My father always smelled of lavender and he always used Rebul,' she said, stroking the bottle as though her father was inside it. Stretched out in bed, her breasts and her creamy skin spread out before me, we talked about lavender. That is, she talked about lavender while I imagined sculpting her.

"So, while I was thinking about that, Belgin was telling me about lavender in a soft, serious voice. That's how I learned that the lavender of Istanbul and the thyme of the Taurus mountains come from the same family. *Labiatae* or something like that, she said. 'I don't understand Latin,' I said. 'I may have become an Istanbullu, but I'm still from Adana, or perhaps I should say Adanatae! Ha!' Belgin responded to my ha with a polite smile, then returned to her botany lecture. That's also when I learned the Turkish family name for lavender and thyme: *Ballıbabagiller*.

"'In English it's also known as the Mint Family, and includes about 210 genera native to the Mediterranean. Lavender is native to more western areas, while thyme is more common in the eastern Mediterranean.'

"'That sounds just like you and me!' I laughed. 'We're both from the Mediterranean, but you're lavender and I'm thyme.' Talk about stating the obvious! But what do you expect from a thick-headed peasant like me! Anyway, she just kept on explaining:

"'Lavender and thyme are related, and in pre-agricultural times had distinct geographical areas to which they were native. But the lines have blurred now, of course.' I couldn't resist: 'Wow, my woman's a regular walking encyclopedia,' I joked. But she was serious, utterly serious. Don't be such an idiot, Ayhan, I said to myself. Here you are, making stupid jokes to a woman who's a professor. How many years have you even been in Istanbul? Here you are, a father even, but you're still a peasant. Through and through. What's a woman like her supposed to do with a guy like you? A guy in love with rocks, a guy who still speaks Turkish with an accent. While you were still a kid she was traveling the world, picking up languages right and left, smelling like Istanbul!

"'One of them has pinkish flowers, the other lilac. I'm sure you know the first is thyme. Lavender's flowers are different shades of purple, some of them quite dark. But you know, Ayhan, what I most love about lavender is the leaves, the silvery-green leaves.'

"I just sat there and listened, stunned and speechless. I'd never seen or heard anything like it. There she was, a woman, a beautiful woman, in my bed, naked . . . and, at the same time, she was every bit the scientist, a professor. She talked about biology the way my mother gave someone a recipe for soup. It blew me away—me, who'd imagined I was modern, who'd accepted that men and women are equal. When I met Belgin, I realized how far I still had to go; that I still divided women into two groups: fuckable and un-fuckable; that I wore my balls like a pair of blinders. Here was the most amazing woman in the world, and she was mine, but it still bothered me that she was five years older than me. I hate to admit it, but it's true. I'm scared shitless! Damn, I'm just as scared of Belgin as I still am of Istanbul!

"Maybe it's because, just like Istanbul, she'll never be completely mine. I'll love her knowing that she's always just out of my reach. Maybe it's because, just like Istanbul, there are corners of her I'll never know? I don't know why that scares me so much. Is it because I'm a man? Is this a guy thing?

"I wish Mom was here. I wish she was alive and here with me now. I'd go down on my knees, kiss her hennaed hands, put my head on her lap. 'Mom, what's your boy supposed to do now? Something this good happens only once a lifetime. It's like the bird of fortune landed right on my head. What am I supposed to do?' She'd probably look at me, smile, and stroke my head. She'd be patient and gentle, as always. Would she say: 'If you love her, go get her—you're a lion of a man. If you love her, if you chose her, there must be a reason?' Or would she say, 'You've got to beat both sides of the drum together, Ayhan. How can you be in synch with each other? You're the son of a cotton picker, she's a daughter of plenty.' I don't know what to do, Mom!

"Maybe I should leave now, go lose myself in the crowds of Istanbul? It would mean I'm a coward, that I have no honor . . . but wouldn't it be best for both of us? She'd be angry, she'd hate me at first. But she'd get on with her life, the life she left behind for me. Later she'd thank me, she'd say it was all for the best, thank God that idiot Ayhan got scared and ran off before it was too late. She'd say that! Wouldn't she? God damn you, Ayhan!"

Standing in front of the panel that clearly indicated the plane carrying Belgin had landed, Ayhan turned tail and raced for the exit. He was in such a hurry that he nearly crashed into the automatic sliding glass doors before they'd fully opened. Inside, it had been air-conditioned and orderly; outside, it was crowded, noisy, and hot. It was a hot summer day in Istanbul, at least over there, in front of the arrivals building at the international terminal, where Ayhan stood. Where Ayhan had stopped so suddenly—all his weight falling onto his front foot—that he nearly fell.

Yes, there Ayhan stood, for just a moment, looking left and right, a stranger, confused and cut off from his surroundings. Istanbul had taught him to deal with loneliness, but this was something much worse.

He was a stranger standing in the middle of a noisy crowd, shuttle bus just to the left, yellow taxis on either side. Swarming around him were hordes of people carrying bags, some with packs on their backs, determined people rushing by. Some smiled as they walked arm-in-arm out into Istanbul. Some looked excited but apprehensive as they consulted guidebooks. The same questions were asked in many languages as tourists were directed, in broken English, to taxis, shuttle buses, and other terminals, airport police on either side of the sliding doors keeping a vigilant eye out for terrorism. The gently smothering heat of Istanbul enveloped them, one and all.

Standing indecisively in front of the doors, Ayhan was too oblivious to realize that he was blocking the way, and that some cursed him under their breaths. He stood there, dazed. Sweat blotched dark patches onto his blue polo shirt, ran in rivulets down his face, dampened his short blue-black hair. He looked like a passenger who'd just awoken from a long flight and suddenly found himself, half-asleep and hungry, thrown out into the city . . .

"Need a taxi, brother?"

Ah, there you go, Ayhan my boy, he thought. Just what you

need. Now get in and go!

"Brother, do you want a taxi or not?"

Get in now! Run! It's all for the best. Do it for Belgin! Go on!

"Hey! You could at least give me an answer."

"You talking to me?"

"At your service, brother!"

Turning his head, Ayhan saw a heavyset middle-aged man, in need of a shave. In contrast to his rough voice, he had gentle brown eyes.

"Made up our mind yet?" the taxi driver asked, with a hint of mockery. When there was still no response, he turned his attention to some other travelers:

"Let me take you home, to your wife and kids. Or I could take you to the Bosphorus to sit down, have a tea, cool off . . ."

The driver had succeeded in catching Ayhan's attention. Encouraged, he continued his patter, growing ever more theatrical: "It's our duty as taxi drivers to reunite citizens with their loved ones. Life's too short to waste time on the bus!"

Ayhan's situation may have been no laughing matter, but he was smiling now, wider and wider. The corners of his full lips curved upwards as his face lit up.

"You're like some kind of walking, talking, psychological hotline!" he said, smiling at the driver.

Having finally received a response from Ayhan, the driver now spoke with an exaggerated Kurdish accent: "You can say that again, brother! Is there anyone in this whore of a city who listens to more troubles, who puts up with more problems, who suffers in more traffic, who sees more of the garbage, the back streets, and neighborhoods far from picture-postcard Istanbul?"

"So she's a whore for you too, huh?" Ayhan asked, with that old, wry smile. "What kind of city is this anyway, and how many different faces does she show to the world?"

"I was just mouthing off, brother. I didn't really mean it. Even if I do miss home from time to time, there's no way I could leave this city. It's true that we drivers see all the worst spots, but we know the best ones, too. What could be better than a glass of cold rakı and a plate of hot fried mussels over in Çengelköy?"

"Fried mussels, huh? Where are you from?"

"I was born in Diyarbakır, brother, but we came here some twenty years ago, looking for work. I suppose I belong here now. Or maybe it's just that I don't belong anywhere else."

"That's it in a nutshell," Ayhan stage-whispered.

"Where are you from? I'd guess you're from out East, too."

Ayhan laughed. "I'm part southern, part eastern. Came here to Istanbul from Adana, the Taurus Mountains. But I'm an Istanbullu now, swear to God!"

When a Japanese tourist came up and suddenly asked in English who was next in line for a taxi, Ayhan automatically indicated he was. The taxi driver took the opportunity to propel Ayhan toward his taxi and open the door. Before he knew it, they were driving off.

"Can't say I've seen many passengers without bags. Well, this is Istanbul. You see it all, sooner or later," the driver said, eyeing his fare in the rearview mirror. "The name's Memet, but everyone calls me Hamo. We get all types, you know, but I can see that you need to get home straight away."

Ayhan was too tired to pay attention.

An elbow propped on the window, "Mind if I smoke?" the driver asked, lighting a cigarette without waiting for an answer. Then he broke out into a Kurdish folk song: "*Agir ketye dilê min, Xew nakeve cave, min tu Çima tu jimin dûr ketî, Bêje ronîya çav min, Rinda min, gewra min . . .*" Burning cinders alight on my soul, sleep comes not to my eyes, tell me my beloved, why are you so far from me . . ."

Ayhan lit a cigarette of his own. Too absorbed in thought to hear the folk song, he sucked on it like a pacifier.

"Look at this traffic! It'll take at least an hour to get to Maslak. Look at that maniac in the sports car!" Hamo shouted out the window: "Hey you! How'd you even manage to sit still nine months in your mother's womb? Get a load of him! Hey, I was driving these streets while you were still in the cradle! By the way, where you going, brother?"

Slumped in his seat, eyes on his shoes, Ayhan had been asking himself the same question for the last few minutes.

"Where am I going?"

"There's another one. Thinks just because he's driving one of those big 4X4s he can do whatever he wants. How are we supposed to get into the EU with people like that?"

"Where am I going?"

"Hey brother, you tell *me* where we're going. We're coming up on an intersection. I need to get into the right lane."

"Stop, Hamo! Take me right back, back to the airport. I've got to get back. She's there. My future. My everything," Ayhan shouted. But Hamo drove on as though he hadn't heard.

"Hamo, are you listening to me? We're going back. Take the quickest way back to the airport."

Angry with the driver for not responding, Ayhan reached out to grab him by the shoulder. But when he lifted his head, he wasn't in a taxi. He was standing in front of the entrance to the international arrivals terminal. A Japanese tourist was getting into a taxi just behind him. The driver stuffing a huge backpack into the trunk was heavyset and middle-aged, and when his gentle brown eyes met Ayhan's, he nodded. The bumper sticker on the taxi read, "Hamo, King of the Road."

9
HEAD SCARVES ARE OUR FREEDOM

"Çamlıca is back to what it was, more like us, more like what it should be. But it wasn't always that way. I remember the wonderful view from the Çamlıca hilltop back when I was a child, back when it was run by Turing, the Touring and Automobile Club of Turkey. Visiting the park facilities there was like being lost and outnumbered in a foreign country. I was little, and there was so much I didn't understand, but I was old enough to know what it felt like to be excluded, looked down on, and—worst of all—ignored. We were Çamlıcalı, born and raised—Istanbullu, through and through. But in those days *they* considered us 'the other,' treated us like the despised members of a minority, like invasive weeds. Cut off from their own people and traditions, *they* would wander around the grounds of Çamlıca with their alcohol and their cigars. So pathetic were they, they thought nothing of treating my mother with contempt and looking down their noses at me, a girl of nine—and all because I wore a head scarf. They couldn't have cared less about hurting our feelings—they'd simply go home and forget all about us. To them, we didn't even exist. We were the invisible ones. *They* were 'Western,' affected, oblivious, and hostile to anyone who wanted to live like a true Muslim. *They* were the ones who ridiculed the İmam Hatip religious schools. They were the unchaste, the ones who outlawed the right to wear head scarves and took away our freedom. They were all the same, those elites. And they expected everyone else to have the same Western affectations, the same lifestyle and even the same ideas!"

All eyes were on the tall, slim woman gracefully swaying into the duty-free shop on white İnci high heels. She was young and fair, and it was only natural that she would draw appreciative glances, but she was also practiced in reading something else in the stares of strangers: solidarity or censure.

Expertly applied liner accentuated the young woman's

enormous dark eyes and enhanced her flawless white skin. Her loose cotton trousers and knee-length tunic were from Zara, a light purple that matched the lilacs on the silk Vakko scarf fastened under her chin, concealing neck, ears and throat. Under the flowery silk scarf, a close-fitting bonnet or skullcap of sorts, made of black fabric, hid every stray strand of hair. Aleynâ Gülsefer was the very picture of Islamic chic, and noticed by all.

"We're people too, with feelings, hopes, and dreams, just like *them*. It's ridiculous that they're scared of us, like we're ogres—but not so scared that they don't still call us 'fish heads' just because we wear head scarves, just because we believe. Don't they stop to think how hurtful it is to paint us as enemies of modernity, to see us as second-class citizens? Not a one of them does! But how could we expect them to? They have no vision, no moral compass—they're misguided and aimless, they don't believe in the hereafter, in hell, or in divine justice. It's foolish to expect the secular elites to think about us! If they could just see themselves for what they are, they would join us on the path of righteousness. But Satan has blinded them to everything but worldly pleasures. Sometimes I pity them, I really do! After all, they're only human, and they, too, are the beloved servants of Allah, peace be upon Him. And, in the end, we're all members of the global community of Muslim faithful.

"Why are they so hung up on appearances, anyway? They say the eyes are the window to the soul. Well, their eyes burn with greed and contempt! I pity them, pity them straight from my heart. But then, when I remember their arrogance and pride, the way they always try to crush us, my heart fills instead with the righteous anger of the wronged! Still, I pray that I might feel merciful. O Lord—*Celle Celâluhu*—forgive me my trespasses! Forgive me my rage! But I'm so angry at them! Who do they think they are, these so-called 'secular progressives,' these 'defenders of contemporary values'? They've completely forgotten about spiritual values, about the roles of wife and mother, and the place of family in society. They think it's modern to fritter away their children's futures. I couldn't help but see some of those television programs they watch, and they filled me with horror and pity. Young women being treated like sex objects and young men being manipulated by those women—everyone joking about adultery, as though it were nothing . . . it's all so empty and crude and meaningless. But they join forces when it comes to us, to the believers. We're the enemy, we're the traitors. As if our veiled grandmothers, along with dervishes, sheikhs, hodjas, and imams, hadn't joined hands to liberate our country under the leadership of Atatürk! They conveniently forget that Atatürk never forced his own wife, Latife *Hanım*, to remove her veil in the name of secularism. What's worse, we're the ones blamed for rising tensions, we're the ones told we have to 'uncover or go,' we're the ones called 'fundamentalist' and blamed for injecting religion into politics! As though this country wasn't 99% Muslim anyway, as though 75% of Turkish women didn't wear some type of head covering . . ."

Because head scarves are barred from most university campuses and classrooms in Turkey, Aleynâ had enlisted the support of her mother, a housewife, in persuading her father, businessman and owner of Gülsefer Textiles, Inc., to allow her to study at a Texas university, a school with a high percentage of Muslim students, many of them veiled. She'd already completed her freshman year in business administration. Thanks to her high school, an İmam Hatip secondary educational institution originally set up to train government-employed imams, but which, unlike other vocational schools, also taught arts and sciences, Aleynâ was proficient in English. She'd also taken additional private courses to prepare for TOEFL, which she'd passed with ease.

With over an hour to go before she boarded her plane to America, Aleynâ had plenty of time to appraise a store display of Kenzo cosmetics. Just as she prepared to reach for a tall, thin bottle decorated with a single red blossom, a hand with lilac-painted nails reached over her shoulder and grabbed it. Deeply annoyed, Aleynâ turned to confront the intruder, who, having already tossed the perfume into a shopping basket, flitted off in a short, spaghetti-strap dress and white sling-backs to the alcohol and spirits section. "*Ya sabır*—God give me patience!" sighed Aleynâ. "*Ya sabır ya Resul Allah!*" she added for good measure.

"No one has any manners anymore! That woman could say 'pardon me,' at least. Perhaps she did it on purpose? To harass me because of my scarf. But would she go to all that trouble? Absolutely! They'll do *anything* to belittle us and to exclude us!"

Aleynâ glanced around to see if anyone else had noticed the little scene, but saw only a few women with bare heads, all of whom avoided her eyes. Aleynâ had long since grown accustomed to furtive stares. Calmly, head held high, she reached out and took a 100ml bottle of Kenzo Flower.

"Those with patience are nearer to God!" she sighed. "Why don't they realize how primitive it is to run around half-naked—how can it be that they don't see that the covering of nakedness has occurred parallel to the march of civilization? It's so sad, the way educated people, supposed defenders of freedom, are so blinded by their half-baked notions of secularism that they deny the obvious . . . How can it be that something so apparent to me isn't equally clear to the professors and pundits and columnists? The only answer is that they're disingenuous, willfully blind to the truth. But how can they live like that? They're so hung up on bare heads that they forget to have an open mind. It is God's blessing for us to be born Muslim, and it is our duty and honor to submit to his will. Islam commands that we cover ourselves. Ours is the only Holy Book that remains unaltered and unabridged, and the Koran clearly advises women not to display their 'ornaments,' except for the hands, face, and feet. An outer display of modesty helps us to focus inward, on purification of the soul, the ultimate aim of our religion. Purification is not an abstract thing. A proper dress code—the 'form' we choose to present the world—is the outward and public manifestation of an inner and personal commitment."

Bottle of perfume in hand, Aleynâ had wandered over to another cosmetics counter. At age twenty, she didn't give the anti-aging creams a second glance, nor did she show any interest in the sunscreens and tanning lotions. At that moment, the lady in the short dress shot past, throwing a bottle of factor 35 sunscreen into a basket containing bottles of whiskey and rakı. A brisk redhead radiating femininity, this bundle of energy also threw off a floral fragrance instantly recognizable to Aleynâ as Kenzo Flower.

"Why don't these secular women believe that we have chosen, of our own free will, as a voluntary act of submission to Allah, to dress modestly and cover our hair? They insist we've been cowed or coerced, that we've been brainwashed since childhood, but they don't stop to consider that they too shape the views of their own children. What's the difference between presenting your child with a head scarf and handing them a bikini? In either case, parents are making lifestyle choices for their offspring. All we want is for our children to grow up to be good Muslims. That's all! How can the pressure and oppression we face for this simple desire be squared with our democratic rights? They call us cult members, bigots, reactionaries. It is *they*, not *we*, who are the reactionaries! Just look at that Kenzo Flower lady, wandering around in public half-naked, drinking alcohol—do we interfere with her in any way? They claim that under sharia *we* wouldn't defend *their* freedom not to wear head scarves, and ask why *they* should defend *our* freedom to wear them. Is it so bad to be governed under Islamic law as laid out by God? Besides, conservatism is on the rise around the globe, not just in Turkey. There's a growing hunger for spiritual values. Why does this cause so much agitation and alarm here in Turkey?

"Take the example of that sculptor—Ayhan something or other. He kicked up such a fuss when they took his naked statues out of a public park. Nude ladies and men with their sexual organs exposed, all on public display in the heart of Istanbul! Yes, I remember reading about him, that sculptor. He apparently came to the conclusion that nudity equals art and freedom. History has shown time and again that women are debased when their modesty is not valued. But that sculptor, whatever his name was, I'm sure it'll come to me in a moment, has become so distanced from his own culture and religion, along with that whole secular crowd, that they see everything through the prism of Western culture. He was on television just the other day . . . Ayhan Pozaner, that's it! I knew I would remember. Anyway, this Ayhan Pozaner claimed that there was a connection between nudity and nature, and between nature and truth, went into this whole philosophical spiel about humanity and a sense of self. And he's a professor, yet! Next thing you know he'll be advocating outright shamelessness, whatever that might mean. By covering ourselves we live in accordance with our dignity as humans. That's what sets us apart from the animals!"

Aleynâ wandered the aisles, sniffing at the various tester perfumes she'd sprayed onto her wrists to kill time, before stopping to select two gift boxes of pistachio Turkish delight for university friends from Japan and Singapore. Heading for the cash register with her three small boxes, Aleynâ saw that long lines had formed, and observed that most baskets and carts were piled high with cigarettes and alcohol. At that moment, a tall man with a shaven head and mossy-green eyes, wearing a dark suit and lilac tie, caught her eye. She guessed he was in his early thirties, and realized that he was monitoring the cash registers and customer lines, indicating to employees with a meaningful glance that the emptied metal baskets should be collected. An employee ID card hanging from his neck read: Jak Safarti—Customer Relations Manager. Sensing that Aleynâ's eyes were on him, the young man turned his head slightly and looked directly at her. Their eyes met.

"What a pretty girl!" was Jak Safarti's first thought. Then his eyes made their way to the two layers of cloth binding her head on this hot summer day. He guiltily averted said eyes but not before noticing that Aleynâ had been eyeballing his ID card. "She's probably judging me," was his next thought. Aleynâ too had turned away as she hastily jumped into the nearest line. The Customer Relations Manager approached her and said, "You only have three items—I'll open another register," indicating one on the end. This attention both pleased and discomfited Aleynâ, who kept those eyes of hers on the floor and responded, "Thank you, but I'll wait my turn."

"But there's no need," Jak Safarti insisted. "Help this young lady out," he called out to a nearby employee. When the new cash register was opened, a number of customers fell into line in front of it.

"Thank you," said Aleynâ, looking into Jak Safarti's aforementioned eyes before glancing down once again at his ID card.

Jak Safarti was used to this. Ever since childhood, he'd known what to expect when someone asked him for his name, and would brace himself for the inevitable reaction to his Jewish name. "Jak," he'd smile. "I'm Jak." After a puzzled pause, he'd often be congratulated with "Ah, good for you. Your Turkish is excellent. No accent at all." When he was much younger, that had been his cue for a spirited explanation of how he was just as Turkish as anyone else. When he got older, he simply smiled and reminded the listener that Turkish was his mother tongue. Still, whenever someone implied that no Turk could possibly be named Jak, he couldn't help himself from thinking "My family has been in Istanbul for five hundred years, and in addition to my mother tongue, which is Turkish, I also speak English, French, Spanish and Italian, and a bit of Ladino, albeit no Hebrew whatsoever. How many years have you been an Istanbullu? And why is your Turkish so bad?" But he kept these thoughts to himself; he knew there was no point in sharing them. Jak Safarti was not what you would call religious, but he had an unswerving faith in the power of laughter. He'd always believed that poking fun at bigotry, at our own mistakes and weaknesses and fears, was the best way to overcome them, that humor and hope go hand in hand, and are our best chance for change and self-improvement. Over the years, many had frowned on this view, regarding it as silly and childish, had been as intolerant of a good laugh as they were intolerant of so much else. But, no matter what anyone else thought, Jak Safarti had no intention of doing without irony and satire, the art of the takedown and the perfect delivery of the send-up.

Jak Safarti could guess at what was going through the mind of the pretty girl standing across from him, a girl who was obviously Muslim and more concerned by his status as a non-Muslim than by his supposedly non-Turkish name. He too was a local, and fully aware—painfully so at times—of how other locals thought. For his part, Jak Safarti had a secular worldview, and saw religion primarily as a form of cultural identity and a source of diversity. These views didn't endear him to the more conservative members of his own community, even though he'd been at the forefront of efforts to prevent the closure of the Ohrida Synagogue in Balat, the district where his grandfather had been born and to which he'd had no other connection. He simply considered the synagogue, which was built by Jews settling in Istanbul from the Macedonian city of Ohri, to be part of Istanbul's cultural heritage, and it was for that purely secular reason that he would, when asked, travel all the way from Kadıköy, on the opposite shore of the city, to help make up the minimum number of ten men in the congregation needed for the synagogue to open for religious services.

These were the thoughts that flashed through his mind as he led Aleynâ to the open register, where she nodded her thanks as she permitted herself a cool, courteous smile.

"She can't get past the fact that I'm a Jew," he said to himself. "She considers me an outsider—she thinks this country only belongs to people like her. That's what she's been taught and that's what she unquestioningly accepts."

In fact, despite the look she'd caught him giving her head scarf, Aleynâ was grateful the store manager had taken so much trouble on her behalf, and was busy with her own thoughts as she opened her wallet to get her credit card: "There, standing right across from me, is the best response to those who won't allow us to live as true Muslims! A Jewish citizen is able to practice his faith in peace, but we aren't! That's precisely the kind of double standard I can't stand!"

Her credit card, issued by the Turkish branch of an international Arab bank her father had chosen because it employed Islamic banking practices, was not in her wallet. "Could I have left it at home?" she thought. "We also accept Turkish lira," Jak offered in his most helpful voice, even as he sighed to himself,

140

"To her, I'm a Jew first, a man second. And that's not going to change for many years, if ever. I'm an infidel and a foreigner, but the real tragedy is that I can't help but see her as something of a stranger too!"

Aware that a line had formed behind her, Aleynâ began to panic and get upset with herself as she started searching through her bag. Were she to call her father, the poor man would of course turn around and drive all the way back to rescue his daughter, but what if she'd forgotten the card at home . . . ?

"If the young lady isn't ready, I wonder if I could pay?" came a woman's voice.

Jak Safarti had other customers to think about, so asked Aleynâ to step to one side, assuring her that she could move to the front of the line when she was ready.

Aleynâ did so, embarrassed and sorry to have made others wait, and increasingly angry with herself for having caused a scene. As she frantically rummaged through her purse she heard a female voice chatting gaily with Jak, who seemed to have forgotten all about her. Annoyed despite herself, she glanced over to see the lady with the purple fingernails and short dress. The perfume thief! Actually, she had quite a pretty face and wore very little makeup. In fact, she looked familiar, like someone Aleynâ had seen somewhere else. But what was most noticeable about this woman, who spoke perfect unaccented Turkish, was the large silver cross dangling from a silver chain.

"Of all the . . . well, I never . . . may Allah bring her to her senses, what else can I say? I'm so sick of these affectations, Muslim girls wearing crosses! What will they think of next? She's probably off to Europe and thinks she'll fit in with her short dresses and her crosses! Well it makes my blood boil!"

"You know, we've got the best airport in Europe. I mean, the ones in Amsterdam and Copenhagen are nice enough, but Istanbul Atatürk is so spacious and well run. Not to mention the friendly service . . ." the woman positively sang.

"She's as irritating as she is affected," sighed Aleynâ, a split second before she finally located her credit card. She heaped upon that initial sigh a longer and larger one of relief. Life without a credit card would have been impossible in America. "Thank God I didn't call Father," she thought. When she glanced over at the register, she saw that the woman with the silver cross was just then handing her credit card to Jak, who exclaimed, "Ahh! Anna Maria Vernier! I knew I recognized you. You're a film critic, right?"

"That's me, all right! I'm just off to Cannes," she said, beaming, obviously pleased to have been recognized.

"I read your column every week, but I'm afraid we don't agree on Tarantino!"

"*Pulp Fiction* is one of my all-time favorites, even if I don't think much of *Kill Bill*," laughed Anna Maria Vernier as she slipped her perfume and whiskey into the plastic carrier bag marked "Atatürk Airport."

"So that's who she is, that journalist, the one who's forever being interviewed about what it's like being a Levantine in Turkey. They're Catholic, no wonder she wears a cross. And no one minds that, do they, but when it comes to my head scarf . . ."

Observing that Aleynâ was waiting, credit card in hand, Jak Safarti said, "Ah, so you've found it! Just come right over here," carefully avoiding physical contact as he guided her to the spot vacated by Anna Maria Vernier and explaining to the waiting customers why Aleynâ was being allowed to return to the front of the line. As Aleynâ was finally relieved of the three items she'd been carrying and her credit card transaction was being completed, Jak Safarti went over to speak to Anna Maria Vernier again. Aleynâ felt excluded, but she was used to it. Any girl who from the age of nine had, with her family's consent and in order to observe the strict letter of the Koran, worn a head scarf, got used to it. But she was still too young and inexperienced not to feel a small pang as she walked toward the shop exit and then on toward the gate where she'd soon board a plane to America.

"Have a good trip. And I hope you'll visit us again," came the voice of Jak Safarti from somewhere behind her.

Pleased by his continued interest, Aleynâ said to herself, "Unfortunately, it's the foreigners who know how others should be treated." But she couldn't help being particularly pleased that the attention had come from an attractive man.

"Thank you," she said, smiling over her left shoulder.

"Let me give you my card. If you're ever here again and you have a problem, I'd be glad to help."

Jack Safarti was a true professional, but even so . . .

"May Allah's greetings be upon you!" she blurted, then blushed deeply, getting angry, extremely angry with herself for having exhibited her feelings to a perfect stranger. A mortified smile on her flushed face, she quickly marched off, berating herself with "That was so unnecessary, Aleynâ. So pointless! You should have just thanked him and gone! He's a store manager. He gives his card to everyone!"

Back at the entrance to the shop, Jak chuckled as the word "Shalom!" somehow slipped out of his mouth. He didn't know if Aleynâ had heard him or not, but he did know that women were remarkably similar when it came to men.

10
AN IDENTITY CRISIS

"They've completely ruined Çamlıca! Massacred what was once a little piece of paradise! Congratulations, and bravo on a job well done! Philistines! Arrivistes! I mean, other cultures, the Arabs included, have a developed aesthetic, a distinctive architectural style that reflects their climate and geography and culture. But when it comes to our religious fanatics, they have absolutely no grasp of the subtleties of taste or style, no original ideas of any kind, for that matter, on the subject of art and architecture. How could they? Even among themselves they haven't yet built a consensus on such fundamental questions as cultural identity. They consider Islam to be *the* defining cultural trait, and wrongly identify Islam with Arab culture, about which they are completely clueless, incapable as they are of reading the Koran in the original Arabic and ignorant as they are when it comes to literature and the arts. They burden their speech with Arabic words but turn their backs on our own Anatolian civilization, including the Bektaşi and Mevlevi cultures, and their uniquely Turkish form of tolerance. They have no appreciation for the Ottoman-Islamic-European cultural synthesis, or the role it played in the flowering of our artistic heritage. Instead, we're left with a crude and incoherent eclecticism, hurriedly cobbled together and thoroughly tasteless, just like the ugly concrete buildings springing up all across Istanbul. Philistines! Do I have to put up with the tastelessness of the country hicks who provide the capital for these blots on the Istanbul cityscape? In the old days, too, peasants streaming into the big city were ignorant of aesthetics, be they cultural or architectural, but they would at least try to learn, to benefit from the cultural offerings of the urban environment; over time, they too would become heirs to the legacy of civilization which is the very definition of a great city like Istanbul. Now, they come here just to fill their pockets by plundering and raping, by destroying and razing, and all in the name of development and modernization.

Vandals! Just look at what you've done! Bravo!"

Two hours earlier, Erol Argunsoy, former chairman of the Istanbul Chamber of Architects, had landed at Atatürk Airport on a regularly scheduled THY flight from Barcelona, where he had been representing Turkey at the Mediterranean Architectural Congress, submitting a presentation on "Urbanization and its Environmental Impact: Projections for the 21st Century." Because the bag containing his passport, credit cards, cell phone, and ID card had been stolen in Spain, the only documentation he had was a temporary card issued by the Turkish Consulate in Barcelona. While still standing in line at passport control, a police officer had invited him to visit the airport police station, to which he'd then been escorted. He had, for nearly two hours, been waiting for his identity to be officially verified. He'd also just learned that immediately to the right of the passport checkpoints through which he normally sailed without a care, a cunning bit of architectural design concealed an entire police station. Although he'd never taken much interest in airport design, except for what he considered to be some minor structural flaws, he was highly impressed by the sleek functionality of the Atatürk building.

"Our religious nuts have grown so narrow-minded and aggressively intolerant that in recent years they've begun ignoring the true pillars of our religion—compassion, community, and charity—even as their hearts have filled with greed and animosity. They resent anyone who doesn't live as they live, dress as they dress. I'm telling you, their fanaticism is almost enough to put you off religion altogether. Islam doesn't simply mean bans on alcohol, enmity against women, and a long list of other taboos. It's a religion rooted in tolerance and subtlety. How have they managed to stray so far from its real roots, as well as our own cultural roots? It was under their watch that the hilltop of Çamlıca, in the very heart of Istanbul, was transformed into a nondescript monument to bad taste that could as easily have been put up anywhere between Iran and Afghanistan. Bravo! Even the Arab visitors are astonished by its crassly absurd inconsistencies, like those women who wrap their heads in two layers of cloth but wear open sandals and blue jeans. Worse, even the fanatics themselves don't think much of the monstrosities they've created: they'd rather flock to the new plazas and shopping malls, places about as far from their medieval mentality as you can get. And they're not content to go singly or in pairs. No, they have a congregationalist herd instinct: group living, group thinking, and group worship. They don't understand urban culture's emphasis on individuality, the interface of city-individual-freedom-democracy. Instead of celebrating personal development through diversity, they continue living as members of a herd, anonymous units of a collective mass, traveling in packs as they compete to snap up whatever they can get their hands on at those 'Satanic' Western-style shopping malls, although so far they lack the numbers to have completely overrun them, as they did Çamlıca! On the other hand, the world they hunger for is nothing like the one they pay lip service to: an Eastern world where women are kept indoors and veiled, and where men wield all the power. In fact, they don't reject modernization at all, and even have a grudging admiration for Western civilization, where a belief in heaven and God doesn't restrict freedom for women. Otherwise, they wouldn't spend a small fortune to send their head-scarved daughters to Western universities, would send them instead to *madrassa*s in Iran, Indonesia, or Egypt. Bravo! Well, the Lord punishes bigots the world over in exactly the same way: 'And the Lord on High condemns all backward bigots to the deepest pits of vulgarity . . . ' Amen!"

Architect Erol Argunsoy wasn't certain of the exact reason he was being detained at the airport police station, but he had learned from the young policeman who served him tea that his papers were being processed on the computer and that the prosecutor would interview him as soon as he was free. Instead of the perpetrator of the theft facing interrogation, it was he himself, the victim, a fact he resented bitterly. He'd have liked nothing more than to complain loudly that just one day after having been subjected to many wearying hours of questions and paperwork, first at the local police station, where not a single person spoke English or Turkish, and then at the Turkish consulate in Barcelona, he, a celebrated architect and all-around distinguished person was now being detained in a police station here in his own country. He'd held his tongue after the young officer serving his tea had looked him up and down—taking in his bowtie, suspenders, stylish short-sleeved shirt, trendy micro-fiber bag, and the silk handkerchief with which he mopped his perspiring brow—and had drawled in a icy tone, "This is standard procedure for all citizens, no exceptions." High blood pressure, extreme heat, and fatigue had combined to make Architect Erol Argunsoy feel decidedly off, but he'd decided not to make a fuss, especially after the policeman's sarcastic emphasis on "all citizens," over what he'd expected would be at most a fifteen-minute ordeal. Sitting on a hard wooden bench, he looked at the photographs of Çamlıca in the THY magazine *Skylife*, remembering the Çamlıca he'd picnicked at sixty years earlier with his mother and grandmother, and then the Çamlıca he'd visited as recently as fifteen years ago, when it was run by Turing, to have coffee and tea with his ex-wife's niece, Belgin, whom he loved like his own daughter—and her nanny, Kete, too.

"Those were the days, back when Turing ran Çamlıca, back when chic ladies didn't shrink from being women, when men were well-dressed and clean-shaven, children obedient and respectful, waiters well-spoken and highly-trained. It was an urban—and urbane—setting in which men were addressed as 'sir' and women as 'madam,' a place where one could be a true Istanbullu, proud to be a resident of a great city where strangers nodded in greeting, a sophisticated social discourse was appreciated and practiced, and recordings of timeless Istanbul songs were played or even occasionally performed live by chamber orchestras. All thanks to the late Çelik *Bey*, that tireless chairman of Turing, who oversaw the restoration of so many Ottoman summer palaces and mansions, transforming them into magical settings popular with the middle class. Oh, those were the days . . ."

The young policeman with the nametag reading Üzeyir Seferihisar asked if he'd like another tea, to which he responded: "Look, officer, how much longer am I going to have to wait here?"

"What do you mean 'longer,' Uncle? It's only been half an hour."

"Uncle, is it?" he thought, making a face, "And what exactly makes me an 'uncle' to him? His feudal background is what, the fact that he's steeped in a culture that insists we're all relatives! Everyone is 'uncle' this and 'aunt' that, like he's still in the village, or as though he brought the village with him! You can't blame him, of course, for having been forced to come to Istanbul to make a living. He may even be honest, may even be a gentleman. Who knows how difficult it's been for him to adjust to city life, how he barely scrapes by on minimum wage, how many mouths he has to feed, even at his young age. We should really be blaming ourselves—we're the ones who have failed to teach him the essentials of urban culture, such as addressing men as *beyefendi* and women as *hanımefendi*, apologizing when you bump into someone on the street, and waiting patiently in line. Each and every one of us shares the blame for the unconscionable degeneration of cultural life in all the cities of Turkey (but most of all in dearest Istanbul) into the monolithic machismo of a frontier town!"

Officer Üzeyir Seferihisar interpreted the grimace on Erol Argunsoy's face as a personal affront, and got annoyed. "They're all like this, stuck up and looking down their noses at the people. Well, this old guy's clearly got it made—he's probably inherited property and money, probably never had to work for a living, never had to worry about his children's future, never had to face a transfer to some strange new place. Just look at him, one of those lords of Istanbul! Well, I've got news for him: times are changing and people like me are sticking up for our rights. Just wait and see, you old idiot, maybe one day you'll get a taste of what normal people have to go through!" he thought to himself in a rush as he left the room.

Erol Argunsoy returned to his magazine and the evocative photos of Çamlıca.

"They just don't get it. They worship Medina as the second holiest place in Islam and the burial place of Mohammed, but what they don't realize is that the very word for civilization, *medeniyet,* is derived from the name of that ancient city. Civilization as we know it did not flourish until cities were founded, but they're insistent on turning even the cities of Turkey into a collection of narrow-minded villages! As soon as they get their hands on a place, they ban alcohol, never stopping to consider that it is in Konya, a province with the strongest prohibitions against the sale of alcohol, that alcohol consumption is highest. They don't stop to consider anything that might lead to an open debate—in their eyes there can be no debate on taboos! If you're such a perfect Muslim, why do you have to ban alcohol? Let anyone who wants to sin, sin. Why should you have to carry them into heaven on your shoulders? Oh, yes. Bravo!"

At that moment, several policemen escorted two young girls who looked like guest workers from Turkmenistan or Kyrgyzstan into the room. "Have a seat," said one of the police in an already fed-up sort of voice, pointing to six wooden chairs lined up under an enormous clock and a photograph of Atatürk. Dressed in knock-offs of the latest designer wear, the girls looked even more terrified when they received a sympathetic smile from Erol Argunsoy.

"They haven't paid their entry fees," a policeman grumbled.

"I swear, brother, my husband's going to pay it!" one of the girls cried in broken Turkish, springing to her feet. Erol Argunsoy was dismayed to hear that a girl who looked all of sixteen was married.

"Her husband!" laughed a policeman. "They find a husband here just so they can get Turkish citizenship."

"I swear, I have a husband," pleaded the girl in a quavering voice.

"Sure you do," said the policeman, who had clearly dealt with similar cases.

"How much is the visa, or fee, or whatever it is . . . I'll pay it!" declared Erol Argunsoy, standing up.

Erol Argunsoy had always done all he could to help children and the poor, through voluntary work and on his own initiative. As an Istanbul University student—engaged to Belgin's aunt, by the way—he'd been a young trainee on a construction site in Sarıyer the day he'd arranged for the adoption of Safiye, the young girl who came down from the hilltop shantytown every day to serve the workers their lunch. His fiancée's family had for generations subscribed to this practice, traditional among wealthy Istanbul families: taking in a girl and raising her as part of the clan. Generally from large, rural families, the girls would be taught to read and write and were expected, until they came of age—when they would be permitted to marry—to help with the housework and look after the children. Critics might argue that the system represented forced labor, was even a modern form of slavery, but Erol Argunsoy had always been proud of his decision to arrange for Safiye to come live with his fiancée's family, and was certain that Belgin's much-loved nurse, who later came to be known as Kete, enjoyed a far better life there than what she would have had to look forward to had she been married off at a young age. Belgin's ex-husband, Mehmet Emin Entek, would frequently voice a dissenting view: "It's interesting that the social-welfare policies advocated by your esteemed uncle include luring a poor Kurdish girl into servitude in exchange for three meals a day. It seems to me to be the perfect example of the very exploitation of the working classes of which I am myself so frequently accused!" Erol Argunsoy knew better than to rise to such bait. He was fully aware that Mehmet Emin Entek resented him not only for opposing so many of his development projects and for questioning his business practices, but—above all else—for continuing to act as a surrogate father to Belgin. As much as he longed to teach Entek a lesson, Erol Argunsoy held his tongue, for he loved Belgin like a daughter and knew that Entek had gone so far as to suggest that he, having divorced Belgin's aunt, should no longer be considered a member of the family.

"No need for that, uncle: they've got money, plenty of money!" jeered Officer Üzeyir Seferihisar. "They just don't want to hand it over."

The frightened eyes of the girls were now fastened on Erol Argunsoy, not the policeman. Aware that in their eyes he was an "old letch" out to exploit them, he spoke in a fatherly tone of voice: "I was most impressed by the handicrafts I saw in Central Asia," he began. The girls looked more terrified than ever:

"We've got our papers—our husbands are outside waiting," cried one of the girls, pulling a fifty euro note out of her pocket. Erol Argunsoy sighed and sat back down on the hard bench, sadly mopping his brow. The other girl also produced a big note, and a few moments later they were processed and gone.

"If there is such a thing as a slave market in the twenty-first century, it's the illegal workers flooding into Turkey from the dictatorships of Central Asia and the Black Sea basin," he lectured to himself, feeling even more dispirited, drained as he was by long hours of travel, long waits at police stations in two different countries, and, finally, by his offer to the girls, which had apparently been woefully misinterpreted. Studiously ignoring Erol Argunsoy, the policeman had moved behind a wooden counter and was refilling a plastic self-inking stamp, his thoughts on his wife of eight years, who was at that moment in labor with their fourth child, as it happens. Only twenty-eight years old, Üzeyir Seferihisar already had three children, all girls, for which reason he had insisted his twenty-four-year-old wife of eight years produce yet another child to try and break this streak. His chief frequently advised his men to have only as many children as they could support, and, since he wouldn't allow his wife to work, a fourth child would be a grave burden. Even so, he prayed to himself, "God willing, this one will be a boy! They'll call me at any moment with the good news!"

He then heard the following words: "Are you telling me that the Turkish police still use those plastic stamps?" He raised his head to see Erol Argunsoy, who'd decided it was time to make conversation with this young Anatolian officer.

"We were using those things when I was a child, sixty years ago. Haven't they been replaced by something more modern?"

"I guess not. See, we're still using them."

"Here we are, in the process of entering the EU, and we've still got the same red tape, the same creaky, authoritarian state. Just look at the way I've been kept waiting here all these hours. It's just this mentality that . . ."

"And who wants to get into the EU? It's not as if the Europeans will give us the right to work and live in Europe. So what good would it do people like me? All they'll do is corrupt our values: they'll let in homosexual marriage, tolerate draft dodgers refusing to do their military service, keep the police from being able to properly interrogate prisoners—we've already lifted the death penalty, as it is! Soon we won't be able to catch and punish any rapist or thief. Who wants the EU? Anyway, we're not part of Europe and we're not Europeans!" he exploded, not even pausing to take breath. He regretted his words the moment they left his mouth, but it was too late. He knew he was a bit of a hothead, just as he knew that he was on the lowest rung of the civil service and so completely expendable. It was stupid to take such risks, especially with a son on the way.

He looked around to make sure no one had heard, but was confronted only by a staring pair of aggrieved eyes, the eyes of that old, pot-bellied architect in his fancy outfit.

"Care for another tea, uncle?" he offered meekly.

Erol Argunsoy shook his head from side to side and pursed his lips, taking his handkerchief out of his pocket to wipe his forehead.

"Look, son," he began, gently and patiently, "Europe isn't the enemy and being European isn't some kind of disease. Hundreds of years before we Turks came to Anatolia, the Byzantines who lived here were part Roman. And if we assume that our ancestors, the Ottomans, didn't put every last Byzantine to the sword, every Ottoman was part Byzantine. DNA studies show that Aegean Turks and Greeks are closely related. The meaning of that is clear. Look, I've been all over the Turkic countries of Central Asia, as well as to Afghanistan, Iran, and numerous Arab countries, and I've had ample opportunity to conduct informal, on-site anthropological and cultural studies. Yes, we Turks do have something of the East about us, and, in cultural terms, our border regions in particular are more Eastern than Western, but you can take it from me, whether you like it or not, that we have been European for at least the past five hundred years."

For the first time, Officer Üzeyir Seferihisar found himself taking the old man seriously. Anyone who talked like that in a Turkish police station must have friends in high places. Continuing to mop at his forehead, Erol Argunsoy kept talking in a weary voice.

"It's not tea I want—I just want my papers processed, or whatever it is you're doing. I've been here for two hours now and I've had it. I was exhausted when I got off the plane and it's hot in here, and I don't feel well, and now rush hour is about to begin. I've got to go all the way to Maçka, and there'll be traffic jams in Akaretler, Fulya, Ihlamur . . ."

"Akaretler, Fulya, Ihlamur . . . As if I'm not an Istanbullu just like him and don't know where anything is! So, what if I'm originally from Yozgat? Stuck-up twits like him think they own the place! Anyway, his papers say he was born in Bitlis. What's with the Istanbullu pretensions? Of course, he did have to go out of his way to tell me how his father was governor of Bitlis when he was born, and all that . . . But what makes him think he's so high and mighty? Too much trouble for him to wait two hours! Poor thing might get stuck in traffic in an air-conditioned chauffeur-driven taxi! Well what about people like me, waiting in line in this heat to squeeze onto overcrowded buses?" were the thoughts running through Üzeyir Seferihisar's head, although he successfully kept his mouth shut this time.

"If you'd had proper identification it would have taken no time at all," was all he said, eyes on the plastic stamp, not once looking up.

"You're not listening to me. I told you, everything was stolen. I have a stamped and signed letter from the Turkish Consulate and you still ask for ID! I've handed you half a dozen membership cards—from Greenpeace, ÇEKÜL, TEMA, ÇYDD . . . and you claim they're no good!"

"We'll accept a driver's license."

"I told you, I don't have one. I support mass transit by taking

154

a taxi, or a ferryboat if I cross to the Asian shore. That way I don't contribute to pollution or traffic problems."

"The law's the law, uncle. Only Turkish citizens can enter the Republic of Turkey without a passport, and they have to prove their citizenship. We've had to keep people here for as long as three days . . ."

Erol Argunsoy glanced at the policeman to see if he was being threatened, but Üzeyir Seferihisar was placidly refilling his stamp, drop by drop.

"Get me a glass of water, would you? Room temperature if you don't mind. My throat's gotten dry waiting here in this heat."

"Poor thing's got a dry throat, has he? And a sore ass from parking on that hard bench, no doubt about that. Bet that fat ass of his didn't get all padded from eating dry bread and raw onions every day . . . if he only knew what it was like to be a cop in this country," he muttered to himself as he left the room. "Room temperature! Like he's ordering around a waiter in a five-star hotel. Europeans and Byzantines and all that shit! Well I'm a Turk and a Muslim and proud of it! Treating me like I'm some refugee from Afghanistan, an asylum seeker in his precious Istanbul. What is it about this city that they won't share with people like me? All I see is thievery, fraud, cheating, drugs, alcohol, porn . . . Everything that was shameful and forbidden back in Yozgat. Are we the ones that brought all that to Istanbul? It's the police and the garbage men who keep this city from falling apart and stinking to high heaven! And then they say they don't like the police, we who keep them safe, on minimum wage, so they can spend all their time in fancy bars and expensive restaurants!"

Erol Argunsoy thanked Üzeyir Seferihisar for bringing the glass of water, drained it in one gulp, cleared his throat, and began speaking in a forceful but level voice:

"I'm certain you'll allow me to make a phone call? I don't want to be a burden to the chief of police or the public prosecutor for a minute longer. Bring me a phone, officer! It's time to put an end to this nonsense!"

Üzeyir Seferihisar was taken aback by the sudden transformation of the grumbling but compliant old man, and decided with a sinking heart that his initial impression had been dead on. He'd taken in the expensive clothing he'd considered ridiculously trendy on such an old man—and then the manicured nails, the large ruby ring, and of course his beautifully spoken Istanbul Turkish—and assumed the moment Erol Argunsoy entered the station that he was the type to "clear things up with a single phone call." But, when the docile man had merely taken a seat on the bench, Officer Üzeyir Seferihisar had decided he'd been mistaken. Now it appeared that the man had simply been pretending to be an ordinary citizen! Himself a truly ordinary citizen of the Republic of Turkey, Officer Üzeyir Seferihisar had long since developed the social survival skills of knowing how to address whom, and when, and in what tone of voice. Those skills now lept into action. "There's a telephone in the back office. Please follow me, sir," he said, hanging his head and slumping slightly, palms pressed against his thighs.

Erol Argunsoy caught the giggling plague, emitting a sound rather like a hiccup as he followed the police officer into the room where he would be allowed a single phone call:

"Deniz!" he said. "Hello darling! Yes, it's me, Erol, just back to Istanbul from Barcelona. The congress was a huge success. Hopefully we'll be hosting it in Istanbul one day. Anyway, I'll tell you all about that later. I'm afraid I'm in a bit of a pickle. I was mugged in Barcelona, passport, cash, the works. Now they're holding me here at the airport police station. Could you find out who's in charge, the name of the commissioner or chief or whatever, so I can finally go home? Yes, about two hours now. No, some things never change! Thanks so much. I'll call you later. Bye."

Back in the waiting room, Erol Argunsoy began to imagine himself at Bebek Bar with a glass of Merlot and a Cuban cigar, looking out over the Bosphorus, which he had begun to miss after less than a week away. The only thing that was going to keep him away from those famed straits would be death itself. Yes, it would be a fate worse than death, never to see the Bosphorus, or dine at an outdoor table, or talk with friends, or listen to music on its shores. His thoughts had taken a decidedly morbid turn, so he turned to one of the joys of his life, that sweet young man, so full of energy and drive, who'd left the village behind, determined to become an Istanbullu. He'd come so far over the last few years, and it certainly wouldn't do to ponder death when someone so young and vital still needed his guidance and his love.

"Exhausted or not, I really should stop by to see him. I've waited this long, delaying my homecoming for another hour won't really matter, and I can always go to Bebek Bar tomorrow . . ." he was thinking when he was interrupted by Officer Üzeyir Seferihisar, who respectfully informed him that the police commissioner would see him now. As they walked down the corridor together, the policeman's cell phone rang, and with an apologetic look he answered.

"What are you saying, Mother? What? A C-section? Why can't she do it the normal way? Do you know how expensive a C-section is? Okay, okay! There's nothing we can do about it. Do you know yet if it's a boy? Well let me know as soon as you find out!"

Assuming the policeman was about to become a father for the first time, Erol Argunsoy prepared to congratulate him, then he thought better of it, fearing a reversion to the role of "uncle." He was tired of living in a part of the world where the line between courteous pleasantry and over-familiarity was so ill-defined and so frequently crossed. Tired! Yes, his beloved homeland could be most taxing . . .

He was on his way in no time. Waiting at the door was the commissioner, who ushered him in with an ingratiating smile and a sharp rebuke to his unfortunate escort: "Why did you keep Erol *Bey* waiting!" Moments later he was presented with a cup of coffee, which he didn't touch, and a stamped document, with which he was whisked through passport control. He was in Istanbul at last! Although it didn't take long to track down his luggage, which had been taken off the carousel and entrusted to an airport official, he was now bone-weary and short of breath. Well, it was nothing a long, hot bath wouldn't cure. But first, a quick visit to a certain barman.

11
MIRRORS

"There was always someone else in the mirror," Belgin shuddered. She was still locked into a stall in the airport bathroom, aching head cradled in her hands, fingers massaging her temples. "Someone who resembled me: a face like mine, the same nose, my eyes. Yet the face staring back at me was not mine—there was something about the expression, the attitude, something alien and remote . . . and dead. And it filled me with dread, that face in the mirror. It wasn't that the reflection was ugly or beautiful, disturbing or pleasing. It wasn't about that. After all, it was undeniably me: my face, my features, my skin. But *I* wasn't there, whatever it is that makes me, *me*, as though I'd lost my shadow, or my soul.

"I was thirteen when this fixation with mirrors began. My mother put it down to the excessive vanity of a young girl on the threshold of womanhood, and worried aloud that I'd neglect my lessons. Poor Kete tried to allay her fears by clucking, 'If the little lamb spends so much time in front of the mirror, she'll get tired of her own face, won't she, Mother Halide?' Dear Kete would drag me away from the mirror and out of the room so my mother couldn't see. But it wasn't what my mother thought: I wasn't merely a precocious young girl developing a premature and unhealthy obsession with her attraction to the opposite sex. But how could I possibly have explained the truth? How do you explain to someone who herself had only ever had the haziest of self images, who had never had the time or even the inclination to develop one, the need to search for yourself in the mirror, to find some part of yourself that seems irretrievably lost? You couldn't. I couldn't.

"There was no sign of me in the mirror: not in our house in Bebek; not in Arnavutköy, in the house shared by Uncle Erol and my aunt; not at Uncle's bachelor flat later, in Maçka; not at Ayda's, in Pangaltı; or in the Nişantaşı flat I shared with Mehmet

Emin Entek; and certainly not at Dame de Sion Lycèe or Bosphorus University . . . There was no one I could tell, but the truth was this: I had disappeared from every mirror in Istanbul. It began the year they killed Father, the year I started having migraines, the year they labeled me 'the girl with the melancholy eyes' (or was it 'melancholic'?). And would you believe that it was this same year I became a captive of the cool, melancholy eyes looking out at the world from every mirror and every photograph? Well, believe it, because it's the truth . . ."

Belgin had lost track of exactly how long she'd been sitting on the toilet seat in that public restroom located just outside passport control, her migraine having given her an excuse to run away from Ulviye Yeniçağ, to avoid her old classmate, Ayda Seferyan, and—most of all—to escape Ayhan, who was no doubt waiting just a few hundred meters away. She'd lost all sense of time: had it been fifteen minutes or one and a half hours since they'd landed? She didn't want to know; she was afraid to find out. The migraine, the walls of the stall and time itself pressed in on her.

Decisions torture the truly indecisive. But Belgin had made her decision two months earlier in New York; she'd accepted that her life had reached a crossroads, a turning point, pregnancy and the subsequent realization that she was ready to be a mother playing no small part. But her decision hinged even more on something else: a filigreed mirror from Mardin.

But now, back in Yeşilköy, battered and buffeted by memories that seemed to rush out at her, ambushing her from the air, sea, and land, she'd lost her resolve. She felt worn and defeated and discouraged, utterly incapable of emerging to face the world and a new life. Rushing in with the flood of memories had been painful, more painful than she'd thought possible, and Belgin realized she would have to quickly review her options and make a new decision. Actually, she didn't have all that many options, which made the decision that much easier: either get up now, walk through passport control, tell Ayhan he's going to be a father, and be propelled into a new life together; or wait in the toilet stall until Ayhan gives up and goes home, then book a flight back and spend the night at an airport hotel. It was that simple; there were no other choices. It was that simple!

The pain had spread to the sockets of her eyes, before which hellish colors whirled and white spots flashed—eyes she knew would be bloodshot and blinking in the bright light. She began breathing exercises, deep and slow, and was already feeling a little better when a tapping on the door dynamited the silence: "Are you okay? Do you need help?"

"Thank you, I'm fine," said Belgin, mortified. Unbidden, an image of her mother popped into her mind—the mother who'd sailed her car into the Bosphorus. That "traffic accident" . . .

"Years later, when Jacqueline Kennedy Onassis was an editor in New York, I found myself standing in the crowd at the opening ceremony of newly restored Grand Central Station. Although I didn't admit it to myself at the time, I was there for mother, as apprehensive and excited as though she herself was going to appear. It's funny when you catch yourself doing the sort of thing you've vowed never to do, it makes you realize how callow you were, once upon a time . . . Anyway, there they were, Jacqueline Kennedy, her lover, Maurice Tempelsman, and her son, John Jr. Seeing her like that, there in the flesh, I got a lump in my throat and blinked back tears. I'd never realized. They really did look alike! Mother would have been ten years younger than Jackie, if she'd lived . . . As I caught sixty-year-old Jacqueline Kennedy exchanging a flirtatious glance with her lover, it hit me: I realized I'd never really made an effort to know the person who was my mother, a woman widowed at thirty, dead at fifty. If I'd stayed in that crowd at Grand Central Station any longer, I might have stormed the platform and thrown my arms around an astonished Jackie O. But I didn't. I ran out of that crowded station, for dear life . . .

"It was the year I couldn't find myself in the mirror that one of the best things in my life happened. Back came Kete, there to help out after my father died, solid, dependable Kete, sleeves rolled up, ready to take charge right around the time I began having my crises with mirrors. First brought to the house a few years before I was born, a young Kurdish girl whose family had 'saved' her by sending her from Van to Istanbul, she was about ten years older than me, my playmate, confidant, nurse, big sister, family, my everything, my precious Kete. I couldn't remember a time she'd been known as Safiye, but I knew it was because of me that she was called Kete, after the Eastern Anatolia *kete* buns she used to bake. Those simple buns filled with fried flour were the one reminder of her home and childhood Kete allowed herself, and I imagine it pleased her to see me devour them by the dozens, even as my mother struggled to steer me away from those 'rustic' buns and make me eat high-protein *börek*, filled with cheese and spinach and mincemeat. But, uh-uh! You couldn't get me away from those little, round buns, a smear of egg yolk luxuriously brushed on top. Piping hot *kete* buns made by my beloved Kete.

"There's no need to take her to the doctor, Mother Halide. Belgin's strong as an ox, praise the Lord. It's just been a bit too much for the little lamb, poor thing, Father Halit Ziya passing away and all, and her growing up so fast. What we need is a lead caster,' she said, somehow convincing my mother to permit a lead-melting ceremony, a folk cure Mother had never even heard of. Kete must have been about twenty-five at the time, but like so many girls from the rural east didn't have a birth certificate, so I can't be sure of her exact age. On good terms with everyone in the neighborhood, all the shopkeepers and tradesmen, Kete rushed out and found a lead-caster Gypsy woman the moment my mother wondered aloud if it would do any good. As my mother and grandmother looked on in astonishment, the Gypsy woman and Kete melted a fistful of lead, draped a sheet over me, and poured the silvery-gray liquid into a metal bowl of water held over my head. There, in my little tent, I listened, intrigued and frightened, to the incantations and the hissing and popping of the lead overhead. Next, the Gypsy woman deciphered the fantastic shapes cast by the molten lead, determined which demons had been my tormentors, and cast them out with a theatrical grimace and a few more darkly muttered prayers. I decided then and there not to wait to see if the spell worked: never again would

I say anything to mother, or anyone else, about losing myself in the mirror. After a few weeks, Grandmother and Mother decided the lead-casting had worked, greatly increasing Kete's standing in the family. I kept my vow for many years to come, until one day, a married woman, I was stupid enough to bring it up with Entek . . ."

From time to time there were more taps on the door of the stall Belgin occupied, but whoever it was would apologize after hearing her say "occupied"; they would shuffle their feet and wait until one of the other two stalls was free. As she sat in her cell, memories and fragments of conversation and images racing through her mind, Belgin could hear the sounds of running water, women chatting in different languages, and shoes clicking across the bathroom floor. The sounds were as sweet to her as a lullaby, and a part of her wanted to be lost and hidden in sleep.

"I searched for years, in Turkish mirrors, in ones made in China, India, America, Denmark, and Brazil: framed and frameless, stained and cracked, decorative and plain, hand-held and full-length. Nothing—I thought I'd vanished forever, replaced by someone else, someone who answered to the name of Belgin, someone who lived and breathed but wasn't me. No one noticed; no one really looked at me. Not really.

"'Did you know that the word for mirror is masculine in French? When Turkish women sit in front of the looking glass they don't realize that, of course. We don't assign gender to objects. Come here, Belgin, come sit in my lap and I'll show you something.' That's how Father and I started our little game with the mirror. I must have been eight or nine. We were living in Bebek, or was it the ambassador's residence in Denmark? I can't remember exactly, not right now . . . If it was the mirror with the silver leaf it must have been the house in Bebek, but I may be imagining it, just because I loved that mirror . . . I still dream about the candleholders on the walls shaped like angels, the porcelain cup with the angel, the wall lamp with silver leaf angels . . . silver and angels . . . like I'm imagining it all . . . But I clearly remember perching on Father's lap like a princess. 'Come on!' he said, 'I'm going to teach you a new game. Look into the mirror and tell me what you see.' I did what he said—I had no problem seeing myself in the mirror back then. 'Look carefully, Belgin, look into your eyes and tell me what you see.' 'Brown eyes,' I giggled. 'There's more,' he insisted, 'look deeper, right into your pupils, and describe what you see!' I concentrated as hard as I could, determined to come up with a clever response that would please Papa, staring into my eyes to find what it was he wanted me to see. And I saw it, and laughed. 'There are little lights burning in my eyes, like sparkles! Like a torch!' I was thrilled. I held the whole world in my hands whenever I held one of his huge ones. I was the happiest girl alive, the best loved, the strongest. Father loved me so much he'd helped me find the light in my eyes. I was loved, and I sensed, even then, that I would never love or be loved in quite the same way again. Me and Papa, the two happiest people in the world! When Mother saw us together she'd smile—never interrupting, she'd smile and quietly withdraw. Or is that only what I *wanted* her to do? Am I making this up? Did Mother really 'catch' us like that?

"'I want you to promise me something, Princess,' Father softly whispered in my ear. I was more than ready to do whatever he said. 'Promise me that, no matter what, you'll never let that light go out—promise me you'll never let anyone put it out! And if anyone does, promise me you'll leave: that person, whoever it is, is your enemy. Remember, that light is yours. It's your most precious possession, and will light you through the darkness, keep you going, keep you alive. It's a divine spark, and its brightness is what makes you, you. Promise me with all your heart, Belgin!' I promised, not only with my heart, but with my whole being. But it was a promise I failed to keep. There came a time when I could only stand by helplessly as the light went out; in the darkness, I could no longer see myself in the mirror.

"Father went before his time, but he couldn't bear to see me suffering, would visit me in my dreams to help . . . I was so despairing I must have turned to him even in my sleep. 'This isn't like you, not like you at all, Princess,' came his disappointed

164

voice. We were in the living room in the house in Bebek. He was forty-three, the age he was when they killed him, but I was now a young woman. He was looking out at his beloved Bosphorus, his back to me, talking fast and furiously. 'What happened to my girl, my clever girl? What happened to the light in your eyes? Didn't you promise me?' He kept his distance and he looked tired. I didn't know what to say, but I was so happy to see him. I'd missed him so much! 'Father, there's someone in my life, someone I trusted completely. He's educated, he's well-bred, he loves me. My husband. But every day I catch him telling another lie. Do men who love still cheat, Father? Why would a successful person need to cheat and lie and prevaricate? Why didn't you teach me about men like him, Father? I'm in trouble. And I'm afraid of being alone,' I said in a flat voice, as though reading aloud. I wanted nothing more than to run over to him, throw my arms around his neck, find shelter in his strength. But I didn't do it. I was afraid he'd disappear if I touched him. 'You've got to face your problems and solve them, Belgin. Don't forget, you weren't raised just for a husband and a good marriage. Get up and go, rekindle the light in your eyes! Go now! I know you can do it!' And he passed through the window, out onto the balcony of the three-story house on Ehram Yokuşu and down the street. Tears streamed from my eyes. I tried to call him back, but couldn't make a sound. Even though it was just a dream, the pain was real, my heart aching, my stomach in knots. From the window, I saw him walking on the shore of the Bosphorus, near the spot where Mother's car flew into the sea. I woke up on the floor, sobbing. The next morning I finally found the courage to call Uncle Erol and ask him to find me a lawyer. There would be no more cheating, no more humiliation, no more sneering at me, my past, my work and my family: I was divorcing Entek.

"Before I could search for the missing light, I had to get rid of the man darkening my world. I knew it wouldn't be easy. And it wasn't. Entek's swollen ego wouldn't let me go without a fight, and I had to endure another year of biting insults and attacks, too distracted and miserable to complete my thesis on time. Finally,

165

we were divorced and I was free. Everyone I knew at that time had gone off to establish new lives. Kete had married a local widower, a shopkeeper, and moved to Sarıyer where she had a baby the following year, as though she was anxious to make up for the all the years she'd devoted to me. Even though she was busy with her infant, Halit Ziya, and her two stepchildren, she was always there to support me. I'd inherited the house in Bebek after my mother died, and had rented it out when I moved to Entek's flat in Nişantaşı. That's why I ended up staying with my uncle Erol, himself in the process of getting a divorce. If it hadn't been for my professor, Yannis Seferis, and Ayda, my old friend from Lycée, I don't know how I would have got through those dark days. Finally, I succeeded in getting myself to New York, safe and sound, to start a new life. But I still couldn't see myself in the mirror. I needed something. Something else! Of course I knew full well that what I most needed was to trust someone again, to allow myself to love and be loved. But I couldn't do it. I'd lost the two people I'd loved and trusted most, my father and the husband I myself had chosen, thinking he was special. I'd managed to avoid the trap of thinking all women were victims and all men villains, but I had learned all too well that the world is full of cowards and fakes. I'd been deceived, and couldn't trust myself not to make the same mistake . . ."

Belgin opened her bag and pulled out a silver filigree hand mirror, a gift from Ayhan. "Look, Belgin," he'd said. "Look at the craftsmanship in the filigree, the influence of thousands of years and dozens of cultures: Mesopotamian, Syriac Christian, Arab, Kurdish, Turkish, Armenian, Roman, Seljuk, Persian . . . Whenever you feel like looking into this mirror, at the most melancholy, most melancholic, most beautiful face in the world, first run your fingers across the back of the mirror—feel it. Appreciate the Arab, the Kurd, the Turk, the Greek, the Iranian—all of them a part of you, part of your heritage. Then, when you look into the mirror, see just how beautiful you are!" he said, in that deep voice of his, crackling, if such was possible, with mischief: "If I couldn't feel all of them inside of me, my sculptures wouldn't be worth shit!"

Not even sure anymore how long she'd been in the locked stall of a restroom at Atatürk Airport, Belgin held up the mirror and looked into it. "Do you think your love of filigree is anything like my love of silver leaf?" she'd asked Ayhan the first time she looked into that mirror. "Technically speaking, yes. They're both made out of gold or silver, but leaf is formed from thin plaques, filigree is made from wire—there's a lot of fake leaf around, but filigree is always genuine: leaf is European, filigree is the masterwork of our own Syriac Christians!" he smiled, eyes sparkling. Actually, the light in Ayhan's eyes wasn't a sparkle *or* a twinkle, but a beam, powerful as a spotlight. And it was in the mirror Ayhan gave Belgin that she had at last been able to see herself, for two years now. When she first noticed it, the light in her eyes shining again after all those years, she wept with joy, had leapt out of bed, and danced right there in front of Ayhan, who was stretched out smoking a cigarette. He watched her, smiling, then roared out in his bass voice: "Just see if I don't capture this moment, just see if I don't retell it in stone: the woman who lost herself in the mirror and how I was chosen to make her happy again." And that was the inspiration behind "Woman and Mirror," the critically acclaimed Ayhan Pozaner piece exhibited in a private gallery in Paris a year later. The following year, the curators for the "Contemporary Turkish Sculpture" exhibition at the Istanbul Modern specifically requested his depiction in Afyon marble of a standing nude figure, faceless, one hand reaching into space, as if to ward off danger, the other holding a mirror out of which a face emerges in relief.

After Entek, Belgin's relationships had been few in number, and she seemed to choose men who were risk averse and incapable of sharing her life. Ayhan had been a breath of fresh air, and the better she'd gotten to know him over those two years, the more she appreciated and loved him. He was comfortable in his own skin, something as easy as it is difficult: easy for anyone who's honest, sincere, and natural; difficult because this capacity inevitably stirs up resentment in those who aren't comfortable in theirs. Ayhan had seemed too good to be true. Some of Belgin's Turkish friends took the opportunity to tell her as much, for her own good, of course. "That sculptor of yours is good-looking enough, but don't you think he's a little rough around the edges? . . . You're a diplomat's daughter, after all . . . be careful . . . in the end, men like him always show their feudal roots." Belgin paid them no mind because she knew better. She had already suffered through a marriage to the kind of man her friends and everyone else would have approved of.

Belgin was old enough and wise enough to know that only the "real thing" could heal her. Having found him, she'd rediscovered herself. She'd also discovered that, for the second time, she was pregnant. This time, even if she was afraid to admit it to herself, she wanted a baby, his baby. But that didn't mean she wasn't afraid of what would happen if they lived in the same city, wasn't afraid that he too would cheat on her one day.

"Well then, we won't live together," he'd said when she confided her fears. "Just what are you getting all worked up about? We'll rent two flats in the same apartment building, or we'll arrange for you to move into the apartment next to mine in Ortaköy, you with your silver leaf and me next door with my filigree . . . How about I drill a hole in the wall and spy on you, on my own wife?" He laughed, long and hard. Husband and wife; mother and father of a child Ayhan didn't even know about yet; a relationship sure to grow stale and confining . . . "Or we'll move to a house with a garden, not too far from your university but some way out of the city. I'll quit my post, I can't stand the Higher Education Board anyway, and set up a workshop in the garden. You'll go off to teach and do your experiments . . . Maybe we'll even grow vegetables and have kids? What do you say?"

"Is anyone in there? I've been waiting here for ages."

Belgin knew it was time to vacate the stall.

"How are we supposed to get into the EU if we can't manage to put enough toilets in an airport bathroom?"

Belgin flushed the toilet so it appeared she'd been using it, slowly stood up, and, with her eyes still closed, smoothed her hair and dress. She took a deep breath and waited for a couple of minutes. She imagined herself passing through passport control, heading straight for an airport hotel, and throwing herself into bed. Yes, that would be best. Best to turn back before it was too late. Safely back in New York, she'd write to Ayhan and apologize. He was a smart guy, even when disappointed and angry; he knew her well enough to understand and forgive. By the time she'd opened her eyes and stepped out of the stall, the bathroom had cleared out. When she turned to the mirror, it was herself she saw. Even through stinging, narrowed eyes, Ayhan or no Ayhan, Belgin could still see herself in the mirror.

12
A MAN, A WOMAN, A CITY

"Do cities resemble women, or do women resemble cities? And who was the joker who first compared women to the sea? Must have been some drunken sailor, then a million idiots decided to take it on board! Shit!" grumbled Ayhan as he lit his last Lucky Strike.

"And there was that conference, in Florence I think, an Italian architect lecturing on 'Urban Design.' He said something along the lines of: 'Historically speaking, it was men who established cities.' I was listening on headphones, a simultaneous translation, and my English wasn't really up to it . . . But I sure did understand the looks on the faces of the female artists and architects in the room. Oh, how they smirked and smiled! They looked at each other, and those women could barely keep from bursting out laughing. If it's really true that men establish cities, perhaps that's why women are compared to cities—men love to organize and govern women, just like cities. Anyway, whether women or cities, they have the same effect on me: they're both to blame for the mess I'm in right now!"

July heat pressed down on the people of Istanbul, slowly suffocating them and taking its time doing it. Ayhan had decided against running off, but couldn't bring himself to go back into the terminal either. It wasn't that he was indecisive. No, he'd always known exactly what he wanted, and pursued it with determination and passion. Just as he'd pursued Belgin—until now, when he'd lost his footing just as she was in reach. There was no other explanation: he'd stumbled, and badly.

"You're scared, my boy! Scared of losing your last best chance, of losing Belgin just as you're winning her . . . scared of messing up just as the dream of a lifetime is about to come true, scared of falling short of perfection, scared of your own romanticism, of your cultural limitations, of disappointing someone you love . . ." he groaned to himself through clenched teeth. "You were just like this when you first came to Istanbul: scared of the city, scared of so much life and beauty, scared of being chewed up and spat out, one of the millions!"

He felt a painful twinge as the forgotten cigarette clenched between thumb and forefinger burned down to his flesh. "Shit!" he remarked, tossing the butt onto the ground and grinding it out with his heel.

"If Belgin saw me do that, she'd put me in my place, tell me that city ways mean treating every street like your own home. And she'd be right. But I'm a child of Adana, too proud to let any woman, even the woman I love, criticize me—especially if she's right. But I wouldn't say a thing, I'd bide my time until later, cause a scene over something stupid, something completely unrelated, or else I'd punish her by not sharing something that gives her joy, try to keep the upper hand, play the strong, silent type even for the woman who's taught me why it's wrong. I might not sleep with her for a couple of nights, might stare moodily at the smoke coming out of my cigarette or even look at another women when we're out in public together. Anything to bring her into line. Just stick it to her: like a snake, like a bee, like a man! Oh, Ayhan, how can you even think like this? You know better. You love her. Stop it!"

He needed another one, was suddenly desperate for another cigarette, even though he'd already smoked double the daily limit he'd set himself after meeting Belgin. He'd have to get a pack immediately, preferably Lucky Strikes . . .

"So what if they don't have Lucky Strikes? Could Dad ever afford anything but roll-ups! Just get in there and make do with whatever you find. There must be a vending machine somewhere!"

In order to get back into the airport again he had to be searched and screened and patted down.

"As if terrorists would dare smuggle bombs or anything else into the airport through all these checkpoints!" he said under his breath, shoeless, legs spread wide, arms held high.

Back in the climate-controlled coolness of the terminal, he

calmed down. He'd always been interested in airport microcosms, fantasizing about inventing a kind of energy-collector that fed on human emotions, that would be located in public places where feelings were most intense, the most obvious choice being airports. Emotions would be harnessed and transformed into energy, putting an end to the era of fossil fuels and nuclear power, as well as the resulting wars, pollution, intrigue, and suffering. As he wandered through the terminal, imagining airports as places where people were transported far and wide, and where the purest, most intense emotional energy was produced, his wandering thoughts careened feverishly along to Foucault's proposed examination of heterotopias, even, before a rather more mundane thought brought him down to earth with a clunk: smoking had recently been banned in the airport.

"It's those goddamn EU regulations!" he snorted. In any case, the available vending machines turned out to contain nothing but soda and junk food, not cigarettes. Completely fed up, Ayhan felt like spitting on the floor—also forbidden, of course! That's when he remembered Barman Baturcan and the cozy little bar where smoking was permitted, even if it meant putting up with those barstools designed for American cowboys. So that's where Ayhan headed, smiling irritably, just thirty minutes after Belgin's plane had landed.

ANNOUNCEMENT ONE

ATTENTION, PLEASE!

ATTENTION, ALL PASSENGERS, LADIES AND GENTLEMEN!

DUE TO UNFORSEEN PROBLEMS WITH OUR COMPUTER SYSTEMS, WE ARE SORRY TO ANNOUNCE THAT ALL INCOMING AND OUTGOING FLIGHTS HAVE BEEN TEMPORARILY SUSPENDED.

PLEASE WAIT OUTSIDE UNTIL FURTHER NOTICE.

PROCEED CALMLY TO THE NEAREST EXIT, TAKING YOUR PERSONAL BELONGINGS WITH YOU.

PLEASE ALLOW THE ELDERLY, HANDICAPPED, AND FAMILIES WITH CHILDREN TO LEAVE FIRST.

PLEASE INFORM AUTHORITIES OF ANY UNATTENDED LUGGAGE.

ON BEHALF OF ATATÜRK AIRPORT, WE APOLOGIZE FOR THE INCONVENIENCE.

ISTANBUL, CITY OF FEAR AND LOVE

My name is Istanbul, and, oh, how I laugh at these reports of computer failure! I am Istanbul, and, oh, what fires and wars, what earthquakes and uprisings I have withstood as my houses of worship are bombed, my treasures plundered, my subjects lynched! I am Istanbul, and, having observed these mortals for thousands of years, their capacity for hatred and destruction no longer surprises me in the least. I am Istanbul, fearless and indestructible.

I was determined this morning to keep my eyes upon my airport until I savored the sight of Belgin sinking to her knees and shedding tears of joy at our reunion. It had even been my intention to linger until she embraced and kissed her Ayhan. But I'm beginning to tire of this pair, one of them running off to imprison herself in a toilet stall, the other confined to his barstool!

They are so predictable, these mortals: it was with not a little amusement that my nostrils caught, yet again, the distilled and pure scent of mortality: love and fear, those two opposing and so typically mortal emotions. For more than millennia, now, for as long as man has sheltered on the shores of the Bosphorus, the smells of sweat, tears, and of love and fear have permeated my very soul, mingling through the ages with the perfume of many and varied blossoms, of ripe fruit, of soil and of fresh air. Diverse perfumes and aromas have come and gone, but those two have remained constant through the ages: love and fear. And what do mortals love and fear even more than me? Themselves and each other. And, I must confess, to my immortal nostrils the fear of love and the fear of death smell very much the same!

I've learned much about fear from my oldest friend, one who was here long before me, one who dwells deep below and whose name, forever linked with mine, has been spoken with dread for century upon century: Konstantiniye Zelzelesi, *better known these days as the Istanbul Earthquake. Although nowhere near as terrifying as my subjects would believe, he is admittedly something of an extremist, serious to a fault, and enraged by frivolity. That said, his favorite pastime is simply to lie undisturbed in peaceful slumber, something he confided in that impressive bass voice of his when last awakened, ever so briefly, in the summer of 1999. He grumbled that his cousins no longer strike terror into the hearts of the residents of other great cities, and was quite harsh in his condemnation of Istanbullu as greedy, dishonest, and fraudulent creatures who are only too happy to blame him for their own foolishness. What most distresses my comrade is that, even in this enlightened age, credence is given to so many of the slanderous rumors circulated in his name. The gossipmongers were hard at work even back in pre-Christian Byzantine, when they interpreted his toss-filled sleep as divine punishment for their sins.*

It was at 3:02 A.M., on the night of 17 August 1999, that the Istanbul Earthquake bellowed like a caged lion. "Whether you call yourselves Roman or Byzantine, Venetian or Crusader, Ottoman or Turk, it does not matter. Whether you be Christian, Muslim, Jew, Shaman, Fire Worshipper, Agnostic, or Atheist . . . Black, Brown, White or Yellow . . . You are all the same, all the same to me!" he roared. A harmless enough fellow, it is only when he's roused from slumber and confronted by foolish complacency that he trembles and rages, shakes and tosses, spreading fear and wreaking havoc . . .

Will these mortals never learn! Even here, at my modern airport, and even now, on this joyous day of homecoming, they are bewildered by the endlessly multiplying inanities of their own making, in this case, something they call "computer failure." Ah, how I regret my eagerness to bask in the love of Belgin of Bebek, only to be subjected instead to that most insipid of scents, fear!

I am Istanbul, and I have no time for banalities like fear! I am Istanbul, Mistress of the Balkans and East Aegean, of the Middle East and Central Asia, of Caucasia and the Eastern Mediterranean. European by birth and disposition, I preside over the ages, Byzantine and Roman, Ottoman and Turk. Call me what you will: Byzantion or Anatonina, New Rome or Constantinople, Konstantiniye or The Sick Man (!) of Europe: I shall remain forever on the shores of the Bosphorus, Queen of All I Survey to the east and to the west, to the north and to the south. And as I have done for centuries, I shall continue to welcome one and all, be they dark beauties with waist-length hair, girls with head scarves, women with veils or hats, or men in caps of fur and turbans of silk, in skull caps and yarmulkes. All are welcome to come and go, but I shall remain unchanged for all eternity, forever crowned in glory, regal and constant as I embrace my Istanbulians . . . I, a city made immortal by the love and fear of mortals.

    I am Istanbul!

14
ISTANBUL DEMANDS ANOTHER VICTIM?

"Have they received some sort of tip? Could it be a bomb? Have I returned to Istanbul only to die here at the airport, and Ayhan with me? Is it my turn now, all these years after landing in Yeşilköy with father's coffin?" were the questions racing through Belgin's mind, one after another, as she found herself frozen to the spot upon hearing the announcement.

Having emerged from the restroom, where, after much agonized contemplation, she'd finally decided to board the first plane back to New York, Belgin had been walking toward the passport control booths when she heard the announcement. She instinctively placed her hands on her belly, quickly calculating that her plane had landed at least an hour earlier and hoping against hope that Ayhan had given up on her, had returned to Ortaköy in the pick-up truck he'd dubbed his "trusty steed." Comforted by the possibility that Ayhan, at least, would be safe, Belgin relaxed slightly. But the moment of relative serenity wasn't to last for long: her dreams of a future with Ayhan had given way to an empty, gnawing void. After the age of forty, shattered dreams are as terrifying as cancer, as insidious as insomnia. But Belgin was still too young to appreciate the implications of her decision.

"Some kind of computer problem, they say. But isn't everything computerized and digitalized these days? Why don't they isolate the problem and take localized measures, or something? Why shut down the entire airport? It sounds like an emergency evacuation to me!" she said to herself, hands on her belly in a gesture that while new to her was as old as time itself. All women, mothers or not, whatever their backgrounds, are reminded monthly of the life force they carry inside themselves. And it is this potential, timeless as life itself, that has enabled women to endure millennia of censure, violence, and exclusion.

Belgin had been one those women who frequently questioned the desirability of bringing a child into an unjust and dangerous

179

world. While still in an unhappy marriage with Entek, she had become pregnant for the first time, a terrible accident that soon found her sitting in the waiting room of a clinic, hand in hand with Kete, both of them weeping. The sense of helplessness she'd suffered as that first child was terminated was the worst of her adult life. She then became an honorary member of that group of women who vaguely consider adoption one day in the distant future. And now she was forty and pregnant. And every time she considered the baby in her womb, she smiled . . .

"What is this, anyway? Just when I'd completely given up on the idea of ever having a child, I toss aside all my rationalizations and justifications and sit here grinning like an inexperienced teenager. What's happening to me? If I've happily succumbed to hormones and maternal instincts, why have I always been so determined to base all my life decisions on logic and reason? If women are, by design, totally enslaved to their so-called natural urges, hasn't it been premature to rejoice over the painful and hard-won progress we've made? We've been fighting for control over own bodies, but how do we battle Mother Nature—and should we?"

Although the announcement was repeated in two languages, none of the other passengers seemed at all panicked, and Belgin wondered if she'd been the only one to suspect a bomb. She remembered how often Entek had accused her of paranoia in the final year of their marriage, even going so far as to tell her she needed treatment.

"You're a maniac!" he said. "You lost your wits the day you got off that plane with your father's casket! And now you're trying to take it out on me! What do you know about real life anyway? You were spoiled rotten growing up in Bebek, then you were taken to La Scala to see the Mona Lisa, to view Incan ruins in Peru. That's not real life! You've got to grab life by the throat and make it work for you! But you've got your head in the clouds, and all your airy-fairy ideas about science and art. The minute you collide with reality, you come and take it out on me. You'd better go get professional help! Honestly, all this nonsense about me and my secretary . . . You maniac!"

There had been happier days, of course. Mehmet Emin Entek had professed himself enchanted with the cultural opportunities afforded Belgin during her blissful globe-trotting childhood: "You were Daddy's little princess, and now, by your leave, milady, I'll make you my queen," he'd said, turning her head with flowers, thoughtful gifts, and theatrical phone calls. As he became better acquainted with Belgin and her life, Mehmet Emin Entek had been forced to confront for the first time the realization that even though his was the wealthier of their two families, his education and upbringing had been in the form of a single-minded investment: the expansion of the family fortune. Contemplation and a sense of his own unimportance didn't come easily to a perfectionist like Mehmet Emin Entek, and it wasn't long before he harbored a seething resentment of everything Belgin represented.

While he delighted in referring to himself as "hyperactive" and a "workaholic," there was another trait that truly defined Mehmet Emin Entek: the fear of being alone. Belgin was able to spend many happy hours completely on her own, listening to music, studying a painting, reading a novel, or simply sitting peacefully, daydreaming. It was the key to her inner calm and strength, but in her husband's eyes it made her dangerously independent, and a rival whose self-possession must be shaken at all costs.

"From the way she holds herself, every breath she takes, she's the epitome of unstudied elegance," he'd thought to himself during their first chance meeting in Erol Argunsoy's office. In her final year of study at prestigious Bosphorus University—niece of the renowned architect, Erol Argunsoy—Mehmet Emin Entek had decided that this girl would certainly look good on his arm. She wasn't what you'd call a classic beauty, nothing like the fashion models he usually ran around with, but she was young and pure and would be easy to mold. Having determined that the match would be extremely advantageous, Mehmet Emin Entek turned his attention to the practical matter of getting the girl. Ten years her senior, he was a man of the world, certainly old enough to appreciate that his age could be transformed into an advantage when it came to a girl who'd never fully recovered from the loss of her father. Entek took it upon himself to research the circumstances of the death of Belgin's father, and by their second meeting, which he'd requested this time, he was ready to set his plan in motion.

"I was impressed by how much he knew about my father. Turkish diplomats were being killed one after another in those days, and their funerals were being turned into huge public demonstrations against terrorism. First came the official ceremony attended by thousands outside of the Foreign Ministry in Ankara, then the funeral procession from Bebek Mosque to Aşiyan Cemetery in Istanbul, that long line of protestors, prayers, tears, rage and sorrow . . . While my mother, aunt, and Uncle Erol went off to the ceremony in Ankara, I was left behind with Kete and my grandmother, who'd been rushed to hospital upon the news of her son's death and would die a few months later. Dressed in a black dress, they'd hastily rustled up, I was allowed to stand next to Mother at the funeral held the following day in Istanbul. Years later, when Entek seemed to recall every detail of that black day and that black dress, how could I have known that he'd combed through newspaper archives just to impress me? I'd never met anyone so calculating and so dishonest. How could I have anticipated any of what was to come? I knew next to nothing about men. Fresh from a mild flirtation with a classmate, I fell right into that old wolf's lap. Even my youth and inexperience were mocked. 'You must be frigid! A modern girl like you, still a virgin as you graduate from university? What's that all about?'

"Entek nearly convinced me that I *was* cold and didn't like sex. Well, I didn't even know what sex was! As my husband, he could have helped me, he could have taught me so much, and even enjoyed doing it. But he didn't—he wouldn't. He preferred to bludgeon me with my own inexperience. That's when he began to shrink in my eyes, when I saw him for the pathetic dictator he was. Unfortunately, it took me a full three years before the grim reality of the man I'd married had sunk in. I was young. I still believed in the sanctity of marriage, in the institution of the family, in the inviolability of a promise, in staying together through sickness and health, through good days and bad . . . They'd taught me that a woman is completed by a man . . . and I believed that too. I also believed that the surest path to happiness depended upon unwavering trust and unquestioning faith, never realizing that they can also be the greatest obstacle to personal development. My parents had taken such care to give me a 'proper' upbringing, but I'd ended up a foolishly naïve girl, even if I was well read and knew which fork to use with my fish! Utterly defenseless against a man like Entek, it was during those abusive years that I became furious with my parents for having done nothing to prepare me for the ugly side of life.

"He was thirty-three when we got married, quite old for a twenty-three-year-old like me, but he was handsome and looked much younger, as was to be expected, I suppose, from someone who promoted himself as relentlessly as he marketed his company. He was so vain: back in the 1990s, when men's cosmetics weren't yet available in Turkey, Entek used to apply women's eye cream every night, have a barber come around to the house to dye his hair, which was already going gray at the temples, and schedule manicures and pedicures once a week. Now that he's over fifty I can just imagine the creams and potions he must be using . . .

"He won me over in no time at all, and when he proposed marriage I answered 'yes' without a second thought. But, unlike me, Uncle Erol had his doubts: 'I'm not so sure, Belgin,' he said. 'Mehmet Emin Entek may be a bright and ambitious young man, but there's something about him, something I can't put my finger on . . . There's something false and flimsy about him, like stage décor or camouflage netting. What does it hide? Why don't you take your time? What's your hurry anyway?' My mother initially opposed the marriage as well, but for entirely different reasons. She emerged from her darkened parlor to warn, 'When girls marry without having earned a diploma first, they drop out of college. Swear to me on your father's grave that you won't marry until you have a degree, Belgin Gümüş!' And promise I did, but the moment I graduated, off I went to the altar. It turns out I was very much in a hurry! I was desperate to strike out on my own and start a new life, and like most Turkish girls I had been led to believe that my independence could be gained only through dependence upon a husband . . . a man just like my father, one I could trust and rely on! Yes, I was that foolish.

"At first, everything seemed to be going my way. I was happily married, and about to gain a position as a molecular biology researcher at Bosphorus University, under the tutelage of Professor Yannis Seferis. Then the nightmare began. Uncle Erol had been right: the façade that was my marriage began to crumble and the stage décor that was my husband's character began to fray. Six months after we were married, perhaps because she'd been absolved of her responsibility for me, mother flew into the Bosphorus in a car . . . A car accident. Ha!"

Passport in hand, Belgin headed for passport control, determined to return to New York on the next flight out. But when she saw the length of the line, her heart sank as she wondered if she'd be able to endure the long wait. Then she remembered the special entrance to the airport hotel a short distance along. That same heart then leapt at the thought of a warm bath and cool white sheets, followed by a deep sleep. She could even book a flight for the following morning at the reception desk, and return to New York rested and calm. Return? Ah, that word again. Yes, she'd go back, she'd return to New York; her final return to Istanbul would be abandoned. All she wanted right now was a bath and bed. That's all! But was it really that easy? Really? She glanced down at her flat stomach, looked down at the baby she already loved. Pressing her lips together, she took a deep breath through her nose. The baby had a father . . .

"Pregnant?" had been Entek's horrified reaction when she told him. They'd been married for three years, but Entek wasn't yet ready to consider having a family.

That was the summer Belgin learned for the first time that there were other women in her husband's life; yes, that was the same summer she found out she was pregnant. It had all started with a joke, the little joke of a confident woman who still believed she had everything under control. Mehmet Emin Entek was away on one of his frequent business trips and had forgotten to take the pajamas he usually wore. "You'll be sexier without them," Belgin had joked on the phone. But instead of laughing, he'd stammered and stuttered. Then he'd gone silent. Finally, defiant and defensive, he'd asked her how long she'd known. So that was it, he wasn't alone in that hotel room! She'd been too stunned to speak, had remained silent for what seemed like hours. Then his icy voice shook her out of it: "Are you going to say something, or are you going to hang up on me?"

That night, she'd tossed and turned before finally admitting to herself that the signs had been there all along. She'd planned to confront Entek calmly and sensibly with the words, "Sex is only one aspect of a relationship, so it's not the cheating that bothers me so much as the deception. There is no place in a loving relationship for deception." Instead, she'd found herself saying, "You're not going to believe this, Entek, but I trusted you. I really did trust you!" That's all she'd said. "I trusted you!" Then she'd gone to the kitchen, made a cup of linden tea, and sat down to drink it, alone. It wasn't at all what Entek had expected, which was a hysterical scene, complete with shouting and tears, while he issued denial after denial. Finally, they'd sit down with a stiff drink and rehash, all night long, their relationship and where they'd gone wrong.

When he finally followed her into the kitchen, and found her calmly sipping tea, he'd slammed his fist onto the table so hard her saucer had rattled and declared, "You're my woman and you're not going anywhere!" Belgin had swallowed hard and blurted out, "I'm pregnant, Entek!" To which Entek had replied, "How do I even know the bastard's mine!" Once again, Belgin fell silent. She bowed her head and bit her lip. If he'd looked closely—if he'd been the kind of man to look closely, that is—he'd have seen that she was in tears. He didn't look, of course. He grabbed the cup from her hand and threw it against the wall.

Belgin had made up her mind. One week later, she arranged for an abortion. "There's no rush, please think again," Kete had pleaded, but to no avail. That same day, Belgin moved all her things to her Uncle Erol's flat in Maçka, where he'd moved after his own marriage failed. Once he'd overcome the shock of having been abandoned, Entek came out swinging, a team of lawyers in tow, as determined as if he were fighting off a hostile corporate takeover. The case dragged on and on, as Belgin was subjected first to censure for having failed to consult her husband before aborting "his" child, then to strong hints by her husband and his legal team suggesting that the paternity of the baby had, in fact, been in question all along.

Several months later, the divorce finalized at last, Belgin began picking up the pieces of her life. Her Uncle Erol was there for her, as were Kete and Professor Yannis Seferis, who helped arrange a full scholarship at a doctorate program at Columbia University, in New York. All three of them were also at the airport the day she flew off to her new life. "Turkey's losing yet another talented person to the brain drain," Professor Seferis had said, as he dabbed at an invisible spot on his shirt cuff. "In this case, I'd say it's a brain escaping from a husband who is himself a drain . . ." Uncle Erol had said, with a bitter laugh. Tears streaming down her cheeks, "Ah, my little lamb's running away from cruel Istanbul, leaving me behind!" Kete had sobbed.

At just the moment Belgin reached into her handbag for a mint, it occurred to her to call Kete on the cell phone presented to her by Ayhan, who'd wrapped it in a lavender bow. "A new life, a new phone, a new number!" he'd declared as he handed her a gift-wrapped box. He'd also immediately entered his own phone number into the phone's contacts list, and made her promise that he would be the first person she called upon landing. Now, phone in hand, she called Kete instead.

"Hello?" came Kete's voice, and suddenly everything was all right, the headache better, Belgin's fears forgotten. It was Kete, and everything would be all right.

"Kete, it's me, Belgin!"

"Oh, my little lamb! So you've landed, then?"

"Yes, I'm here. I'm here in Yeşilköy, in Istanbul!"

"So you're here. Well, getting you here was the hard part.

186

Everything will be fine now. Are you all right? You sound a little tired."

"I'm fine, Kete. Don't worry. All things considered, I'm fine . . ."

"All things considered? What's that supposed to mean? If it's the shutdown, don't worry about it. Just ignore what they're saying . . ."

"Kete, there's something I want to tell you. I was going do it in person, but . . . I have to tell you now . . . It's all been a bit much for me . . . You remember how, when I was little, you used to tell me to chase away the black clouds . . ."

Kete knew Belgin well enough to understand that something was seriously wrong.

"Come on, tell me what it is . . . You're worrying me . . ."

"I'm pregnant, Kete!" Belgin said, just like that. And then she said nothing. But Belgin's silence told Kete all she needed to know.

"Pregnant at this age, can you believe it?" Belgin continued. "I found out last week . . . but I haven't told anyone, even Ayhan . . . you're the first to know . . ." The words rushed out, then she took a deep breath audible even to Kete, who was holding her own breath on the other end of the line. This time, it was Kete who fell silent.

"Kete? Kete, are you there?" Belgin cried anxiously. "Kete?"

"Oh, that I should live to see the day! My little lamb, and now she's having a little lamb all her own! Praise Allah for letting me live to see this day!" Kete shouted. Although she couldn't see Kete, Belgin knew the woman would be rocking from side to side, fists tightly clenched. What she didn't know and couldn't see was that Kete was also shedding tears of joy.

"But . . ." Belgin said. "But I'm not sure . . . At my age . . . I'm not sure . . . Bringing a child into a world like ours . . . I'm not sure it's right, Kete . . . And it's not a baby yet, it's just a tiny speck, an embryo . . ."

"What do you mean, 'not sure'?" Kete demanded. "What do you mean, 'at my age'?" Kete lowered her voice and spoke more calmly. "Of course you're sure. If you weren't sure, you wouldn't

187

have brought your baby all the way to Istanbul. If you didn't want it, you would have terminated it immediately. I know you. And you're the perfect age to become a mother. You're only forty, right at the beginning of a woman's best years, Belgin."

"Of course I considered an abortion, though Bush was doing his best to make this as difficult as possible . . ." was what Belgin almost blurted out. But she didn't. She couldn't. She held her tongue. Holding her tongue, Belgin was silent because she herself understood that she had in fact already made up her mind. She wanted this baby. That much was clear . . .

"I'm scared, Kete, so scared . . . Everything could go wrong. I could get hurt again, and even worse this time . . . There are some things I still haven't worked out. It's like . . . like a knot in my stomach or a lump in my throat—and it won't go away, Kete."

"Don't, Belgin. Don't be scared. Whatever you do, don't be scared. Your baby has come home, you brought it all the way to Istanbul. And your baby has a father, a great uncle, an aunt and its very own Kete, its grandmother, right here in Istanbul," said Kete. Then she paused. Kete stopped for a moment because she'd heard something in Belgin's voice, something a little alarming . . . She'd raised Belgin almost single-handedly, and knew all too well that she was as proud as her mother, Jackie-Halide *Hanım*, and as stubborn as Kete herself.

"Kete? Are you there?" Belgin asked. Once again, Kete sensed a hard edge to Belgin's voice, a determined tone that meant something big was coming.

"Kete, I want to make a deal with you. If you're able to finally forgive your parents for sending you to Istanbul, if you can do that, and really mean it, I'll do my best to forgive my past, and myself, and start a new life with Ayhan and our baby. Is it a deal, Kete?"

It was the first direct reference Belgin had ever made to Kete's past and her failure to resolve it. Once again, Belgin had acted like a daughter, like Kete's own child, and picked at a scab as only a child can do.

"If you don't agree, Kete, I'm taking the next plane back to

New York. I'm serious. Kete? Kete, are you there?"

After a few seconds of silence, Kete finally spoke. "I'm here, Belgin."

"Kete, what I need you to understand is that I'm as scared as you, and it's as hard for me to believe in Ayhan and in love and in myself as it is for you to finally forgive your parents. But it's something we both need to do. Kete, is it a deal?"

Kete had put her fist on her chest, right over the hard knot that formed there every time she remembered that long-ago day, that bus ride to Istanbul, all alone. She held her breath, afraid to speak, afraid of her own voice, which would surely crack, betraying the depths of her pain . . . When she did speak, at last, it was about the announcement.

"We'll talk about all this later. Right now, I want you to listen to me!" she said, in stern nanny mode. "Don't panic. Just go straight to the nearest exit, tell the police that you're pregnant and get out of the airport as quickly as possible!"

"Kete, where are you? You're not . . ."

"Where do you think I am? I'm where you are. Did you think I'd stay at home the day you finally returned to Istanbul?"

"Kete, you're in Yeşilköy?"

"Of course I am."

"There might be a bomb! Get out right now!"

"Shut up and listen to me, Belgin. There's no bomb, but I still want you to leave the airport right away. Will you do that?"

"Kete? Hello? Kete, can you hear me!" The line had suddenly gone dead, followed by an unusual beeping sound. Slipping her phone back into her handbag, Belgin decided to wait a few moments before calling again. "She's here, she's here waiting for me, dearest Kete . . ."

"May God keep you safe, you and your baby," Kete murmured, one hand pressing the phone against her breast, the other one clenched into a fist, still oblivious to her surroundings and the people streaming toward the exits. Would she be able to forgive? Could she forget that long ago day, and the bitterness and sense of loss that had grown inside her like a tumor? But what if

189

Belgin was serious, and really would turn round and return to New York, just like that? Why, oh why, had that crazy girl chosen this moment to dredge up Kete's past?

On the other side of passport control, not more than a few hundred meters from where Kete sat, Belgin felt a renewed sense of purpose with regard to the plans she had made with Ayhan. She got up and began striding toward the passport control booths, but had barely taken three steps when she saw that the passengers already in line were dispersing. When she asked one why, he snapped bitterly, "They're closing passport control—we have to wait somewhere else. Why don't they just tell us what's really going on!"

Always composed, at least to an outside observer, Belgin solemnly nodded as she thought to herself: "So, we're stuck here, in Yeşilköy, the baby and me!" She gritted her teeth, caressed her belly, and braced herself for the worst.

15
ISTANBUL, DON'T TAKE THE ONE I LOVE

"That's all I need right now. Shit!" Ayhan had cursed, before his thoughts turned to Belgin, who was even now here at the airport and possibly in danger.

Ten minutes earlier, Ayhan had found himself, once again, in front of the electronic panel assuring him in flashing red letters that the THY flight from New York had indeed landed. He stood there, stock-still, staring. "It's true, I almost ran away," he said to himself. "But look, I came back. I didn't give up, I've never given up!" But he knew he'd stumbled, there was no denying that when it had come time for the reunion with Belgin he'd panicked. And now, even though he'd looked everywhere, in every corner of the arrivals lounge, there was no sign of her. Perhaps he sensed where Belgin was, for he'd waited for quite some time in front of the women's bathroom, his heart leaping every time the door opened and someone came out. And now, as he watched so many of those around him embrace loved ones, remorse changed to longing and then to envy. Finally, he felt like he just had to have another cigarette.

Might Belgin have left already? Left him? Could she have deliberately left him behind as she left the airport? And if he had missed her, where would she have gone? It had all been planned, he'd spent weeks thinking about it; how had it gone so horribly wrong? They were going to get into his blue pick-up, drive along the coast of the Sea of Marmara, across the bridge, Golden Horn at their feet, finally arriving in Ortaköy, at the apartment and workshop he'd knocked together out of two flats. Once there, he was literally going to sweep her off her feet, kiss his angel at last. But so much for best laid plans: he didn't even know where she was now. "Shit, Ayhan," he muttered. "You've ruined everything!"

Where could she have gone? He knew her uncle, the famous architect, lived in Maçka. She might be there. And then there was her nanny Kete, who lived in Sarıyer. Who else did Belgin know in Istanbul? She'd rented out the house in Bebek, it wouldn't be empty until the fall. She'd talked a lot about her old professor, Professor Seferis. He lived in Kurtuluş, didn't he? Would she have called him up; did she know him well enough to say she'd just arrived in Istanbul, that no one had met her at the airport? No, she'd call up a girlfriend, that friend she'd gone to school with . . . Ayda! Yes, that was her name. They'd all gone to the opera together one night, his first time, and he hadn't thought much of the music but he remembered liking her, or at least her name. He'd blurted it out. "If I had a girl, I'd call her Ayda," he'd said. Then there was an awkward silence: he'd begun thinking about Berfin, the daughter he'd lost; Belgin's thoughts had turned to her first child, the daughter she'd terminated.

But if Belgin had left the airport, surely he'd have seen her. He'd been standing in front of the main exit. No, she couldn't have left; she must be here, inside, still! Unless she'd never boarded that plane in New York, been as frightened as he was, equally terrified at the thought of starting a new life together, a new life with an idiot like him, a macho man, a peasant . . . She was smart enough to see through him, perceptive enough to know him better than he knew himself. She'd have sensed that he wasn't ready to go through with it, known that he was a coward at heart, not ready enough, not good enough, not man enough!

These thoughts running through his head, his feet propelled him to the only place he knew he could smoke, the airport bar. As he sat down on one of those despised stools, he didn't even realize his hands were clenched into fists. Barman Baturcan was too busy chatting and laughing with an elderly gentleman in a bowtie and suspenders to notice him. "Just get a load of that kid," Ayhan smiled despite himself. "He sure knows how to pick 'em." The old fellow looked familiar, but he couldn't quite place him, and was too distracted to try. Ayhan sat there for a moment, to use his own words, "a denervated organic mass," until Baturcan finally came over with a welcoming smile.

"Hey, Ayhan *Bey*, where's Belgin *Hanım*? Anything wrong?" he asked, direct as an old friend.

"We haven't hooked up yet, Baturcan," Ayhan sighed. "But I'll be yours for life if you could rustle me up a cigarette. I'm out of steam and out of fuel . . ."

"Can do. Got any preferences?"

"Lucky Strike if you can manage it, but beggars can't be choosers," Ayhan laughed, a mirthless chuckle, unconvincing and tense.

"Just a sec," said Baturcan, darting up to the man in the bowtie, nearly pressing his lips to his ear as he whispered something. Ayhan gave the man a closer look, certain he'd seen him somewhere, but still unable to place him. The man turned his attention to Ayhan, bowed his head in greeting and dug into his bag, producing an entire carton of Lucky Strikes. "Shit! My luck must be turning!" Ayhan thought as a beaming Baturcan returned with a packet of his favorite brand.

"It's your lucky day, Ayhan *Bey*! You'd better run straight off to a casino or go find Belgin. Can you believe it? Erol *Bey*'s a regular here you see, and he just happened to arrive with a carton of Lucky Strikes he picked up for an MP friend of his. And here you are, wanting the exact same thing!" Then he leaned forward as though whispering a confidence: "Erol *Bey* only smokes cigars, you see."

Ayhan ripped open the box like it contained the answer to all his troubles. Taking out a cigarette and lighting it, he scolded himself: "Time to give up, Ayhan. Here you are planning to marry Belgin and you're still smoking like a peasant." Then he took a long drag. And another. He looked up to tell Baturcan to thank the lifesaver in the bowtie, but the barman had already flown back to his "regular customer." Ayhan was happy to see that the frequent flyer with friends in high places was so good to the barman, who looked as though he'd been reunited with a long lost lover . . .

That was the moment the announcement advising all passengers to leave the airport was made. "That's all I need right now. Shit!" Ayhan cursed, before his thoughts turned to Belgin, who was here at the airport and possibly in danger. He leapt to his feet. And then it happened. Something sudden and unexpected: he felt better. In that moment he remembered that it was the chaotic energy of the city that fed him, that gave him the strength to remain calm in times of great crisis. His professors had always said that about him, had grudgingly admitted that he was "at his most productive under stress." Chaos! Yes, it had always been that way, he'd thrived on the overwhelming confusion of this great city, as though just below the muddled, boiling surface was a miraculous pool of cool, clear water, one from which he drank and was fortified, mind miraculously cleared. And the woman he loved was like the city that nourished him: exacting and beautiful, complex and one of a kind. He'd known since childhood that he tended to fly off the handle, to exaggerate and enthuse until he'd worked himself into a frenzy, and, finally, into a panic. He'd even been warned by his old professor, Şefik Hodja, to channel his unbridled enthusiasm into his work, and not to allow it to take over his life. That's exactly what had happened here at the airport; he'd allowed himself to spin out of control. But he was better now. He took a deep breath. He'd ride it out; he'd find Belgin and take her home. Stubbing out his cigarette, he stuffed the pack into his back pocket.

He turned back to say good-bye to Mr. Bowtie and Baturcan, but the barman was pale as a ghost and busy at the cash register, processing the checks thrust at him by customers eager to race outside, some of them convinced that a terrorist attack was imminent. As was so often the case, Ayhan had achieved a sense of calm purpose just as everyone else around him began to fall apart. "They're the normal ones," he said, shaking his head ruefully. "You're the only one that thrives on chaos." But what he saw then directly contradicted that statement: Bowtie Man remained in his seat, off on another planet as he puffed on a cigar and sipped his whiskey. Baturcan waved his arms excitedly and shouted out to Ayhan, "Personnel are being evacuated last." Pumping his fist in the air as a show of encouragement and solidarity, Ayhan jogged away from the bar. Then he remembered the phone he'd given Belgin to use in Istanbul. "You idiot, Ayhan, where are your brains!" he told himelf, not breaking stride as he excitedly reached into the pocket of his black jeans to extract his own late model cell phone, which was switched off, even though he could have sworn he'd turned it on that morning as he left home. He quickly punched in his PIN code, located "Belgin Istanbul" in his contact list and selected the "call" option. How could it be? Belgin's phone was busy! Belgin was right here, in Istanbul, talking to someone else! He listened to his voice mail: nothing. Hundreds of meaningless messages had been recorded on that tiny chip, but not a single word from Belgin. It was impossible! He called again: busy. "Not only has she called someone else, she's having a good long chat!" He frowned, scratched his nose and gritted his teeth.

"Shit, Ayhan," he said to himself, "You really do love her. You're jealous, that's what you are. Jealous."

He was startled out of his thoughts by a voice shouting: "Please remain calm, everything is under control." It was an airport security guard, wireless transceiver in hand. Completely focused on his phone, Ayhan had been swept along with the crowd and now found himself right in front of the exit. The mounting tension was palpable as well-dressed Turks and foreigners toting bags jostled their way toward the automatic sliding doors. Japanese in town for the music festival, Americans in shorts, northern Europeans here to attend the match against Galatasaray, European Turks visiting their families in Turkey: everyone was intent on getting through those doors as quickly as possible.

"The foreigners probably all think that because they're in a Muslim country this is Islamic terrorism," Ayhan said, wincing.

The airport had conspicuously filled with security guards and policemen with dogs, a sure indication that something had gone awry. In the midst of the chaos, Ayhan made an observation: the passengers dressed as migrant workers, as well as their working-class relatives in the arrivals hall, looked calmer than anyone else. As though they knew nothing could happen to them. Or that it already had. "Have they grown immune to fear, or is it just fatalism?" Ayhan asked himself. "Do people with diminished expectations find it easier to keep a cool head when danger threatens? Is

195

it something like the acceptance I felt when I learned my mother was dying of cancer?" Even as these thoughts ran through his head, his mind was elsewhere, on his silent cell phone and on Belgin's busy one.

"I've been waiting here for her for hours, and what does she do, she gets on the phone with someone else! What's going on here? It's not fair!

"Actually, it's not hours, it's years that I've been waiting for her, years that I've been dreaming of Belgin. Perhaps I didn't yet know her name, or perhaps I imagined a woman with a different name, but it was her all right. She was the one, always has been."

Ayhan extricated himself from the crowd, and as he made his way back to the bar, he noticed an elderly woman sitting on a gray metal bench, completely oblivious to all the fuss. Serene as a yogi, accepting as a Sufi, dignified as a Greek goddess, she sat on the bench with a cell phone plastered to her ear, all smiles. She was one of those women everyone in Turkey, of whatever class or background, encounters at some point in their life: dark, medium height, late middle-age, pious, pure of heart, stubbornly self-sacrificing for those they love, adept, and molded by the ages: just your average Anatolian earth mother, with the tranquil tenacity of the roots of an oak. Ayhan had known many such women from his days back in the village, but something about this one was different, and it immediately caught his eye: those shoes! She was quite thin, her white hair fashionably styled, a simple lavender dress falling to just below the knee. But those stubby low-heeled shoes, those wonderfully inappropriate bright red slippers! It was a miracle! Could it be her? Yes, it had to be!

"It's Kete—Belgin's Kete!" shouted Ayhan, thrilled as though he'd seen his own mother.

196

16
BURY ME WHERE I WAS BORN

"Really! This is too much! What's the likelihood of something like this happening? Could it really be a computer failure, like the announcement said—or, God forbid, is it something far more serious? No, no it can't be—no point in getting alarmed over nothing. They wouldn't do something as stupid as that, not when we're on the verge of joining the EU; even terrorists wouldn't do something so stupid!" Professor Yannis told himself, inhaling through his teeth. He had been slowly making his way to the gate for his flight to Athens when he heard the announcement. Riveted to the spot for a few moments, he was just beginning to formulate a few reassuring sentences in his head when the nearby exit signs began flashing red. The flashing lights may have brought to mind the sirens associated with a full-scale emergency, which is perhaps why so many travelers suddenly grew so tense. In fact, there was not a sound except the low hum of many voices rising in pitch and volume. Professor Seferis begun running his hands down the sleeves of his jacket and along the fronts of his trousers, an unconscious gesture, as though he was brushing dust off his clothes or wiping dirt off his hands. An obsessive-compulsive, at that moment the Professor was more concerned about contamination than about the possible threat to his life, was already calculating how many people would brush against him, spreading disease, as he squeezed through the exit.

Ironically, his lifelong fixation on germs allowed him to remain far more focused and calm than if he'd continued speculating on the mysterious announcement. His breathing slowed, his heartbeat returned to normal, and he decided to return to the relative cleanliness of the wooden bench from which he'd recently risen, taking care to sit in precisely the same spot and to place his bag not on the dirty floor, but right next to him on the wooden bench. From the snatches of animated conversation he overheard in the three languages he understood best, Turkish,

197

Greek, and English, he was able to ascertain that many feared a bomb and were busily convincing themselves and each other that the stringent security measures adopted at any airport would surely keep them safe. Professor Seferis heard brash Greek speakers, most likely passengers who had been preparing to board the Athens flight with him. He looked over and saw a young Greek couple, clearly tourists, lamenting their decision to visit Istanbul in the first place. Professor Seferis's first impulse was to go up and reassure them in their native tongue, to inform them in assured and courteous tones that terrorist attacks are just as likely in "civilized" cities like New York, London, and Madrid—if not even more so. Ostensibly, he wished to comfort them, but he was in fact motivated by the urge to protect Istanbul, to protect the good name of He Polis, Konstantiniyye, Istanbul. He'd been doing it all his life, ever since he was a boy, without regard to the identity of the critic or how the critic chose to label him: Turk, Istanbullu, Rum, infidel, non-Muslim, Turkomeritis, minority, Greek . . . Those who disparaged his city never stopped to consider that he had once been little Yanni, that he'd been born and raised in the district of Tatavlı, now known as Kurtuluş, and that his core identity and sense of self was bound up in his fiercely protective love of a city with which he was inseparably identified. He'd always risen to the challenge, ready for combat. But now, at this very moment, here at the airport, with the exit signs flashing away, he felt exhausted by the years constantly defending his city against those who would not, could not, understand and appreciate it.

"It's as though I feel I have to rehabilitate this city," he murmured to himself. "I've also felt I had to rescue it from the smears and ignorant lies of my own relatives, my own countrymen, even my own worst moments . . . Here I am, at this stage of life, worn out, stuck between two countries, and still defending this city and myself!

"And then I catch myself referring to New York and London as 'civilized,' as though I'm excusing Istanbul by implying that it somehow isn't up to par with the great cities of the West." He became cross with himself. Yes, that was the state of things—Professor Yannis Seferis was cross with himself because he realized he'd been preparing to disparage Istanbul in the name of protecting her from outsiders. Perhaps he'd done the same thing before? Perhaps this wasn't the first time he'd sold his city out. With a grim nod of self-accusation, he compressed his lips and sulked.

On the next bench over, a tall, slender blonde in her mid-forties had just awakened from a deep sleep and through bleary eyes was trying to make sense of the commotion: police dogs sniffing at bags, everyone on their feet, travelers streaming toward the emergency doors, above which an exit sign was flashing. She turned to the middle-aged man on the next bench over, apparently the only other person who had remained seated, and called out to him in imperfect but fluent Turkish:

"Excuse me, what's happening here?"

Professor Yannis Seferis found himself looking at Istanbullu Susan, and smiled. She was even more attractive, face all smooth despite the alarm in her eyes. He was quite pleased to find that while everyone else was beating a retreat, shouting and overexcited, he and the American woman had remained behind, just the two of them: Yannis and Susan!

"Oh, it's you! Don't worry—it's nothing serious. There's been an announcement, you see; we've all been advised to leave the airport. You're free to panic if you like, or you can just shrug it off, like me. I mean, if someone really *has* planted a bomb, and if it really *does* blow the place to high heaven, it's not as if there's anything we can do about it, is there?"

"Excuse me?"

"What I'm trying to say, Madame, is that there's no point in making a big deal of our fears—a great truth adults utterly fail to teach us as children."

The scholarly-looking little man and his carefree manner of speaking were so at odds with each other that at first Susan thought she hadn't heard him correctly. If there had been a bomb scare, which is what he'd seemed to indicate, how could he be sitting here so calmly? She suspected her Turkish of having let her down, yet again.

"Excuse me, do you speak English?"

"Yes, I do, but your Turkish is excellent. And I'd love to hear more," said the Professor, with a roguish twinkle in his eye.

Susan Constance decided they'd met previously, and was embarrassed at not being able to place this man among the thousands of clients she routinely dealt with through her travel agency.

"I've just woken up . . . I'm a little groggy . . ." she began, buying herself time.

"Yes, you were sound asleep, dreaming away with a lovely smile on your lovely face." Istanbullu Susan was now absolutely certain they must have met previously, but she still couldn't place him. For his part, the Professor was thoroughly enjoying this new Yanni and wished it hadn't taken so long for him to emerge. Well, not for nothing did both Turks and Greeks refer with such frequency to the world around us being one of illusions . . . "*Yalan Dünya! Palio Dunias! Payyo Dünyas!*"

"Could you tell me again exactly what that announcement was about?"

"They said something about the computer systems being down. It must be serious, or they wouldn't have asked us to evacuate the airport."

"Oh my God! It must be a terrorist attack!" screeched Susan, springing to action and likewise to her feet. But no one gave the startled American so much as a second glance.

"Don't worry, Istanbul can handle it," said the Professor, mocking her gently.

"But we're all gonna die! Jesus Christ! Come on, let's get out of here!"

"Where can we go? Look at the crowds. It isn't as though anyone can help us. If it's our fate to go . . . well, I'm not saying this is going to happen . . . but you could do worse than to go with me, Professor Yannis Seferis, at your side."

Susan quickly scanned her companion's face for signs of duplicity, and was surprised to see he was perfectly calm, deadly serious, and possibly even a professor after all, just as he'd claimed. She sat back down.

"As far as my being the last person you'll ever see, I won't be so presumptuous as to pretend to know whether you should curse your fate or count your lucky stars. What I can tell you is this: I'm not a bad sort. When it comes to food, music, coffee, and cities, I pride myself on my discerning tastes. For example, there's nothing like a good bottle of Cabernet Sauvignon. That ought to prove my bona fides. You can keep your California wines, so uniformly pleasant and innocuous; give me a glass of something that surprises not only from year to year, but from bottle to bottle . . . not unlike people, no?"

Encouraged by the bemused smile on Susan's face, Yannis Seferis continued, "I admit that I can be a bit testy at times, and I've always been tidy to a fault, I won't deny it . . . But—and you're not going to believe this—I've changed! I saw how meaningless it all was and I changed, just like that! No more counting cracks in the sidewalk, no more wiping down door handles with sanitizing tissues, and I'll certainly never again refuse to share a bottle of water with a lovely lady like you . . ."

Here he paused to give Susan a significant stare. "Enough, I said to myself! Enough with Aunt Eleni. To hell with the lot of you!"

Susan couldn't help being intrigued by the Professor, this naughty boy, this flirtatious wolf, this mad philosopher holding forth on the meaning of life. But she was growing impatient as she listened, an eye on the people rushing past, and finally decided the poor thing was definitely in shock after all, and the time had come to take things in hand.

She extended one of hers. "Come on, Professor. Why don't we go outside, the two of us, together. If this turns out to have been a big hoax, we'll have a good laugh about it later."

"I shall follow your lead, Madame."

As Susan Constance propelled Professor Yannis Seferis toward the nearest exit, he nearly caught himself calculating the total square footage of the floor tiles between the bench and the door.

201

But he resisted. Buoyed as he was by the mischievous grin lingering on his lips and the warm touch of the hand on his elbow, he was absolutely determined to enjoy every moment of Susan's company—for as long as it lasted.

17
WELCOME TO ISTANBUL

"So, Kete's come all the way to Yeşilköy?" said Belgin with a smile, all too aware that she was breaking into her first heartfelt smile of the day—consigning any previous ones we might have mentioned to the dustbin of insincerity. But when she realized the passport booth directly in front of her was now closed, her smile faded as she sank down onto the nearest bench, "So, Kete's come all the way to Yeşilköy to surprise me, and now that she's heard the announcement . . ."

Kete loved to give surprises. When Belgin was a girl, she was forever producing toys, chocolates, and *kete* rolls just at the moment Belgin needed them most. Belgin had tried to reciprocate, of course, even though she sensed that Kete didn't like being the recipient of surprises herself. Perhaps being "saved" by her parents, and sent off alone on a bus bound for Istanbul from Van, had been enough of a surprise to last her a lifetime.

But Kete's ability to surprise was still going strong, and still took the form of thoughtfully chosen gifts. She'd outdone herself with her latest surprise, stunning Belgin, who had asked herself, "Whatever will she think of next?"

On one of the Sundays, always in the evening to get the cheapest rate, that she'd been telephoning Kete since moving to New York, she'd passed on a description of Ayhan's flat. He'd described it to her the previous week, in typically exhaustive and vivid detail, thrilled that he'd just combined an old garage with his living quarters to create a true "atelier/apartment" nothing like the cramped one-room flats that pass as "studio apartments" in big cities these days.

About a month later, Kete suddenly remarked, during one of their long Sunday chats: "You know that boyfriend of yours, that sculptor, Ayhan. Well, I think you finally found the right one. Take it from me, he's the one!" No doubt delighting in the puzzled silence on the other side, Kete had held her tongue until

Belgin protested, "But you haven't even met him yet, Kete."

Kete continued, in the matter-of-fact tone of a wife telling her husband about an expedition to the fish market, "What do you mean, I haven't met him yet? Like you said, all you have to do is go to the main road in Ortaköy, then turn up the street on the right just after Yapı Kredi Bank and walk to the top of the hill. There it was, and the building's even called 'Ayhan Apartments' . . . No one could miss it, and certainly not me. I just marched right up and rang the bell, just like that!"

Rang the bell? "What do you mean you just rang the bell?" This was terrible! It would seem like she'd sent Kete to check out Ayhan, to get a second opinion and scout out his home. That's not why she'd so carefully described Ayhan's flat to Kete. That wasn't it at all . . . or was it? It wasn't the first time Belgin suspected Kete not only of being able to read her mind, but of being able to detect the secret desires of her subconscious. It was the kind of thing a mother would do; but it was also the kind of thing that no child, of any age, can ever permit!

If pressed, Kete would simply have responded, "Ah Belgin, you don't have to give birth to have a child. Think about it, my little lamb, think of those mothers who throw their own lambs to the wolves, supposedly to 'save' them. I know every twitch of your nose and every hair on your head, and no harm will come to any of them as long as I'm around." Belgin let it drop.

"As the old saying goes, 'know a lion from his den.' Well, I thought, first let's have a look at the neighborhood he chose to live in—since he's one of the Istanbullu who actually has a choice. You know me, I don't go in for those neighborhoods full of phonies, Nişantaşı and the like. They're too . . . overdone for my tastes, something like that . . . And I liked Nişantaşı even less after you went there to live there with Entek. Don't think I don't appreciate clean streets and nice buildings. Take your late father, Halit Ziya: he was perfectly in place in Bebek because he was just like Bebek: openhearted and generous, full of life but a real gentleman. And Ortaköy's just right for Ayhan, too. But I'm getting ahead of myself here." Kete took a deep breath. "Anyway, one day, I got onto the bus in Sarıyer, traveled all the way down the Bosphorus, seeing again how beautiful it is, Rumeli Fortress, Aşiyan, Bebek . . . I had my face pressed against the window the whole way. It was a rainy day, cold and misty, but I wasn't worried about the weather, got out right in the middle of Ortaköy. First I had a good look around, walked over to the tea gardens, the quay, the mosque. It was kind of noisy there by the water, but you could spot the real people of Ortaköy, the quiet ones who live back away from the coast, further up the hill. So, I followed your instructions and found Ayhan Apartments and pressed the button right next to his name: Ayhan Pozaner. Nothing, not a tick. He must be out I thought, but I pressed the button again a few times, just to make sure. Then I was buzzed in, and, standing in a doorway on the ground floor, I saw a young man, half-asleep, in a dirty T-shirt and sweatpants. He's just like you said: dark, handsome, Eastern. Even asleep on his feet, those lips were curved into a smile; again, it was just like you said. I knew it was him. I felt like I'd known him for years. He looked at me, and then he looked at me again, like he had no idea who I was. Well, how could he have? Than his eyes landed on my red shoes. He mumbled something, but not to me, to himself. He must be one of those guys who talks to himself a lot, like your Uncle Erol. 'Hello!' he said. That's when I knew, Belgin: he's got this strange old woman on his doorstep and there's none of that 'can I help you' or 'what do you want.' Just a smile and a 'hello,' just like that! Can you imagine what Entek would have done, if he could even be bothered to answer the door himself? Well that's how Ayhan scored his first point with me. I replied with my own 'hello,' of course, and waited. He smiled and said, 'Welcome, but are you sure it's me you're looking for?' I smiled right back, but I was smiling because I knew that this time my little lamb had found a good man with a good heart. If that wouldn't make me smile, what would! "Son, you're Ayhan, aren't you?" I asked, just like that. "I am, but not the Ayhan who owns the building. I'm the one who isn't rich, the other Ayhan!" he said, still smiling. I didn't have the heart to drag it out one moment longer. 'I'm Belgin's nanny, big sister, mother . . . you can call me Kete!' You should have seen him!

205

As thrilled as if his own mother had appeared on the doorstep. The way he threw his arms around me, picked me up and carried on. I thought he was going to break my ribs. Take it from me, only a man full of love can hug like that!"

That was Kete. The Kete who switched off all the lights for one minute every night during the Susurluk scandal, the Kete who overrode her husband's protests to give flowers to the Saturday Mothers gathered in Galatasaray, the Kete who supported Women's Day marches and telephoned in to radio and television programs, determined to help right a wrong. Kete was something else. And this, her most recent endeavor, had been a long bus-ride all the way to the other side of Istanbul, to the airport in Yeşilköy.

"And he's so in love with you! That man Ayhan loves you heart and soul, plain and simple . . . I can't tell you how I felt when I finally left Ortaköy, like I was floating back up the Bosphorus to Sarıyer. The next week I said I was going out to the cemetery, and I visited the family plot. I prayed at the graves of Father Halit Ziya, your grandmother and Mother Jackie-Halide, telling them not to worry, that you'd be safe. 'She finally found a real man, a real husband,' I said. 'Amen.' Now they're all resting in peace . . ."

Listening to Kete's adventures with Ayhan, Belgin had bitten her lip, too embarrassed to say a word. She'd been raised in a culture that frowns on overly girlish excitement in grown women, but, finally, she couldn't resist asking her old nanny, "Do you think I look five years older than him?" Through hysterical laughter Kete had managed to get out: "Oh Belgin, oh my little lamb, you're sooo old . . . Listen to you! The two of you are still kids. You haven't even begun your lives yet!" Belgin regretted having said anything, even before Kete continued with, "And anyway, that devil Entek was ten years older. If age differences are so important to you, why didn't you worry about it then? Besides, you know what they say: a man with an older wife is sure to get rich. Ayhan might end up buying the whole apartment building. Wouldn't that be convenient? It's even named after him already!"

"So, Kete's come all the way to Yeşilköy to meet me," thought

206

Belgin, smiling despite the computer breakdown and in the face of the closed passport booth. "But after hearing that announcement . . . surely once she's heard that announcement . . ."

It had been a roller coaster of a day, and her spirits plummeted once more when she looked up and saw police dogs nosing a piece of hand luggage. She knew the dogs were trained to sniff out explosives as well as drugs . . . "Welcome to Istanbul," she whispered to herself. "Welcome, indeed."

18
GET OUT OF THE MUD, ISTANBUL

"That's Kete, that's Belgin's Kete!" exclaimed Ayhan. It was Kete, absolutely, and now everything would be all right. Ayhan was filled with relief, transported far from the panic-stricken arrivals hall, scene of fear and failure, back to his first glimpse of those red slippers, those muddied red slippers, in the hallway of Ayhan Apartments . . .

People who assume that an abundance of natural talent is by definition a great blessing are people who are too healthy to understand that overwhelming talent can, well, overwhelm. Ayhan had at times considered himself to be cursed, not blessed. It takes an unusually active imagination to "talk to stones" and to contend with an unbidden avalanche of images and imaginary constructs. All through his life, Ayhan had experienced periods of feverish restlessness, viewed sympathetically only by his mother and later appreciated fully only by a handful of fellow sufferers of similar temperament. Visions triggered by certain images gave rise to emotions and sensations which left him disoriented and isolated, as though he were seeing the world through a curtain, now translucent, now flashing colors, now moving patterns. As a boy, he'd firmly believed he'd been cursed with some strange illness, attacks of which made him short of breath and dizzy. It was only when he learned to manipulate stone and wood that he learned how to feel better. But the sense of disorientation remained, bringing melancholy in its train. It was why he'd chosen to spend so much time alone, and was also the reason he hadn't felt lonely. The child of a family of limited means living in Çukurova, a plain of unlimited fertility, Ayhan's imagination had enriched his boyhood. Bits of vegetation floating in the river became ships; leaves turned into bearded men in green robes; clouds were the cotton fields, workers and all, whirling up into the sky; stars were rockets shooting up from America past the moon to Mars and beyond; his mother's feet were the tall buildings of Adana, her corns and

209

calluses their windows; the inscriptions on ancient shards of clay at the nearby Aslantepe archaeological digs were Ottoman epitaphs on old tombstones, were gold-embroidered inscriptions on the black silk curtain covering the Kaaba, were engravings on a goblet of sharbat being sipped by a black-bearded holy man alone in a cave . . . Ayhan didn't yet realize that the act of drawing or sculpting the images taking shape in his mind was thought and imagination rendered into form. It would be many years before he would see Rodin's *Gates of Hell*.

And it was many years later that the sight of a pair of red slippers instantly revived in his mind's eye the image of that other pair of slippers, red and mud-spattered. He'd been transported.

"Oh how we all talk up Istanbul, but the mud on those shoes looks exactly like the mud you'd see on a pair of clodhoppers in a cotton field in Adana," he thought. Ever since those outdoor summer cinema days in Adana, where, too poor for tickets, they'd sit on the ground, back behind the screen, watching reversed images of Ayhan Işık-Belgin Doruk films flicker in the night, he'd had such high expectations of Istanbul, expectations replaced by wonder when he'd finally arrived in the city, eager to become an Istanbullu. But every winter came the mud, sloshing through the city streets, fouling shoes and spattering trouser legs, begriming and besmirching. "Shit, will I ever get away from mud!"

Ayhan wasn't the type to shrink from getting dirty, and he was only too happy to muddy his hands on a potter's wheel or while kneading clay, but the mud on his shoes was something else altogether. It had come to represent poverty, despair, and suffering—perhaps all of them a natural part of life in a village—but the indiscriminate smearing of both the neglected slum quarters and the well-fed districts of a city like Istanbul? After walking the streets of some of the great capitals of Europe and seeing that mud wasn't necessarily a part of the daily slog, even though winters there were even wetter and colder than back home, Ayhan began to see muddy shoes as a metaphor for "life in the Third World," the result of centuries of poor administration, a lack of planning and general carelessness.

"Hey Istanbul, all ready to take a twirl on the stage in 2010, for your turn as European Capital of Culture: Well when are you going to get your skirts out of the gutter, old girl? You haven't even learned how to wash your hands and face!" Such had been his thoughts the day he saw those muddy red slippers standing outside the door of his atelier on the floor below his flat in Ortaköy. He'd nodded off in his studio while waiting for his cleaning lady to finish work upstairs, and, when she didn't answer the door, assumed she'd left. When he finally opened the studio door, blinking and groggy, he saw a middle-aged woman with clear eyes and a pair of shoes so muddy the red leather below barely showed through. The woman followed his eyes down to her shoes, as though noticing their condition for the first time, before raising her eyes to look into his. He was trying to remember where he'd come across a depiction of the muddy streets of Paris in the 1800s. It was probably either *Les Misérables* or *Notre-Dame de Paris*, but whichever one it was, what had stuck in his mind was the mud, so much so that when his literature teacher at Darüşşafaka had assigned them a composition he'd seriously considered writing an essay on "Mud and the City."

Ayhan had quickly regained enough presence of mind to smile and say "hello" to the woman studying him from head to toe, for he was the kind of man who assumes every stranger deserves just that: a smile and a "hello." "You must be Ayhan," she'd said, beaming. "You must be Belgin's Ayhan!" And that's exactly what he was, "Belgin's Ayhan."

"That's Kete, Belgin's Kete!" exclaimed Ayhan, back at the airport. But this time it was Kete who'd become lost in thought, distracted, all her attention focused on the cell phone pressed against her ear. As Ayhan stood there, only a foot or so away from Kete, wondering who she was speaking to, and hoping his guess was right, a suitcase wheeled along by a passenger racing for the exits slammed into his leg, throwing him off balance, nearly causing him to fall, and jarring him into the here and now: "We've got to get out of here!" he shouted to Kete, who was still talking on the phone.

211

19
THY WILL BE DONE

"*Bismillahi Rahmani Rahim*! What's all this about a computer problem? It had better not be a bomb, God forbid. Although that's certainly what it sounds like to me . . . And if it is a bomb, I suppose they'll go and blame it on the Muslims again . . ." sighed Aleynâ Gülsefer—another in the chorus of sighs.

She'd heard the announcement while standing in front of a monitor telling her which gate to proceed to. In her left hand was a colorful *Istanbul Atatürk Airport Duty Free* carrier bag, decorated along the edges with emblems meant to ward off the evil eye, and containing her Kenzo Flower perfume and two boxes of Turkish delight; in her right hand, she was holding the business card given to her by Jak Safarti, manager of the duty-free shop. She'd been silently reciting İhlas and Fatiha, two verses from the Koran, so at first she assumed that she had been too preoccupied for the announcement to register, and that she may have misunderstood. As a graduate of an İmam Hatip high school, and a person who'd also benefited from the informal religious training provided by her family, Aleynâ knew her suras by heart, and considered it her duty to enlighten those who tended to confuse their Kulhüvallahi with their İhlas, the verse she'd just recited.

As the buzz of alarmed voices speaking several languages grew louder and her heart began to beat faster, she tried to remain calm, aware that stress and excitement could trigger an asthma attack. The recitation of a second Fatiha failed to achieve peace of mind. Like most asthmatics, she'd learned the importance of minimizing stress; self-possessed beyond her years, that's exactly what she set out to do.

But Aleynâ was distressed by the knowledge that there are three particular words that are all too often placed side-by-side, and invite the same misplaced conclusion in any language: *terör*, *bomba*, and *Islam*. A girl who'd grown up believing that true believers are at best treated like unwanted stepchildren in modern

Turkey, and had been so ever since the founding of the secular Republic, her distress had grown even more acute after the rising chorus of criticism directed at Islam from the West, using the pretext of 9/11. Still, she'd been a happy and well-adjusted child overall, and it was only in recent years that it had begun to wear on her, this constantly being misunderstood, this forever having to fight for what she felt was a basic human right. Tenacious and persevering, she'd been determined to remain calm and strong while fighting the good fight, which in recent years had somehow become almost entirely centered on what she chose to wear on her head. But Aleynâ was, after all, only twenty years old, and her constant state of battle readiness had taken its toll, even as she considered her unflinching ability to soldier on as a sign of God's grace.

"Good can come out of evil, but only for those able to distinguish clearly between the two, for those blessed with a sense of 'love and thanksgiving,'" she told herself. After all, the reason she was in the airport to board a plane to America was that she was attending university there because her head scarf was banned on campuses in her own country. Aleynâ Gülsefer firmly believed that were she now to be killed by a bomb as a result of having followed God's command to seek knowledge and enlightenment, she would most certainly die a martyr.

Head high, shoulders back, she did what she always did in moments of stress: she recited a verse of Fatiha and then drew slow, deep breaths. Asthma and the malicious glances of unbelievers would be repulsed!

"Don't worry, Aleynâ, Allah sees you and tests you. He knows and protects those who believe and persevere," she whispered to herself.

Amid a concerned chorus of "What happened?" and "Where are we supposed to go?" in English and Turkish, she pushed those thoughts to one side and began looking for an exit. There were not yet any signs of overt panic, but that didn't mean the situation couldn't deteriorate at any moment. Flashing arrows indicated that exits were located to both her left and her right. As a true believer, the decision she faced was a momentous one, yet another test, one that could lead her to salvation or destruction. She felt a chill as she thought of her mother, father, and little sister. If she died here today, her father would blame her mother for sending Aleynâ to America. But, just like her mother, once she set her mind on something she would follow through. She pulled herself together and took a deep breath. Yes, she was still able to take slow, deep breaths!

"Fate!" she whispered to herself, "There's no denying destiny: that which is written on our foreheads at birth will come to be, no matter what we do! And if I was destined to die here today as a martyr, that too shall come to pass." The thought calmed her; the acceptance of the inevitable and the heightened awareness of being in a given place at a given time helped her to achieve a degree of serenity. At a minimum, she no longer feared an asthma attack. She glanced at the business card in her hand: Jak Safarti. The duty-free shop was to her right. Muslims always favor right over left: the angel Münkâr awaits at the right shoulder; the *amel defteri*, a sacred record of lifelong vice and virtue, is delivered on the right; one steps into the bathroom left foot forward and the left hand is used for cleansing after urination or defecation . . . and it was probably a complete coincidence that Jak Safarti was now located to Aleynâ's right. Automatically placing her right foot forward as she said "Bismillahirrahmani Rahim!" Aleynâ began walking toward one of the two nearest exits. About forty meters along, she found herself surrounded by a group of tourists who had abandoned their shopping baskets in the rush to get out of the duty-free shop. Standing at the entrance, calm and poised, was Jack Safarti, reassuring the tourists in several languages. Aleynâ quickly took in his well-cut black suit and spicy fragrance (now what was it?). "Actually, what makes him so attractive is his sense of calm," Aleynâ told herself, "and his ability to maintain a respectful but courteous distance . . ." Her next thought was like a stab to the heart: "He may be the last person I ever see . . ." It wasn't that she had anything against Jak Safarti, it was the thought of never again seeing her parents and sister. Her eyes closed for a moment. "And if he weren't Jewish?" was the thought

215

she banished from her mind a split second later. "It's the devil's work—Allah is testing me yet again! A true Muslim must never discriminate on the grounds of religion or race! It is forbidden!"

When Aleynâ opened her eyes to the sight of several people solicitously asking her if she was all right, she grew embarrassed, flushed pink and began perspiring. Even though she'd grown accustomed to drawing the unwanted attention of strangers, some part of her believed it was sinful to do so. One of the men looking on with concern was Jak Safarti, and she couldn't help smiling at him as though at an old acquaintance, if not an old friend.

"Are you all right?" asked Jak.

"Thank you, I'm fine. I was overcome for a moment. I'm fine now."

As their eyes met, they both smiled a shy, slightly guilty smile. Then they both looked at the passengers scurrying for the exits. Even under the circumstances, Aleynâ imagined Jak thinking, "She may be Muslim, but she's all right, I guess," and felt hurt.

"Don't worry, Atatürk Airport is probably the safest place in Turkey, with the most professional security team anywhere. And by now there are probably plainclothes policemen all over the place as well. Don't be afraid," Jak whispered to Aleynâ.

She wasn't afraid. Aleynâ wasn't afraid of being martyred, but she was disturbed by just how much she seemed to be appreciating the attentions of a complete stranger, and a man at that.

"Keep going straight ahead and take the first exit on the right; it leads to the Airport Hotel. That's probably your safest bet right now. And if you're ever here again, under more usual circumstances, I'd be happy to be at your service," Jak said in a low, noncommittal voice.

"But when are you going to leave, Jak *Bey*?" Aleynâ found herself asking him, upon which she immediately asked herself if it wouldn't have been better to address him as "*Bay* Jak." Would he have assumed that she'd used the more formal address because he practiced a different religion, and would he have minded? It was at that moment that she realized that she'd had no experience in dealing with her non-Muslim fellow countrymen, and that her family, true believers all, didn't number a single one of them among their acquaintances. Not one. Had it been by choice, or was it merely coincidence? What about the guide books and historical accounts of "Muslims, Christians, and Jews" having lived for centuries in Istanbul "side by side." And why hadn't this realization occurred to her before, especially considering that she took so much interest in the varied backgrounds and religions of her group of friends at the university in America? She'd been taught to take great pride in the Ottoman Empire; how had her ancestors managed to live together in such tolerance and peace?

"Airport employees are being evacuated last," Jak said quietly.

"He might die . . ." thought Aleynâ. "He knows he might die, but he's perfectly calm about it. Perhaps he's a man of deep faith, like me? Or is it that he's good at hiding his feelings, also like me . . ."

"*Hakkınızı helal edin*!" Aleynâ blurted, once again finding herself involuntarily using a phrase that had implications only for Muslims. Under Jak's astonished eyes, Aleynâ hurried off with an embarrassed smile toward the exit. She'd done it again! What claims did she have over the manager of a shop she'd only just met, and how had she expected him to respond? Empty, unnecessary, foolish words!

"If mother had heard me she'd have been furious . . . I can't believe you did that! And especially since . . ." she said to herself. "Especially since . . ." Since she considered herself to be a "modern Muslim woman," why hadn't she waited for Jak to respond? Why had she run away? If she felt guilty, it meant she'd done something wrong. "What do I have to feel guilty about?" she asked herself indignantly. Did *they* feel guilty about what Israel was doing to the Palestinians? And why was it such a crime for her to identify primarily as a Muslim when they identified themselves as Jews first, Turks second? Why was that museum she'd visited in New York called the Museum of Jewish Heritage, not the "American-Jewish Museum"? She stopped in her tracks, mind racing. "It's just another example of Western double standards! They ostracize Islam, but they consider Jews to be an integral part of Western culture. Everyone's against us—real Muslims can expect understanding only from other Muslims!" Strangely relieved by the certainty of that grimly comforting conclusion, Aleynâ resumed walking toward the exit.

When she overheard other travelers talking about the closure of all sections of passport control, she forgot her ruminations and everything else. So, it was no longer possible to return to the departures hall where she'd last seen her mother, her father, her sister. They were probably back home in Çamlıca by now, sitting in their spacious kitchen drinking tea and eating cookies baked by the live-in servants her grandfather had brought to Istanbul from his village. They were probably talking about her right now, rightfully proud that the first member of their family was about to graduate from university, in America, and a girl no less! Everyone that is but her father, who'd expected her to stay at home and provide grandchildren to whom he would teach the Koran. "Why are you being so stubborn?" he'd said to his wife. "If Aleynâ is determined to work, there's nothing in our religion to prevent it. But she'll get married first, and then, with her husband's blessing, she can work at our company, where women are free to wear head scarves, unlike in state offices. Praise Be to God, business is going well and there's plenty of work for her. Why should the girl go all the way to America?" But Aleynâ's mother had sided with her, and that was the end of it.

If her father heard news of a bomb or—God let it be so—a computer failure at the airport, his already high blood pressure would probably shoot up. God save him, he might even fall ill. She fought the temptation to telephone her family, reluctantly telling herself not to cause needless panic. And were she to cry when she heard their voices, her father would feel even worse . . . no, she wouldn't phone . . .

The best course of action would be to emerge from the airport safe and sound. God permitting, even if the passport section was closed . . . Closed! Officially, she was no longer on Turkish soil, was trapped in an international zone in which a bomb had possibly been planted. She recited another verse of Fatiha, and for the tenth time checked to make sure her nasal spray was in the side flap of her handbag. Noticing at that moment a pair of girls in long ivory coats, some distance away and arm-in-arm, and also wearing turban-style head scarves, she was as overjoyed as though she'd spotted long-lost relatives, but they were too busy talking and walking to notice her. Perhaps they're on their way to America just like me, to study because of their head scarves?" she wondered.

"Somebody call a doctor! She's out cold! Quick, go get help!" Aleynâ swiveled her head to the left, in the direction of the cries, and saw a group gathering in front of a jewelry store. Through the assorted onlookers she caught a glimpse of a figure on the floor, a woman, barelegged and prostrate. Pulling a spare scarf out of her handbag, Aleynâ pushed her way through the crowd to quickly cover the woman's legs. Kneeling on either side of her were an elderly female tourist and a woman clearly identifiable as a guest worker in Europe, both of them shouting, "doctor!" in English, Turkish, and what sounded like German accents. Aleynâ flinched when she saw that the woman stretched out on the floor was none other than Anna Maria Vernier, the film critic who'd snatched her Kenzo Flower perfume in the duty-free shop. Gasping and wheezing, Anna Maria looked directly at Aleynâ through wide, staring eyes. "She's having an asthma attack!" Aleynâ shouted.

In seconds, Aleynâ was kneeling on the floor, gently cupping the back of Anna Maria's head with one hand while she operated her inhaler with the other. "Miss, are you a doctor?" a security guard asked. "Perhaps it isn't asthma. You'd better wait for a doctor!" But Anna Maria was already breathing more freely, and within a few seconds she was well enough to smile at Aleynâ, gratitude showing in her eyes.

"It's nothing. Anyone would have done the same," Aleynâ said, her comment misinterpreted by Anna Maria as "I'd have done the same for anyone."

As Anna Maria slowly rose to a sitting position, Aleynâ kept a supportive arm round her back, eyes traveling once more to the silver cross swaying above Anna Maria's cleavage.

"Have we met before?" Anna Maria asked, weakly, but carefully enunciating each syllable.

"I've read a few of your articles," Aleynâ admitted as she helped the film critic to her feet.

"Ah, I remember you now, we use the same perfume! Isn't that so?" smiled Anna Maria, the color returning to her cheeks, well enough now to act playful.

Aleynâ allowed herself a nod in the affirmative. So, Anna Maria *had* spotted Aleynâ in the shop . . . And had known exactly what she was doing . . .

20
CIAO, ISTANBUL

"Now you're in for it! Imagine it's really a bomb, and it explodes, killing dozens—imagine how many decades it would take for Turkey to clear its name!" winced Anna Maria Vernier when she heard the announcement.

"If the same thing happened in the metros of—say—London or Tokyo, there would be a concerted effort not only to wash away the blood, but a general cleansing, psychic and political, with life soon returning to normal—tourism, art and science continuing as always, completely unscathed . . . But that's not what would happen here!" she thought, exhaling several times, as though trying to blow out one of those trick birthday candles.

"If Uncle Giovanni were here, he'd say, 'Here we go again. I've got a donkey's luck!' Anna Maria tried to smile at the memory of her uncle, but she was breathing even more heavily now. She drew another deep breath, but felt no better and, as an asthma sufferer most of her life, knew she'd better remain calm.

"They'll ask me all about it at the panel tomorrow: Turkey caught between East and West, Turkey's EU aspirations, Turkey's identity crisis . . . I can hear them all now. Then we'll move on to Islam and terrorism, and on and on. You'd think the members of IRA and ETA were Muslims too! You know, I've got half a mind not to show up in Cannes tomorrow. It isn't as though any time or questions will be devoted to 'Turkish Cinema: Generation Next.'"

Carrying a duty-free bag containing a bottle of whiskey, a bottle of rakı, a few boxes of Turkish delight, a vial of sunblock, and a box of Kenzo Flower perfume, Anna Maria Vernier had been window-shopping in front of an exclusive jewelry store at the time of the announcement. At first, she was overwhelmed by a series of speculative but highly unwelcome scenarios concerning her reception in Cannes, and it was only a few moments later that she began considering the very real danger she possibly faced at that moment. Her family had been in the film industry for generations (Westerners were always amazed to learn that the first Turkish film was shot in 1917), and often joked that they had begun to view life itself as a film, maintaining a studied distance that wasn't always healthy. And it was perhaps for that very reason that Anna Maria's thoughts turned first to her country's international reputation and her obligation to uphold it, and only later to the immediate and personal, the fact that if her flight were cancelled she wouldn't even be arriving in Cannes as scheduled, let alone called upon to defend her country.

Each and every citizen of Turkey goes abroad burdened with the baggage of "Turkey's international reputation," but Anna Maria also had to contend with being a Levantine, a state of mind and being she had come to believe could only be fully appreciated by a fellow Levantine. But that had never protected her from having to explain at length, both to foreigners abroad and to fellow Turks at home, with whom she shared a common language and national destiny, what and who she was, and what it meant to her.

"No, I'm not an immigrant. I didn't migrate to Istanbul! My grandfather's grandfather, and his grandfather before him, were all Istanbullu. No, I'm not a Muslim, but I think you'll appreciate that Istanbul wasn't founded by Muslims or even for Muslims. No, I'm not a foreigner, I'm a Turk of Levantine extraction. Yes, my roots stretch back to thirteenth-century Istanbul, to a Venetian family that emigrated to what was then Constantinople. You see, even when the Byzantine Empire gave way to the Ottoman, the Venetians and Genovese maintained their trading privileges and social relations. Yes, of course there were many more Levantines in Istanbul back then, especially in the Pera district. No, Turkish is my mother tongue every bit as much as Italian! I'm not a foreigner, I tell you, even if my name is Anna Maria, which happens to be just as 'Turkish' as what you know today as the district of Galata. Why don't I move to Italy? You must be joking! Why would I do that? Why do you live here? Well, that's why I do. And I'm not going anywhere!"

It was exhausting . . . Even if she simply smiled knowingly when congratulated on her unaccented Turkish, or smiled tensely when asked if she'd ever considered converting to Islam, the conversation would all too often veer off into the supposed inevitability of her 'return' to Italy, and she would come face to face with the contradictions inherent in the concept of a 'local foreigner.' It was tiring indeed, but in her thirty years she had never considered, even for a moment, leaving her country, friends, childhood memories, roots and identity behind.

"Really, you'd think they owned the place and the rest us were aliens visiting from outer space!"

Anna Maria Vernier returned to the dramatic potential of the announcement, imagining it as the opening of a film and reviewing in her mind the many motion pictures featuring scenes of mayhem and panic. Once again, she became so immersed in her thoughts that she was quite cut off from her actual surroundings. Once again, she betrayed her roots in a family of dreamers. While her great-grandfather, Sergio, had been an architect, most of his descendants were in some way connected to the arts, some more tenuously than others: Grandfather Vittorio had been deputy manager of the Elhamra Cinema when the great Atatürk himself attended the Turkish premiere of Chaplin's *Modern Times*; Uncle Giovanni was a film historian and critic, and had encouraged his niece to follow in his footsteps; Cousin Maria Rita was an acclaimed pianist, and there were many other artists and musicians in the family, all of them Istanbullu or İzmirli, all of them "locals!"

"And to think that so many Turks know nothing about fish, have never tried seafood, can't swim—have not a single memory or impression or association that is in any way connected to the sea, and here, in a city that has expanded to the shores of two seas, and in a country lapped by the waters of the Mediterranean, Aegean and Black Sea. They know nothing about the Bosphorus, Galata, the Golden Horn, or Pera; they know nothing about their own history and don't care to know more . . . And I won't even go into the ones who would like to transform Istanbul into

223

just another modern Middle Eastern city, not even realizing that, from Damascus to Cairo, not a single city has thrived on a single language, culture or religion. What's more, Istanbul isn't just any city, or even Middle Eastern. Sometimes I'm tempted to open my mouth and shout: Istanbul was cosmopolitan before the word had even been coined; a homogenous culture would smother her to death, goddamn it! *Dio vi stramaledica*!"

And at that moment, she really did open her mouth. But there was no shouting: she stood there, mouth open, gasping like a netted fish, chest heaving, but telling herself she was all right, knowing panic would only make things worse. Reaching into her bag, she felt for her inhaler, locating it just as the attack subsided. Yes, it was there if she needed it.

"Take that girl in the shop, the one wearing the turban. What was that all about? Layer after layer of clothing, head wrapped up like a mummy—and in this heat! Feet naked in those expensive sandals, but too virtuous to expose the underside of her chin! Women like her wander the streets of Istanbul holding themselves up as models of virtue, but there she is choosing Kenzo Flower, a perfume specifically designed to turn men's heads. So proudly pious is she, she no doubt imagines she represents the poor and downtrodden. If that isn't false pride, I don't know what is! If she had it her way, Istanbul would be a city of twelve million devout Muslims, all of the women covered like her and resigned to their abusive husbands, the streets running with the blood of sheep during the Feast of Sacrifice, all restaurants closed by day during Ramadan, all students enrolled at İmam Hatip type *medresse*s, Tekel liquor shops selling nothing but rosewater and sharbat! Well, it'll never happen. This is a city of many voices, many faiths, many languages and many cultures, and that's what makes it special, and that's the way it's going to stay . . ."

As if an asthma attack wouldn't be bad enough, Anna Maria was on the verge of hyperventilating, so infuriated had she become when she considered the threat posed to her lifestyle and her city. But she still left her inhaler in her handbag, as an emergency measure of last resort. Her thoughts then turned to her husband, a

Muslim she'd married with the consent of her family, but over the objections of his. She'd been expected to convert, but despite having refused to do so, was eventually accepted by her parents-in-law as their Catholic daughter. Anna Maria and her husband-to-be had cunningly pointed out that the mother of as eminent a person as Fatih Sultan Mehmet himself, the conqueror of Constantinople, had died without converting, and was even now buried in a cemetery reserved for Christians. That may have been what did the trick, but they would never know for sure. And it never stopped her father-in-law, a retired lieutenant, from adopting an accusatory tone as he railed in her presence about the role "foreign elements" had played in the collapse of the Ottoman Empire, elements, he argued, who had secured an unfair hold on the economy and were not above collaborating with rival European powers.

The irony was that neither the lieutenant himself, nor indeed his son, had ever visited a mosque. And as for Anna Maria, she celebrated mass only on Christmas Eve, and had astonished her Uncle Giovanni as much as her in-laws when she'd taken to wearing a silver cross. She'd explained it as an act of defiance, declaring, "I'm wearing this cross as a political symbol, just like the turban those girls wear. It's my country as much as theirs, and the public sphere is the public sphere!"

As her increasingly severe wheezing signaled an imminent attack, Anna Maria exclaimed aloud: "I hate it!" The people hurrying past toward the flashing exit sign paid her outburst no mind, although a police dog did seem to prick up its ears for a moment. She was just reaching into her handbag when she felt her shopping bag slip through her fingers: "Am I falling?" she wondered. "My husband'll be so upset . . ."

"She fainted! A woman's passed out! Quick, go get help!" she heard a moment later. It was true that she'd momentarily blacked out, but she was conscious that she was now stretched out on the floor, and astonished upon realizing this: it had never happened before. "She's having an epileptic fit!" cried someone else. Because her head was thrown back, she was having even more difficulty breathing. If someone would help her sit up, she'd ask for the inhaler in her bag. Two sprays and she'd be fine. But she was wheezing too hard to give voice to her thoughts.

And then she saw her, a girl in a head scarf. She was spreading one of those loathsome head scarves across Anna Maria's bare legs. "Save my life, not my honor!" she wanted to scream, but was able to produce nothing but a wheeze of protest, indistinguishable from its fellows, its meaning no doubt lost on her Good Samaritan.

The head-scarf girl gently slipped an arm under the back of Anna Maria's head, carefully lifting her up a few inches, greatly easing her discomfort. That's when she recognized her: the girl from the shop! The moment their eyes met Aleynâ shouted: "It's asthma. She's having an attack!" She fished out an inhaler from her own handbag, shook it, and sprayed it into Anna Maria's mouth. Through years of habit, she held the spray in her lungs before exhaling with a low whistle. Another puff and Anna Maria was able, with the girl's help, to sit up. The whole thing was over in moments. The only indication that there had ever been a crisis was the gathered crowd and the stinging rebuke of the security official ringing in Aleynâ's ears. Aleynâ knew it had been wrong of her to administer medication without waiting for the medical team to arrive. She hung her head and flushed pink, but she remained at Anna Maria's side, even as the crowd dispersed, leaving the two women together. Anna Maria tried and failed to read the label on the inhaler, but managed to rasp:

"Thank you, I've got one in my bag, but it came on too quick!"

"You seem much better now. Are you sure you're all right? May the Lord . . ."

"Mine's atopic," Anna Maria interrupted, anxious to find out the name of medication she'd just inhaled. "Mine too," Aleynâ said, as she helped Anna Maria to her feet, a firm hand on her arm in case she got dizzy. Had anyone taken the time to observe the two women, they would have seen a girl in a scarf, her feet and face the only exposed parts of her body, and a woman in a short sundress wearing a silver cross slowly walking arm-in-arm toward the emergency exit doors, having discovered that they were both atopic and partial to Kenzo Flower.

"If I'd been you, I wouldn't have had the guts to assist anyone without consulting a doctor. I mean, I wouldn't have risked it. You certainly are brave!" smiled Anna Maria.

Aleynâ glanced over at Anna Maria to see if she was being sarcastic, and wasn't certain whether or not she was. Sensing that she'd somehow upset her companion, Anna Maria changed the subject.

"Do you think it's really nothing but the computers being down?"

"God only knows!" she replied, eyes shifting to Anna Maria's cross. "It is He who knows and protects."

"Well, I think the police might have a minor role to play as well," Anna Maria ventured with a dry cough.

Aleynâ had hung her head; no one saw the smile playing across her lips.

"They say these are going to be banned in France. I might have to take it off when I get there," threw in Anna Maria, fingering her cross. There was no discernable tensing in the arm linked with Anna Maria's, as Aleynâ contented herself with an indecipherable nod. And on the two women marched toward the exit, arm in arm.

21

ISTANBUL, MY PROMISED LAND

"It's all over, Jak *Bey*!" Jak Safarti said to himself. "End of the road! Everyone's terrified—they'll have no problem controlling us now!"

A few moments earlier the shop had been full of foreigners and Turks carrying shopping baskets full of slender-necked bottles, chocolate, Turkish delight, cigarettes, perfume and cigars, selected either for their own enjoyment or for their loved ones. A single ambiguous announcement had been enough to send most of them running. Standing near the cash registers to facilitate the flow of customers, duty-free shop manager Jak Safarti found boxes and bottles being flung into his arms as off they went, headed for the exits.

"We've been cursed," he said to himself with a resigned sigh, shaking his head. "They hoped for the worst, and here it is; their prayers have been answered. And what could be worse than fear?" But it was only seconds later that the word "prayer" set off a familiar tickling in his nostrils, a sure sign that a joke was coming on . . . One day, a woman shows up at the Rabbi's door with two female parrots and says, "Rabbi, I've got a terrible problem I need you to help me with. It's these stubborn parrots of mine. They know only two sentences: 'Hi, I'm a whore' and 'What can I do for you?' It's so embarrassing, and I haven't been able to teach them anything else. I'd hoped to teach them a prayer or two, you know how pious I am. Please help!" The Rabbi comforts the woman by telling her that his own two male parrots will lead her wayward birds down the path of righteousness. But the moment the woman places the cage of borrowed parrots next to her own birds, and leaves the room, they begin the familiar refrain: "Hi, I'm a whore / What can I do for you?" The two male parrots, who had been busily learning a new prayer, exclaim in unison: "Praise the Lord! Our prayers have been answered at last!"

Jak Safarti smiled despite himself, just as his father would have done. His mother, however, would have shaken her head disapprovingly as she accused the two men of "dodging reality" by "hiding behind humor." They'd been doing it for years, father and son, ever since Jak was a boy: exchanging gags and yarns, perfecting timing, building off each other, getting it just right. There was one joke they particularly delighted in, and told only when mother wasn't around:—How do you define "boy wonder"?—a so-so student with a Jewish mother!

The duty-free shop had nearly emptied out, and Jak Safarti observed that his personnel were growing uneasy. "Listen everyone, keep in mind that we're perfectly safe here. Let's gather up all these shopping baskets and start putting goods back on the shelves. We're not in danger. They'll evacuate us soon enough, if need be," he said, measured and reassuring. His employees visibly relaxed. Jak was a master at getting himself across without waving his arms about or raising his voice, the result of his upbringing, and that of his parents and their parents before them. Ever since he was a boy, his mother had urged him to become a manager of some sort, a position in which he excelled, even now, as his inner voice worried and nagged:

"Of course no one believes it's nothing but a computer failure. Not anymore. Not these days. We've all switched into survival mode: too many bombs, too many body searches, too many security measures, too terrorized to think straight. If someone had fallen down here in this shop, they'd probably have been trampled. Here we are, at the beginning of this brave new millennium, and terrorism has already won; they're trying to persuade us peace and democracy are luxuries we can't afford," he thought, heaving a sigh. Then he noticed that a tourist was having difficulty pushing her wheelchair-bound husband past the theft detectors at the shop exit, and raced to help her. As he reassured the couple, in English, that there was no need to panic and that the security measures at the airport were on a par with any, anywhere in the world, he noticed that the elderly woman was looking directly at his nametag. She spoke a few words of what he took to be Hebrew, continuing in English when she saw he didn't understand:

"Thank you for your help. I'd have expected you to speak Hebrew. Anyway, this is our first time in Istanbul and we just love it. We live in Israel now, immigrated about twenty years ago."

"Ah, wonderful. I do hope you're happy there, and I hope you'll visit us again in Istanbul one day. There's no cause for alarm, you're perfectly safe here," he continued, his hand on the woman's back as he pointed out the nearest exit.

"We're used to this kind of thing. We've forgotten how to panic," said the woman with a rueful smile.

"They make me crazy! Not every Jew speaks Hebrew or chooses to live in Israel . . . The same way not all Muslims speak Arabic, or Catholics know Latin! And as for settling in Israel, well, *Aliyah* may be a fundamental concept of Zionism, but that doesn't mean . . ."

An approaching plainclothes policeman nodded to Jak, who winked to let him know everything was under control. The policeman, who was indistinguishable from an average passenger, walked off.

"Perhaps they've been tipped off? Perhaps this really is a bomb scare?" Jak worried momentarily, relaxing when he told himself that the policeman had seemed perfectly at ease. "No, not with all these security measures in place. At worst, there's an isolated disturbance of some kind." He spotted a mother and child who'd dropped their shopping bag at the entrance to the shop and were picking up the contents strewn across the floor. After helping them, he gave the girl a lollipop from the display stand next to a register. As she looked at him, he remembered his cousin's little girl, both of them killed in the bombing of the Neva Shalom Synagogue the previous year. His cousin had been deeply religious, and a constant critic of Jak's secular ways. Every year, he'd urged Jak to accompany him on his summer holiday to the Promised Land. But, just like so many of his Muslim compatriots, Jak never said no to stuffed mussels, occasionally ate bacon with his eggs, and rarely set foot in a house of worship. But he was respectful of his cousin's beliefs, even if there was a point of contention upon which the two of them could never agree: Jak advocated a two-

231

state solution with pre-1967 borders. "Sooner or later, a Palestinian state will be established, so we might as well begin learning to live peacefully. It's the only chance we have. Then, and only then, will peace come to the Promised Land," he'd say. "Listen to you," would come his cousin's retort. "Still a leftist, still an idealist, head off in the clouds. Haven't you ever wondered why so many Jews played the violin, but so few the piano? It's because we were always on the run!"

Although they rarely agreed on political matters or philosophical questions, his cousin decided that every community and every family needed at least one black sheep, an eccentric romantic to help them refine their own views. He didn't always treat Jak with respect, but could often be heard proudly remarking, "He's the manager of the airport duty-free shop!" And they both supported the Fenerbahçe football team, attending matches together, chanting and cheering side by side. Another thing they shared was a sense of humor, and even if the cousin didn't approve of rabbis being made the butt of jokes, he was determined not to let Jak get the better of him, and would listen silently before countering with a joke of his own.

"As the Rabbi's wife went off to market," Jak began one day, "she left behind a box, telling her husband not to peek inside of it. Now the Rabbi was an honest man, but he was, after all, only human. Opening the lid to the box he saw three eggs and 2000 Turkish lira. When his wife returned, he admitted having peeked, and asked her the meaning of the box's contents. Whenever one of your sermons bored me, I'd buy an egg, his wife explained. Oh, said the Rabbi, heaving a sigh of relief. Only three boring sermons, not bad if I say so myself. What about the 2000 lira? Oh that, says the wife. Every time the eggs make an even dozen I sell them at the market." The cousin had laughed—grudgingly, but he had laughed.

"Ever hear the one about the atheist Jew?" began his counterattack. "An atheist Jew falls in love with a girl but she tells him she's sorry, her parents are true believers and will never consent to give him her hand in marriage." Every time this cousin spoke the word "atheist" he would fix his eyes on Jak to study the word's effect—but Jak never reacted. "'Ah, dear mother, the man I love is an atheist and he doesn't even believe in Hell,' the girl confides to her mother one day. 'Don't worry, darling' the mother assures her, 'we'll have him believing in Hell in no time!' Hah ha ha!"

"What do you mean, an atheist Jew?" Jak had wanted to ask, once the anecdote—mercifully short—was over. But he didn't bother, because even when it came to his beloved cousin, he'd long since come to the conclusion that strongly held religious views exclude a lightly held sense of irony.

Of course, Jak's cousin wasn't the only one who complained about his failure to appreciate the bonds of family and community, and who criticized him for being a bachelor of thirty who occasionally dated women from outside the faith. The young people of today had no respect for tradition, were losing their culture! The community elders weren't unlike literary critics who, every decade or so, solemnly pronounce the novel as an art form, to be dead. "Look, if in the face of nonstop disaster, natural and man-made, horror and holocaust, mankind has endured, survived, and even thrived, it is for one reason and one reason only: change. Even as we adapt and change as a species, and at breakneck speed, why do so many of us dig in our heels and resist social change of any kind?" he'd ask his mother, father, cousin, and friends. But his protestations failed to mend the growing rift with his family and community; he hadn't been cast out, but he was certainly no longer as welcome as before, and was perfectly aware that a growing number of the members of the congregation wished to have nothing more to do with him. He had grown to accept that as a minority within a minority he must conform or be ostracized. And as for the wider community, he could only hope to be spoken of as "Jewish, but a good person."

Jak spotted Aleynâ among the swelling crowd of worried travelers streaming toward the exits the same moment she noticed him. When he saw how pale she'd grown his first impulse was to help, and he acted on it by advising her to go directly to the airport hotel, having been told earlier by a policeman that there was a strong chance that all passengers would be gathered there. As he spoke to her, he'd nearly placed a reassuring hand on her back, but refrained from physical contact, aware as he was that it could easily be misconstrued. Their brief conversation had been friendly and routine, one he could have had with anyone, but just as Aleynâ prepared to go she blurted out, "*Hakkınızı helal edin!*" surprising both Jak and herself. He smiled. Deeply touched, forgetting for a moment the tensions caused by the announcement and the passengers rushing off toward the flashing exit signs, Jak smiled a crooked smile and whispered, "*Helal olsun!*"

The exchange with Aleynâ had been a blessing and an absolution, a ritual request and response designed to resolve whatever may have been wrong between them. Even though the system technically applies only to fellow Muslims, if only because non-Muslims would not understand the system or even the words, Jak Safarti was familiar with both and had automatically made the response required.

A moment later, back in the shop, Jak Safarti managed to find the credit slip signed by the head-scarved girl he'd just helped. "*Helal olsun*, Aleynâ *Hanım—helal olsun*, cousin!" he whispered.

22
UNSEAL YOUR GATES

"Have they given up on us? Could they have decided to just write us off?" Belgin anxiously thought to herself. A quick calculation of the possible reasons behind and ramifications of the vaguely worded announcement, which had been ominously followed by the closure of the passport booths, appeared to confirm her initial reaction and her worst fears. Although her head ached with renewed intensity, an outside observer would have seen only a calm and collected woman, the Belgin best summarized by the folk song Ayhan sometimes whispered into her ear: "The leaves of the willow are slim and soft / I burn inside, while cool without."

"Our passports haven't been processed, which means we haven't officially entered Turkey yet," she told herself, again. Belgin knew what it was to be an outsider, had always been on the fringes, had even preferred not to be a member of any group, clique or club, but she had also known the loneliness of the outsider. And at this moment, being stuck in the margins could spell danger. In fact, she wouldn't have been at all surprised if the rubbish bin right next to her turned out to contain a bomb.

"They wouldn't just abandon us here for bureaucratic or diplomatic reasons, would they?" They wouldn't just leave us?" she pondered, just as a whiff of lavender reached her nostrils. She smiled despite herself: the magical scent of lavender was working its spell yet again, and never failed to raise her spirits. Like nearly everyone in Turkey, she, too, appreciated a refreshing splash of lemon eau de cologne, a ritual widely observed when welcoming guests, sending off restaurant customers or as a staple of long-distance bus travel, during which, every few hours, passengers extend cupped palms to an attendant proffering cologne from a bottle. Belgin had even tried orange, lilac and pine cologne, as well as novelties like tobacco, tea and banana, but nothing compared to lavender. Nothing.

The reactions of her American friends in New York always

amused her: not only were they surprised to be greeted at the door with a splash of cologne, some of them were even more bemused by her obsession with a fragrance they associated with a musty bygone era. She'd quickly learned that the fresh, spicy smell she associated with her father, with the city of her birth, and with the Mediterranean, had connotations unheard of in Turkey: lavender and old lace, creaky but stately ladies with faded lavender hair, the lavender color of alternative sexual lifestyles . . . Literary critics even referred derisively to "lavender prose"!

"Didn't the same thing happen exactly twenty-eight years ago, here in Yeşilköy, when we returned with father's casket? Didn't I smell lavender then, too? Is this just a coincidence?" she wondered, perplexed but pleased nonetheless. She felt a strong urge to discover the source of the fragrance, and even stood up to have a look around. But she saw only a few tense and weary travelers, none of them the type likely to smell of lavender. Annoyed with herself, Belgin sat down and began biting her lip. Was she losing her mind?

And even if she had identified the source, what difference would it make? Would that person, whoever he was, have enfolded her in a lavender embrace, like her father! She remembered having wished that lavender was sold in little emergency capsules that she could break open when she needed a "hit," even if she was at the North Pole or in the middle of the Sahara Desert. Later, in New York, her therapist had dubbed her fantasy the "lavender effect."

"A belief in the total acceptance of reality is as futile as a belief in life without fantasy, or dreams that you can preprogram before you go to sleep. A thirteen-year-old child may accept the reality of death, but certainly can't be expected to understand its implications. And the expectation of full acceptance and understanding of something so unfathomable would itself lead to trauma . . ." she sighed.

"Just look what you've done to me, Belgin! You went and got me addicted to lavender, too!" Ayhan had joked. "I'd never heard of the stuff, the flower or the cologne, believe it or not, but I still

236

managed to have a perfectly happy childhood. Well, how was I to know that one day I'd fall in love with a girl from Bebek who was a lavender junkie, just like her father . . .

"The next thing I know, I find myself at the Rebul shop on İstiklal Caddesi, wondering just what it is they're selling. I mean, is it some kind of magic potion? So I ask the guy there, I say, 'Tell me, sir, what's the secret of your scent?' . . . Don't laugh, Belgin! I'm trying to tell you the results of my field research, you being a scientist and all. Hey, stop laughing! Actually, keep on going. You don't smile enough, and when you do, you're even more beautiful . . ." And with that, Ayhan had thrown his arms around her and kissed her full on the mouth, smelling all the while of . . . lavender.

Thinking about it in the airport, Belgin laughed aloud, and realized, not for the first time, how good Ayhan had been for her. And would be for her.

He'd released her and returned to his lecture, taking enormous satisfaction in reversing their usual roles. "I bet you didn't know Rebul was founded in 1895 by Jean Cesare Reboul, as—give me a second to get my tongue around this—*Grande Pharmacie Parisien*, one of the first drugstores in all of Beyoğlu. But when our Levantine chemist, Monsieur Reboul got old, he had no heirs. So what did he do? He turned over the business to Kemal Müderrisoğlu in the same year Atatürk passed away. And the Reboul name remains with us today as 'Rebul.' Who says Ayhan doesn't do his research?"

Belgin impulsively reached into her purse and pulled out a little plastic flask of lavender cologne. Impatiently twisting off the top, she spilled some into each of her palms, then held the bottle to her nose, breathing deeply, as though her life depended on it, filling her nostrils with the intoxicating scent of memories: the house in Bebek, her father, her grandmother, her mother, Kete, Ayhan, and the baby she was carrying.

"If it's a girl, let's name her *Lavanta!*" was the thought that flashed through her mind. A girl named Lavender! A girl with raven-black hair, naturally, and eyes like a foal, graceful as a deer, independent as a cat, free as an eagle, clever as a jinn, and playful as an otter. Nothing less! Her lips would be curled into a permanent smile, just like Ayhan's, and she'd have a little comma of a nose, just like her mother's. But how did she know it would be a girl? She didn't. And when, exactly, had she become so eager to have a child? She didn't know the answer to that question, either. And if it was a boy, why should she mind? She had no idea. Sometimes, the questions we're least prepared to answer are the ones we pose to ourselves, Belgin realized, and not for the first time.

She was distracted from her thoughts by a group of policemen moving toward the passport booths, thereby raising everyone's hopes that they would soon be reopened. A few dozen stateless passengers even formed a quick line, but the police simply continued speaking on their transmitters, without a word of explanation or clarification. While there was a great deal of grumbling and many of the passengers wore tense expressions, nerves no doubt strained by the flashing red exit lights, there wasn't a general air of panic. At least not yet. Belgin's lavender reveries had calmed her down, but she, too, was feeling ill at ease and growing increasingly resentful when one of the young policemen suddenly announced to the little assembly that everything was under control and that all passengers without entry stamps would soon be transferred to a more secure area. The announcement was made in Turkish, only serving to further exasperate those who couldn't speak that language.

"Nothing's changed!" Belgin exclaimed in a low voice, the expression on her face still as impassive as ever. "A huge modern airport has replaced the old one, but the police still don't know any foreign languages. Well, here we go again."

Belgin stepped in to offer her services as a translator, joining a few other Turks in explaining to the international visitors what the police had said. The effort of communicating with strangers had been too much, and she stumbled on the way back to her seat. A young policeman caught her by the arm.

"Are you all right, ma'am?" he asked.

"I'm fine, thanks," was all Belgin had intended to say, but

when she opened her mouth to speak, the words, "I'm pregnant!" came out instead, causing her to blush in embarrassment.

The policeman barked into his receiver, "We've got a pregnant woman here. She's not well. Send help!"

"Really, I'm fine," Belgin insisted. "I got a bit dizzy, is all." The policeman assumed the woman's bashfulness was a reflection of her delicacy and good breeding, and would never have guessed what had really embarrassed her. Belgin realized how much she had suppressed her maternal instincts, and the real reason that she had decided motherhood was not for her: was it that her own mother had seemed so confused and incapable; could it have been Kete's deep sorrow over having been separated from her own mother at such a young age; or might it have been Mehmet Emin Entek, who'd jeered, "Whose bastard are you carrying, anyway?" when she'd told him she was pregnant for the first time?

"My wife's pregnant too. God willing, she's giving me a son this time," confided the policeman with a proud smile.

"Congratulations!" Belgin automatically offered. For the first time in her life, she was discussing pregnancy and motherhood, and with a policeman no less. But she continued:

"It's possible these days to determine the sex of the fetus. All you need is an ultrasound scan, although it's not particularly effective in detecting Down's, contrary to what people say."

"We didn't bother. When we did have scanning done, all three turned out to be girls, so I was against it this time. I told the missus it just brings us bad luck."

Belgin's eyes met those of the policeman for just the briefest of moments, and the look they exchanged was inscrutable to them both. It had just occurred to the policeman that his wife had had trimester check-ups, and may well have had a scan in secret. But if the baby had been a boy, surely, she'd have told him? For her part, Belgin was reminded of how much she wanted a girl, and remembered how devoted Ayhan said he had been to the daughter from his first marriage. Then she looked at the policeman and tried to imagine what it would be like growing up unwanted, just for being a girl.

Growing up without a father's love! It was incomprehensible to her; even though she'd lost her father early, his love had always been with her, protecting her, making her feel safe. How could any girl do without that?

"It's strange," she thought to herself. "After Kete, the first person I'm telling is a complete stranger, a policeman."

"I'm afraid you won't be able to contact your husband," the policeman said. "All the networks are down."

"What?"

"You remember, the same thing happened after the earthquake in '99. When everyone gets on the phone at once the system collapses, just like that."

That information didn't stop Belgin from reaching into her purse for the cell phone that Ayhan had given her and pressing the "call" button. But the policeman was right: all she heard was a strange beep. She tried again. Nothing.

Belgin suddenly felt nauseous, and when she began to retch the policeman whisked her off to the ladies' bathroom in record time. "Don't worry, it's just morning sickness. My wife had it all the time," he said, holding the door open for her. "I'll page a doctor. You'll be fine."

Belgin found herself back in the same bathroom and the same stall into which she had shut herself earlier in the day for what had seemed like hours. She began to vomit. A few moments later, as she rinsed her mouth and splashed cold water onto her face, her thoughts turned back to the policeman, and how kind he had been. She'd been more than ready to condemn him as one of the men who at best ignored their daughters, at worst abused them. Even so, he'd been there and he'd helped her, and she wanted to thank him, even congratulate him, if he'd received news of the birth of his fourth child. She could distinctly remember the name on his tag: Üzeyir Seferihisar. Yes, she'd find him.

"We've got to get out of here!" Ayhan had shouted to Kete, only to see that she was too engrossed in her phone conversation to take notice of him or anything else. "She's talking to Belgin, she must be talking to Belgin," he thought. "Only a mother talking to her child would be so cut off from what was going on around her . . ."

It was Belgin who had said that motherhood isn't simply a matter of giving birth. They were standing in front of the window of her studio apartment on the twenty-seventh floor and she was talking about her mother's car accident. Almost as an aside she'd said, "Giving birth is one thing, being a mother is another . . ." So matter-of-factly, just like that, but Ayhan had been completely taken aback—well, just astonished, really. Motherhood was a sacred concept and all mothers were beyond reproach! Surely motherhood couldn't be expressed in dry clinical terms, biological or sociological: mothers were mothers, and they were there to offer unconditional love and protection, never judging, never criticizing and certainly never complaining. That's just the way it was. And that's why the only woman who ever loved a man unconditionally was his mother!

"She was the kind of woman who is completed only by a man, and I suppose she was happy with father and that they loved each other. I can only suppose they were happy together, since no one really knows what goes on between two people in a relationship, especially when it's been formalized by marriage, do they, Ayhan?" Belgin said.

"Father was away so often: I wonder if there were other women? Well, I'll never know. But, anyway, Jackie-Halide never recovered from the loss of father. Her generation didn't consider widows to be single women or allow them to have any personal needs, let alone sex."

Ayhan thought about his own mother, who had died of

uterine cancer at a relatively young age when he was still a boy, and reached the painful conclusion that he had never seen her as anything but his mother, and certainly not as a woman or as an individual. After that "mountain of a man," her husband, who, for all his restlessness and faults, had managed to bring home some money from time to time, had wasted away before their very eyes, dying within a few months, his unkempt and worn-out wife had become a widow. They said his father had died "because of cigarettes and drink." They'd washed the corpse and buried him. Years later, when Ayhan sadly remembered how difficult those times had been, how the burden on his mother's shoulders had grown still heavier, he'd never once considered his mother's sex life. It simply wouldn't have occurred to him to do so. As though his mother were made of flesh and blood, but genderless. If his father had been a widower, and had wished to bring home a young bride and new mother, he wouldn't have protested. He might not have been happy about it, but he wouldn't have had strong objections. What's more, his mother was widowed at only forty-four, three years older than Belgin was now . . . And he'd observed at firsthand that when Belgin cast aside her unwrinkled dresses and her professorial air, she was a passionate and responsive woman, that much at least he had learned.

When, a year after his father's death, relatives had helped his two older brothers migrate to Europe, one to France and one to Austria, and when a few years later their sister joined them as workers on the European minimum wage, the money they sent was enough to spare their long-suffering mother further toil in the cotton fields. She found further solace and peace of mind when Ayhan, the youngest of the three children still at home, was sent to Istanbul to study at Darüşşafaka. Whenever Ayhan came home for the summer, he'd regale his mother with tales of Istanbul, that magnificent city and its people, that huge city whose streets and buildings and shops were even grander than anything found in Adana. "*Abooo*, I hope my little Ayhan doesn't get lost there," his mother would fret while Ayhan laughed at her fears. He'd begin missing her even as he waved good-bye from the window of the bus that would take him back to Istanbul, and dreamed of the day when he could get his mother a flat with running water and central heating, the places he'd take her when she visited him in Istanbul . . . touring the island of Büyükada by phaeton or cruising up the Bosphorus by ferryboat . . .

"A tractor accident! My big brother was driving it. They say he was driving too fast and it tipped over . . . and he was crushed, dead. They say mother just couldn't handle it. That's what they said later, that it was too much for her. Well, what mother could be expected to handle the death of her son? But that didn't mean she had to suddenly get cancer. I mean, there's no connection is there, Belgin? You know all about those things. Anyway, mother died soon afterward, six months after my brother's accident. She seemed as healthy as can be, as healthy as can be expected for a woman with seven kids and a hard life that is, but the cancer had eaten away at her. Cancer of the womb. She'd had seven kids and perhaps as many miscarriages, maybe her womb just gave out? You know about cancer and oncology and all that stuff, Belgin. Tell me, was it fair for a woman who'd always been a mother first and foremost to be struck right in the womb? Would you believe they didn't even tell me until the summer, months after she'd been buried? They were afraid I'd be too upset all alone in Istanbul, and would give up my studies. Well, I didn't cry at all when I finally found out. Can you believe that? My heart seemed to be made of rock . . . like those rocks I talk to and chisel . . . It was only two years later, while I was visiting my brother in France, that I cried like a baby, thousands of miles from Adana . . . If we hadn't been so poor, she'd have gone to a doctor, she'd have had access to birth control. She might still be alive today. That's poverty for you, Belgin: death and loss!"

As snowflakes fell outside the window of that tiny studio flat in Manhattan, Belgin and Ayhan had held each other, embracing each other and the mothers that were no longer with them. Ayhan had always felt like an orphan, but that day, as he held Belgin tight in his arms, he appreciated for the first time what she had gone through growing up as an orphan.

"Of course, poverty's terrible, Ayhan," she'd murmured, nuzzling Ayhan's neck. "It's an embarrassment to mankind, there's no doubt about that. But even if I never went hungry, death and loss are things I've lived through too."

"You know what they say, dear: 'money can't buy happiness'! And some kinds of happiness are free however you slice it. Let me get you out of that dress and I'll show you what I mean . . ." he'd joked, lightening the mood. But the smile Belgin gave him was sadly unreceptive, and he decided to return to their conversation.

"'Money can't buy happiness'—I learned the truth of that cliché too, Belgin. I had enough money to buy all the books and CDs and magazines I wanted, enough to visit museums in Paris and Florence, enough to get a house and enough to send gifts to my nephews and nieces . . . And I also learned the truth of another old saw, about hearts of glass . . ." Ayhan said, trailing off. He looked out at the snowflakes drifting down from the gray sky outside the window, and imagined that each of them was a tiny glass heart . . . Belgin, too, looked out and saw only falling snow; then she looked at Ayhan and saw the wistful smile she knew so well, and that suited him so much. She summed up her thoughts on motherhood:

"Not all mothers are capable of motherhood, but maternal love can come from another woman, one who hasn't given birth to you. That's how I feel about Kete, and that's why I say she's my real mother."

"Ah, Ayhan, my boy Ayhan. There you were, standing right in front of me, and I didn't even see you!" Kete cried as she stood up and threw her arms around him. As hundreds of travelers streamed toward various exits throughout the international terminal of Atatürk Airport, Kete's conversation with Belgin had suddenly been cut off. "Godspeed, to you and to your baby, my little lamb . . ." Kete had whispered into the silent phone, pressing it against her heart. But when she heard her name, she lifted her eyes, saw Ayhan, and embraced him with all the unconditional love of a true mother. She wrapped her arms around him and touched his heart, his heart of glass.

24
IT ALL BEGAN WITH LOVE FOR A CITY

"I suppose this is it, Istanbul . . . So, it's here in Yeşilköy that I'm meant to bid you farewell, is it?" had been Architect Erol Argunsoy's first reaction upon hearing the announcement.

Now completely exhausted by the intense four-day program he'd endured in Barcelona, coupled with the stress of making a presentation, the futile quest for a new passport, the two-hour wait at the airport police station and the subsequent infuriating search for his luggage, which he'd discovered propped against the wall near a baggage carousel, Erol Argunsoy was definitely feeling the worse for wear, his high blood pressure adding to his discomfort by manifesting itself in the form of an aching head and throbbing temples. It was one of those days when everything seemed destined to go wrong. As a porter loaded his luggage, weighed down with half a dozen books, onto a metal trolley, he'd dodged into a duty-free shop to pick up a couple of bottles of French wine and a box of cigars for himself, as well as a carton of cigarettes for a distinguished friend. Instead of leaping into a taxi and heading straight home to Maçka, where he'd originally planned to take his medication and a leisurely cool bath, he went directly to a bar in the arrivals hall of the international terminal and ordered a nicely chilled glass of Sauvignon Blanc ("those delightful Sultaniye grapes, straight out of blessed Anatolia"). Lighting a cigar, he struck up conversation with the dear friend he'd last chatted with at the same bar five days earlier: Barman Baturcan.

Erol Argunsoy had always helped others. Whether through sitting on the board of NGOs set up to assist street children or battered women, articles penned in support of environmental groups, or through more informal channels, he was a firm believer in assisting others as a simple "neighborly act" of kindness and cooperation, and as a way by which to foster a spirit of community in an urban environment. He was, however, honest enough with himself and others to admit that the decision to

245

assist the Black Sea waiter who'd served him at a seafood restaurant in Kumkapı was not based entirely upon charitable considerations. Waiter Baturcan had immediately betrayed his village roots with his thick accent, as well as the disarmingly quirky sense of humor that shone through his efforts to studiously de-bone a sea bream. But it was Baturcan's hungry determination to become a real Istanbullu that had attracted Erol Argunsoy's attention, and brought him back to the restaurant time and again. To be honest—and that is what he tried to be with himself and those he loved—there was one thing about the good-looking waiter, known at the time as İlyas, that most set him apart from the other young men who had enjoyed the guidance of the elderly architect: he had never hidden the fact that he was gay. Erol Argunsoy did not wish to seem opportunistic, and had at first contented himself with enrolling Baturcan in a morning high school diploma equivalency course, as well as assisting him and a friend to move from Sirkeci to the district of their dreams, Cihangir. He also informed the young man that love for the city would come only through deep familiarity, for which reason he secured his companionship for many of the daily excursions he so enjoyed. And as he guided Baturcan through the city, he sought also to guide his thoughts and shape his perceptions, steering him toward a fuller appreciation of the peoples and cultures that he saw as an integral part of the buildings, streets, squares, coastlines, palaces, mosques, churches and quarters.

"Take the Maiden's Tower, Baturcan. Yes, it's a beautiful island lighthouse, standing guard at the entrance to the lower Bosphorus, but what makes it so special is the legends that have sprung up around it, the heroes and heroines that are our ancestors! And it doesn't matter if they were Roman or Greek or Ottoman—we should consider everyone who lived on these lands to be our ancestors, yours and mine. You won't find the Nordic homogeneity of Scandinavia here, or the southern tendency toward the extermination and Westernization of the locals and aborigines. Seed and blood have truly mixed here, Baturcan, here in the Tower of Babel that is Istanbul! You came to Istanbul a country boy, but if you understand and accept what I tell you, it is within your power—yes, yours too!—to become an Istanbullu!" he'd proclaim. But even as he preached the virtues of tolerance, he knew all too well what others so often said behind his back: "Erol wastes his time on foundations and civil initiatives, but I suppose he's a good person at heart!"

Paying no mind to his detractors, he'd forged ahead with his latest mission. And if Baturcan had been able to study, had learned how to become an Istanbullu, had found a better job as a barman, had moved from Sirkeci to Cihangir, and—most importantly of all—had been able to call his life his own, it was all due to none other than Erol Argunsoy. And, of course, it was none other than Erol Argunsoy who was absolutely smitten with the boy.

Glass of white wine in hand, Erol Argunsoy was now feeling much better. He was relaxed and enjoying the attentions of Baturcan; that is, until a dark handsome man in his forties entered and gave the barman a friendly nod . . . Erol had never been the jealous type, not when he was married to Belgin's aunt and not during the infrequent affairs he'd had during his second bachelorhood, but, perhaps due to his total infatuation with the barman, or possibly as the result of several taxing days, he found himself troubled. And more than a little annoyed. He studied the striking interloper: shiny black hair, cut short; dripping charisma; a trim, muscular body that no doubt drove the ladies wild. Simply dressed in jeans and white sports shoes, the man was probably older than he looked. "He's got to be at least forty," Erol Argunsoy reassured himself. The man looked familiar and had the easy assurance that usually comes with success. Erol decided he must be a TV actor, one of the "village types" so much in vogue these days. Then he considered the effect a brush with fame would have on Baturcan's impressionable young mind, and felt even more vexed than previously. An expert at masking his feelings, he sipped his chilled white wine and turned his attention to the match being shown on one of the four giant plasma screens. Perfectly aware that Erol had no interest in football, Barman Baturcan finished serving a beer and came over to nonchalantly mention that the stranger he'd saluted was a famous sculptor, the one whose nude statues had been vandalized in an Istanbul park. "Oh, really . . ." murmured or muttered Erol Argunsoy, seemingly uninterested even as he remembered that he'd seen that same sculptor interviewed on television, and been duly impressed by his views on aesthetics and morality in art. Sensing dissatisfaction, Barman Baturcan went on to masterfully insert the fact that if the sculptor seemed overexcited it was probably only because he was waiting for his girlfriend, due to arrive in from New York at any moment. He considered any additional information to be superfluous, and didn't mention the woman's name. In fact, he didn't say another word, was uncharacteristically un-chatty. He hadn't gone into details because he naturally had no idea of the effect the name of that woman would have had on her uncle, Erol Argunsoy. It was one of those moments, one of those missed opportunities. And Belgin could have written or phoned her Uncle to tell him exactly when she was arriving; she could have told him her lover's name and profession. But she, too, had chosen caution. Still guilty over having confided so many troubling details about her ex-husband, and determined to spare her uncle any more unnecessary worry this time around, she hadn't even told him Ayhan's name. A casual reference to "an academic, five years younger than me," had been all she'd said on the phone to Erol. Even so, he'd responded with, "Please, Belgin, whatever you do, go slowly! Let me meet him first, let me see him in the flesh and get a feel for him. Then you can decide what to do. Oh God, I hope he's not like the first one!" That's when Belgin had decided it might be best to return to Istanbul first, and arrange an introduction to Ayhan only later. She and Kete had thought a "surprise" might be best for all concerned, and had imagined the look on Uncle Erol's face when the happy couple showed up on his doorstep. It was one of those moments . . . like so many other moments in life, a moment full of plans and schemes, dreams and surprises. But as it happened, it turned out to be one of those moments in life when things just don't work out as expected.

Once he'd learned that the sculptor was waiting for a woman, a woman he loved, Erol Argunsoy relaxed, and was happy to send over a pack of Lucky Strikes. The man nodded his thanks, warm and sincere: Erol Argunsoy was completely won over, and Baturcan could now relax as well. The little episode had ended on a high note and all were enjoying the moment when the announcement came.

"I suppose this is it, Istanbul . . . So, it's here in Yeşilköy that I'm meant to bid you farewell, is it?" was Architect Erol Argunsoy's first reaction upon hearing the announcement, as he ignored the stabbing pain in his chest.

"A computer problem, huh!" he gasped, swallowing hard, as though something was stuck in his throat.

"I'm sure it's nothing serious," Baturcan comforted him, now directly opposite and smiling one of his most beautiful smiles.

"Ah, Baturcan, ah, dear boy . . . If only you knew how I'll miss your innocence!" Erol Argunsoy smiled back through a grimace. The pain in his chest had spread to his arm, and was now stealing round to his back. Struck by the sorrow in his mentor's eyes, Baturcan leaned over to whisper, "Or do you mean? . . . Could it be serious? God forbid, could it be a bomb?" The moment the words had left his mouth he clapped his hand over said mouth in horror.

"Ah, my boy, so innocent yet so knowing—you've understood, haven't you, that while a computer failure might cause the cancellation of flights, it's no cause to evacuate the airport?" Erol Argunsoy replied in a low voice, straining to maintain his composure. Most of the customers had already grown alarmed; some were rushing out of the bar without waiting for their change. With great difficulty, Erol Argunsoy turned to see the sculptor punching buttons on his cell phone as he waved good-bye to Baturcan and left the bar. He took another puff of his cigar and another sip of wine as he thought to himself, "Now that's a man in love. See how worried he is." But the stabbing pain in his left arm cut his thoughts short. The bar was now empty, and Baturcan watched, face drained of color, as a policeman and his dog began circling the premises. He turned toward Erol Argunsoy and their

249

eyes met. With a loving look, Erol whispered, "Don't worry . . . nothing will happen to you, to you or to Istanbul . . ." Baturcan, unable to hear what Erol was saying, came running over, brimming over with concern.

"Don't be afraid, Baturcan. You're young and Istanbul's strong! You'll both be fine . . . but I . . ."

"Don't talk like that, Erol *Bey*," Baturcan stammered, face clouded, eyes misty, a veritable storm front. "What would I do without you?" The despised tic in his shoulder kicked in, the tic that indicated that something was going wrong—the involuntary twitching that had been the cause of so much ridicule. Baturcan had just turned his head, partly to forget about his shoulder and partly to see what the bar manager and plainclothes policeman behind him were talking about, when he heard a loud thump followed almost immediately by a shout from the manager. When he turned to look, he saw Erol Argunsoy, who'd been sitting directly across from him, sprawled across the floor.

"Help, quick! He's got high blood pressure!" Baturcan sung out, unaware that the piercing cry ringing in his ears was coming out of his own mouth. A policeman raced over, squatted next to Erol Argunsoy, and began barking directions into his walkie-talkie: " . . . elderly male, might be a heart attack, possibly inebriated, Bar One in the arrivals hall!"

"Quick, call an ambulance. Do something! Save him!" screeched Baturcan, twitching uncontrollably as he alternately waved his arms and beat his thighs with his fists. "Has he had a heart attack? Get an ambulance, get a doctor, somebody save him for God's sake!"

"Calm down, we're doing everything we can. We've got an ambulance standing by, and a doctor . . . We'll have a medical team here the second we get permission to open the doors. Try to stay calm."

"But this is an emergency! Aren't there any doctors on call in the airport? Open the doors," Baturcan shouted, completely losing what control he had retained during his previously reported hysterics.

The policeman seemed to be berating whoever was on the other end of his walkie-talkie, but he'd moved to a far corner of the bar so this exchange wouldn't be heard. The dog sniffed at Erol Argunsoy's hand, and released a mournful yelp, then a pained howl, like a dirge.

"Open the doors, save him! He's an important man. There's nobody like him in all Istanbul! Save him!" cried Baturcan, now adding tears to his repetoire as he danced and twitched.

A second policeman knelt next to Erol Argunsoy's body and checked his pulse . . . "He's dead," he pronounced, voice flat.

An anguished cry broke from Baturcan's chest, climbed up to his lips, threw itself from this precipice, and then hurtled through the bar, reverberating off the walls and echoing as far away as the arrivals hall:

"No, Erol *Bey*, don't leave me, Erol *Bey*!"

25
LIFE AND TIMES AT THE AIRPORT

"Some kind of computer problem, huh . . ." had been Barman Baturcan's reaction when he heard the announcement, shrugging his shoulders and getting back to work. "They'll fix it soon enough. The technology here is as good as anywhere in the world. Life in the airport will be back to normal in no time." Baturcan smiled nonchalantly, but couldn't help noticing that Architect Erol Argunsoy, who'd been sipping a glass of white wine at the bar, appeared to be taking the news much more seriously. Once he finished with this customer, he'd go straight over.

The "normal life" in the airport that Baturcan had been thinking of was anything but normal, however. Although the flow of Barman Baturcan's own life had accelerated considerably since he and his family had exchanged the slow-moving village life in Trabzon for the hectic pace of Istanbul, he himself had continued on "eastern time" even as he worked punishing shifts at a taverna in Kumkapı. But as soon as he first set foot in the airport, the folk songs, fables, dirges and legends that had shaped him and his people for thousands of years were banished, seemed to evaporate in this strange new environment in which time seemed to have a character all its own, not time, but Time. Here at Atatürk Airport, the regulated, channeled flow of time surged relentlessly onward, heedless of the rhythms of the East, or the Middle East, or the Mediterranean, or the Orient. Time in the airport wasn't at all like time anywhere else in Turkey: it was exotic and Western and its own master: Time was a force to be reckoned with.

The airport was like a bell jar, a hermetically sealed environment with its own rules and laws. It was ultra-modern and unlike anything he'd ever seen before, located within Istanbul, but not at all of Istanbul—or anywhere else. It was completely independent of its neighboring districts and quarters, a living machine, regulated and digitalized. It was a self-contained, artificial city, one that produced its own air and water, one whose lifeblood flowed through pipes and along circuits. And contained within this mechanical monster—so masculine and terrifying and compelling—were tens of thousands of scurrying organisms, emotional creatures propelled by pain and joy, hopes and memories.

"Atatürk Airport is a giant metal whale! A huge machine that lives and breathes!" Barman Baturcan had once remarked about this intimidating mechanical city he so loved, throughout which 30,000 employees and 150,000 travelers circulate every day.

Within a smoothly functioning sterile environment, Atatürk Airport caters to its denizens: those messy creatures, those frantic beings, many of whom are at their best and at their worst, precisely here, in the airport, where all experience is heightened and emotionally strained: the coming and going, separating and reuniting, abandonment and abandoning, the setting off for new horizons and returning home after long absences, the waiting to go and the waiting to arrive and the waiters with no prospect of going anywhere at all; some running from loneliness and some running off to be alone; wanderers and drifters, movers and shakers, modern-day nomads and explorers; finders and seekers, exiles and refugees, buyers and sellers; peddlers of goods and traffickers in ideas. Here, in the airport, are you and I, and them, and us . . .

Architect Erol Argunsoy had been amused by Baturcan's description of Atatürk Airport as a "giant metal whale." He had his own ideas on the subject of the airport as a microcosm, and had been more than happy to share them with the young waiter, chief among them the startling notion of airports being a prototype for the cities of tomorrow, mega-cities that will come to have the artificial intelligence necessary to run themselves, independent of their residents. Baturcan had listened respectfully, almost as puzzled as he'd been when Erol *Bey* had proclaimed that it was not Man that had created cities, but cities that had created Man. "But!" he'd added (and there was always a "but"), "the cities I refer to were all Mediterranean cities, of course. Only the cities of the Mediterranean allowed man to flourish in abundance and to achieve his greatest potential." Baturcan privately wondered if

254

Man hadn't flourished in places like India and China as well, but thought it best not to contradict his mentor.

"Well," was what Baturcan had said, "I'm not quite sure what you mean, but one way Atatürk Airport is like a city is that I'm free to be myself here. I mean, I never have to worry about being gay . . . !"

"That's because we Istanbullu have failed to create a city where everyone is free," Erol Argunsoy had agreed, nodding wisely in appreciation of his pupil's keen insight even as he mistakenly assumed that Baturcan meant that life at the airport was less restrictive than that in the city it served. "We may be 'free' here in the airport, but keep in mind that the airport isn't a place where people live, it's a place they pass through, like a gate, the biggest gate in the walls surrounding Istanbul. But a gate can't be a city, no matter how big it is. Oh, and there's something else about the airport: Big Brother is everywhere, and he's probably keeping an eye on us from one of his cameras right now, Baturcan!"

Here, again, Baturcan didn't feel in complete agreement with Erol Argunsoy. For all its problems, Istanbul *had* allowed him to be free, freer than he'd dreamt possible. It was true that he had never gone hungry in his village. And yes, the air was fresh and the water was pure (and free), but there was no indoor plumbing. He'd been constantly surrounded by family, friends and neighbors, all of them ready to help at a moment's notice—but only insofar as you lived and thought and believed as they did. Girls were married off with or without their consent, and most young men, too, found that their spouses had been chosen by their families . . .

Baturcan had been ten when he realized he was attracted to other boys, but he was old enough to sense that if anyone else knew, he would be made to suffer for it. But he suffered nonetheless, assuring himself he was going to burn in hell, crying until dawn, shaking with fear. Things changed for the better after he moved to Istanbul with his family. Allowed out on the streets of that great city, he sensed that there were others like him, but they weren't afraid or suffering like him. He began telling himself,

"Allah wouldn't have created me like this if it was wrong," even if, in his heart of hearts, he wasn't yet convinced. It wasn't until his father died that he allowed himself his first sexual experience with a man. By then, he'd dropped out of high school and begun working as a waiter to help his family make ends meet. His increased responsibilities had opened the door to increased independence, and one night he was finally ready to go to a gay bar. It was on that night that he had learned what it was like to be in a room filled with other openly gay men, many of whom openly desired him. Baturcan had stumbled home at dawn, with a huge smile on his face . . .

Acceptance of his sexuality was only one step on the path that Baturcan, formerly known as İlyas, had chosen in his quest to become a "modern and urban" citizen of Turkey, the kind of person he identified as in possession of unlimited freedom. He was tired of shouldering the burden of the various identities and labels that were being foisted upon him: Muslim-Turk, homosexual, a Laz born in the Black Sea, a Middle Easterner with roots in both Central Asia and Europe. How wonderful it would be to cast all those labels aside, to become a true Istanbullu, cultured and sophisticated, rooted yet international! But it wasn't easy. And he'd been in Istanbul long enough to know that many so-called moderate, free-thinking Istanbullu would have dismissed him with, "He's not bad, for a homo!"

"If I hadn't met Erol *Bey*, I wouldn't have changed nearly as fast, and I wouldn't have been so happy about it . . ." he thought to himself as Erol Argunsoy toasted him from the other side of the bar. Although he sincerely admired and appreciated his mentor, he also felt strangely guilty, even now, and the tic in his shoulder became more pronounced. He'd been unable to reciprocate. Sexuality was something else, and everyone's skin had its own feel, its own touch, its own attraction—or lack thereof. Erol *Bey* had never openly pressured Baturcan, had contented himself with watching him and talking with him. But there had been someone else, a businessman who had sat on that same barstool some months ago, a handsome married man with two kids who had stolen Baturcan's heart. He was twenty years younger than Erol *Bey*, and the touch of his skin, well, it was something else, something impossible to explain or put into words. Baturcan knew he wasn't cheating, not by the strictest definition of the word, but that didn't stop him from feeling guilty, any more than it stopped him from seeing his new lover as often as possible.

After becoming a frequent visitor to that skyscraper studio apartment in Levent that the businessman kept available for his extramarital assignations, Baturcan had been told that gay men of Erol *Bey*'s generation, for all their culture and status, still seemed to consider it a sacred duty to hide their homosexuality. Lying in bed, they'd joked about recreating the Ottoman days of old, the days when love between men was commonplace and out in the open. They'd even gone so far as to imagine what it would have been like if one of them had been a sultan, the other one his favorite servant . . .

So it was with mixed feelings of guilt and loss that Baturcan wept as he accompanied the stretcher to the ambulance, too much in shock to look over in the direction of the deafening crash coming from the main exit. Just moments ago, wineglass in one hand, cigar in the other, Erol *Bey* had been tenderly smiling at him from across the bar . . .

26
MY BABY FROM BEBEK

"Ah Kete, mother Kete, if only you'd let me know. I'd have thrown you onto my trusty steed and brought you here myself!" roared Ayhan as he embraced Kete. Thrilled as she was to see Ayhan, Kete remembered the reproach darkening Belgin's last words, and was unsure how much to tell him.

"Dear boy, let me get a good look at you, my black-eyed boy!" Kete said, a tear—no less!— running down each cheek.

Ayhan assumed the tears were for him and was deeply touched. Just as they were beginning to talk about how much they'd both missed Belgin, a heartrending scream came from the bar Ayhan had been sitting in moments earlier. Startled by the anguished cry, they exchanged fearful glances.

"What's going on?" Kete asked, frowning, grabbing Ayhan's arm as he made to run back to the bar. "Hold on, Ayhan, you can't go running off every time an alarm goes off or someone screams. You've got a baby to think about now!"

Ayhan froze at first, telling himself he'd misheard Kete's words, so shocked that he forgot all about the bar. "What do you mean?" he asked. He thought for a moment. He scratched his chin. "Kete, what on earth are you talking about?" he asked again, even as Kete's sparkling, glistening eyes gave him his answer. "Belgin's pregnant?" Pleased as he was, he was unable to fight off a twinge of disappointment: Belgin hadn't told him herself. That's when Kete realized she'd blundered, and quickly backtracked with:

"Yes she is, dear boy. There were some things she had to sort out before she told you. Some things she's taken care of now. Everything's going to be all right," Kete said, rubbing Ayhan's back with one hand while she held a clenched hand to her own heart with the other.

Confused by her words, Ayhan asked, "Is there a problem? Is Belgin okay? What's going on? Why am I always the last to know?" Remembering his fruitless efforts to contact her, he then asked: "Is she okay? Her phone was busy . . ."

"Don't worry. Everything's all right now; she's fine and so is the baby . . . I'm telling you this for a reason . . . Trust me, just look at your Kete, with her hand on her heart, your blockhead Kete who's got things of her own to sort out. If I say everything's all right, it is! We're going to be happy, all of us are going to be happy!"

Ayhan knew something was up, but he'd also learned that Belgin and the baby were well, so he decided now was not the time to dwell on her failure to call him first upon arriving in Istanbul, or to given him the news of their child himself. It was something Belgin had decided to keep from him, and since Kete was the first person she'd spoken to, it was only natural that she'd been the first one to receive the news. Having dispelled his envy and his doubts, his thoughts returned to the situation at hand.

"Kete, we've got to get her out of her. There might be a bomb!" he said, not even noticing the blanketed body on the stretcher being carried past by two medical attendants. Had he looked over, he would also have seen a plainclothes policeman, a police dog and Barman Baturcan, silently weeping as he accompanied the stretcher.

"Considering all the orphans and abused children in the world, wouldn't it make more sense to adopt?" Belgin had asked him in London, where they'd spent five days together on the pretext of attending the "Turks: Journey of a Thousand Years" exhibition at the Royal Academy. They'd been examining an embroidered robe once worn by a sultan while, Ayhan spoke of the importance of a Western exhibition that implicitly recognized the Ottoman Empire as a great civilization at a time when the so-called "clash of civilizations" was all the rage. Belgin had cut him off, had suddenly interrupted him to bring up . . . babies. It's true that a tiny caftan stitched with silver-thread gilt was also on display before them, but it was clear that Belgin had been thinking about the subject of babies for some time, and had seized upon the princeling's finery as the first tenuous link. They'd only recently begun openly talking about starting a "new life" together in Istanbul, and Belgin's words at the exhibition had worried Ayhan. Any talk of children still pained him, as it reminded him of the daughter he'd lost, of Berfin, and of the guilt he still felt for having allowed a seven-year-old girl to travel on a plane alone. "Well then, we'll adopt a Kurdish girl and a Tibetan boy, Belgin!" he'd said, aware even as he spoke that he was smiling stupidly. Belgin had glanced at him to see if he was serious, and he'd avoided her eyes. And now, months later, having learned here, at Atatürk Airport, that Belgin was pregnant, Ayhan finally appreciated the significance of that moment. He'd avoided her eyes and he'd avoided the subject, and what he wondered now was: had Belgin actually wanted to have a child with him, even then? Had she been testing the waters, perhaps unknown even to herself? Had she dropped the subject only because he'd looked away, misunderstanding why he'd done so? Was it true that women often resort to indirect channels through which to express themselves? So, even then, Belgin had loved and trusted him enough to consider starting a family, and he'd been such an ass about it!

"I'm an idiot!" he mumbled into his chest. "Of course, she didn't tell me first. I've got to talk to her; I've got to tell her I understand now." But the network was still down.

"The phone's not working, Kete!" he grumbled. Kete knew how he felt. She knew what it had been like on September 11 when she'd tried to reach Belgin, knew what it had been like on the day of the August 17 earthquake, when she'd tried to reach Uncle Erol, Ayda and Yannis Hodja. But she'd kept her cool then, and she was calm now as she placed a hand on Ayhan's arm and said, "It'll be all right, Ayhan. We'll all get out of here safe and sound. Calm down. Everyone's luck turns one day, and it's Belgin's turn to know happiness. I feel it. It's high time fortune smiled on that girl!"

Ayhan smiled appreciatively at the slim, white-haired, dark-skinned little woman next to him, glanced down at her red slippers, took a deep breath and looked around him. The only obvious sign of panic was the growing crowd in front of the main exit, but the woman he loved and their child were on the other side of passport control, in possible danger and inaccessible by phone. To make matters worse, smoking was forbidden.

"If I can't trust Kete, who can I trust!" he comforted himself, just as a terrible crash resembling an explosion came from the direction of the exit doors.

27
TEMPERAMENTAL AS THE SOUTH WIND

"Perhaps it's my fault? Perhaps I demand the impossible from men, make them insecure and unhappy?" Belgin asked herself as she dried her hands and prepared once again to leave the all-too-familiar bathroom.

"Belgin, as long as you consider your father to be one of the men in your life, I'll feel like a pedophile! Strike him off your list and let me breathe easy!" Ayhan had said once, the usual smile on his face standing in marked contrast to the seriousness of his tone. "Look, it's great—thanks to you I've learned to accept that parents are people too, with sexual needs and problems of their own. But, Belgin, this son of a cotton picker still says that it's only normal to view your mother and your father as essentially non-sexual beings, or how else can you be expected to kiss them, hug them? And with a father as wonderful as yours, how can any man hope to compete, my cruel angel!"

"How can I be expected to cross my father off the list of men in my life? Is it really any different for men? Don't they all consider their mothers to be unattainable, the very pinnacle of womanliness?" Belgin now fretted in the airport bathroom. Lifting her head, she looked at her face in the mirror. Her hair was mussed, her curls quite limp, her lips cracked. Dark shadows had appeared under her eyes, which were bloodshot, and the lines at the corners of the eyes and her mouth seemed to announce, "We're here for good, and we're not going anywhere!" Belgin had been able to see herself in the mirror for only the past two years, and at the moment she wasn't certain it was altogether desirable to be able to do so. But her thoughts soon turned from her appearance to the questions that had so often run through her head:

"Little girls raised on fairy tales are taught to believe in magic and dreams, and that anything they desire may one day be theirs. But the role of provider and rescuer is always assigned to a boy or a man. And for centuries, little girls have been insidiously brainwashed through these fairy tales so they'll grow up to be stupid women who await a man to give them love, security and devotion. Even the smartest women fall under the spell of those tales, and if so many women die bitter and disappointed, it's because their Prince Charming never arrived and was never real to begin with. But the fact remains: a woman is only ever truly loved by one man, her father. No other man is capable of treating her with the same tenderness and honesty!"

Belgin closed her eyes and lightly rested her hands on the basin.

"Why doesn't someone say, 'Hey, girls of the twentieth century! There's no such thing! Have you ever seen a boy raised on Cinderella or Sleeping Beauty? All you've got in life is your father, and, if you're lucky, he at least will be the one man you meet who might resemble one of those storybook princes.

"'Girls, it's time you accepted that men are designed differently from us, that niceties and details simply pass them by. Adjust your expectations accordingly! We lost the battle thousands of years ago: it's a man's world, and we dress, behave, and live as they wish us to. No, you can't be expected to give up men, but stop it with the foolish fantasies, girls of the world, wherever you may be!'"

Leaning on the basin in the empty bathroom, Belgin closed her eyes for a moment and tried to clear her mind, even as various images flashed up before her mind's eye: the unloved daughters of Officer Üzeyir Seferihisar, the baby in her own womb, her father, her ex-husband Entek, and the man she now loved with all her heart, Ayhan. Belgin was besieged by images, worn out by memories and overwhelmed by competing emotions.

"I won't expect Ayhan to become a father. I won't hope for him to exceed his own capacities, abilities, and feelings. I won't demand that, in addition to being my lover, friend, and husband, he also take on the role of father of our child. It's time to leave fairy tales behind. But that doesn't mean I'll allow anyone to look down on you, to hurt you, to tear you to pieces. That much I can promise you, Lavanta!" she said, placing her hands on her belly.

"Baby Lavanta!" This time, she pronounced the name aloud. "Unlike me, you'll have a clear-headed mother who isn't afraid, and who doesn't wait for her fairy-tale prince. You'll have a mother who isn't afraid, who will fear nothing: not Istanbul, not love, and not men!"

The sound of a distant crash or a collision of some kind jolted Belgin from her thoughts. "An earthquake?" was her first reaction, as she leaned against the wall and looked for a safe place to crouch down. Then she decided it was probably a bomb, the bomb that had led to the suspension of all flights and delayed her re-entry into Istanbul.

"Ayhan? Kete? . . . What if the bomb went off near them!" Belgin hurried out of the bathroom and back into the spacious hall. She felt as though she'd been at the airport for weeks, walking its corridors, sitting on the toilet seat, staring into the mirror, wrestling with her memories and her fears. Even worse, it seemed now that she might never leave at all! So it was with a sense of déjà vu that she hurried out of the bathroom, the only difference being that this time she nearly collided with Üzeyir Seferihisar, the policeman, who'd been waiting just outside the door. Yes, there he was, still waiting.

28
GIVING ISTANBUL A COLONIC

"What's all this nonsense about 'couldn't there have been a nicer announcement,' oh those poor travelers and their shattered nerves . . . Tsk tsk tsk . . . Everyone's always complaining about something! It doesn't matter what we do, how hard we try, everyone hates the police. They all look down their noses at us!" Üzeyir Seferihisar had grumbled to himself when he heard the announcement in the police station at Atatürk Airport, where he'd been anxiously awaiting news of the imminent birth of his fourth child.

"But the second they're in trouble or worried about something, who do they all run to? The police. We're the ones who have to flush the filth out of the guts of this city. If it weren't for us, they'd be swimming in shit!"

Üzeyir Seferihisar had been on the force for eight years and he knew that Turkish intelligence had been pursuing various leads for weeks, all of which pointed to a planned terrorist attack upon the airport. The National Intelligence Organization and the police had been working together on the case for several months, resulting, during the past four days alone, in the arrest of ten suspects in Istanbul, Ankara, and Konya. The authorities had decided against releasing any information to the general public until the case was wrapped up. And on this particular day, security forces were on red alert: they'd received a series of tip-offs that terrorists were planning an attack on the airport, most likely by concealing explosives in their hand luggage; various security cameras had also captured the entry into the airport of three suspicious types through two different entrances. There was no concrete information as to the identity of the terrorists or their motives, but intelligence experts believed they conformed to the usual profile of "A cell based in either the West or the East who, for ideological reasons or as a result of their links to extremist religious groups, seeks to launch an attack upon the Republic of Turkey, the only secular, democratic, and Muslim state in the world."

Üzeyir Seferihisar prided himself on his calmness and sense of caution, two qualities instilled into him by his conservative, traditional upbringing in a small Anatolian city. Even knowing what he knew today, and as deeply annoyed as he was that today's red alert had coincided with the expected birth of his fourth child, he'd presented to the world his usual air of dignified self-possession. That was, until he'd had to deal with the patronizing attitude of that "old dandy" with the lost passport, Erol Argunsoy, the possibility of being demoted to a way-station out in deepest Anatolia and dozens of travelers alarmed by the announcement.

"Not only are you expected to put up with the bad breath of hundreds of people just to collect a pathetic salary, knowing full well that if you're killed in the line of duty no one will look after your family, you're also expected to provide 'service with a smile.' It's really too much! You'd think we were being handed trays of baklava all day long but were too stingy to share a drop of honey-syrup with the good citizens of our country! So we get blamed for clubbing left-wingers, for violating human rights, for failing to turn a blind eye to religious extremists . . . don't they understand how that makes us feel? We're good Muslims the same as everybody else, and we're not about to let our country go to hell or to be overrun by separatists, puppets, and traitors! If it weren't for us, who'd protect our country's honor?" he ranted silently, even as he checked his watch and wondered for the hundredth time if he was now the proud father of a man-child.

"Of all the times for the GSM networks to go down!" he grumbled. Officer Üzeyir Seferihisar was standing outside the door of the bathroom to which he had escorted a pregnant lady, determined to deliver her to her husband, safe and sound, at the first opportunity.

"Of all the rotten luck! Just when I thought I'd seen the back of Mr. Fancypants Erol Argunsoy, *this* happens! Sometimes I wonder why I do it. God, when I think of all I have to put up with: on the one hand, we're paid barely enough to get by—on the other hand, we've got to deal with every kind of lowlife scum, traitor, thief, rapist, molester, pimp and whore you can think of. And as if that weren't bad enough, you've got to put up with these guys with friends in high places who think they can get away with anything with one phone call. And worst of all, some of them can!"

The receiver in his hand crackled to life: Details of a "contingency plan" were provided, and the best wishes of Atatürk Airport Chief of Police Emir Araslan conveyed to all the officers on duty at that moment.

"At least he's different!" Üzeyir Seferihisar thought to himself, brightening somewhat. "Our chief is different. He knows how to treat people right. He might speak foreign languages and have all those years under his belt working in narcotics—and they say he even has an international pilot's license—but he doesn't lord it up over us. I've never even seen him raise his voice. You know, if I have a son, I think I'll name him Emir, after my chief."

As a colleague led a sniffer dog over toward the passport area, he shot Üzeyir a questioning look. Gesturing with his head to the bathroom door, "A pregnant lady got sick," he said. The other policeman nodded grimly as he marched off.

The "pregnant lady" had been in the toilet for longer than seemed necessary to Üzeyir, and he suddenly found his suspicions aroused. She didn't look like a terrorist, but he knew that these days anyone aged eighteen to thirty-five fit the general profile of "terrorist." He hesitantly tapped on the door and asked in a low voice, "Are you okay, ma'am. Do you need help?" But Belgin was too preoccupied to hear him.

"Working here is like working in Yozgat city, it's as least as big when you consider that there are 30,000 permanent employees here, along with 120,000 visitors every day. It's true Yozgat province has a population of about 600,000 if you count all the villages and districts, but 120,000 people, all kinds of people, at an airport!" the policeman thought to himself, impressed as always.

"Ma'am, are you okay? Do you want me to go get help?" he asked, knocking more forcefully this time. He was genuinely concerned, as he would be about any woman with child, but as a

269

professional on a "red alert" day it was also his job to be highly vigilant. And if the pregnant lady did turn out to be other than what she seemed, well, he'd take her out without a second glance at the tears in her eyes! For all his complaints about his job, he'd been fascinated since childhood with the uniform, and with the gun and power that came with it, something he never denied.

A deafening noise came from the duty free area and he also heard screams. The "pregnant lady" came rushing out of the toilet, and Police Officer Üzeyir Seferihisar's suspicions vanished when he observed that she'd instinctively placed her hands on her belly.

"Don't worry, ma'am, I'll get you out of here!" he announced, taking pleasure in the reassuring tone of his own voice as he simultaneously wondered whether his son been born yet . . .

29
TOO YOUNG TO DIE

"Fuck! Why does this shit always happen to me! I'm sick of it!" cried Tijen Derya, clenching her hands into such tight fists that her long, painted nails dug into her palms. When she heard the announcement, she was still searching for her missing cell phone, and had asked a series of airport officials if an expensive Nokia 611 had turned up, relating its features in some detail: "WAP, camera, Bluetooth, MP3 player, USB port . . ." In her rage and panic, there wasn't a trace of the image she'd cultivated over the past two years: the "level-headed, unruffled, cool, and powerful" executive assistant had been replaced by a fuming teenager.

"So what are we supposed to do now? Some hooligan decides to plant a bomb in the airport and we're supposed to just take it, get blasted to bits without so much as a word? God fucking damn it!" She automatically reached into her handbag for a cigarette, stopping herself when she remembered smoking was forbidden. "Fuck them all! Don't do this, don't do that, don't sleep with him, don't say that! How long am I supposed to put up with this? Do I have to wait until I'm in my forties, menopausal, and the butt of all sorts of dirty jokes made by horny teenagers—well, it's possible—before I can finally do what I want? See if I don't light up right here and now. Just try to stop me!"

"You smoke too much, sweetie. At your age, your breath should still smell like fresh milk. But it stinks, Tijen, honey. I think you ought to know," Mehmet Emin Entek had been telling her with increasing regularity. It only made her smoke more—to spite Entek, her mother, her father, annoying coworkers, her landlord, taxi drivers, and anyone else who tried to get in her way. When she was only five her mother had poked her in the back and declared with some exasperation, "The only way to get this one to do what you want is to tell her to do the opposite," and she'd been the same ever since. So much so that she took a perverse pride in criticism, even viewing it as an ill-defined personal triumph of some kind . . .

"Look, if you stop smoking that poison I'll get you a nice little car. Flame red or sea blue, what do you say?"

"I'll try honey, I've been planning to give it up anyway, you know . . ." Tijen had said. But what she'd really been thinking was, "Do you think you can buy me off with some cheap little car? You old fart, you, the famous businessman Mehmet Emin Entek! You've lost your touch, sweetie, you're on automatic pilot when it comes to getting girls . . . Sure, I'll smile and nod, but the market you're so fond of banging on about has its rules and laws. Those who accept those rules go out in the world to do battle; those who don't can just crawl back home. The market says: 1. Trying to "stand on your own two feet" doesn't cut it anymore. If you squander your youth and good looks trying to climb up the corporate ladder, you'll just end up a miserable old career woman and spinster. 2. If you've got a nice face and figure, play it up, even with cosmetic surgery if necessary, and go the movie, television, fashion, singer route. And don't forget to save up your pennies, cause whatever you get won't last long. 3. If you're not pretty enough for 2., use your wits and your youth to become an executive secretary, then concentrate on landing a rich husband. You've only got until about age thirty, thirty-five tops. That's the market, and that's how it works. Don't say I didn't warn you."

Having unsuccessfully fumbled through her handbag for a cigarette, Tijen considered, but thought better of, going back to the bathroom to look there. "As if I haven't got enough on my plate as it is in this fucking airport!"

"And I'll enroll you in a driving course. I can see you now in your cute little car, showing off in front of your friends and your mother . . ."

"Cute little car! Why don't you enroll me in kindergarten while you're at it? You're out of your mind, Entek . . . I know, I know, you think it's still the 1970s and that you're still young, but that's *your* problem darling, not mine . . . Times have changed and so have you. Girls these days aren't looking for a father figure, they're looking for a sugar daddy. That kind of thing only happens in

272

the movies, the movies our mothers were raised on, kindly old men marrying grateful young virgins. Girls today know exactly what's what, and down to the last detail. What you'll get me is a four-door metallic gray executive sedan! A six-cylinder BMW with a sunroof, CD player, leather seats, the works. That would set you back fifty or sixty thousand euros or so. Or, if you really want to try and drive a hard bargain, I might settle for a Honda Accord, also metallic gray, going on the Internet these days for about 60,000 lira. And I'll probably be dead by forty, so I want it now. Anyway, who cares about cars and things when you're that old? It's already too late."

"I'm trying to give them up, Entek," she would say aloud, "but not for a car, for you."

"How many times have I told you not to call me Entek. Stop it! At work and in the street it's Mehmet Emin *Bey*, but it's Mehmet Emin when we're alone, Tijen honey. Oh, and another thing, don't ever call me Memetti again!"

"Oh, for fuck's sake. Whatever you say, boss! All that nonsense about 'the only woman who ever called him Entek,' that ex-wife of his. I couldn't believe it when they told me to never even mention her, but I think I get it now. It's another scenario straight out of an old movie! A rich and handsome husband keeps cheating on his wife, but unlike the other women he's known, she's got balls enough to divorce him. Ta-da, end of Part One. Then fast-forward many years. The woman's gone off to another city, another continent, but the philanderer can't stop thinking about her, that woman, Belgin. That's it! Simple as that. Of course, that's not the way he tells it. According to him, she was a real ball-breaker, and conceited to boot. So, tell me, if the second version is true, why can't I mention her name? Why is he so touchy when he should be happy to be rid of her? But no, it's Belgin this and Belgin that: Belgin grew up in Bebek; Belgin went to Bosphorus University; Belgin lives in New York, loves opera, smells of lavender! I've had it with Belgin! Not that I blame her for ditching Entek—she had enough money to just walk away, after all. It's Entek who pisses me off. Don't you get it, she left you, divorced you, went off to start a new life. Get over it! And if your ego can't handle the facts, don't take it out on me, sweetie!"

Finally having located, in a side pocket, her nearly depleted stash of cigarettes, Tijen's face visibly relaxed as she stuck one in her mouth. While she favored Marlboro Lights, Entek was forever bringing her cartons of Eves and Davidoff Slims, brands he considered more feminine.

"I hate these long, thin ones! A smoke should be a smoke, not some clove-scented garbage or whatever, with flowers on it. It's just like him to try to change my brand, the same way he's trying to change everything about me, to mold me into someone I'm not: like that saying goes, 'bend the branch while it's still flexible.' Does he think he's going to turn me into his precious Belgin? Well, he can forget it—I'll never be one of those brainy, egghead, *entel* ladies . . . a professor or whatever she is.

"Belgin Gümüş. I can picture her now, and I haven't even seen a photograph. He claims he threw them all out, but I don't believe that for a second. He's got them locked away somewhere in his private cupboard or my name's not Tijen Derya. He says she's like the Turkish version of Catherine Deneuve mixed with Belgin Doruk. I didn't even know who the hell Deneuve was until I looked her up on the Internet. And as for Belgin Doruk, well, I've seen her in old movies on TV, a regular Snow White she was, a typical sweet, pie-eyed, virginal Turkish girl. And anyway, Catherine Deneuve looks like her only exposure to sex would have been a flasher in a raincoat, while Belgin Doruk could pop out ten brats and she'd still look like a virgin . . . Zero sex appeal, either of them."

Tijen pulled out a Zippo lighter inscribed with a scorpion.

"I'd have preferred one of those jeweled ones, with Swarovski crystals, but it's just like him to get me this one, and that only because I yelled at him for not remembering I'm a Scorpio. Just wait till we get married, sweetie. That's when we'll see who wears the pants. I'm like nothing you've ever seen, and if you think you can get rid of me, you've got another thing coming, Mr. Entek!"

"Madam, there's no smoking here! Please go to the smoking

lounge—it's right over there," a security guard barked.

"Sorry, I forgot," was Tijen's sour response, as she placed her lighter and unlit cigarette back into her handbag and muttered through clenched teeth:

"Fuck! Fuck you all! Like anyone ever follows rules in Turkey. I swear, one of these days I'm going to smoke a whole pack, right here, then I'll just pay the fine, whatever it is. These airport workers are too much. When I think of that woman in the bathroom . . ."

Increasingly distressed and increasingly in need of nicotine, Tijen gritted her teeth and promised herself a brighter future, with the prospect of marriage in only a year. At that moment, one of the passengers hurrying past bumped into her shoulder, hard.

"Hey! Watch it! What's the rush anyway?" she said, too preoccupied with the loss of her phone and her inability to smoke to pay much attention to the dozens of people racing for the exits. She looked up and saw that the THY plane from Moscow had landed fifteen minutes earlier.

"Damn it! He's probably given up on me by now. He'll make me pay for this by flirting with the new assistant or worse. Well, so be it, he's not getting rid of me so easy. I'd better get to a phone, though, the sooner the better."

Through the sliding glass panels of the arrivals hall stepped newly arrived passengers, many of whom quickly embraced waiting relatives and just as quickly headed for the exit. But Tijen remained oblivious to the low-key panic spreading through the airport.

"Well, this is the only way out, so I suppose if I stay here he's bound to see me," she thought. "He'll still be mad about the phone, but if I'm here to throw my arms around him he'll forgive me soon enough. He's such a sucker for that sort of thing."

Tijen found herself in the middle of a growing and increasingly unruly crowd, as passengers and the people waiting for them jostled and shoved, everyone eager to get out of the airport as quickly as possible.

"Hey! You're crushing me!" Tijen shouted, but nobody paid

any attention.

"There's no need for alarm. Proceed in an orderly fashion," warned a policeman, and, for the first time, and contrary to this order, Tijen got alarmed. She considered calling her mother to ask if there had been any news of a problem at the airport, but remembered she'd lost her phone. Again, she instinctively reached for a cigarette, and, again, she cursed the ban. Then, suddenly, it all became too much, and annoyance gave way to fear, an emotion Tijen was unusually adept at holding at bay. But these were unusual circumstances, and fear was soon joined by outright dread. For a moment she even had trouble breathing. It was almost like that long-ago day back home in Narenciye, a lower-middle class district of Antalya that she considered common and was embarrassed to live in, when her mother, angry over something she'd said, informed Tijen that her father was actually her stepfather, and not a blood relative at all. For some reason, even though she endlessly criticized her father, she'd been overcome by a sense of fear, rejection. Her mother had been scrubbing the floor, and she remembered the smell of bleach filling her nostrils and turning her stomach. She was thirteen at the time, longing for a life in a better neighborhood, smart clothes, holidays in Bodrum, all she could eat at Mystic Pizza, an occasional Big Mac, and, of course, the chance to see Istanbul. Her only reply was "Why didn't you find a better husband?" but she'd been badly shaken. She was the only dark-skinned member of the family, and now understood why. Still only a child, she'd been praying for a richer, more elegant, blonder world; it had now been revealed that the assumptions she'd made about her own despised world had been wrong. The smell of bleach—sodium hypochlorite— seemed to cling to her, her aversion to it so strong that she never again went to a swimming pool. That smell, the smell of rejection and fear of the future. Fear of the future! A whiff of bleach had struck Tijen as she was jostled by the crowd, and she was nauseated. A woman somewhere behind her spoke what she knew to be Russian, bringing her to her senses, reminding her of Mehmet Emin Entek, the man she was going to marry, the man who was

276

going to secure her future. "Nothing will happen to him—he always finds a way. He's got a plan B," she thought. But should her lover's resourcefulness be a source of pride to her, or did it mean that she would have to face all of the impending dangers on her own, totally alone? Actually, she knew the answer to that question, but she was too young and too determined to be honest with herself. "But surely he wouldn't just leave me here . . . I mean more to him than that," she thought, swallowing hard as she was whacked by a bag being trundled along by an overweight tourist.

"Fuck you, asshole! Watch where you're going!"

That's when Tijen noticed the growing numbers of uniformed policemen and their sniffer dogs, which could only mean a bomb. Dogs and bombs and the smell of bleach. Danger and the urge to flee; Entek, and the need to wait; Entek, and her whole future. A police dog came directly up to her, sniffing, wet nose touching her bare leg. "Hey, get off me!" she screamed. A young policeman restrained the dog and gave her a reassuring wink, but Tijen had had enough. Turning toward the flashing exit sign, she ran for her life, and couldn't have cared less at that moment about Entek, her sneering mother, her stepfather, her lost phone, or anything else. Getting out of the airport was the only thing that mattered.

Tijen wasn't the only one panicking at that moment: the swelling crowd in front of the double sliding glass doors shoved and pushed, surging forward a few steps and back a few more. Policemen shouted out for calm and spoke into their wireless receivers, asking passengers to form a line and requesting backup. "What are you waiting for, open the other doors," someone shouted first in Turkish, then in English. There were also cries for help, screams, curses, and shouting. But the policemen hadn't received official orders, and were more concerned with ensuring no one sneaked *in* than with getting everyone out. Bureaucracy, a faulty chain of command, group hysteria, general panic, paranoia fuelled by international terrorism, a heatwave, the stress of travel, and a sense of claustrophobia: all combined to create fertile ground for a disaster. Tijen Derya was one of the people now jammed into the inner doorway.

"Hey, I can't move. Come on, keep moving! Look, I'm stuck!"

"We're all stuck, idiot!" someone shouted. Then other cries rose up:

"Help! I've got a bad heart!"

"Please, help me!"

"My child can't breathe!"

"Is this it? Am I going to die here in a doorway?" Tijen thought. "Fuck! Is this any way to go? I haven't even begun to live yet. This can't be happening . . ."

With a fear-induced spurt of adrenalin, she thrashed even harder, but it did no good, her legs growing even more entangled, her left ankle now twisted and smarting.

Several ambulances pulled up in front of the terminal as the elderly woman next to Tijen fainted and slumped against her right arm.

"I don't want to die," she bawled, unaware of the mascara now running down her cheeks. "I want to live, I want to be Mrs. Tijen Entek . . ."

A woman just in front of Tijen screamed that her leg had been broken just as permission came to open a second set of doors. But the doors could no longer withstand the pressure, and several large panes of thick glass came crashing down onto the people below. From the crashing impact, those in the vicinity assumed a bomb had exploded, with many of them diving to the ground, forearms held up to protect their faces. Tijen was in shock, too shocked to realize that a large piece of glass had bounced off the back of her head. It had all happened so quickly that she also hadn't even noticed that lying among the shards of shattered glass littering the floor was most of her right arm. Nor had she yet looked down to see the blood, her own blood, spurting out of the stump of her arm.

"If I get out of here alive, I think I'll change my name," she was thinking. "I've never liked 'Tijen.' Özlem would be nice. Özlem Entek! And I *will* get out of this alive! I haven't come this far for nothing, not after all that dieting, all that work . . . I even gave up Big Macs! I'm too young to die!" she moaned as the burning sensation spread throughout her body, and she collapsed in upon herself, everything going dark.

Albeit not before she finally noticed her severed arm.

30
FALSE WORLD, FALSE ISTANBUL

"In the name of Allah! What's going on?" bathroom attendant Hasret Sefertaş muttered to herself when she heard the announcement. "Has some lowlife tossed a bomb into a garbage bin or what? Was it written on my forehead that I'm to die here in cruel Istanbul, as a janitor? Or is Allah punishing me for having taken Tijen's phone? No, that can't be it, God forbid such a thing! I've never stolen anything in my life, and God's my witness. If you go thieving around in this life, you're sure to roast in the afterlife. But I didn't steal that hussy's phone anyway, just wanted to teach her a lesson. And I dropped it off at lost and found. As God is my witness, that's all I meant, I swear it . . . And anyway, the bitch didn't buy that phone through honest work. No, it was someone else's hard work that got it for her . . . That girl's enough to make you sin in broad daylight . . . Well, you won't catch me doing anything like that again . . ."

After dropping off Tijen Derya's phone, Hasret had been planning to go to the changing rooms in the basement, where she'd take off her blue uniform and put on an ankle-length black skirt, short-sleeved flowered shirt, and low-heeled, stubby white shoes, before loosely knotting a hand-embroidered scarf with traditional pinking under her chin and waiting for the service bus that would take her to Bahçelievler. The announcement made her stop dead in her tracks, uncertain whether it was best to proceed with her original plan or to head for the nearest exit, uniform and all, instead.

"Is it really some computer problem like they say, or is it a bomb?" she wondered, unable to make a decision. She could almost hear her husband criticizing her as usual for her indecisiveness, and said aloud, "That's enough out of you! This could be a matter of life and death!

"And if I do die here, they'll report that 'bathroom attendant H.S. was killed at the airport.' Something like, 'she was a bathroom attendant, but she was a good woman'! Who knows how many times I've cleaned up after them, and those ungrateful reporters won't even bother to write my name out in the paper. Or worse, they'll use the ugly photo on my employee ID! Not only will my poor girls be broken up over losing their mother, they'll be embarrassed at everyone knowing I was a toilet scrubber. I happen to know my younger one tells her school friends only that 'Mom works at the airport.' And if I do die, what'll happen to the kids. That no-account husband of mine is too lazy to look after them. He'll go off to his village in Kayseri, boast about his grand house back in Istanbul so he can trap some poor barelegged girl into marrying him. I swear that's what he'll do! Ah, ah, is that any way to treat me! Did you ever stop to think who bought the flat you live in, the one you keep running down? It was me, cleaning up after other people's shit, so I could make the monthly payments. But you couldn't care less, could you? No, you'll be out and about, having the time of your life, trying to impress that girl with trips to Süleymaniye Mosque, and the Bosphorus, and the Maiden's Tower. Have you ever taken me anywhere? Just one trip to Sultanahmet Mosque or Hagia Sophia? No! And your young bride will pull my girl out of school, make her clean up after you and cook your meals. Well, you better watch your step, you whore. Once you marry him, you'll see what I have to put up. You should have seen him when he was young, keeping me up all night, wrapping those strong arms of his around me and shaking me like a rag doll. Ah, those were the days! We were still back in the village then, all that clean air and fresh water, living with my mom and dad . . . Back before we moved to cruel Istanbul . . ."

In the two years Hasret Sefertaş had been working at the airport, she'd never seen so many police dogs and security officials, the exit lights had never flashed as they were doing now, and no passengers had rushed to the doors in panic. The sight made her even more indecisive, and not a little afraid.

"If I go straight out, my head will be bare! How can I do that? But if I go downstairs to change my clothes, I might get blown up, and my husband will marry some snot-nosed girl and my daughter won't finish school. What am I supposed to do?"

The flashing lights brought to mind ambulances, firefighters, and police cars, and something told Hasret to head directly for the exits, bareheaded or not. Without even being aware of it, she'd been taking several steps toward the one open door, then several more steps in the opposite direction, toward the stairs. In the time she'd been aimlessly wandering, she could have changed out of her uniform, but, like so many around her, she was in a state of semi-shock, and becoming increasingly panicked the more the policemen shouted for calm and order. Among the milling throng, which reminded her of a crowd surging through the turnstiles at a football match, she thought she caught a glimpse of Tijen Derya. "Oh no," she cried, "It's her. God's punishing you for taking her phone!" But she was drawn closer and closer to the double glass doors, as though hypnotized by the flailing bodies trying to force themselves through an impossibly narrow space.

"Allah, I swear if I get out of this alive, I'll never complain again. And I won't wait for my husband to show me around or my girls to grow up. I'll just set out one day and see what this city has to offer. And once my younger girl's finished school, found a job, married, and I'm ready to retire, I'm going straight back to the village. Please Lord, let me die and be buried in my own village!"

A tall, well-dressed man in expensive dark sunglasses wheeled a trolley past Hasret and toward the second set of exit doors, which remained closed. After showing a policeman the piece of paper in his hand, he was permitted to leave.

"Ah, Allah, you're not helping out the rich even at a time like this, are you?" were the words that slipped out of Hasret's mouth, forcing her to instantly repent for having questioned the will of the Divine. At about the same moment, a police dog pressed his wet nose against Hasret's hand and there was a terrific crash as the glass doors collapsed on top of the crowd stuck in the doorway. Hasret opened her mouth but no sound came out. The cries and screams of the wounded and maimed ringing in her eyes, she looked on, transfixed, as though watching a reality program or footage from Baghdad, until she identified a young girl, blood spattered across her short skirt and legs, arm severed above the elbow, more blood gushing from the stump, and still more seeping from the severed arm on the floor. The girl slowly looked down at what was left of her arm, then at the floor, before her knees buckled and she slumped over onto several other wounded people lying on the floor. That's when Hasret came to her senses, suddenly became aware once again of where she was and what was happening.

"My God! That really is Tijen! Oh, the poor thing!" she shouted. The second set of exit doors was now opened, and a team of medics rushed in to treat the wounded.

"Run, quick, help her!" cried Hasret, who was now at Tijen's side, and who followed as the medics bore her out on a stretcher, a tourniquet on her arm and the severed limb packed in ice. One of the medics turned to Hasret and asked, "Are you a relative?"

"That's Tijen Derya. She works at Entek, Inc. She's from Antalya," answered Hasret, in one breath. The medic took the response as an answer in the affirmative, and the next thing she knew, Hasret was boarding the ambulance and on her way to the hospital.

In the back of the ambulance, sirens screaming, lights flashing, a medical team frantically worked to stabilize the patient by inserting a catheter into a vein in her healthy arm. An intravenous drip infusion was desperately needed to expand her intravascular volume. They were monitoring her blood pressure and pulse, of course, and Hasret heard frequent references to something called "hypovolemic shock." All thoughts of her head scarf, husband, and toilet-scrubbing job were swept from her mind. Hasret stared at Tijen, beating her knees and wailing, "Please don't let her die, Allah. She's so young and knows so little. It's those TV shows making everyone so greedy. She hasn't even lived yet . . . In the name of her father and mother, forgive her Allah!"

As a medic handed her a tissue to wipe her tears, Hasret asked, "She won't die, will she, brother?" With a long sigh, the medic replied, "Well, if she recovers from the shock induced by loss of blood . . . There's reason for hope." Then he added, "Are you two very close?" Sirens screaming in the background, her blue uniformed smeared with blood, tears streaming down her face, Hasret managed to choke out, "Yeah, you bet we're close. Here, in cruel Istanbul, you could say Tijen and me were sisters!"

31
A CAPTAIN OF INDUSTRY JUMPS SHIP

"Goddamn it, that's all I need! This isn't exactly my lucky day. Everything started going wrong when I couldn't get through to that idiot Tijen!" Mehmet Emin Entek had mumbled when he heard the announcement. "Just imagine what'll happen when they start evacuating. Rubbing shoulders with all those sweaty people. Even the ones who've migrated to Europe don't bother washing. They stink!" he continued, remembering his brief encounter moments earlier with the Berlin-based worker Sabriye Bektaş.

"If Tijen had answered, I'd be long gone by now. She's probably lost her phone again. Actually, it was mine, I'm the one who got it for her!"

At the time of the announcement, Mehmet Emin Entek had been in one of the duty-free shops in the baggage claim area of the arrivals hall, where he'd already selected a jar of "next generation anti-aging serum" eye cream for himself and a tube of corrective cosmetics concealer for Tijen ("twenty-four, and still pimply!"), as well as a couple of boxes of cigars and two one-liter bottles of whiskey. He'd been looking for a "classy" brand of cigarettes, something feminine and elegant, and was standing in front of a stack of Davidoff Classic Slims when news of the computer system failure first came to his attention. Since he was about to leave the airport in any case, he felt no real sense of alarm; but when he noticed that some of the customers were abandoning their shopping baskets and racing directly for the exits, he began to consider the possibility of something serious. At the prospect of danger, he decided to abandon the fruitless game of phone tag with Tijen in favor of calling his private chauffeur. It wouldn't do to be indecisive, and he had spoiled that girl, she who was so obviously eager to "jump up a class" in record time. Yes, there was no doubt that he'd spoiled her, and he'd even begun to suspect that he'd been less than successful in "grooming her into something of worth";

287

that suspicion brought with it a nagging doubt concerning his own powers, and forced him to confront the fact that he wasn't getting any younger. He'd become more sensitive on the subject of age, and found himself annoyed by even joking references to "young guns" and "old coots" and the very word "Viagra." Out would come one of his well-polished maxims: "A young man is just an unripe version of a mature man, that's all."

His chauffeur answered on the first ring, and informed his master that the car was waiting outside, as arranged by Tijen, who had wanted to ensure that it was ready and waiting at least two hours before Entek's flight was scheduled to land. He added that he had been unable to reach Tijen *Hanım*, but had noticed an unusual number of police cars and ambulances waiting outside the airport, for which reason he would be so bold as to suggest that Mehmet *Bey* and Tijen *Hanım* proceed to the vehicle as quickly as possible.

Mehmet Emin Entek decided to review his situation one last time before making a final decision. Strolling nonchalantly over to the checkout counter, he extended a fistful of euros at the young woman at the cash register:

"Some idiot's probably spotted an unattended bag and reported a bomb. Security's so tight these days," he thought to himself. "Would the terrorists really do something that stupid . . . ?" The word "terrorist" reminded him of the assassination of Halit Ziya Gümüş, and his thoughts turned infuriatingly to his daughter Belgin. "She never used my surname, not even once!" he said aloud, allowing the cashier to inspect his passport, a "green" one technically allocated only to high-ranking bureaucrats and their families. As she rang up his purchases, the cashier turned to a colleague and asked when they would be allowed to leave. Entek was annoyed that she hadn't given him or his passport so much as a second glance. He sensed that he'd been getting less attention in recent years, and it bothered him more than he'd admit.

"Don't worry, they'll soon announce that everything is under control. You're in good hands here at the airport," proclaimed this major partner in Entek, Inc., using a low voice that was both authoritative and soothing, and that, combined with a rakish charm and a glint in his eye, was designed to impress the impressionable.

The look he turned upon the young cashier was that of a man who was impish, dashing, and energetic: prepared for a fling at a moment's notice, a bit of a prankster yet possessed of an old-fashioned courtliness, able to keep up with and appreciate the changing times, not to mention thoroughly entertaining to boot! This last quality was of the utmost importance, and he was frequently heard to emphasize its significance to his young male employees, the suggestion being that he himself was a master of the art.

Even as he puffed himself up with pride over his little performance in the duty-free shop, he suddenly remembered that dry pronouncement of Belgin's uncle: "I hope this groom of ours realizes that a man who becomes known for clownish womanizing in his youth will be known solely as a buffoon in his later years!" Yes, that's what he'd said, that great protector of the environment and champion of Turkish architecture, Master Erol Argunsoy!

"But just look at him now, in his later years! They say he's a faggot!" Entek spouted to himself. No, he wasn't at all like the other men his age, nearly all of them hen-pecked middle-aged types. Young girls still adored him; he'd had two successful marriages and was about to become engaged with someone under twenty-five. After all, any woman over thirty was certain to have been betrayed by a man at least once, and would therefore be loaded with baggage, grim and suspicious, and immune to his romantic charms. "Always choose a woman under thirty," was another staple of the freely offered advice he gave to the men in his office.

But the cashier appeared unimpressed as she counted out his change, placed his purchases into a bag, stapled on a receipt, and glanced right past him to see who was next in line. As though he were just any ordinary customer, any ordinary man. Mehmet Emin Entek told himself that the girl had quite simply become unhinged by the extraordinary events now taking place at the airport, but still feeling the need to prove himself, he glanced at the nametag on the cashier's chest, deepened his voice, and casually asked:

"In the business world, we often encounter unknown and unexpected risks. It gets the blood flowing, the adrenaline too, and forces us to draw on all our powers of resourcefulness. It also heightens whatever beauty we see, Sinem *Hanım*!"

Hearing her name, the woman raised her head and looked directly at Mehmet Emin Entek for the first time. Apprehension could be read in her large green eyes, but other than that they contained not a single emotion: nothing. In fact, they didn't even register having seen Entek.

"Excuse me, were you talking to me?" she asked politely. Without waiting for a response, she turned to a young male colleague and said, "Why don't they let us leave *now* . . ."

"I'm not old enough to be looked right through!" Entek kept up his muttering as he stormed out of the shop. "I still look at least a full decade younger than I really am!" He looked around for a porter to relieve him of his laptop, Samsonite bag, and now the shopping bags dangling from his left hand, but there were none to be seen. Having to carry his own luggage was yet another insult added to the injuries of this long day, yet he strode determinedly over to the line of metal trolleys, chained one to the other, and handed the attendant a five euro note with a magnanimous flourish, signaling "keep the change." Inwardly, though, he fumed over the fact that the trolleys weren't complementary as they were in nearly all other airports throughout the world. He noted the growing number of sniffer dogs, pacing security guards, and policemen, but it was his unsatisfactory encounter with the cashier that was causing his stomach to burn. He decided to take one of his antacid tablets the moment he was outside, but had to wait while a dog nosed his baggage.

Pushing the trolley, he discovered that what he had taken for a handle was, in fact, a braking device, which led him to wonder if the cleverly designed trolley was produced in Turkey and, if so, how much profit it generated. Normally, such thoughts lifted his spirits, but today, as he pushed his own luggage, alone, Mehmet

Emin Entek was uncharacteristically dejected.

"Just look at this! How did this happen to me? I won't be made a fool of!" he said to himself. He was depressed now, feeling that dreaded sense of despair descend; the feeling that usually lurked only on the fringes, somewhere in the shadows, had waylaid him. It was something he feared as much as failure, a deep sense of desolation, a black cloud that swept in, leaving him enervated and listless for days. He'd suffered it—whatever *it* was— since childhood, on some days so badly that he couldn't even go to school. While his mother had shrugged it off, certain nothing could be seriously wrong with her little darling, there was another woman much later in his life who'd suggested therapy. "Perhaps that's why you're so obsessed with success, Entek," Belgin had said. "Perhaps you might be compensating for something?" It was classic Belgin, so open, so understanding! He'd snapped, "I see you've moved on from genetics to psychology!"

"They were all on salary," he now said sadly to himself. "That includes Tijen, and all the other girls I've gone out with, or even married. When we met, I was paying their salaries and they were all taking orders from their boss. All but Belgin!"

As he passed out of customs and through the large sliding glass doors into the arrivals hall, he felt even worse when he saw no one was there to meet him. His eyes searched in vain for Tijen, but what he did see was something he'd never come across before: the hall seemed deserted except for a huge panicked crowd in front of the only exit opening out onto the parking area, mainly reserved for taxis and shuttle buses. Only a few people sat on the metal benches inside, and they were obviously restlessly awaiting the arrival of their overseas visitors or families. There were no lines in front of the Avis, Hertz, and Budget car rental agencies, and none in front of the currency exchange bureau, the banks or the hotel reservation desk. Mehmet Emin Entek clearly understood for the first time the gravity of the situation, and called his chauffeur once again. There was a strange beeping sound, and he surmised that the telecommunications network was down as well.

"Or have they really planted a bomb here at this brand-new

airport?" he thought. "This is the work of the enemies of a liberal economy, the conservative opponents of the EU, the so-called nationalists! It's probably someone like that idiot uncle of Belgin's, Erol Argunsoy, pining for the good old days of the Ottoman Empire. Well if a bomb does go off, that's the end of the economy, of our prestige in Moscow, of our contracts and our tourism sector. Goddamn you all! They should have thrown the lot of you out of the country!"

He was startled by someone right next to him shouting, "Don't panic! There's no cause for alarm!" It was one of the security officials roaming the hall with a walkie-talkie. The rush of bodies to the exit reminded him of a modern ballet, a huge production, a frenzied interpretation of the bustle of airport life. Mehmet Emin Entek, known for thinking only of business, couldn't help but imagine how pleased Belgin would have been to hear how his thoughts had turned to art and culture.

"Please, remain calm. We'll be opening the other doors shortly!" rang out the shout of a policeman. But it was as though no one heard him. Further along, Mehmet Emin Entek noticed a dark, handsome young man impatiently punching buttons on his cell phone. "I bet he's trying to reach a woman as well!" he said to himself, smiling ruefully. But the smile faded from his lips as he considered how much younger the man was than himself. The man had looked familiar, but he couldn't quite place him. An actor? A journalist. Then the same dark man came eye-to-eye with a woman sitting on a metal bench and Entek forgot everything for a moment. He was stunned, all his attention now on the calm, dignified, middle-aged woman, who herself was entirely focused upon whomever it was she was speaking to on the phone. On her feet, she wore red leather slippers.

"Kete?" Mehmet Emin Entek whispered, for no one's benefit. Could it be her? Kete, who he hadn't seen for so many years? Belgin's Kete. What could she be doing here, and all alone? More importantly, who could she be waiting for? When his eyes met Kete's, she stiffened, ended her conversation, and fixing him an icy look she slowly mouthed a single word:

"Phony!"

Mehmet Emin Entek felt like he'd been slapped full across the face, a face momentarily drained of color. He was about to go up to her and give her a piece of his mind when something totally unexpected happened: Kete stood up and looked directly and unblinkingly into the face of the man standing directly in front of her.

Dismissed and defeated, Mehmet Emin Entek gritted his teeth as he turned his back on Kete and pushed his metal trolley toward the exit. "It's all that idiot Tijen's fault," he said through clenched teeth. His face had gone from white to purple. "Kete saw me on my own. All alone!"

The crowd in front of the exit had grown larger and the angry shouting louder. Mehmet Emin Entek had no intention of joining the milling throng—as though he were just another newly arrived passenger! A strategic thinker, ever ready and able to turn misfortune to best advantage, he began plotting more attractive alternatives to what appeared to be the single available way out, even as yells turned to cries of pain. But for all his composure, Entek had been deeply rattled by Kete, his own mood swings and the necessity of dealing all alone with the extraordinary circumstances of his arrival. The thought of Kete telling Belgin that she had seen him completely unaccompanied, and pushing his own trolley, also disturbed him. He decided right then and there that if he escaped unscathed he would marry Tijen, idiot or not. But first, he must escape. Taking a pair of black Gucci sunglasses out of his breast pocket, he put them on. Then he began waving the green passport he held in his left hand as he strode toward the second, as yet unopened, pair of sliding doors.

"Open that door, son!" he commanded the police officer stationed in front of the doors. The policeman hesitated, but decided it would be too risky to confront the well-dressed, middle-aged man, who was at worst some rich guy trying to bluff his way out, but might as easily have well-connected friends. Were he to antagonize this man, he could find himself demoted to a rural station with no way to look after his family. But if he opened the doors without first getting the "okay" from his superiors, he might face the same fate. He opened the doors, allowing Mehmet Emin Entek to pass through them with a triumphant look, then quickly relocked them. Making his way past the line of waiting ambulances, shuttle buses and police cars, Mehmet Emin Entek was unable to locate or telephone his chauffeur, and decided to hail a taxi. The driver at the front of the line, a short, well-set man with a two-day beard, snapped to attention, and with surprising deftness grabbed the trolley, opened the passenger door to his vehicle, and ushered his fare inside. As he loaded the man's luggage into the baggage compartment, decorated with a "King of the Road" decal, he speculated on the rank and identity of this person who had managed to stroll right out of the airport, every hair in place. Safely inside the taxi, something occurred to Mehmet Emin Entek for the first time that day, a painfully obvious thought that sent him reeling: "Belgin's in there! My God, Belgin's in the airport, and there's a bomb!"

32
RINDA MIN ISTANBUL*

"Hey, blessed Istanbul! The last thing you needed was some disaster at the airport, here in your little corner of paradise!" muttered Hamo the driver, turning the ignition of his Hyundai Accent taxi. Like most Istanbul taxi drivers, he was an expert at instantly sizing up in the rearview mirror anyone who got into his vehicle, and considered himself an unfailing judge of character. "Who knows how many will die, how many will go hungry because of this?" was the rhetorical question he posed to the middle-aged man in the back seat, having quickly taken in the wavy silver hair, expensive watch and well-manicured nails. Hoping to come eye to eye with his man, whose assured manner indicated he was accustomed to giving orders, and who, as the only person to emerge from the mob gathered in front of the single exit, might have inside information on what exactly was happening inside, Hamo ventured, "We need tourists to come here if we expect to support our families." But there was no response. Hamo glanced in the rearview mirror again and saw that his fare was miles away, left hand cupping his chin, index finger pressed against his mouth. Driver Hamo Türk was as anxious as anyone to learn what was really behind the mysterious announcement, and had been speculating busily with the other drivers at the airport taxi stand, as well as with passengers emerging from the airport and the friends and relatives waiting outside. As he'd tossed the expensive leather suitcase with the Moscow-Istanbul tags into his trunk, he'd expected his latest customer to shed some light on the strange event.

"Look, brother—police cars, ambulances, fire trucks everywhere. Something's up, but I can't quite put my finger on it yet!" he tried again. But Mehmet Emin Entek was thinking, and didn't even raise his head to acknowledge this patter. Had he taken a

---

* "My Beautiful Istanbul" (Kurdish)

look, he would have seen a stocky middle-aged man of medium height, with auburn hair, brown skin, and weary bloodshot eyes. He may even have noted the contrast between the rough tone of the driver's accented Turkish and the gentle expression in his mossy-green eyes. But he paid no attention, the eyes behind his dark Gucci glasses neither looking nor seeing, oblivious as usual to anything outside of his own personal concerns.

"I've been living in Istanbul for going on thirty years now, and have been a taxi driver for just about as long, but I've never seen anything like the heavy security they've got at the airport now. And if it isn't a bomb of some kind my name's not Hamo!" added the driver as he gently braked. The flow of traffic just outside the arrivals terminal had slowed to a crawl.

"Look at that! Won't even let us onto the road! *Xwedê qahar û xezeba xwe bike*!* Istanbul's gone right down the drain, filled up with all the wrong sorts of people. Old Istanbul's disappeared without a trace, and so have the real Istanbullu . . . Look's like we'll be here for a while . . ." he grumbled, reaching for a cigarette but thinking better of it when he considered that the hotshot in the back seat might object. His act of self-denial and gentle braking had left Hamo Türk feeling quite proud of himself.

Meanwhile, Mehmet Emin Entek, who was accustomed to being ferried about by his own chauffeur in his own car, had completely forgotten he was in a taxi, and was thinking about the expression on Kete's face. But it wasn't his wounded ego that so preoccupied him at this moment, it was the near certainty that the person Kete awaited could be no one but Belgin. If Kete was at the airport, it could only mean that Belgin had returned to Istanbul after all these years. Belgin was here, in Istanbul. And if Belgin was inside the airport, her life could be at risk. The thought of harm coming to Belgin troubled him deeply, much more than he would have thought possible. He was astonished to find that he was nearly prepared to say a prayer on her behalf. "Belgin . . . Ah, Belgin . . . Ah!" he whistled through clenched teeth. He felt

* Roughly equivalent to "Damn it!" (Kurdish)

296

helpless, an uncomfortably unfamiliar emotion he, in fact, associated with Belgin. And, at that moment, she was inside the airport and in danger and there was nothing he could do! And he was worrying about her, even though he hadn't spared a second thought for the safety of Tijen, the woman he expected to marry.

"Just look at this traffic, *beyefendi*! It'll take at least an hour to get Maslak!" complained Driver Hamo, having calculated that by using the Turkish equivalent for "sir" he'd be more likely to get a response than with the overly familiar "brother" . . .

"And here we are planning to get into the EU, all that talk about starting talks and so on . . . Well, take it from me, they'll never let us in *beyefendi*. No way! I mean, I'm sure you know better than me, but do you really think they'll agree to let the EU grow by seventy million people overnight? I mean, look at Istanbul today, all these families having seven or eight kids, children out in the streets selling tissues. I'm sure you've got kids of your own—may the Lord bless them all, they're what brings joy to life, they are—but how on earth can parents send their kids out into the dark streets of a monster like Istanbul? And if you want to know about life on the dark side, just ask a taxi driver like me. Teenagers out doing drugs, little children rented out to purse-snatching rings, whores (excuse the language) of both sexes trolling for trade, the homeless, drunks, a whole bunch of losers with no hope and no tomorrow, all stuck here in this whore (again, apologies) of a city, Istanbul. I'm telling you, if I just took the time to write it all down, well, you'd have a bestseller on your hands, you would!"

The optimistic Hamo took his important customer's silence as agreement, even though a quick glance in the rearview mirror had revealed that the man in the back seat was now lightly pinching his lips between his thumb and his index finger, and didn't seem to be paying attention at all.

"Ah, *beyefendi*, when I think of all those journalists and 'lifestyle' correspondents living it up in their glass towers, and just think of all they could learn if they spent just one night with me traveling around the city. And think of the pictures they'd get! There's a lot more to Istanbul than five or six restaurants, ten nightclubs, a few dozen blondes, and a handful of rich men. But you've got to have courage to get out into the real city— you need a heart like an ox, big and strong. All that talk about Istanbul being the best city in the world, the most beautiful in Europe . . . well, let me take you on a tour of the back streets of Laleli, Tarlabaşı, Beyoğlu, Eminönü, Bakırköy. Or take a look at some places around dawn, places like Maçka Park, Gezi Park and Belgrade Forest. You wouldn't even recognize them, would you, sir?"

Hamo had managed to squeeze onto the main road, and even though traffic was barely moving, he felt somewhat better, certainly well enough to continue with his vivid description of the city's underbelly.

"The poor outsiders still think Istanbul's streets are paved with gold, and to the city they trudge, bringing their families with them. Okay, so maybe their villages were burned down and their relatives mysteriously gunned down, maybe they're threatened by the terrorists on the one hand and shunned by the state on the other, caught between the two, without a roof over their heads, a school for their kids or a job of any kind . . . no one's denying life is tough! But Istanbul's kind of like a truck, it has the capacity to carry just so much and so many, you know. Anytime, anyone over in our parts gets into trouble or finds they can't make ends meet, they jump at the chance to come here, to Istanbul. 'Find me a job, Brother Hamo,' they say, 'as a driver or whatever.' How am I supposed to do that? Do you think it's easy to become a taxi driver in a city where one out of ten people travel by taxi? I try to tell them that there are about 17,600 taxis cruising the streets of Istanbul at any given time, carrying an average of about one and a half million people every twenty-four hours. But they don't get it, they just stare at me like oxen!"

Hamo, for all his much vaunted ability to analyze people, had failed to realize that the passenger in the back seat was totally oblivious to anything he had to say, and under normal circumstances would long since have told him to shut up. But there was one thing Hamo *did* know: ten years earlier, it would have been impossible for him to speak freely about the subjects he so casually brought up today. He was enjoying the chance to speak his mind, and a pair of human ears in the back seat gave him the excuse he needed to do so.

"How can you possibly explain to these dimwits, who truly believe they can scrape together the 10,000 lira for a taxi medallion, that even in Istanbul, a city two million tourists visit every year, being a driver is hell? Believe me, it's the most dangerous job there is, after being a policeman. In the last year, seventy-eight drivers have been bumped off for a fistful of change, just like that, in cold blood. And even if they catch the killers, they get let out again. Our laws are shit, they really are . . ."

"I wonder how Belgin is doing? She's always hated that airport. She probably has migraine . . . and she's all alone . . ." Mehmet Emin Entek was thinking there in the back seat. But what really worried him was something he hadn't yet admitted to himself: however hard he tried to dismiss Belgin, she remained the main reference point of his life—and he was terrified of losing her for good and all.

"It's about time they decided to upgrade our taxis as part of getting into the EU. Just imagine clean, air-conditioned, modern cars," said Hamo, proudly stroking the steering wheel of his Hyundai.

"Thanks to this I earn my daily bread, even if I'm still making monthly payments . . . I even provide magazines and newspapers for my customers. You could say I've already entered the EU in my own small way. The Association of Taxi Drivers should give me a medal! Ha ha!"

"Is Belgin all alone . . . ?"

Hamo Türk was just about to ask his fare where they were going, when they heard a tremendous crash coming from the international terminal to their rear.

"Allah!" shouted Hamo Türk as he slammed on the brakes, simultaneously swerving to the right just in time to avoid hitting the vehicle in front, which had stopped just as suddenly.

His customer spoke for the first time: "Was that a bomb?"

"I couldn't tell you, sir. God forbid it was! The bastards! It's a disgrace it is, a disgrace to Istanbul and to all of us. Those traitors!" cried Hamo, his eyes filling with tears. "God damn those terrorists!" he continued. "You know, even if it was Hezbullah who did it, everyone will still blame it on the PKK. Just you wait, sir, you'll see I'm right. I'm a Kurd myself, and I've never been ashamed of my culture or my language. Anyway, when it comes to the safety of our country it makes no difference if you're Kurd or Laz, Sunni or Allawi . . . My grandfather was killed on the battlefield in Sakarya. This land belongs to all of us!" Hamo was on a roll, and he couldn't help feeling hurt at the memory of having overheard certain of his colleagues remark, "He's a Kurd, but he's still a good guy!"

"I've got friends who get mad at me, say I've 'assimilated.' They think they can insult me by claiming I've lost my Kurdishness. I don't listen to them, but I do believe that the government's got to invest in the Kurdish areas of this country. I mean, if the state pushes its own people around, of course, they'll give up and won't want to work. You know what I mean?"

He didn't. In fact, Mehmet Emin Entek hadn't listened to or understood a single word so far.

"If anyone gets hurt, foreigners will say Turkey's full of Muslim terrorists, and some Turks will blame it on the Kurds. Damn them all! Why are we always the ones to suffer!" Hamo nearly shouted, punching his steering wheel for good measure.

Mehmet Emin Entek was trying to get through to his chauffeur to find out what had happened at the airport, and so to Belgin. "I can't believe it, the network's still down!" he observed in his usual mutter. It still hadn't occurred to him to try his lover and personal assistant, Tijen Derya, once again . . .

Meanwhile, Hamo was switching through the radio stations, all of which were playing music. "That's funny . . ." he said to himself. "If a bomb had gone off, wouldn't there be a news report?"

As they inched along in heavy traffic, the shriek of an approaching ambulance grew louder and louder. It was an indication that something serious had happened, and as the flashing lights became brighter and the traffic parted to make way for it, the hearts of both of the men in Hamo's taxi got heavier by the moment.

Mehmet Emin Entek's head was throbbing and his ears were ringing. Annoyed, finally, by the talkative driver, he lifted his head to tell Hamo to be quiet, only to see him chatting to the taxi driver in the next lane over.

"He doesn't know anything either, sir. Well, let's at least hope that ambulance makes it to the hospital in time. Think of the poor family . . ." said Hamo sadly as the flashing lights retreated into the distance.

"Let's hope so!" whispered Mehmet Emin Entek, astonished to find that he was having trouble swallowing. It was as though his tonsils had suddenly swollen up. He knew he had to pull himself together, just as he knew how much he prided himself on his ability to emerge victorious from any situation—the more difficult the better. But, for the first time in his adult life, he didn't feel like bothering. It was almost as though he'd stepped outside himself and was simply observing the middle-aged man in the back seat of a yellow taxi in Istanbul traffic—and found that man wanting.

"Those damn killers! Curse them all!" said Hamo, peering into the rearview mirror as he solemnly announced, "They've turned off the sirens. May Allah grant peace to the family of the departed."

At first, Mehmet Emin Entek seemed to clutch at the hiccup that was leaving his throat, but in the next moment he lost control. The same man who'd boasted that he hadn't shed a tear at his own mother's funeral had doubled over, sobbing. With Hamo casting worried glances into the mirror, Entek cried and he cried.

Hamo was at last at a loss for words. As he shifted gears and maneuvered into the next lane over he murmured, "Well, I've seen it all today! First the guy from Adana who made me take him right back to the airport, and then this guy! Oh well, Hamo, it's all in a day's work . . ."

33

BAT BY NIGHT, SEAGULL BY DAY

"Promise me that you'll never be cruel on purpose!" Kete had said. Those were the exact words she'd used: "cruel on purpose."

As Kete and Ayhan began getting to know each other in the studio where she'd arrived in her muddy red shoes to see the prospective bridegroom in person, she'd asked him, over *kete* buns, which she'd made herself, and tea, the preparation of which she'd supervised, to make her that promise. The studio was a mess, filled with dirt and dust and half-finished projects. Kete couldn't have known how unusual it was for Ayhan to receive a guest in his studio—and without having showered first. She simply looked on with the air of a mother-in-law as he quickly cleared off a couple of chairs and some space on a low table. It was late afternoon on one of those days in late winter when it seems spring will never come, a cold gray day, damp and muddy. But somehow, none of that mattered, neither the abruptness of his guest's arrival, the cluttered condition of the studio, his sleepy unwashed state nor the hawk-like eyes of Kete as he made tea. Ayhan had experienced the strangest sensation the first time he set eyes on Kete. It was as though they'd been reunited, as though he'd known her all his life, and had spent many years missing her. Kete had spoken those words the moment she sat down: "Ayhan, promise me you won't be cruel to her on purpose; don't make my heart beat like the wings of a bird, day and night, worrying about her. I know you're only human and we all make mistakes. But deliberate cruelty is something else, something I'll never forgive or understand! She's like a daughter to me, Ayhan, and I want my girl to be happy." Her agitated voice contained the hint of a threat, the whisper of a plea, and an abundance of concern. It was real; it was the voice of someone speaking an unvarnished truth.

"Deliberate cruelty, huh!" Ayhan had thought to himself, feeling as though he'd been rudely shaken awake from a dream and transported back to his cluttered studio. But the woman with the red shoes was still there, staring at him. "That's some pretty heavy shit!" he muttered under his breath. But what rattled him most was that the "heavy" words had come from an unremarkable looking woman with white hair who—as far as he knew from Belgin– hadn't even finished primary school and who'd spent her entire life cooking, cleaning and looking after children. Ayhan had always thought that motherhood embodies virtues like love, patience and self-sacrifice, but doesn't necessarily enhance the ability to grasp abstract ideas or human psychology. He'd compounded this mistake by judging all women on their potential to make good mothers and wives, with intellectual qualities of secondary importance. But Ayhan had learned a lot in Istanbul, particularly through his hasty and confusing first marriage to the young classmate who would soon give birth to his daughter, Berfin. He went into that marriage considering himself to be a real progressive, with advanced ideas on gender equality, but was soon to discover that he expected his young wife, a city girl with a career, to satisfy herself with the life of a full-time wife and mother. Wasn't motherhood sacred? Why wasn't it enough for her? And how could it be that, even as the mother of a young daughter, she had the same sexual desires and career ambitions?

But by the time Ayhan met Belgin he was a man rapidly approaching forty, and mature enough to realize he still had much to learn on the subject of women and so much else. He still had a long way to go, but Belgin was so inaccessible, that somehow none of his parochial taboos, prejudices, and misogyny applied to her: simply, she seemed beyond reproach. As a result, their relationship had been smooth sailing, even if he had no idea how long it would last. He truly had no idea! He'd come to terms with Belgin, one way or another, but what would he do about Kete? Kete had been a latecomer to the Gümüş family, and hadn't been raised and educated as Belgin had been. Ayhan, too, had come from a humble background, but he'd gained an excellent education and had enjoyed the freedom to make mistakes that is permitted only to men. It was as he got to know Kete that Ayhan realized how narrow-minded he'd been. For Kete, "art and philosophy" were practical matters she dealt with on a daily basis. She'd grown up in a household where she was treated as an equal, where intelligence was appreciated and curiosity encouraged. Even now, as a wife and mother with her own household, Kete relished challenges and opportunities for growth. And if she was a remarkable woman, it wasn't because of the delicious *kete* she baked, her abandonment as a child or the suffering she'd endured: what made Kete remarkable was that through it all, she'd been true to herself, and strong and courageous enough to grow and learn and change.

On the evening of the day they'd met, Ayhan escorted Kete as far as the street, hugged her and kissed her on both cheeks, received permission to kiss her hand, and sent her on her way with the broad smile of a boy who's just been petted and adored by his mother. Back at home, that smile lingering on his lips, he settled onto the sofa, determined to prolong for as long as possible a sensation he hadn't felt since the death of his own mother: the bliss of a cat luxuriating in the sun. "You're a lucky guy, Ayhan," he purred. "Not only did you go and fall in love with a woman like Istanbul, but, as an added bonus, this Kete of hers smells just like your own mother. Later, back at work on his current project, he pondered the promise Kete had extracted:

"Deliberate cruelty? What's that supposed to mean? Only perverts and fascists hurt other people on purpose, so why did Kete say that to me?" he asked himself. "Besides, a leftist like me could never hurt anyone . . ." He hadn't even finished composing that last sentence in his head before he realized how naïve he was being. He thought about the way so-called democrats persecuted Gypsies, transvestites, and street kids, excusing themselves with "but they deserve it." What was that if not deliberate cruelty? Those who looked the other way when the infamous Wealth Tax was imposed on non-Muslim minorities in Turkey in the 1940s, in the years when Europeans were ignoring the shipment of their neighbors to concentration camps, had also been guilty of deliberate cruelty. And what about what was happening in Iraq . . . But he wasn't *personally* responsible for any of that, was he? Then

305

he remembered his first wife, the most beautiful girl in the Fine Arts Department, the mother of Berfin, also in her early twenties, those crazy years when they'd been young, when their love rocked the world, or something like that; when they spent hours making love, morning, noon, and night, everywhere they could, and all the time . . . In that filthy mildewed basement apartment . . . they'd been so happy. What happened? How was it that at a time when they were inseparable, they'd found they couldn't stand each other? Had divorce been an easy way out, just four years after they'd met, two years after they'd married? What had been the exact process that turned them into two people who raged and shouted on the telephone at the mere mention of Berfin, and why had that process been so infused with bitterness and pain? Was it freedom from a "bad marriage" they'd sought, had that been what had made separation "inevitable"? That must have been it, that's the very definition of separation, breaking away and leaving something behind in a bid for freedom. But it's a lie! Only in books and films do endings and separations lead to more freedom! For Ayhan, that first separation, and all the ones that followed, had only made him feel heavier, slower and wearier.

In the end, what had happened after that first separation, that "end," that bid for freedom? Berfin had been forced to live in Ankara, with her mother and grandparents. Ayhan hadn't prevented, hadn't been able to prevent, a small child from being separated from her father, and had guiltily admitted to himself that as much as he missed his daughter, he found it easier to breath at home without her mother. And somehow, he'd been unable to find the time to visit her in Ankara. And somehow, Berfin's mother had been unable to find the time to visit him in Istanbul. Finally, Berfin had been entrusted to a flight attendant and sent to Istanbul on her own, and that plane, of all planes, had been the one that had crashed. Berfin's plane had crashed! Berfin was dead! And Berfin's mother was never the same . . . That was what had happened. Berfin had died alone, aged seven. Seven!

"You wanted to be free, Ayhan, didn't you? No responsibilities, endless horizons. You chased after the most beautiful girl at school, married her, and then, when your child was born, you panicked and you ruined everything. Well, that part of your life will always be with you. You had a wonderful wife, a healthy baby, and what did you do, Ayhan? You screwed it up. You thought you were too young to be 'a married man with children' and you knowingly sabotaged your life and the lives of those you loved. You turned your back on her, ignored her, didn't touch her, didn't make love to her, didn't speak to her, didn't listen to her . . . Even while you were living together in the same house, you'd already abandoned her! You complained about not being happy, but you wouldn't let her make you happy. You didn't want to be happy with her, and you did everything you could to make *her* leave *you*. Worst of all, you turned your wife into a prison guardian even though it wasn't her you resented: it was the institution of marriage. And you weren't being honest when you told her about the 'other woman,' Ayhan. You knew exactly what you were doing when you broke her heart! You had to shake her off, as well as your daughter, so you'd be 'free' for new loves, new journeys, new projects, new toys. You planned it. You did it on purpose. It was deliberate and cruel. Deliberate cruelty."

Ayhan put down his chisel and took off his mask. He sat down next to the base of the sculpture he'd been working on, put his face in his hands and wept silently. He always felt bad when he thought about his marriage and the heartbreaking memory of Berfin could easily move him to tears, but what he felt now was far worse. He'd always excused his role in his failed marriage as youthful ignorance, but he'd finally admitted to himself that it was deliberate cruelty, even as he also found the courage and clarity to realize that so much of what had been done to him, too, by best friends, brothers and lovers had also been just that: deliberate cruelty.

"What have you done to me, Kete? Did I have to face all this?" he shouted. Then he cried as a man can only cry when he's alone—or so one has been told. He cried in his studio, all alone, thinking of Berfin, his mother, Kete and Belgin. And as he cried he couldn't help wondering whether or not either of them, himself or Belgin, would ever suffer deliberate cruelty at the hands of the other . . .

It was dark outside by the time he was ready to wipe his eyes and nose with the back of his hand, and get up. He turned on the lights, washed his face and put on a Tolga Çandar CD, setting it to his favorite Aegean folksong, "A Pair of Partridges."

"Ah, Istanbul," he grumbled as he picked up a chisel. "You're forever expecting Istanbullu to offer you another sacrificial victim! You're like a bat, a shining jet-black bat that spends its nights flitting through the back alleys, only to turn into a pure white seagull racing the ferryboats by day . . . Which of us could ever be more guilty of deliberate cruelty than you, Istanbul?" His grumble faded into a sigh as he closed his eyes.

Opening them again, Ayhan turned to Kete, who was sitting next to him in the arrivals hall of Atatürk Airport, and said, "So, that means Berfin's going to have a sister or a brother?" There was an explosive crash, and Ayhan threw himself onto Kete, pulling her head against his chest.

"Shit! The terrorists have made it into the airport!" he said, fighting the urge to spit on the floor.

34
LAVENDER, JUDAS, AND TULIP

"When we make love, he whispers my name into my ear!" Belgin remembered. Her lips involuntarily parted, and she felt a warm wetness between her legs. "Ayhan whispers my name when we make love!" she remembered again.

She'd read somewhere that apprehension of death can force people to confront issues they've avoided; perhaps it had been in a novel, or it may have been a poem or a line in a film. In any case, like so many ideas concerning love and death, hers were as likely to have been articulated by a writer. Was this one of those rare moments, when she would confront the prospect of death at first hand? Did death await her?

A well-bred woman, and quite conservative when it came to subjects of an intimate and sexual nature, Belgin looked around to ensure that no one was aware of the thoughts going through her mind. "It's the same in all classes, women aren't supposed to entertain erotic thoughts! . . . The only difference is that my class frowns on it as simply being uncouth, while other classes consider it to be a moral issue! For me, it's inappropriate; for them, it's a sin!" She frowned as it occurred to her for the first time, on this extraordinary day during which so many of her half-formed ideas had gelled and crystallized, that the men who forbade women to partake of any pleasure in sex are the men who themselves took a perverse sexual pleasure in that same denial.

Sitting on a metal bench under the strict but well-meaning orders of Officer Üzeyir, who'd told her not to move until things had calmed down, Belgin decided that if she ever got out of the airport in one piece, she would devote her lectures not only to biology and genetics, but to "cultural genetics" as well. That mysterious loud crash had convinced her, along with so many other passengers, that there really had been a bomb, and that it had exploded. She'd feared not only for Kete and Ayhan, but for herself and baby Lavanta. But, along with fear and the apprehension of death, she'd been flooded with a strange and unexpected wave of sexual desire.

"Women are like flowers, so delicate and beautiful! They should be looked after with the greatest care," her father would often repeat, like so many others in Turkey, male and female. Whenever he trotted out this well-worn sentiment, women of a certain generation, and even some of the younger ones, would nod appreciatively as smiles blossomed on their faces. Although Belgin was only a child at the time, she knew that flowers were vegetation, were merely sweet-smelling weeds that had the added virtue of being pleasing to the eye. She couldn't help wondering whose responsibility it was to tend these flowers. "Men, of course, Belgin!" her father had said with a smile and a loving pat to the head of his little budding beauty.

"Take Istanbul for example: Istanbul is like a Judas tree." That had led to a long and vivid comparison between the low tree with its masses of magenta blossoms and the city of Istanbul. It turned out that cities, too, were like flowers, especially Lady Judas Tree herself: Istanbul.

But Grandmother had dissented, expressing her firm opinion that if Istanbul was a flower, it was most certainly a tulip: "Judas blossoms are for the street, but the tulip is noble and purely Turkish. Why do you think Ottoman seals incorporated the tulip! If women are like flowers, and I agree with you on that point, different flowers represent different virtues. Dear boy, how could a lowly blossom with such a checkered past possibly represent Istanbul!"

"How many grandmothers have died happy? How many women, who in their youth were tender and delicate as flowers, have been able to lie on their deathbeds deeply contented? I'm not talking about the happiness of the bright-eyed, smiling old lady who sits silently in the corner, an ancient, loving being who is beyond gender as she rejoices to herself, 'Despite everything, I made it. I'm alive, and through all the pain and betrayal I've protected my family, made thousands of sacrifices to keep them together.' I'm talking about a woman who has known fulfillment

310

as a woman, who has known what it is to be loved and valued and—this is the important bit—*pleasured*. How many of the sweet old biddies laid up in bed can look back on their sex lives with a smile? Are there any at all who can do so?" Belgin asked herself, astonished that these thoughts might well be her last on this earth.

"How many of the women who aren't scorned as 'loose,' the virgins and mothers constantly compared to flowers, how many of them will ever know real sexual pleasure?" Belgin asked herself with yet another sigh. "Why is it that only gullible young girls are considered desirable, while capable and self-aware women are perceived as being dangerous and threatening? Why are intelligent women valued only when they acquire the status of grandmother?"

"So, are men gardeners then?" was what she'd asked her father, provoking a loud burst of laughter. An expression of distaste on his face, he'd replied, "No, dear, men aren't gardeners. If anything, they're the bugs in the flowerbed." As father and daughter discussed flowers and men and bugs, Jackie-Halide *Hanım* had sat in silence, perhaps too much of a noble tulip herself to voice her own opinions. But as shy as Kete was, she would always find a way to join in, and if the subject was flowers, she would always talk of lavender.

"It's not for me to speak up, Grandmother, but you know how I always tell you that I don't remember being able to smell anything when I first came to Istanbul? Well, that was until I got a whiff of Halit Ziya *Bey*'s lavender cologne. I felt all refreshed and clean, and I've loved that smell ever since. There's nothing like lavender to pick up your spirits. If you ask me, that's the smell of Istanbul. Istanbul is lavender."

The soft voice of Officer Üzeyir Seferihisar intruded politely upon Belgin's musings: "Your name is Belgin Gümüş, isn't it, ma'am? And you did arrive on a THY flight from New York?"

"That's right," ventured Belgin, fearing the worst: could it be bad news . . . Ayhan and Kete?

"I wanted to surprise you, so I asked a policeman friend of

311

mine to help me out. But I'm afraid we haven't been able to find anyone in the arrivals hall by the name of Mr. Gümüş."

"Mr. Gümüş?" Belgin repeated. "Who's that?"

"Why, your husband, of course. The baby's father!"

35

PAREV, DEAREST ISTANBUL

"Oh, come on! I've only just arrived back in Istanbul, in *Sireli Bolis,*" and now this!" Ayda Seferyan had groaned when she heard the announcement.

A French teacher at Dame de Sion Lycèe, Ayda Seferyan was returning from Paris after entrusting her daughter, Sibel, to the safekeeping of her older brother, Sarkis, who had remained in that city, never even coming home to visit since he'd gone abroad as a child to attend boarding school. She'd been overjoyed to see Belgin, and considered it a good omen to have witnessed the return of the childhood friend who'd fled Istanbul some thirteen years before, vowing never to return. But Ayda's spirits had sunk again upon hearing the unsettling announcement.

Actually, she'd been feeling a bit down even before the announcement, sorry that she'd been forced to leave Belgin all alone in the restroom. She knew all about Belgin's incapacitating migraines; she'd suffered them even as a schoolgirl. She also knew that once Belgin had made up her mind nothing could dissuade her. But she still couldn't understand why Belgin was so determined to suffer alone and in silence, and why they couldn't have left the airport together. Something was up, she was sure of it. And that's why even after she'd had her passport stamped and been greeted by her brother, Aret, they'd decided to linger in the arrivals hall until Belgin appeared.

"There's something she's not telling me," Ayda worried aloud to her brother. "We've been friends all these years, Belgin's in trouble, believe me. Fine, she had migraine, her eyes were swollen and she was pale—but isn't that all the more reason to get out of the airport as quickly as possible—instead of locking yourself into a toilet stall? She was perfectly friendly, as always, but you

---

* "Hello" (Armenian)
** "Dear city" (Armenian)

know how stubborn she is! Would you believe she looks exactly the same, hasn't changed a bit. Just like Jackie-Halide *Hanım*! Thin as can be, the same curls, cool as a cucumber—but like she needs a hug or something, you know what I mean? Look at me, Aret, I'm at least ten kilos heavier, all that running around after mother, Sibel and my students, no time to look after myself . . ."

Aret rubbed his belly and winked at his older sister, and they both burst out laughing. They were always laughing like that, and anyone who didn't know them well would have assumed they took absolutely nothing seriously. Even Belgin had failed to realize until years later that their ability to make a joke of life itself, which was something she'd always admired and envied, was a survival instinct developed over generations, and reflected their status as members of a minority.

"Aret, I know the car's not in the long-term lot, but it won't take much longer. I mean, she can't stay in there forever, can she? We've got to be here for her." And Ayda's family had indeed always been there for Belgin, especially in the dark years after her father's death.

It was as the siblings waited and joked and worried about their car being towed away that the announcement had come. At first they thought it had to be a bad joke, but when their eyes met neither one was laughing.

"Oh, come on! I've only just arrived back in Istanbul, in *Sireli Bolis*, and now this!" groaned Ayda.

"Calm down, don't jump to conclusions," her brother said, now even more worried about the car and fully aware that if they'd left the airport as originally planned, they'd have been back home in Şişli by now. But Aret was no more willing to abandon Belgin than Ayda was.

"There's a new girl in our class, Daddy. Her name's Belgin, and they had her sit next to me. She gets a lot of extra attention cause she came midway through the semester, but she already knows English and Spanish, and they say she'll learn French in no time. She's so pretty, like a movie star. But really shy. She never talks to anyone. Her dad died last year. They all whisper about her: 'Her dad was martyred by the terrorists, that's why she's so sad.'" Then Ayda turned to her father, looked him directly in the eye and said, "They say ASALA killed him. What's that, Daddy, and what's it got to do with me?"

Ayda was twelve the first time she asked her father that question. She was old enough, of course, to sense that "it" did indeed have something to do with her, at least in the eyes of society. She knew her family was different: they went to church instead of the mosque, celebrated Noel instead of Ramadan Bayramı, had a cross on the wall instead of a Koran in pride of place on a lectern; their women didn't cover up in church, all the daughters of all the families in their community were sent to school and when they came of age they were always free to choose their own spouses—if only from among the community. She knew they were different, but, as a girl, she didn't *feel* any different, certainly not at all like an outsider or a foreigner. It was true that they spoke Armenian at home, so they wouldn't forget it, but Ayda considered it to be just another language, like the French or English she was learning at school, or the Turkish she spoke out on the street. She belonged here and she was an Istanbullu, that much she knew. Just as she knew they had no problems with their neighbors. Her mother would serve lunch as soon as she heard the call to prayer coming from the mosque next door, they'd exchange greetings with their neighbors on Muslim holidays and accept gifts of candy or freshly slaughtered lamb, reciprocating at Easter time with painted eggs. But on that day, at school, something had happened: the other children had suggested that she was in some way responsible for the death of Belgin's father. And there had to be a good explanation for it!

Ayda's father and mother had exchanged glances, taken a deep breath and sent Aret to his room. It was that most dreaded of moments for parents: having to explain to a child the unexplainable. When Ayda's mother went off to keep Aret company, even locking the door behind her with an ominous click, Ayda's heart began beating faster. She knew something important must be coming, something terrible. Her father had coughed dryly, clearing his throat, getting his thoughts in order. She never, ever, forgot the first words he spoke, there in the living room, sitting across from each other on the sofa: "Ayda, the problem is that we're Armenian!"

So? So what? "Of course we're Armenian. How could that be a problem?" Ayda had asked. "Ayda," her father continued, slowly and gently, "we've been living here with the Turks for hundreds of years. But then, a long time ago, long before you were born, some terrible things happened, and many people suffered. But this is our home. We belong here. The thing is, some people on both sides don't want us to live together. I don't know how to put this: there are some Armenians, especially outside of Turkey, who, unfortunately, have been killing Turkish diplomats. It's not something we support in any way!" We. Us. So it was "us" and "them," was it? Couldn't you be both Armenian and Turkish? Did you have to pick one or the other?

"Unfortunately"—it was the second time he'd used that word—"some of them are blaming it on the Armenians in Turkey. Just like Turks don't all think the same way, we Armenians don't either. But, unfortunately"—the third time—"life's not always fair. That's why we took our name off the buzzer by the front door of our building."

Ayda studied her father, and she saw fear. And like so many children, she associated fear with cowardice, and hated her father for it.

"Well, isn't Sarkis living in France? Is he one of those overseas Armenians you're talking about?"

"Sarkis has unfortunately"—four!—"been overly affected by the diaspora. He's . . . drifted away from us. I've lost my oldest son, and, unfortunately"—by now Ayda had stopped counting—"there's nothing I can do about it. Your big brother is my biggest failure and my greatest disappointment. Unfortunately. I don't know what I did wrong, but I'll never forgive myself," said watch-repairman Artin Seferyan as his eyes filled with tears.

Although Ayda was too young to fully comprehend the ramifications of what her father had told her, bewildered as she was

316

by even the softened version of matters heretofore discussed by her parents only in whispers and behind closed doors, it was the string of "unfortunatelys" and the sight of her father as a defeated man that had disturbed her the most as she asked through her tears:

"But what am I supposed to do, Father? I'm an Armenian, and that's that. Should I tell my friends at school that none of this has anything to do with me? Tell me what I'm supposed to do!"

Kissing Ayda on the forehead, her father had said, "We don't choose where we're born or who we are. I've already lost a son, and I don't think I could bear it if anything like that happens again. Listen carefully to your father: Don't ever be ashamed of your roots, don't deny or apologize for who you are. And as for that new girl, Belgin, be the best friend to her you can. Trust me, it's important for you both."

Ayda Seferyan arrived at school the next day a little sadder but strangely reassured. She was an Armenian and a Christian and an Istanbullu, and she remained so for the rest of her life. Over time, Belgin became like a sister to her, so close that she didn't even get jealous when her father paid so much attention to her new friend. At university she fell in love with a fellow student; he wasn't an Armenian, but he was as secular as she. Many of her relatives on the Gregorian side of the family bitterly opposed their marriage, as did the groom's Muslim family, as a result of which they spent what should have been the happiest years of their young lives constantly defending and explaining, knowing they were right, but worn out by the constant effort and the erosion of the respect they'd previously felt for their elders. And unfortunately (that word again!), by the time Sibel, their daughter, had turned six, the young couple, secular humanists both, could no longer deny that in Turkey, whether you're Turkish or Armenian, it is the happiness of the extended family that determines the duration of a marriage, not the happiness of the couple themselves. The marriage ended, and each of them later married spouses approved by their respective families, only for each of them to divorce a second time . . .

317

"This place is too secure for anyone to have smuggled in a bomb," Aret said soothingly. "There must be some threat to the planes, a disturbance on the runway or something." Ayda had been distracted, and blinked blankly in response, at which Aret felt the need to reassure her further. "It's not a bomb I'm worried about, it's the car. Wouldn't it be best to wait outside in the car for Belgin?"

When there was no response from Ayda, Aret resorted to his famous black humor: "Well, with all the terrorist organizations running around these days, at least they won't try to pin it on us!" Ayda reacted with a disapproving frown.

Then a number of policemen and their dogs appeared in the hall just as red lights began flashing above one of the exits. In a matter of moments, the crowd went from uneasy to agitated to panicked.

"Come on, Ayda, we've got to get out of here. We'll wait for Belgin in the car. She's smart enough to look after herself!"

Smart enough? So, do only stupid people find themselves trapped or in need of help? Does danger discriminate between "smart" and "stupid"?

"Go and save the car, Aret. Belgin and I will join you later," Ayda replied with chilling calm. Aret knew his older sister well enough to say, "Don't be silly. I'm not about to leave you here on your own. And anyway, they've only opened one door and everyone's rushed for it like it's a line for free Ramadan pita. It's better to wait here than to get crushed over there."

As they both looked toward the exit, they saw that Aret hadn't been exaggerating: the passengers had indeed turned into a crushing mob. Taking Ayda by the arm, Aret tugged her trolley along with his free hand, heading for a quieter area of the arrivals hall.

"There are some things you can't renounce, Ayda! You're an Armenian. Face the facts!" her mother had shouted, angrier than she had ever seen her.

"I'm not saying I want you to become like your brother Sarkis, full of hate and thinking only of revenge, but there are still certain things you can't deny. My uncle was from Barizaglı, the original name of Bahçecik, the town in İzmit. He was a doctor and he served in the Ottoman army to defend Gallipoli. But . . ." Her mother began sobbing, choking on her words as she flashed a look of reproach upon her twelve-year-old daughter. A look Ayda would carry with her for the rest of her life. "But he was thrown out of work and left homeless in 1922. When he escaped to a Greek island, he learned that his entire family had been killed. His whole family! How could this happen, and to a man who served his country, Ayda. Can there be a worse disaster than that? You're still an Armenian and you always will be. Never forget!"

Ayda hadn't thrown her arms around her weeping mother, nor had she been able to assure her that the past was the past and that nothing like that could ever happen again. She felt as though she had been turned to stone, temporarily unable to move or feel, and she never again discussed that day with her mother. There had been a similar scene, though, many years later, when as a married woman she'd exploded: "I won't allow my outlook on life to be affected by what happened before I was even born. I've had enough of hatred and vengeance and I want to live in peace as a modern Istanbullu. Enough!"

Even as a girl, that's what she'd tried to do. She'd soon become fast friends with Belgin, just as her father had wished, but Ayda Seferyan had no idea what effect that friendship was having on the Gümüş household. At first, Jackie-Halide *Hanım* didn't and couldn't approve of close relations between her daughter, "the daughter of a diplomat killed by Armenians," and "that Armenian girl." It had been Uncle Erol who'd intervened, pointing out that it was just this attitude that had led to all Turks indiscriminately being stamped as "barbarians," and over time, unbeknownst to the Seferyan family, Jackie-Halide allowed that Ayda was "an Armenian, but a good girl." That was the first secret Belgin had kept from Ayda; the second was the real reason she had wanted to be left alone in the toilet stall.

Even Kete, who was twenty-five at the time, had spoken hurtful words on the subject of Armenians: "It doesn't pay to talk too

319

much—it could even be dangerous. But they say, back in the village in Van, that a long time ago many Turks were murdered by Armenians. My aunt's neighbor said she was only a girl at the time, and she told us all about it, with tears rolling down her cheeks. They didn't do anything to our family, because we were Kurdish . . . But they found a mass grave near our village . . . and that neighbor said she'd lost her whole family. I was young, so when I saw a grown woman crying like that, well, I started bawling, too." That's what Kete had said, Belgin's Kete, who was more like an older sister and friend than a nanny. She'd been serving *kete* buns one weekend when Ayda was staying, and just blurted it out as she poured the tea. The two girls had exchanged glances filled with hurt and sorrow. That was just like Kete back then, forever putting her foot in her mouth and saying the wrong things. There were many occasions when Kete was summoned by Jackie-Halide and politely informed that certain information concerning the Gümüş family was to remain private, after which Kete would go directly to her bedroom, red-faced and mortified.

"I'm worried about Sibel, Aret. What if she takes after her Uncle Sarkis? You know, when I was in Paris, he started shouting at me, saying, 'I can't believe you, Ayda. You're completely assimilated. Just look at Sibel: what kind of name is that? Were you too frightened to give her an Armenian name?'"

Aret was surprised that Ayda chose that moment to bring up assimilation and their brother Sarkis. There they were, in an airport in which a bomb might go off at any moment! And Ayda had chosen to bring up one of the most sensitive subjects in Turkey! He'd recently been having his doubts about his sister's emotional stability. She'd even suggested that upon retirement, she wouldn't give private lessons like all the other teachers her age, but would open a yoga school instead, and she'd been saving up for a course in India, so she could develop her "spirituality," whatever that meant. Ayda was alone, very alone. She had no lovers and never talked of remarrying. To her brother, she seemed to be one of a growing army of lonely women over forty. It was strange, for she was the one who had always spoken so glowingly of the importance of having "a companion for life, someone you can share all your joys and sorrows with." But she was alone, her daughter now far away, making Aret particularly happy to hear that her great friend was back in town for good.

"On my last night in Paris, I sat Sibel down across from me and told her about that night my father had sat me down to say, 'The problem is that we're Armenian.' I think it's time that changed, I don't want our being Armenian to be a problem anymore. I want to live in a country where we can all be ourselves, and all be different, equal and free. I also told her that she was under no obligation to make friends only with Armenians while she was in France, and to remember that her uncle was wrong if he still believed violence would change anything. Let him know that's what you believe, I said, but try not to hurt his feelings. Do you think I did the right thing, Aret?" she asked.

"Okay, okay, Ayda! Yes, you're right, now leave it alone! Calm down, would you! And would you hold on a minute? Let's sit somewhere quiet and wait until they open another exit," he told his sister, struggling with her bags as she marched along talking a mile a minute. "Wait, Ayda! Can't you see how many people are trying to get out of that door?" That's when they heard the bloodcurdling wail coming from the bar. The anguished cry of a man in pain. They stopped in their tracks, as did nearly everyone else who heard it, before being swept up by the general commotion and panic.

Aret called the Swatch branch he managed to tell them he'd be late, but he couldn't get through. It's just like the earthquake, he thought, but said nothing to Ayda, not wanting to alarm her further. As he tapped his foot and wondered what to do next, Ayda pointed to a middle-aged woman on a nearby bench.

"Aret, do you see that woman over there, with the red shoes? She looks just like Kete. It *is* Kete! Right there, talking to the dark man. She's probably waiting for Belgin!"

"I haven't seen Kete for years. Are you sure that's her?"

A covered stretcher was borne out of the bar by two medics, startling Ayda, who took a step backward. The siblings avoided each other's eyes, trying their best also to ignore the tall man with the ponytail and earring who wept as he walked next to the stretcher. They had to get out! Immediately! But there was still no sign of Belgin, and they couldn't leave without her . . .

"It's Kete, I'm telling you," cried Ayda running toward the woman. Aret followed with the heavily laden trolley, and had nearly caught up when there was a sound like a bomb, no, more like breaking glass, like a ton of glass had been shattered with terrific force. Aret leapt toward his sister, pulling her to the ground with him. After a few seconds, they slowly got up. When they looked in the direction of the moans and screams, they saw that the huge pane of glass over the sliding exit doors had fallen onto the crowd below, and that tens of people had been hurt, perhaps seriously.

"I'll go see if there's anything I can do. Promise to stay here," Aret told his sister. "Or better still, go over to Kete and wait for me there. All right?" Tears in her eyes, Ayda nodded gratefully and headed straight for Kete, pulling her cell phone out of her pocket in case Aret needed to reach her.

She'd barely taken a step when the phone was snatched out of her hand by an extremely agitated woman. "Sister, in the name of Allah, Mohammed, and Ali, could you let me use your phone? Doesn't anyone help anyone else anymore?" The woman looked like she was in shock as she began to frantically press buttons, talking to herself all the while. "It's even worse here than in Germany. No one helps strangers anymore . . ."

36
ISTANBULLU, ISTANBULITE, ISTANBULESQUE

"What do men want? Except for that one particular thing, that obvious one, the one we're all chasing after, what exactly is it that men want? God, you're an idiot, Ayhan! Is there any other man in the world who would think about something like this at a time like this?" Ayhan muttered to himself with an irritable grin. He was stretched out naked on the crisp white sheets of a bed in a hotel in Rome, luxuriating in the sensation of total relaxation. Moments earlier, just as the sun was rising, Belgin had risen from that same bed and headed to the bathroom to wash away his perfume, their perfume, the hours of lovemaking that clung to her skin and hair. She'd soon emerge from the shower, smelling once again like a serious, composed scientist, the only trace of her nighttime self, the warm depression still visible in the sheets. Only an hour remained before the woman who'd lay in Ayhan's arms the entire night, at times murmuring in her sleep, at times crying out in orgasm, would be making a presentation at the "International Congress of Genetics and Biotechnology." But they still had one precious hour, sixty minutes in which to breakfast, to laugh and to caress. This woman Ayhan had known for two years, and for whose warm body he'd crossed oceans and continents, was nothing like the other women. He felt a new contentment, even as he appreciated more than ever the joys of being a man. What amazed him most was that one woman could give him so much, could be so many things to him all at once. Did this deep satisfaction, this self-confidence, this sense of joy, come from his ability to give joy to a woman like Belgin? For three days now, they'd been staying in room number fourteen at the Gladiatori Hotel in Rome, enjoying spring, the Mediterranean and love. The Mediterranean, spring and love! It was the final rendezvous before they'd meet in Istanbul to start a new life together.

"What is it that men want? What do we really want? Why is it that everyone is always wondering what women want, but we men never stop to ask ourselves what we want? Are woman so complicated and intense? Are their desires and needs such a great mystery, at least to us men? And are we men so transparent and basic that our wants are clear for all to see? Is it simply assumed that our worlds revolve around screwing a few more women, getting more money, grabbing for more and more? Are we really that basic?" Ayhan snorted, so loudly that Belgin called out from the bathroom:

"What'd you say, Ayhan? I didn't catch that."

"Nothing, darling. I'm just cursing myself out and wondering how you could love a man like me." Belgin had turned off the shower in order to hear him better, and smiled at his words. "Hang on a second. I'll be out in a minute, and I'll tell you exactly what I love about you. Hang on!"

Impatient, he glanced out of the open window opposite and saw the sea sparkling in the morning light and the Coliseum perched proudly on a green hill. Ayhan suddenly remembered he wasn't in Istanbul. They hadn't yet wandered through Istanbul, communed with Istanbul, made love in Istanbul . . . But it wasn't long before they would, before summer would come and everything would be Istanbullu, Istanbulite, Istanbulesque. Ayhan smiled as he got out of bed and went over to the window for a better look at the Coliseum.

"You're a real beauty," he said, addressing the heap of stone on that distant hill. "A real beauty after all these years. After all you've seen, violence and fear, laughter and love, there you are, still standing tall on one of the seven hills, seven hills just like in Istanbul. You know what, seeing you makes me miss her, makes me miss your sister to the east."

Hearing the shower had been turned off again, Ayhan cut short his conversation with the Coliseum. After all, while Belgin was at the congress, he'd have most of the day to himself, free to talk to marble and brick and weathered stone. His thoughts returned to Belgin and the question of women and men, and what they want.

"Ayhan, are you all right?" Belgin called out from the bathroom, so accustomed was she to hearing a continuous patter.

"I'm fine, but if you stay in there any longer, you'll be late," he warned. "Oh, and what have you decided to do about dinner tonight? Are we going to meet with that professor of yours, Yannis Seferis?" As he folded his underwear and put it on the end table, he tensed at the sight of an unused package of condoms. What had they done last night? Had Belgin finally started taking the pill, as they'd discussed, and was that why they hadn't bothered with protection? How could they have been so careless; that wasn't at all like Belgin . . . Or had he used other condoms? What if Belgin became pregnant? Ayhan was astonished to find that the idea didn't frighten him at all. Even so, he looked under the bed and tore aside the bedclothes, searching for used condoms. There were none. Had Belgin flushed them down the toilet? No, she'd never flush plastic down the toilet. Cursing as he tore back the double set of sheets tightly tucked, English-style, under the foot of the bed, he accidentally knocked a book off the nightstand, a Margaret Atwood novel Belgin must have been reading on the plane. As he picked it up off the floor and placed it back on the nightstand, a flower fell out. It was a pink little blossom, cherry, just going brown around the edges. Ayhan stared at the delicate little flower resting shyly in the palm of his hand. It was the flower he'd jumped up and plucked from a branch three days earlier, out walking in Rome with Belgin, the flower he'd presented to her like a lovesick schoolboy. She'd pressed it in the pages of her book! She, Professor Belgin Gümüş, had kept the flower given her by sculptor Ayhan Pozaner!

"She's still a girl, still just a girl at heart," Ayhan smiled to himself as his eyes filled with tears and he abruptly sat on the edge of the bed he'd been ransacking for a used rubber. "For all her cool composure, she's as fresh and tender as a girl." He'd been touched and overjoyed at the sight of that single blossom, but anyone observing Ayhan at that moment would have thought he looked terribly sad. They would have been wrong: Ayhan was, in fact, terrified, utterly terrified . . .

Ayhan had slept with many women younger, more beautiful

and more impressionable than Belgin. Many of them had been inexperienced enough to melt at his touch; most of them had been young enough to be bowled over by the slightest evidence of his success; some of them had been striking enough to be a model. But none of them had been like Belgin. Belgin was something else.

When, a moment later, Belgin walked out of the bathroom wrapped in a white robe, she found Ayhan sitting on the edge of the messed up bed, completely naked. She looked at him, not indicating in any way that what she saw surprised her, and walked over to the window, sensing that he needed a moment to collect his thoughts. As she looked out at the Coliseum and dried her hair with a towel, Ayhan came up behind her, pulled her close against him and kissed the wet hair on the crown of her head. "I wouldn't mind one bit, girl or boy, not one bit," he murmured.

Belgin had no idea what he meant, but she let it go. She'd learned to allow Ayhan to think aloud, and didn't expect to make sense of everything he said at moments such as this. "I could always give my presentation on an empty stomach," she took up his murmur as she turned and threw her arms around Ayhan's neck. And it was with the greatest tenderness that Ayhan pulled her even closer, as close as he dared. As close as he dared.

"Mr. Gümüş? You are Mr. Gümüş, aren't you, sir? Here's your key. Third floor, room fourteen. Ms. Gümüş asked us to inform you that she'd be in the congress hall until 17:30. Welcome to Rome, sir!" Ayhan repeated once again, for Belgin's entertainment, the incident at reception, complete with a convincing Italian accent, laughing aloud each time. "Get a load of that guy! Just because we're staying in the same room, he assumes that I'm your husband and my surname is Gümüş. What a cliché! Italy's no different from Turkey!"

Several weeks earlier, when Belgin had told Ayhan on the phone that she would be attending a congress in Rome, he'd responded right on cue with: "You know what, Belgin, Rome's only about a two-and-a-half hour flight from Istanbul, and the airfare's not out of reach for a humble stone carver like myself. They say, 'all roads lead to Rome,' so I might just track you down there, catch you in my arms, take all your clothes off, smell you, tickle you, kiss you, and use every advanced technique at my disposal to do some other things that I won't mention on the phone right now . . . what do you say?" Belgin had assented, rather coolly, and only a man like Ayhan would have understood how overjoyed she was at that moment. And it was when Ayhan arrived at the boutique hotel on the appointed day and asked reception for a message from one Ms. Belgin Gümüş that he'd been greeted as her husband.

It was spring, it was the Mediterranean, it was their last meeting before Belgin would return to Istanbul. It was spring, and they were head over heels in love: scattered and blissful, incurable and incorrigible, overwhelmed and fearless, cautious and abandoned, determinedly realistic and hopelessly romantic. They were all of those things, and they were madly in love. It was spring in the Mediterranean and Belgin and Ayhan lived love, spoke love, drank love, ate love and made love at every opportunity. And neither of them knew that, there in Rome, on that spring day, Belgin would become pregnant.

Ever practical and cautious, Belgin should have known better, while Ayhan had already lost a daughter and had no intention of becoming a father again. But that didn't stop Belgin from becoming pregnant that day in Rome. Fearful of the side effects of the pill, Belgin had preferred that Ayhan use a condom, a preference that had caused some disagreement. Like so many men, he'd argued that a shrink-wrapped penis was unnatural and desensitizing, no matter the colors, flavors and lubricants of the condoms Belgin always brought from New York. Their sex life was still amazing, on that point they agreed. And as Belgin overcame her natural reserve, her pleasure grew, increasing his, as together they scaled new heights, new sensations, new plateaus. Ayhan loved urging her to articulate what she was feeling. "Do you like that, Belgin, tell me again, I couldn't hear you, tell me again . . ." he'd coax, with more kisses and more caresses for as long as she whispered, "Yes, yes, yes! I feel wonderful! More, more!"

Sex with her ex-husband, Entek, had centered on his "performance," as though he were a gymnast and her role was to cheer him on from the sidelines as he exerted himself, sweaty and grim, determined to outdo himself once more. While Entek loved talk of sex, endlessly subjecting her to anecdotes and jokes, in English and Turkish, laughing loudly even before he'd even reached the punch line, he had never, the entire time they'd been married, made love with Belgin twice in a row. He'd always have a ready excuse to leap out of bed, as though terrified that Belgin would demand another "performance" before he'd caught his second wind.

By the time Belgin met Ayhan at that exhibition in New York, she was no longer the tense, unhappy woman Mehmet Emin Entek had so frequently accused of being "cold, frigid, and unresponsive." Ayhan, too, had grown over the years, and was now enlightened enough to appreciate that an obsession with virginity was as damaging to men as it was to women. He was also a man who was confident enough to declare, "Well, who wants to make love to a corpse?" whenever conversation turned to the virtues of a compliant, shy, repressed, "good" girl.

Belgin and Ayhan had both made considerable sexual and intellectual progress, but it was their emotional state, their capacity for trust and dependence, that plagued them both in the early stages of their budding relationship. It was months before they found the courage to open up to each other, propelled and emboldened by the force of their love.

"Women don't like oral sex or anal sex! They only do it for their partner or for money!" Belgin declared in that room at the Gladiatori Hotel, her body entwined with Ayhan's. "What? Are you telling me you were faking it a minute ago?" Ayhan shouted, mortified at the thought he'd somehow pressured Belgin.

"No darling, that's not at all what I meant!" she hastened to add. It hadn't been her intention to hurt Ayhan, a man who seemed to be forever finding new ways to fulfill her. "I was just trying to let you in on a little secret not many men know. As for what we . . . were doing . . . a minute ago . . . I know how much you like oral sex, and when I see you like that, feel you like that, well, then I can't help liking it too . . ." she smiled.

Ayhan relaxed. "Oh, what a relief! You've talked your way out of it, but don't ever do that again! I really will die in your arms if you say things like that, and it won't be out of pleasure!"

"I'm sorry, I suppose it's time I stopped acting as though I was behind a lectern. Could you help me with that?" she said, snuggling closer and kissing him on the ear.

After responding with a nibble of his own, Ayhan whispered, "Come on then, I'm all ready to help any way I can!"

But Belgin was in professorial mode and returned to her presentation. Sitting up, bare-breasted, tousled and suddenly serious, she said, "All I meant was that I wouldn't necessarily choose to perform oral sex, not on my own. I mean, the clitoris alone has about eight thousand nerve endings, it's really nothing but a bundle of nerves designed to give women pleasure, Ayhan! And it's located in the vagina, not in the back of the throat or . . . back there!"

Ayhan still hadn't got used to Belgin's scientific approach and running commentary on positions and organs, and he reacted as he always did, with a roar of laughter: "Belgin, thanks to you I'm going to end up a gynecologist or an obstetrician! Now lie back down and tell me all I need to know about that clitoris of yours. You'll never find a student as eager as me!" It was when Ayhan whispered Belgin's name into her ear that she would completely lose control and actually be at a loss for words. "Come here, Belgin . . ." he whispered again, and she went to him, into him, allowing him deep inside, deeper than anyone had ever gone, holding him tight. Ayhan could feel it every time, as he was enfolded and welcomed, and he knew that women do not "give" themselves to men, they welcome them. Without this acceptance and reception, lovemaking can only be basic sex, and Ayhan was so grateful to be welcomed back into that warm, wet, privileged place that he didn't bother with a condom. Belgin didn't bother, either. There had been no words, no discussion, but neither of them had bothered with a condom. And that was when Belgin became pregnant.

"Do you need anything else, ma'am?" was the question that intruded upon Belgin's thoughts as she sat on a metal bench in the airport. She looked up to see Officer Üzeyir Seferihisar, but failed to recognize him for a moment. "Oh, thank you. I'm fine. But I'd appreciate it if you'd tell me what that explosion was!" she asked politely.

"Don't worry, ma'am, there's nothing to be scared of. They'll explain everything soon enough," he said as he hastened over to help an elderly woman sit down. The airport official who offered Belgin a glass of orange juice from a large tray of refreshments was more forthcoming, telling her that a pane of falling glass had injured a few people. As usual, it was up to Belgin and a few others to pass this bit of unofficial information along to the worried foreign passengers.

Üzeyir Seferihisar returned to her side a few moments later to tell her that everyone waiting in passport control was to be transferred to the domestic terminal. "When I told my chief we had a pregnant lady, he said we could rustle up a pillow and a blanket, and to make sure you were comfortable." Belgin looked him in the eye and saw an honest man doing a difficult job, and thought to herself, once again, that the real drama of Turkey was sharing a country with well-intentioned people all living together in very different eras with very different world views. She hoped that her grandchildren, if not the child she carried, would be able to live in a country where time wasn't so fragmented, where cities and towns and villages all used the same calendar and the same clock, where people would be free and equal!

"Thank you so much for all your help. I hope that your baby grows up with loving parents, whether it's a boy or a girl!" she told the policeman, surprising even herself with her generous tone and words that could have been spoken by Kete. Still hoping for a boy, Üzeyir Seferihisar nodded his appreciation for her wishes. Belgin watched him as he walked off, she waited and watched.

38
WATCH YOUR STEP

"What's that supposed to mean?" Sabriye Bektaş had thought to herself. "If something's broken, why don't they just fix it? Why make an announcement? Well, whatever's going on, I bet that secret agent at the baggage carousel knew all about it . . ." Towing an enormous suitcase upon which a large box tightly wrapped in plastic teetered precariously, she'd slowly plodded through customs, struggling to balance the two bags she'd slung one over each shoulder. Then, just as her eyes were searching for her uncle's son, Hasan Hüseyin, and she was preparing to heave a sigh of relief as she was spared her burden, the announcement had come.

Sabriye had in fact been burdened with baggage from birth, but had spent her life as uncomplainingly as she was at that moment, weighed down with the things she'd spent the entire previous night packing in Berlin. She'd been fifteen when she'd learned that people can turn into monsters in the blink of an eye and can cut down their neighbors at the slightest provocation, imagined or real. She'd carried this baggage for many long years, and perhaps that was the reason she seemed so resigned to her fatigue and the heavy suitcases, laden with gifts, as always, that she unfailingly lugged back to Turkey once a year: Sabriye was in permanent survival mode.

She'd never been a particularly religious woman, but that hadn't stopped her from becoming one of the foremost Allawi activists in all of Germany. Life had intervened, life had forced her to question her identity, life had sent her first to Istanbul and then onward to Germany. Life. But was it really life's fault that Sabriye had been a high school student in Maraş in 1979 when rumors had spread like wildfire and the detonation of a bomb in a cinema had been blamed on the "Communist Allawi." Had life dictated that her favorite teacher was one of the two men lynched in their own homes the next day, and that thousands had turned out for their funerals, chanting, "No mosque services for communists and Allawi!" As shops were pillaged and neighbors killed and homes burned down, Sabriye's father had fled to Istanbul with his three daughters, and Sabriye's life would never be the same again.

She remembered the night they'd arrived at the home of relatives in one of the poorest neighborhoods of Istanbul. "Papa, why do they hate us so?" she'd demanded. "Don't we believe in Mohammed? Don't we love our country?" Her father had no easy answers, just stared at the wall, the ceiling, the floor. It was her uncle's son, Hasan Hüseyin, who answered her questions many years later in Istanbul:

"I'm tired of all this talk about what it means to be an Allawi! Why don't people get onto the Internet and read up on it? Is it so hard, or do they prefer to stay as ignorant as ever, forcing us to jump up and down and insist that we're Muslim, same as them. This is our country, too, and I'm sick and tired of the way we have to keep defending ourselves. They've been persecuting us for centuries, centuries over which we've mastered the art of passive resistance, but I say it's time to speak up and take action! We're the descendants of the Turkmen, of traditions thousands of years old. We're the ones who continued speaking pure Turkish even when the rest of the country was swept by all things Ottoman. We're the guarantors of democracy in this country, Sabriye, because democracy starts at home and we're the ones who have always treated each other as equals—including our women . . ."

Sabriye had listened carefully to her uncle's son, and had taken his advice. Back in Germany, she'd sought out others in her community, other misplaced souls who'd left everything behind and had begun, thousands of miles from their villages and cities, to pick up the pieces again. She found herself identifying with her Allawi heritage more and more with each passing year, and became a leading proponent of her culture. But she was still too scarred to allow her memories to turn to those horrible events in Maraş in 1979, to that day she'd lost her innocence and her home.

Whenever she found herself missing her homeland, and it

happened less and less as the years rolled by, she'd find herself thinking not of Maraş, but of Istanbul, and of the many trips she'd made by ferryboat, crossing from Karaköy to Kadıköy and back again. She'd even begun to see Istanbul herself as a huge ferryboat, a ferryboat so big that it encompassed the entire city. Istanbul was a ferryboat sailing along under plump white clouds. Istanbul was the seagulls racing alongside the boats, screeching in gratitude for the bits of sesame roll passengers tossed up into the air. Istanbul was a vast, festive, colorful, crowded, noisy ferryboat-city, forever crossing from Europe to Asia, a Noah's ark filled with people of all races and religions, a brilliant blue bridge stretching from Maraş to Berlin, a life-affirming voyage, just as it had been all those years ago, when her parents had taken her to the hospital on the opposite shore twice a week, and nursed her back to life.

Sitting on a bench in the arrivals hall of Atatürk Airport, thinking of Istanbul and ferryboats while waiting for Hasan Hüseyin, Sabriye was rudely jolted back to reality by a wet nose on her leg. She didn't like dogs, perhaps because she associated them with policemen, and flinched. The dog may have sensed her fear, and began sniffing in earnest at her bags and box, drawing the unwelcome attention of the policeman holding his leash. When asked for her passport, she respectfully handed him her German one. After a cursory examination, he handed it back and asked her to open the box on the floor at her feet. The box was full of toys, and had been painstakingly wrapped in plastic, but Sabriye hauled it up onto her lap and patiently dug at the masking tape with her nails. Having examined its contents, the policeman thanked her and left. Sabriye's encounter with dogs and authority had rattled her, and she grew quite alarmed when she noticed the flashing exit signs. She decided to call Hasan Hüseyin, and was dismayed to find that her phone didn't seem to be working. Rising to her feet, she glanced over at the growing crowd in front of the exit door and decided she'd never get out alone, especially with the torn box of toys. That's when the scream reached her ears, the cry of a man in pain. A cry that sounded like the cries and shrieks

335

and wails back in Maraş, the ones coming from her neighbors' houses. She punched out Hasan Hüseyin's number again, frantically this time, before glancing up to see a tall, well-dressed man in dark sunglasses. She knew him. She knew that man, he was the one at the baggage carousel who'd known her name. As she watched him being ushered through an exit she'd assumed was closed, a stretcher was carried past, followed by a weeping young man. "This isn't Maraş, you'll be all right, you'll get out of here," she said to herself, willing calm, drawing on all her resources. But it was after she was nearly deafened by an explosion that she completely lost her wits. The last thing she remembered was grabbing a cell phone out of the hand of a complete stranger and being desperate to reach Hasan Hüseyin, in the name of Allah, Mohammed, and Ali . . .

39
EVERYTHING CHANGES

"God willing, it's nothing serious!" Kete had thought as she held her breath upon hearing the announcement. "Watch over my little lamb, Allah—may she smile once again, oh, merciful God!" But she'd barely had time to draw breath when her phone rang and everything changed. Belgin had called to tell her that she was going to be a grandmother, but had then brought up her past, something they never spoke of, and asked her to forgive her parents. Belgin had seemed to believe that only if Kete managed to forgive her parents, would she herself be able to start a new life in Istanbul with Ayhan and the baby. Had she been serious? Belgin was as proud as her mother, and every bit as stubborn as her Kete. Could Kete forgive and forget, all these years later? Could the knot in her breast be made to dissolve away, even now . . . ?

Kete had long ago accepted that her parents had had her best interests at heart when they'd put her on that bus in Van and sent her to her uncle's in Istanbul. She also knew that if she had remained in Van, she would have been married off while still a girl, and may even be dead by now, worn out by a cruel husband and a dozen children. But she'd never found it in her to forgive either her mother, now long dead, or her father, who'd remarried. Whenever she thought about them, she'd hear a voice in her head, the voice of her childhood self, saying, "They don't want me. They're sending me away." And now, as she sat here in Atatürk Airport, a grown woman in her late fifties, married and with children of her own, she was being asked to absolve her parents. "I wonder if Belgin thinks her suffering compares to mine? Could hers have been so bad?" she thought to herself.

Kete sighed heavily. "Ah, ah, why do we always make things so difficult?" she sighed. But what if Belgin was serious? Would she really return to New York? Kete nearly choked at the thought, grew pale and panicked. It had been her responsibility to look after Belgin, Father Halit Ziya and Mother Jackie-Halide expected it of her. How could she be the one to stand in the way of her lamb's happiness? Would it be so difficult to do as Belgin asked? Her throat constricted and her chest tightened and she did what she always did at such moments: she looked down at her red slippers. Years earlier, even before she'd gone to live with the Gümüş family, back when she was still delivering lunch to the construction site where her uncle worked, she'd seen a pair of red shoes, shiny red patent leather shoes worn by a little girl her age, a pretty girl, a happy girl . . . And she'd had an obsession with red shoes ever since. No one knew her secret, not even Belgin or her son, Halit Ziya . . . but every time she felt alone or scared, every time she overheard someone saying, "She's a good girl, for a servant," she'd look down at her red shoes and remember that happy girl. Now a middle-aged woman with gray hair, Kete did what she had done so many times before: She looked down at her red shoes and she felt better. But when she looked up she felt better still.

"Ahhh, Ayhan! My black-eyed Ayhan!" she screamed. She pounded at the melting knot in her chest, rose to her feet and embraced Ayhan, refreshed and a bit dizzy, a single tear appearing on each cheek, tears she'd shed not for Ayhan but for herself, her mother and her father. "There's no need to cry, Mother Kete!" Ayhan said as he hugged her, not even noticing the fist on her chest, and unlikely to understand even if he had.

Ayhan had been told the news, had tried and failed to reach Belgin on his phone, had urged Kete to leave the airport in case there really was a bomb. But Kete had sat him down and told him the time had come for Belgin to smile again. Then she'd said the words she had been holding inside for so long: "Don't worry, Ayhan. Everything changes. We'll all be gone. Only Istanbul will stay forever." Those were Kete's exact words in July of 2005 at Atatürk Airport. It had seemed a strange thing to say, even to her own ears, but she repeated those three sentences and realized how much better they made her feel. Ayhan just looked at her, unsure of what she meant, his mind on Belgin and how to reach her. But Kete knew that everything would be all right. Kete knew the time had come!

And as Ayhan and Kete sat there, Erol Argunsoy had a heart attack, Barman Baturcan screamed, Mehmet Emin Entek fled through a door, Hamo the driver hit the road again, Tijen Derya lost her arm, Hasret Sefertaş wept in an ambulance, and Sabriye Bektaş snatched a cell phone out of Ayda Seferyan's hand.

A few minutes later, Ayhan and Kete were joined on that metal bench by Ayda, Sabriye, and Aret. And as Kete looked at the little group and nodded sagely, she realized that new lives, new dreams and new tomorrows happen only if old disappointments and old sorrows are washed clean, and forgiveness offered. Of course, it hadn't been her mother and father she'd needed to forgive, it was herself, and that's why it had been so hard.

"Enough!" thought Kete to herself, glancing one by one at Ayhan, Ayda, Aret and Sabriye. "Enough!" she said aloud, thinking of Belgin and the baby. "Enough of hatred and spite and being cut off from each other! It's time for new beginnings and new horizons and a baby shall be born!" The others looked at Kete, and each of them thought she was talking about them. That's what they thought . . .

ANNOUNCEMENT TWO

ATTENTION, PLEASE, ALL PASSENGERS, LADIES AND GENTLEMEN.

THE COMPUTER FAILURE HAS BEEN RESOLVED. ALL SUSPENDED FLIGHTS ARE BEING RESCHEDULED.

ON BEHALF OF ATATÜRK AIRPORT, WE WOULD LIKE TO APOLOGIZE FOR THE INCONVENIENCE AND TO THANK YOU FOR YOUR COOPERATION AND UNDERSTANDING.

SHUTTLE BUSES ARE STANDING BY OUTSIDE THE FRONT ENTRANCE OF THE MAIN TERMINAL BUILDING. ALL INTERNATIONAL AND TRANSIT PASSENGERS ARE TO BE TRANSPORTED BY SHUTTLE BUS TO THE DOMESTIC TERMINAL, WHERE YOUR PASSPORTS WILL BE PROCESSED.

WE THANK YOU ONCE AGAIN FOR YOUR COOPERATION AND UNDERSTANDING.

40
FULL CIRCLE

"Today, I understood what happened," Belgin rejoiced. "Today, something happened to me, and, finally, I understood . . ."

Until today, it had usually been only after much time and great suffering that she had finally understood the meaning of so much that had happened. But here today, in Istanbul again after thirteen years, it hadn't taken her days or years to understand. As she boarded the shuttle bus for the domestic terminal, "Could anything be better than this?" she smiled to herself. The smile spread to her face.

The bus filled with passengers, all of them worn by an hour of tense waiting. She'd occupied one of the few seats, and gave it to an elderly woman. Rising to her feet, she turned her face to the window, fixed her eyes on the blue sky and searched for a cloud. Belgin searched for a cloud. When she spotted a cluster almost directly overhead, she was as overjoyed as someone finding a ray of light in an hour of darkness. Ecstatic. As a child, she'd played games of "Where do clouds go?" with her father. Together, noses pressed against the glass of a house in a city, they'd invented stories about the journey of this and that cloud. There was no difference between a cloud in Istanbul and a cloud in Copenhagen, between one in Rome and one in Buenos Aires. They were all in motion. And then, one day, she understood that clouds didn't go anywhere at all; they were transformed. And the realization that had struck Belgin today was something like that: there was no such thing as a final return, and never had been. It was all a fabrication, something our minds dream up. Yes, Belgin had returned to Istanbul; yes, she was in love; yes, she carried a child; yes, she wanted to start a new life. And yes, along with her hopes and desires came terrible fear, the fear it would all end in disappointment. But there was no such thing as a "final return," nor was there a "final ending." The words "beginning," "ending," and "final" were dreamed up by the same minds that came up with "definite" and "perfect." Because clouds go nowhere, waves don't disappear, and the tides turn, ebbing and flowing. Flux and motion, eternal and constant. That's all . . .

A bus transporting Professor Yannis Seferis, Susan Constance, Aleynâ Gülsefer and Anna Maria Vernier crossed the path of the one on which Belgin stood, face against the glass, watching the clouds. After so many years of endless analysis, she had begun listening to her inner voice, and she was flooded with gratitude as she watched the clouds. After all, her inner voice had only been repeating what she'd already known to be true. And now, for the first time, she listened and she understood.

"There is no final return—we live and we turn. Full circle!" she said, eyes on the sky. That's what Belgin said. The shuttle bus stopped in front of the domestic terminal. Before entering with the other passengers, she stopped for a moment out on the tarmac, lifted her face and looked at the clouds. Belgin raised her head. And looked.

And so it came to pass.

I am finished for today, here at my airport, to which I turned my attention for a few hours of amusement. As always, the mortals have failed to astonish me . . . But perhaps Belgin has understood, has seen herself anew today, here . . . Who knows? These mortals imagine themselves to be living in an age of science and reason, in the twenty-first century, but still they squirm in prisons of their own making, constructed of their own fears. And they continue as they have for millennia, creating and feeding their beloved fear, worshipping it, sacrificing to it. Would that they could see themselves for what they really are, could observe themselves with the detachment reserved for their history books . . . But this they can not do, these mortals, alas!

And so these mortals come and go. But I have been here for thousands of years. I am Istanbul, and toward my embrace have rushed emperors and slaves, sultans and laborers, saints and heretics, heroes and heathens, mystics and knaves, the blessed and the wretched, soldiers and philosophers, the highborn and the homeless, concubines and convicts, the lovelorn and the lost, the weary and the wise, idealists and opportunists, sages and cynics, fools and philanderers, romantics and raconteurs. I am Istanbul, and I am the city, too, of garbage scavengers, the homeless, glue sniffers, street children, whores, pimps, gays, transvestites and gypsies, of the wise and cunning, the enlightened and the crazed, a city of idealists and opportunists and starstruck romantics. City of them all, I recline across two continents, one leg flung across Europe, the other across Asia, and through me courses the waters of the Bosphorus and crowning me are my seven hills. I am Istanbul, and after 2,700 years I am the only woman on Earth invulnerable to menopause!

My name is Istanbul.

Buket Uzuner was born in Ankara in 1955. She is the author of short stories, travel writing, and novels, as well as being trained as a molecular biologist and environmental scientist. She has studied and worked at universities in Turkey, Norway, the United States, and Finland, and was a fellow at the University of Iowa International Writing Program in 1996. She has won numerous awards, including the Yunus Nadi Prize for her novel *The Sound of Fishsteps* in 1993, and the University of Istanbul named *The Mediterranean Waltz* Best Novel of 1998. She currently lives in Istanbul with her son.

Born in Salt Lake City in 1964, Kenneth J. Dakan is a freelance translator and voice-over artist whose translations include Ayşe Kulin's *Farewell: A Mansion in Occupied Istanbul*, Ece Temelkuran's *Deep Mountain: Across the Turkish-Armenian Divide*, Perihan Mağden's *Escape*, and Mehmet Murat Somer's *The Prophet Murders*, *The Kiss Murder*, and *The Gigolo Murder*.

SELECTED DALKEY ARCHIVE TITLES

FOR A FULL LIST OF PUBLICATIONS, VISIT:
www.dalkeyarchive.com

SELECTED DALKEY ARCHIVE TITLES

The Third Policeman.
CLAUDE OLLIER, *The Mise-en-Scène.*
Wert and the Life Without End.
GIOVANNI ORELLI, *Walaschek's Dream.*
PATRIK OUŘEDNÍK, *Europeana.*
The Opportune Moment, 1855.
BORIS PAHOR, *Necropolis.*
FERNANDO DEL PASO, *News from the Empire.*
Palinuro of Mexico.
ROBERT PINGET, *The Inquisitory.*
Mahu or The Material.
Trio.
MANUEL PUIG, *Betrayed by Rita Hayworth.*
The Buenos Aires Affair.
Heartbreak Tango.
RAYMOND QUENEAU, *The Last Days.*
Odile.
Pierrot Mon Ami.
Saint Glinglin.
ANN QUIN, *Berg.*
Passages.
Three.
Tripticks.
ISHMAEL REED, *The Free-Lance Pallbearers.*
The Last Days of Louisiana Red.
Ishmael Reed: The Plays.
Juice!
Reckless Eyeballing.
The Terrible Threes.
The Terrible Twos.
Yellow Back Radio Broke-Down.
JASIA REICHARDT, *15 Journeys Warsaw*
to London.
NOËLLE REVAZ, *With the Animals.*
JOÃO UBALDO RIBEIRO, *House of the*
Fortunate Buddhas.
JEAN RICARDOU, *Place Names.*
RAINER MARIA RILKE, *The Notebooks of*
Malte Laurids Brigge.
JULIÁN RÍOS, *The House of Ulysses.*
Larva: A Midsummer Night's Babel.
Poundemonium.
Procession of Shadows.
AUGUSTO ROA BASTOS, *I the Supreme.*
DANIËL ROBBERECHTS, *Arriving in Avignon.*
JEAN ROLIN, *The Explosion of the*
Radiator Hose.
OLIVIER ROLIN, *Hotel Crystal.*
ALIX CLEO ROUBAUD, *Alix's Journal.*
JACQUES ROUBAUD, *The Form of a*
City Changes Faster, Alas, Than
the Human Heart.
The Great Fire of London.
Hortense in Exile.
Hortense Is Abducted.
The Loop.
Mathematics:
The Plurality of Worlds of Lewis.
The Princess Hoppy.
Some Thing Black.
RAYMOND ROUSSEL, *Impressions of Africa.*
VEDRANA RUDAN, *Night.*
STIG SÆTERBAKKEN, *Siamese.*
Self Control.
LYDIE SALVAYRE, *The Company of Ghosts.*
The Lecture.
The Power of Flies.
LUIS RAFAEL SÁNCHEZ,
Macho Camacho's Beat.
SEVERO SARDUY, *Cobra & Maitreya.*

NATHALIE SARRAUTE,
Do You Hear Them?
Martereau.
The Planetarium.
ARNO SCHMIDT, *Collected Novellas.*
Collected Stories.
Nobodaddy's Children.
Two Novels.
ASAF SCHURR, *Motti.*
GAIL SCOTT, *My Paris.*
DAMION SEARLS, *What We Were Doing*
and Where We Were Going.
JUNE AKERS SEESE,
Is This What Other Women Feel Too?
What Waiting Really Means.
BERNARD SHARE, *Inish.*
Transit.
VIKTOR SHKLOVSKY, *Bowstring.*
Knight's Move.
A Sentimental Journey:
Memoirs 1917–1922.
Energy of Delusion: A Book on Plot.
Literature and Cinematography.
Theory of Prose.
Third Factory.
Zoo, or Letters Not about Love.
PIERRE SINIAC, *The Collaborators.*
KJERSTI A. SKOMSVOLD, *The Faster I Walk,*
the Smaller I Am.
JOSEF ŠKVORECKÝ, *The Engineer of*
Human Souls.
GILBERT SORRENTINO,
Aberration of Starlight.
Blue Pastoral.
Crystal Vision.
Imaginative Qualities of Actual
Things.
Mulligan Stew.
Pack of Lies.
Red the Fiend.
The Sky Changes.
Something Said.
Splendide-Hôtel.
Steelwork.
Under the Shadow.
W. M. SPACKMAN, *The Complete Fiction.*
ANDRZEJ STASIUK, *Dukla.*
Fado.
GERTRUDE STEIN, *The Making of Americans.*
A Novel of Thank You.
LARS SVENDSEN, *A Philosophy of Evil.*
PIOTR SZEWC, *Annihilation.*
GONÇALO M. TAVARES, *Jerusalem.*
Joseph Walser's Machine.
Learning to Pray in the Age of
Technique.
LUCIAN DAN TEODOROVICI,
Our Circus Presents . . .
NIKANOR TERATOLOGEN, *Assisted Living.*
STEFAN THEMERSON, *Hobson's Island.*
The Mystery of the Sardine.
Tom Harris.
TAEKO TOMIOKA, *Building Waves.*
JOHN TOOMEY, *Sleepwalker.*
JEAN-PHILIPPE TOUSSAINT, *The Bathroom.*
Camera.
Monsieur.
Reticence.
Running Away.
Self-Portrait Abroad.
Television.
The Truth about Marie.

SELECTED DALKEY ARCHIVE TITLES